Missing Persons

MISSING PERSONS

D. K. Smith

Cedar Point Press

RIDEAU LAKES   KANSAS CITY

First Cedar Point Hardcover Edition 2017

Published in the United States by Cedar Point Press
www.cedarpointpress.com

Smith, Donald Kimball
Missing Persons / D. K. Smith. –1st Cedar Point hardcover ed.

ISBN 978-0-9914737-0-0

cover photo: David Papazian/Stockbyte/Gettyimages

for Annie
once again

Part One:

Fathers and Sons

1.

My father had a talent for sleep that was the one remarkable thing about him. He devoted himself to it twelve, thirteen, fourteen hours a night. He'd come home from the store at five-thirty and putter in the garden till dinner, then as soon as he could he would drift up to his bedroom and remain among his deep and shadowy dreams until morning. It worried me at first, in those early months. I was afraid he would keep sleeping longer and longer until he lost himself completely and would never find his way back. But eventually I got used to it. I realized that, in many respects, given all that had happened, it wasn't such a bad response. Where someone else might have started drinking or shouting or carrying on, where another man might have gotten angry or bitter or just terribly sad, Henry Bailey slept. It became a central fact of our lives. One of those things you come to count on.

So when I came home from work one night in early June I wasn't expecting anything. It had been one of those slow, slack nights that even the seediest of bars will occasionally suffer, and I'd spent most of it drinking de-caf coffee and playing pool with Tiny Alice. By eleven-thirty it seemed easier just to go home. I parked on the street and climbed out of the truck, and only then did I notice the flickering glow spilling out over the steps of the porch.

I had become so attuned to the possibility of disaster, so accepted it as the currency of our life together, that I started forward without hesitation. I was suddenly sure I'd left the stove on or the kettle, or some lamp had fallen over, and all I could see was the image of Henry trapped in the rising flames, where even his dreams couldn't protect him. But as I hurried forward, some small, less frantic part of my brain grew aware that the night breeze remained strangely clear, carrying along with the usual mixed scents of lilac and mock orange, not a single hint of smoke.

And then I heard the music.

A number of things occurred to me in that long, unspooling moment. Thieves. Housebreakers. Burglars bursting in and... what? Robbing us blind to music? Because another of those facts that could be counted on about Henry was that he didn't play the stereo. I wasn't even sure he knew how. But here was proof that someone, at least, had both the necessary expertise and an ear for the finer things in life because, creeping forward into the shadow of a drooping lilac, I heard the thin, treacly line of Benny Goodman's clarinet twining through the air. And there was Henry, wide awake and resplendent in my favorite tuxedo.

It was a wonderful tux, a twenty-five year old thrift shop number in unrepentant burgundy with black pocket flaps and satin lapels as wide as your hand. It had been a gift from my mother, though not to me, and I cherished it for its inestimable powers of reassurance. I tried to save it for special occasions.

Though, clearly, this evening was nothing if not special. There was Henry, who hadn't been awake this late in half a dozen years, standing mantled in burgundy gabardine, between a bottle of champagne up to its neck in ice and the palest woman I had ever seen. She had short black hair and black lips and a ridiculously short pink dress with broad epaulets and black bows down the front like a series of military decorations. Its vaguely martial aspect seemed at odds with the long, pale legs, as if she'd been awarded the medals during a battle in which she'd acquitted herself bravely, but had somehow lost her pants.

She was squinting slightly in the candlelight. "You know, I can't promise anything."

"I'm not asking for promises," said Henry.

"It's not as easy as you make it sound."

"I'm not trying to make it sound easy."

"Well, it's not."

He smiled.

I had never thought of my father as handsome. If he had a smile that tended to find answering smiles in other people, that had always been more a handicap than anything. As a boy I'd been embarrassed time and again by his indiscriminate friendliness. He would fall into conversation while standing in line at the bank or the post office or the grocery store, and from an early age I had come to feel like his keeper, tugging on a shirt or an arm to draw him away before he could embarrass us both. But now he stood there in that killer tuxedo, just a shade too snug around the middle, and leaned over the champagne, rolling the neck of the bottle between his hands with the uneasy concentration of someone who has seen it done, more or less like that, in some movie long ago. "Do you think it's ready?"

"Well, if it's not," she said, "I am."

He lifted the bottle, glazed and dripping, and after an uncertain moment clamped it resolutely under one arm and began to worry at the cork. The ice bucket, which had looked surprisingly urbane until just this moment, was revealed in the bottle's absence as the white plastic wastebasket from the upstairs bathroom. The woman didn't seem to notice. She stood, head cocked, nodding to the music, and her body disclosed itself beneath the pink dress in a series of odd and awkward angles: a jutting hip, a thin elbow, the long syncopation of one tapping leg. "This is nice," she said.

"I can turn it down."

"I said I liked it."

Prying one edge of the foil from the neck of the bottle, he tore it off in a long, ragged spiral, which he held dangling for an instant like something vaguely disreputable before slipping it into his pocket. Then he pried off the little wire basket and, bracing himself like a lumberjack, gripped the wine in both hands with his thumbs against the cork. Just like in the movies.

Nothing happened. He leaned forward slightly, putting his

weight into the job, straining at the cork. The woman watched, her hands twitching, a frown slowly darkening her face. The pink dress swung impatiently. "What are you doing?"

"Almost there."

"If you just...."

With a muffled, anticlimactic pop the cork came free. Henry turned with a modest flourish and from the table handed her an empty glass, pinching it by the narrow stem as if offering her a posy. Even from a distance I recognized the glasses: a pair of crystal flutes, heavy and delicate. They'd been up in a closet in their own little box, packed in old and graying tissue, for as long as I could remember.

He started pouring, but too quickly. The wine exploded toward the rim. "Careful!" she said.

"I've got it." And quick as thought he plunged one clean if careworn finger into the mounting foam. It hesitated and then subsided.

The woman was frowning. "Here's a clue."

"Sorry."

"For future reference?"

"I'm sorry."

"It's probably better if you keep any body parts out of the wine. At least on the first date."

Henry smiled gamely. "I guess I'm a little nervous."

"Forget it." But she was looking more kindly now. "Just relax. You're doing fine."

He filled his own glass more carefully and took a tiny doubtful sip. "How is it?"

"Not bad. A little longer in the fridge wouldn't hurt."

He nodded, digesting the information. Then after a moment, "Thanks," he said. "For coming, I mean. It means a lot to me. I wasn't sure you would."

She frowned again and took another ruminative sip.

"You want to sit down?" Henry gestured at the bench swing, hanging from two chains at the end of the porch.

"Those things make me sea-sick."

"I could bring out some chairs."

She considered him for a moment, frowning judgment weighing him in the balance, then she offered up a thin, reluctant smile. "You do this sort of thing often?"

"Are you kidding? All the time. Can't you tell?"

"Well, it's been a while for me. I can't make any promises."

"You said that."

"I'm saying it again."

"Okay."

"I just don't want you getting your hopes up."

"It's too late. I was born with my hopes up." The heavy crystal glinted in his hand as he took another sip.

As if she noticed it, too, the woman held her own glass to the light. "These are nice. Did you buy them for the occasion?"

"A wedding present. I don't use them very often."

She hesitated. "You're not going to get hurt, are you?"

"You can let me worry about that."

"Are you sure?"

He turned. "I think it's time for a refill."

"No thanks. One's my limit."

"You can't say no to champagne."

She laid a thin hand over her glass. "No," she said. "Really."

But Henry, all but gleaming in the candlelight, drew the bottle out of its wastebasket and raised it high. "The night is still young."

"Don't."

"Move it or lose it."

"Stop."

"You're going to make me spill."

"Cut it out!"

But he knew not to stop, tilting the bottle further and further until she snatched her hand away, laughing, to catch the wine as it fell. "For God's sake, Henry!" But she was smiling now, swaying ever so slightly, ear turned to the music. "Is that a saxophone?"

"Clarinet. Benny Goodman plays a clarinet."

"It's like the tail of a kite."

"Exactly," he said. "It's just like that."

I stood there staring, wondering if in the candlelight with the music playing and the champagne catching each golden glimmer as if electrically charged, this woman had any idea what kind of a man my father was. If she could tell that he'd never poured a glass of champagne in his life, that the jacket he wore didn't really fit, that all he knew about Benny Goodman was the instrument he played. I wondered if under all these conditions she could recognize what a complete flake he could actually be. But all she said gazing up with a lilt in her voice like a ruffling caress was, "How tall are you?"

"Five-ten."

Henry Bailey, Sr., had been five foot seven at age sixteen, five-eight at twenty, and five-eight-and-a-half from twenty-one to fifty-one. But she didn't seem to notice. "That's a good height," she said. "Do you want to dance?"

"I'm not much for dancing."

"It's easy."

"Not for me."

With a smile she stepped closer, raising her champagne flute and touching it to his. It gave a little timorous clink. "Just follow the glasses," she said, and slipped her left hand onto his shoulder.

With his wine held like a bouquet in his left hand Henry laid his other lightly on her slender waist. She began to move her glass slowly through the air, as if tracing the kite tail of the music. He moved his own to match. Their feet shuffled to the rhythm in something that, while not precisely dancing, was closer than anything my father had ever done before.

"Isn't that amazing," he murmured.

The music wound on, and the two of them swayed together following the movement of the sparkling crystal. And as they moved, each occasional stutter or uncertain step produced the thin, fragile ding of the glasses colliding.

At last the clarinet gave a final little swoop and died. The two figures stood there, uncertainly, then stepped apart, and together they peered in through the open window at the stereo, as if uncertain what came next. After a moment Henry whispered something, and she laughed. "If you say so."

He stepped inside and then a moment later re-emerged.

"More clarinet?" she asked.

"I don't think so. He doesn't seem to be holding anything." He held up the empty CD case. "Wait, here it is. Saxophone."

"Good," she murmured. "Saxophone is so sexy."

That seemed to take him aback. He hesitated as, from the living room, Stanley Turrentine's sexy saxophone poured itself out into the candlelight. Her face was pale beneath the black hair and dark-painted lips. She laughed again, and my father smiled uneasily as if he hadn't the slightest idea what to do next.

I crept silently around to the back of the house and in through the kitchen and up the stairs, pursued all the while by the soft, rising thread of the music. Years ago we had divided the second floor more or less in half. To the right was what I still thought of, despite the best intentions, as my parents' room. To the left was the bathroom, and further still, two other rooms, front and back. They weren't large, but there was plenty of space to mill around in. One was my bedroom.

Into the other, gradually, without ever actually deciding to, we had moved all the furniture, all the books and clothing and knickknacks we couldn't bear to have in the rest of the house. All her favorite chairs, a bright pink and floral rug she'd gotten at a flea market, a few paintings she'd bought over the years, a small mahogany secretary she had picked up at an auction and refinished herself. We just piled everything into the middle of the room and closed the door. But eventually I had set about rearranging things, pushing the boxes into the corner, laying down the rug, putting up the pictures. It had been odd at first to see all those things suddenly condensed into one place, but gradually I began to spend more and more time in there. Sometimes I would read. Sometimes I would just sit.

I used to pretend my mother had died. I sat in her chair and made up complicated stories, full of incident and detail, turning them over in my mind and playing out a whole array of tragic deaths. I would read about disasters in the newspaper and imagine that my mother had been involved, that I had just read her name among the list of victims or seen her photograph—a smiling portrait taken during some birthday or family occasion and supplied by her grieving husband and son—and that the shock of her death was only slowly settling into my mind. I imagined her in a car accident, running head-on into a telephone pole, or crashing into the ocean aboard a 767, or falling as the random victim of some crazy hold-up at the Seven-Eleven.

I didn't dwell on the details. What I imagined as I sat in her chair, which at some moments still carried the faint hint of her perfume like the echo of a muffled cry, as if she'd spoken into the fabric and the sound even now was rising in little whispers.... What I imagined was that she had perished on her way home and in the last instant, when she realized she would never see her beloved husband and child again, she had been struck by the most bitter sadness. That's what I thought. That's what I would pretend. But this was early on, when she'd only been gone a year, two years, three, and I was slowly having to realize she wasn't coming back, and I thought how much easier it would have been if, one way or another, she had been taken against her will.

I never told Henry any of this. I wasn't sure he'd understand. I never really knew what his thoughts were. It wasn't anything we talked about, and my father never really came into the parlor, never sat in her chair. Though sometimes I caught sight of him frozen for a moment in mid-gesture, blank-faced and staring as if there were something he was trying to follow in the distance.

It always gave me a stab of worry, and one afternoon I asked him. He was hunched, motionless in the garden with his trowel hanging limply from one hand

"Henry?" I said. "Henry! Are you okay?"

He shook his head, but only to clear it. "I was just thinking," he said, but with so much obvious sadness that I didn't have to ask about what. We just stood there, two people tied together by the silence, as I waited for him to move again, to straighten up and stand, just to be on the safe side, just to make sure it wasn't a stroke or a coronary or some blockage in the brain, just to make sure it was still only heartbreak.

But now? What was I supposed to make of it now? This wasn't a coronary or a stroke, and maybe worst of all, it wasn't heartbreak. I sat upstairs in the dark and listened through the open window to the sweet and sexy sound of the saxophone. And every few minutes, if I held my breath, I could make out the thin sharp clink of champagne glasses colliding, like the sound of a tiny and very distant car crash.

2.

Henry, in the morning, had a flight pattern as fixed and intricate as a honey bee's. He would walk into the kitchen and, winter or summer, dark or light, turn on the lamp by the stove. Then he'd switch on the back burner, pick up the kettle, and bank left toward the sink. As the kettle filled he'd select the large blue and white mug from its hook and, completing a counterclockwise pirouette, take two steps forward to set the mug down on the cutting board before opening the cupboard and taking down the economy-sized jar of Postum. Only then would he veer back to the stove to place the kettle on its, by this time glowing, element. Then a complete turn, three hundred and sixty degrees, during which he'd select a bowl from the cupboard, the yogurt from the fridge, and a single, under-ripe banana, and he could begin. Three large spoonfuls of yogurt, and the spoon would be washed and returned to the drawer. The banana would be peeled and sliced onto the yogurt, and the knife would join the spoon. At this point, and only then, as if he'd been trying to hide it from himself all along, Henry would open the cupboard and take down a jar of wheat germ, sprinkle a large spoonful over the top, and put it away without ever setting it down. By this time the kettle would be boiling.

My own routine was less intricate, but no less fixed. A large cup of coffee and a bowl of cereal, followed by another cup of coffee, and, stunned by the early morning, I would sit at the table and watch Henry bustle through his routine, warmed by the prospect of such smooth reliability and by the companionable knowledge that, in the end, it was only the smallest things that could be counted on.

This morning, though, as I came down the stairs Henry

emerged from the kitchen without bowl, spoon, or Postum. He sniffed the fragrant steam rising from his mug. "Smells almost good enough to drink."

I hesitated. "Is that my coffee?"

"I made lots. I didn't think you'd mind."

"That's real, you know. Caffeine and everything."

"You're telling me." He took an appreciative sip.

"Won't it keep you up?"

"It's morning. I'm supposed to be up."

"But what about your blood pressure?"

"My blood pressure's fine."

"Did the doctor say that?"

"I said that. And I'll tell you what else." He smiled mischievously. "I'm about to make some eggs."

"Henry," I said with an answering smile, so we could both pretend I was only joking. "You're frightening me."

Six years ago, the summer I turned eighteen, when Elizabeth Drew Bailey drove away and never returned, it had caught us by surprise. By that I mean the two of us, Henry and me. I can't say for sure about Elizabeth.

In that last year of high school I'd been considering a number of colleges, arranging them in my mind by location and by their relative distances away: Palo Alto, Providence, New York City. Growing up I'd always thought of the mid-west as the center of the country in the same sense that the molten core of iron and magma was the center of the world: bleak, inhospitable, and equidistant from anyplace that might actually support life. So when I'd thought about college I'd never considered the classes I might take or the occupation I'd prepare for. I thought only of how far away the schools were, how many miles between here and there, as if one of those movie signposts stood in the middle of my bedroom—9000 miles to Singapore, 5000 miles to Timbuktu—pointing in every direction but this one.

But then, with all those applications spread across my desk

like so many travel brochures, the aforementioned Elizabeth Drew, who had graced the Bailey household for more than twenty years, climbed into her car and drove away. And because in the larger karmic scheme of things there were only a limited number of tickets to make that big trip out of town, after she left I stayed. And because going to the local college would have, in some small way, salvaged something from the disaster, I turned my back on that as well. It was like one of those card games, where the last one left at the table gets stuck holding all the losers. I had known for years I'd been playing the game, but I hadn't realized my mother was until she left. And there I was, alone at the table with Henry, who hadn't even known such a game existed.

In place of a note or forwarding address Elizabeth had left a pan of lasagna wrapped in foil in the fridge with instructions for cooking and additional instructions for assembling a salad from the ingredients filling the crisper. She offered no comment on events, unless you considered the fact that, in preparing the meal for a forty-five year old man with high blood pressure and the beginnings of a weight problem, she had added extra cheese and far too much salt.

That first night we ate the dinner, believing perhaps it was all just a misunderstanding that would clear itself up with a decent meal and a good night's sleep. But the second night it seemed more real, and neither of us was hungry. After a week I threw the rest of it away.

At first we survived on sad little entrées with extravagant names: lobster newburg, shrimp croquettes, Salisbury steak. They slid, frozen and stiff, from cheerful boxes and didn't so much cook as soften and heat. And when we eventually started eating real dinners it was only because I cooked them. I searched through the cupboards and found my mother's cookbooks, worn and faded and stained with food, and from these I prepared a series of familiar casseroles which we ate together, hunched around one end of the dining room, as if crowded into a corner by the pressure of the empty table.

Together we moved through each day in a state of constant surprise, as if inhabiting that instant just after a balloon has popped and before our answering gasps. I hovered around my father, doing what I could while trying not to see the depth of sadness in his face. Once at work he was fine. He slipped into his old routine. But at home he seemed to be re-discovering with every minute the terrible news, and I waited anxiously for our hearts to break. But there was something in his unutterable grief that gave me a kind of emotional leeway, a shell-shocked objectivity that carried me through. And at the end of each day, when he finally trudged up to bed, I felt as if I'd delivered him safely to harbor, leaving me only the evenings to get through on my own.

Gradually, though, as the first sharp sadness dulled into a kind of stunned bewilderment, we settled into our new life, embracing it together like a language only the two of us spoke. I took over the shopping, the cooking, I did the laundry. And after a while it began to seem a comfort, all the things I was doing for us. But over time Henry developed some alarming symptoms. In addition to washing every dish immediately after using it and tidying the house each day until it looked so clean and brittle that the slightest thing out of place might have caused it to crack, he occasionally became dizzy. He would slow to a halt, his cheeks turning pale and a gleam of moisture condensing on his face. And his left arm went numb for almost twenty minutes one afternoon in the store. Just numb, for no reason. I came upon him, in the home appliance aisle, staring down at it, slowly moving his fingers as if by remote control.

"The funniest thing just happened," he whispered.

We drove to the emergency room.

It was stress, the doctor said. That's all. Henry just needed to relax. Take some sensible precautions. Cut out caffeine. Try to keep that blood pressure down.

But now he sat sipping his coffee as if he'd never heard of

hypertension or sadness or Postum. "I was thinking about an omelet," he said cheerfully.

"What about the yogurt and wheatgerm?"

"We've even got a little bacon."

"No, we don't."

"I bought it yesterday. And some mushrooms. What do you say? If we play our cards right we may even have some cheese here somewhere."

I sat very still, watching as if at any moment my father might tear off his clothes, or collapse, or go running outside making noises like a locomotive, but all he did was walk to the fridge and take out the eggs, the bacon, the mushrooms, and a chunk of cheddar cheese. Then he drew out the frying pan and set it on the stove.

The bacon sizzled going in. "Too hot," I called. "Pan's too hot!"

But he didn't seem to hear. He shook his head, marveling. "When was the last time we had bacon?"

"When was the last time you went to the doctor?"

"A little bacon won't kill me."

"Who says?"

But he just smiled. Standing by the stove he poked at the bacon, arranging it with the shy, overeager gestures that come out between old friends who haven't seen each other for a while, as the house filled with an aroma too cozy and appetizing to be real. He started whistling something jazzy and syncopated under his breath.

"What's that you're whistling?"

"Was I whistling? Sorry."

"It's okay. It's nice," I said. "So, how was your evening?"

He glanced up, a sudden study in blandness. "Oh. It was okay."

"Just an average night at home?"

"More or less." He fussed over the bacon, lining it up in the pan. Then very casually, "What time did you get in? I didn't hear you."

"Pretty late."

He considered that. "I just watched a little TV. You know me. Went to bed early."

"Anything good on?"

"Just the usual. Pretty much just the news. How about you?"

"And then you went to bed early?"

"You like cheese, right?"

"That's my cheese. I'm the one who bought it."

He picked it up and started grating. "Just a little too much cheese, and a little too much salt," my father was saying. "That's the secret." He reached for the eggs.

"Henry? Is there anything we should talk about?"

He hesitated, and a small, embarrassed grin stole across his face. "I suppose you mean Mona."

"Her name's Mona?"

"Yeah. Isn't that great?"

"Who is she?" I asked.

"Just a friend."

"How'd you meet?"

"Oh... through a friend of a friend. You know how it is."

But I realized that, after all these years, I had no idea at all how it was.

And then he was whistling again as he picked up a fork and beat the eggs into a froth. He was smiling to himself, almost laughing. When had I last heard him laugh? "Mona," he muttered with evident satisfaction. "You don't hear names like that any more." And he dumped the eggs into the too-hot pan with a rush and a rising hiss.

3.

We drove to work, the truck rattling over potholes like a coffee can full of old screws, and parked in the alley under the faded sign my grandfather had painted sixty-five years ago. The B in Bailey's had flaked off into an inverted R, and the words Hardware and Other Dried Goods looked faded and old-fashioned against the brick. The sign had been there a long time, but instead of a sense of permanence it managed to give only an impression of grim stubbornness, like the scuffed and narrow farmhouses that still remained, wedged between the strip malls on Route 6 west of town. Each time I saw it, it struck me as a kind of warning: the dangers of remaining behind after everyone else has left. But Henry didn't notice. Powered by a hearty breakfast and genuine caffeinated coffee, he hopped out of the truck and unlocked the heavy steel door. He was whistling under his breath as he flicked on the lights.

It's hard not to see the hardware business as a kind of judgment on my family. As a young man my great-grandfather Benjamin uprooted his wife and infant son and dragged them twelve hundred awkward miles west from Connecticut, drawn by the promise of rich land just beyond the Mississippi and by the certainty that the one thing he didn't want to be in this life was a farmer. Most of his friends and family wondered why he had to go so far. There must be easier, less inconvenient places not to farm. But Benjamin had a plan. Whatever else their faults, the Baileys have always been big on plans that escaped the straightforward. If you wanted to make a place for yourself in a job that didn't involve farming, you needed to find a place where all those jobs weren't already taken. A place, in fact, where everybody else was so busy farming, they needed the sort of services only a determined non-farmer could provide. Benjamin went to work in a black-smith shop, then a feed shop, then a dry-goods store. His son, when it came his turn, blundered into hardware, and that's where we've stayed, in a store in the center of town, as far as possible from the rolling ocean of farmland that vanished to the horizon in all directions—a family of castaways living on an island and determined to ignore the sea.

The store became a Rorschach Test for the Bailey unconscious. For Henry, despite everything, it remained a sanctuary, an arena of promises waiting to be kept. A tiny thermo-couple might hang on its hook for years gathering nothing but dust until someone came in with a broken furnace, and then it became the only crucial thing in the store. A small wire of steel had no use at all until you broke the cotter pin on the blade of your lawnmower. Under Henry's watchful eye the whole store remained a symbol of hope and repair. Contractors, students, home fix-it screw-ups— each one looking for that single solution: a roll of sealing tape, thirty-three inches of three-eighths copper pipe, fifteen feet of telephone cable, a pair of wire-cutters, a new deadbolt. They all went away happy with the only answer they needed cradled in their hands.

But me, I'd never liked the store. It made me uneasy. All the different bits and fragments gathered together in drawers, as if a roomful of complex machinery had simply fallen to bits. Where Henry saw order and plenitude—five hundred countersunk #6 wood screws, a thousand rubber washers sorted by size—I saw all the separate pieces, revealing nothing so much as the tendency of every object in the world to come apart.

This morning I took my place at the cash register, and between customers I watched my father. After last night I don't know what I thought I'd see. Something stranger, maybe, or more familiar. But it was only Henry, just Henry, in a worn blue work shirt, khakis, and an ancient carpenter's apron. But it was Henry with a brand new skip in his step. Despite the mind-numbing boredom of the monthly inventory, he was nodding and smiling with a clipboard in his hand, trailing short whistled snippets of Benny Goodman like a thin string of eighth-notes hanging in the air.

Happiness is a funny thing. It's so light and insubstantial, like a sparkler bouncing its little stars off everything, while sadness has all the complexity, all the weight and accumulating importance, of snow to the Eskimos. I don't know how long it had been since I'd seen Henry happy. I couldn't remember a time. It was like a fish remembering the world before water. And though, watching him now, I could see he was enjoying it, I didn't know what to do. The only time there had been something even remotely similar, he hadn't looked anything like this. It had been five years ago and had involved a woman named Edith Mullins.

She worked at the Hallmark shop at the mall, and she was maybe five years older than Henry. A widow, a little heavy-set, with sandy hair that she washed and curled every week and a closetful of pantsuits in a rainbow of colors. She was perfectly nice, and even a year after Elizabeth's departure she was very sympathetic to my father's loss. She brought casseroles. She brought the occasional apple pie. Then one evening I left them sitting in our kitchen discussing the recent increase in city water bills, and in the morning her car was still out front.

I was shocked. And a little outraged. It had only been a year since Elizabeth had left. What could he be thinking? He was lonely, I knew. Of course he was lonely. We were both lonely. But at least we were lonely together. Wasn't that enough?

The next day I watched Henry at the store unpacking boxes, arranging a new shipment of house paint on the shelves. I was looking for some difference in his behavior, some evidence that he was moving beyond our tragedy, some sign that he was leaving me behind. But he worked through the day with the same trudging thoroughness he'd managed for the last year, and that evening, though he announced he was going out for dinner and put on a clean shirt and fresh pair of khakis, he was back by seven-thirty and asleep by eight.

And that's how it went. Edith continued to stop by, dropping off a plate of cookies or a small pile of neatly folded laundry, which she carried without hesitation in through the back door and up to Henry's room. And one warm Sunday afternoon I came home to find my father sitting on the sofa absorbed in *The New York Times* while Edith, looking solid and matronly in a white slip and bra, was standing at the ironing board working her way through a pile of his shirts. Among all the things Elizabeth Bailey had never done, ironing in her underwear stood near the top of the list.

Maybe Henry realized that, or maybe it was something else. Maybe it was just the added loneliness of realizing you were lonely in a stranger's company. But whatever the reason, within a month Edith was gone. Henry was back in his garden after work, or reading his catalogs or watching the news by himself. And once again, worriedly, I tried to gauge the effect. But there seemed none at all. If he was depressed or relieved or disappointed at this new departure he gave no sign. He seemed no happier, but at least no sadder than before. And when I finally worked up the courage to ask about her, long after the fact, all Henry said was that Edith was very comforting and a very good friend. And I told myself that despite the sadness and the loneliness, at least we had each other, and I tried not to be relieved.

But I was. Because the problem with happiness is that it's nothing you can share. I don't care what people say: laughter is contagious, smile and the world smiles with you. It's not like grief. Shared sadness lends a kind of solid comfort, a common foundation that makes you both a little steadier. But happiness. I don't know. Maybe I've just forgotten how it works.

By three-thirty I had sold two packs of batteries, a hot glue gun, a box of fluorescent bulbs, an extension cord, and three sets of blades for an electric saber saw, and I was standing at the register building a wobbly tower of small rubber Stress-o Dolls when the door opened with a cheery jingle. I glanced up. It was a woman of about my age, looking as if she'd gotten dressed in the dark out of some stranger's closet. She wore a loose orange t-shirt that didn't quite reach down to the lime-green cargo pants hanging on her hips and a black biker jacket so large and stiff it made her look like a turtle too thin for its shell.

"Can I help you?"

She was less than medium height and a little less than pretty, with a nose broader than it needed to be and a stubborn jaw. She wore heavy, black-framed glasses like a roadblock on her nose and in her left nostril, gleaming, the thin silver sliver of a ring. "Is this Bailey's Hardware?"

"We like to think so."

"You should have a sign out front."

"We do."

"Then you should make it bigger." Her lips were thin. They gave her an air of measured consideration, as if even in this brief time she'd formed a reasoned opinion of all my short-comings.

"So, you're what?" I said. "Some kind of sign consultant?"

"I'm looking for the owner."

"That would be me, in a manner of speaking. What can I do for you?"

She lifted one of the little Stress-o Dolls from the pile on the counter. When you clutched it the eyes, nose, and tongue bugged out as if its whole little rubber head might explode. She gave the bulbous nose a contemplative flick, then turned it to me and squeezed. "Henry Bailey," she said, speaking clearly so that even the slowest members of the audience could follow along. "Is he in?"

"Can I tell him what this is about?"

"No."

I said, "Why don't you take a seat in the waiting room, and I'll see if I can find him."

But just at that moment, following his inventory of paint, polyurethane, and mineral spirits to the end of aisle seven, Henry moseyed into view.

"You're in luck," I said. "Mr. Bailey can see you now."

"Thank you."

She dropped the doll into its box and strode toward the back of the store, and I was thinking, Let Henry handle this. He needs a little aggravation. But then he glanced up, clipboard in hand, and gave her a wide and welcoming smile as if she were right there on his list, precisely the very item that he had just been looking for.

I picked up the doll she had dropped and I turned the little rubber face, and together we watched her go. She might not have been exactly pretty. But she wasn't Edith Mullins, either. And as she turned, the pale curve of her hip, surprised between waistband and shirt, offered just the hint of a body less angular than I had imagined. It put me in mind of that short pink dress in the candlelight, and I felt the slippery flick of some sudden feeling, just the little tail of something, beyond irritation though not entirely unrelated.

She looked pleased to see Henry, though they didn't kiss. He looked unfazed by the bright assault of her clothes. She half-stood, half-perched on a shelf of coffee-makers, and my father held his clipboard in both hands as if suddenly moved to conduct a public opinion poll right there in his own store. He seemed happy with her answers.

My mother wore beautiful clothes, elegant clothes, that she would buy at consignment shops and vintage clothing stores and the summer sales, coming out of the shabby chaos of cast-offs and remainders with that one, perfect outfit that must surely have been there by accident. She wore a shade of lipstick they no longer make; or at least, they no longer call it the same thing. Summer Rose, it was called. And for a while, after she left, I would linger in the cosmetic aisle of the local drugstore just to make sure it was still there. But I never thought to buy it. And when Revlon came out with their new spring colors, it was gone, and I could no longer remember whether it was closer to Antique Pink or Dusty Fuchsia.

I read once that nothing is ever forgotten. Even the briefest and most transitory memory is stored in the chemicals of your brain so that although you can't retrieve it, it remains there somewhere, lurking in your cells. I try to think of that as a comfort: that memory outlasts even your own power to recall. But it's an empty sort of comfort. Over the years I've held onto the idea of my mother, though I can no longer remember exactly what she looked like. Almost from the moment she'd gone I began to have trouble conjuring up the individual aspects of her, as if she'd left an outline behind but had taken the details with her. One morning I couldn't remember how she wore her hair, or the shape of her nose. I couldn't remember her chin. I held on as tightly as I could, but I'd feel her slipping away. Her perfume, her voice, the way she walked, the way she laughed. Every detail fading until all that remained was some large and vague approximation of everything that had vanished.

Yet, even if I didn't remember, I could still measure the space she had taken up by the sudden weight of sadness that rushed in to fill it. More than her appearance, her absence was the shape I built my life around. I preserved her the way a sculptor preserves the shape of a wax statue in a hardened mold. The statue melts and slips away, but the mold retains the image in reverse. A kind of lost wax process of the heart. And I was grateful in a way. At least I had that much. At least, I thought, we both did.

But in that moment looking at Henry, I could no longer tell what he remembered, or what he'd forgotten. He was nodding and smiling. Then Mona whispered something, and he laughed out loud, a sudden, startled sound that might have surprised him as much as me, because he glanced up a little sheepishly. Then he held up his open hand to me—back in five—and before I could say a word he and Mona were hurrying up the aisle. At the door he turned with a little wave, and just in case there were any doubt where he was headed he mouthed the word "lunch" like a secret he didn't want anyone else in the empty store to hear.

I checked my watch. Lunch? At a quarter to four?

But the heavy door was already easing itself closed, and I stood there like one of those audience members in a magic show who only gradually realizes the missing card has been pinned to his back all this time.

I was around the counter and hurrying toward the door. I cracked it open. In the alley beside the truck there was a red Mustang with the top down and a parking ticket bent under the wiper. Mona plucked up the paper and crumpled it, then settled into the driver's seat. Henry smilingly closed her door, then he scampered around to the passenger side. He was still settling in as the car started moving, backing out, turning. I had a last glimpse of him, laughing and hurrying to get his seat belt buckled, as the car roared past.

4.

When I say "lunch" what I usually mean is a sandwich or a slice of pizza or a burger. On special occasions maybe a little chinese. Often I take a book or a magazine and read with my meal, so I come back to the store refreshed. When Henry left I spent far too much of the rest of the afternoon wondering what exactly he meant by lunch, and waiting for him to come back so I could make a point of not asking.

In retrospect, maybe I should have just minded my own business. Let Henry lead his life while I led mine. But in a sense that was part of the problem, part of what made it so hard. All those years of sad and lonely casseroles, of long, silent evenings with Henry asleep upstairs, of somehow ensuring we both made it through each ragged day... it blurred the boundaries. So it wasn't simply that I couldn't tell Henry's business from mine. It was worse than that. He had somehow become just about all the business I had.

When he still wasn't back at ten after six I left his clipboard leaning against the end of aisle seven, in case he had trouble remembering where he'd left off, and doused the lights. I drove home through the center of town, not searching exactly—that would have been ridiculous—but keeping my eyes open, just in case. There was no real possibility of spotting him; it wasn't that small a town. Just small enough that I could think I might. So I drove as slowly as traffic allowed and paused at every intersection to look up and down without any real hope or expectation, and in the process I managed to spread my attention so thin I missed my final turn and had to go all the way down Bloomington, bouncing over the uneven bricks, and come back on Linn Street past the laundromat, the fire station, and Rusty's

Blue Diner.

The Blue Diner was, technically speaking, neither a diner nor blue. It had begun life as an old airstream trailer perched on cinder blocks and painted a dark, flat color which, in the old black and white photographs, had to be taken on faith. Then the '74 tornado came and wrapped it like a model train halfway around a neighboring oak, leaving the tree more or less undamaged and the trailer anything but. Now the diner took up the ground floor of a three-story yellow brick building, and the only thing less blue was the bright red Mustang convertible parked by the curb out front.

It wasn't a restaurant I ate in as a rule, though I'd driven past it a thousand times. This was the sort of town where you drove past everything a thousand times. But tonight I stopped and parked and stepped gingerly inside, remembering only at the last minute to put on a look of genuine amazement at the prospect of coming upon my father here where I least expected him. There were wooden booths lining one wall, a row of tables along the other, and in the middle a narrow, U-shaped counter like a referee's box where the current owner, a solid, squarish woman with pale cinnamon hair, reigned over the low and ongoing clamor with an expression of monumental indifference.

I had never actually met her before, though there were stories which you didn't need to eat there to hear. She was said to have lost a husband, though how, exactly, remained unclear. One version had him running away, fleeing his wife and the state in the middle of the night only to come to a sudden halt against the front grill of a semi- just outside of Lincoln, Nebraska. Another implied she might have driven him away, and a third, somewhere between the two, suggested both the involvement of another woman and the likelihood that Rusty might have helped him along, not simply into the next state, but into the next world as well. Since the collision was reportedly coupled with a sizable insurance policy, that was the reigning favorite. And though the owner herself declined to comment, her appearance was said to lend credence to the story. Everyone agreed, she wasn't the sort of woman who would take a lot of crap.

Dinner was in full career, and the aroma of the current Blackboard Special, pork roast with applesauce and stovetop stuffing, hung heavily on the air. There were a handful of reclusive souls scattered around, hunching meditatively in their seats, as Rusty patiently ignored them. She stood at the counter paper clipping a small xerox of the evening's specials to a stack of laminated menus.

There was no sign of Henry, or his lunch date. I stood looking around, table by table, as if there were somewhere they could hide beneath the bright fluorescent glare, until Rusty glanced up and fastened her indifferent gaze upon me. A moment's hesitation and I settled at the counter.

"Know what you want?" she asked.

"Just coffee."

"We serve food, too."

"Thanks," I said. "I ate before I came."

She was frowning. She had reached the end of the pile and now stood there with three extra menus unmarred by the night's specials.

I tried a sympathetic smile. "Lose count?"

"What?"

"The menus."

Still frowning she said, "I thought you didn't want one."

"No, I just... No. Thanks. Just the coffee."

She gave me a look that said it was too early in the evening for whatever it was I was doing. Then, filling a mug, she put it down with a thump that sloshed a little wave of coffee over the rim, and then stood gazing down at the spreading puddle though she made no move to wipe it up.

"I'm looking for a couple," I said.

She raised her eyes.

"Of people," I added, as if that might be the confusing part.

"I'm trying to find them. I thought they might be here."

"This is a restaurant."

"Yes. See, I thought they might be eating." She regarded me as if even this was hard to believe, but I pressed on. "He's in his early fifties, dark-hair. Thinning. Kind of ordinary looking. Not as tall as he says he is."

"Is this some kind of joke?"

"No, see… She's maybe half his age. Too thin. With an earring in her nose."

"An earring?"

"Okay. A nose ring."

Rusty glanced around at the few scattered customers. "You see 'em here?"

"No. That's the thing. I'm looking for them--"

"You the husband?"

"Excuse me?"

"What's it to you?" she inquired patiently.

"Oh. I'm just a curious by-stander."

"You know how many people come in every day?"

"She was wearing orange and green. Don't ask me why. And a black jacket. Leather. One of those biker numbers…"

I could see her attention beginning to wander.

"And short hair. Black and straight. And a pale face. Not that pretty. I mean, not bad. But not as pretty as you'd think. And the nose ring," I finished, my voice trailing off less compellingly than I might have wished.

Rusty shrugged, "Sorry," and she started to turn away.

"His name is Henry. Did I say that already?"

"Honey, they could all be named Henry." She started gathering up the menus.

In a booth behind me a guy in a red lumberjack shirt, much too warm for the day, looked up. He stared hard at me for a moment, as if trying to recall who it was I reminded him of, and I leaned forward eagerly. "Have you seen--?"

"No." He held up his coffee cup. "But I could use a refill. You mind letting her majesty know?"

I turned back to Rusty. "She was young. Did I mention that? Young enough to be his daughter. See, that's what I'm getting at. Way too young...."

Rusty set the coffee pot on the counter before me. "You want to pour that?"

"Mona," I said, picking up the pot. "Her name's Mona. Mona something or other. I don't know her last name."

"Mona?"

"Mona something."

Rusty looked disgusted. "Well, for God's sake! Why didn't you just say so instead of dancing all over the place? She's not here."

I stood there, whatever expression I might have started with drooping a little now. "I know she's not here. I mean, I can see she's not. But the thing is, her car is out front."

She nodded at the lumberjack. He was still holding out his cup. "Do you mind?"

I stepped over and filled it. "But you know her?" I said.

"Mona." She repeated it as though the name itself annoyed her. "As if."

"But you've seen her lately? With some guy maybe? Dark-haired, thinning--"

"Where's the cream?" asked the lumberjack.

I passed him the cream. "Dark-haired. Thinning on top--"

"Yeah, yeah. I heard. And not that tall. Tell you the truth, I don't know. This man, that man. I can't keep track." She took back the coffee pot and put it on the burner. "Maybe that makes me a bad mother. So what?"

"What?"

"I don't tell her who she dates. And she doesn't tell me."

I was shaking my head. "I'm sorry, but...."

"Sometimes that's the best you can hope for with kids. You know?"

I settled back onto my stool and picked up my cup. It was

cold. Coffee dripped from the bottom. "You got any kids?" she asked.

"No."

She sighed. "What can you do?"

"I don't suppose you have any idea where she might be now?"

"You tried her office?"

"Her office?"

Rusty pointed behind me again, but when I turned, the guy in the lumberjack shirt was perfectly absorbed in his nearly-full cup, and there was no sign of any office. "Upstairs," she said.

"Upstairs?"

"You hard of hearing or something?"

"I didn't used to think so."

She spoke slowly and with emphasis. "Out the door. Turn left. Open the door. Up the stairs. Knock on the door."

"Thanks," I said. I turned.

"You're planning to pay for that, right?"

Hurriedly I pulled out my wallet.

"And while you're at it...." She reached under the counter and held out a short, ragged stack of pink message slips. "Give her these, why don't you."

5

It is one of the least helpful laws of metaphysics that you never know something is lost until you try to find it. For six years
Henry and I couldn't have lived more closely if we'd been man-
acled together. He was always right there, the most predictable
of men, so that everything about him seemed obvious and clear.
I may have been unsure of myself over the years, mired in the
tangle of muddles and mistakes that was the ongoing evidence
of all I was doing wrong, but I'd always been sure of Henry;
sure of everything about him. But now, here I was. And the mere
fact of looking for him suddenly conjured up a whole range of
uncertainties that adhered to my father like a new set of feathers.

I stood outside on the sidewalk with the collection of pink
message slips in my fist, thinking maybe I should just go home.
I hadn't actually agreed to deliver them. At least, not quite. And
I could still leave. There was definitely a way of looking at this
in which whatever was going on in the office upstairs could fall
outside the category of what was, strictly speaking, my business.
But I was thinking about Henry, conducting his little survey at
the end of the paint aisle, and about that pleased, half-sheepish
wave as he left the store. And I found myself striding up a steep
bank of stairs, carpeted in something dark and mud-colored,
with a sense of slow burning irritation that I couldn't put a name
to but which seemed its own justification.

At the top, a narrow hallway stretched away to the left past
an open window and not one closed door, but three. I hovered
there a moment, considering the arrangement. It was as cryptic
as the face of a stranger, and I was just wishing Rusty had been
more precise in her sarcasm when an angry voice drifted down
from above.

"What the hell do you mean? I don't care how busy you are! You promised!"

It was a voice of full-throated outrage, and I was struck, even from a distance, by its new familiarity. Anger had always been a little shameful when I was growing up. No one shouted. On those rare occasions when some argument bubbled up, it always ended in a long and awkward silence as if my parents had unexpectedly found themselves on unfamiliar ground and were feeling their way back. But this voice was sharp and unapologetic.

"God damn it! You gave me your word!" Mona shouted. "You are such a pain in the ass!"

There was something in the near-operatic projection, the unabashed purity of her tone, that sent a thrill of appalled appreciation through the delicate bones of my ears. In his own pleasant and inoffensive way no one could, on occasion, be more irritating than Henry, and it gave me a small glow of vindication to hear someone else say so. As I turned and started up the next flight of stairs I found myself wondering what exactly my father had promised.

The third floor was identical to the second except there were only two doors on the hallway and the window was closed. One of the doors, however, was open, and I crept forward to listen. Henry had always been quiet. He seldom raised his voice, always speaking as if calmness were a language without which he couldn't make himself heard. But now, in the silence punctuating Mona's shouts, it seemed my father had perfected his talent all the way into quaking silence.

I sidled up to the door. I wasn't sure what to expect. The two of them facing off over the ineffaceable evidence of an unmade bed? At the very least a room in disarray, as if that voice alone could have scattered clothing and knocked lamps off their tables. But through the narrow crack of the door, the room looked as orderly as a doctor's waiting room. There was a gray steel desk that might have come out of an old insurance office, an easy chair, a long gray sofa. And that was it. No sign of Henry, no clothing scattered, no telltale clues of passionate abandon. The only thing untidy was the voice.

"Bullshit! That's bullshit! You're there in the cards. The goddam two of swords crossing the Knight of Cups! That's a loser at love with a criminal past. Who else is it going to be?"

A loser at love? I thought as I sidled closer. Poor Henry. But what could you expect when…?

"Goddammit, Carlisle!"

Carlisle? I stopped.

The possibility for making one of life's really substantial mistakes comes more rarely than you might think. It appears suddenly, unexpectedly, like that moment of stark and echoing silence just before the thunder. I started to back away, moving with the slow, molasses-heavy tread that grips you in the worst of your dreams. If I got to the stairs, I could at least claim to be on my way somewhere else.

But at that moment the door was snatched open, and Mona stood on the threshold under a large white towel. She was holding the phone with one hand and drying her hair with the other, and the higher her voice rose, the harder she rubbed. "Well, screw you, too! Are you kidding? You can ride off a goddam bridge for all I care!"

She switched off the phone as if snapping its little neck, then gave her hair one last furious swipe and whipped the towel back into the depths of the otherwise tidy apartment, revealing a wild head of dark hair every bit as angry as she was. I had last seen it lying straight and flat, but now it erupted into a permed and fluffy tangle like an explosion of black goose down. She bent and snatched up a brown grocery bag from the floor. Then, slamming the door behind her, she stepped out into the hallway and ran almost straight into me.

"Jesus Christ!" She was squinting furiously, patting her pockets with her free hand until she drew out the heavy, black-framed glasses and jammed them onto her nose. "Who the hell are you?"

I stood there with what wanted very much to be a smile on my face and tried to think of something to say. The moment for an introduction seemed to have long come and gone, since I'd been thinking about her more or less continuously for the last twenty-four hours. Besides, she was dating my father, and in the informal bonds of modern romance that made us practically related. So, for a number of reasons of which she was completely unaware, we were already entangled within a slippery net of familiarity before I even opened my mouth.

I offer this as a kind of explanation, because what I finally said was, "What have you done to your hair?"

She glared at me. "What? It's a perm. Haven't you ever seen a perm before?"

The wild disorder of it put me in mind of a black dandelion. "Is it supposed to look like that?"

"It's a goddam perm. What do you think it's supposed to look like?" But even as she said it, her hand was patting at the wild hair, trying to smooth it down.

"It's nice," I said, finally coming to my senses, though not, of course, in time.

"Nice? It's not nice. Nice is a couple of barrettes and a pair of Mary Janes. This is fashion. Oh, forget it." And as if suddenly realizing how much of her attention I'd already wasted, she started to push past me, heading for the stairs.

At this point, too, I could have escaped but, "Wait," I called.

She stopped and turned. "Do I know you?"

"We met at the hardware store. This afternoon."

"Oh, right." And then something seemed to occur to her. "I don't suppose you've ever been in jail?"

I hesitated, a little more wide-eyed than I'd have liked. "Not exactly. At least, not for very long."

"How's your love life?" But she didn't seem to need my answer on that. "What's your name?"

"Harry."

"Well, listen, Harry. I need a little help here. How would you like to make fifty bucks?"

Mona drove as if she were furious with her car, accelerating wildly, braking only when she had to, taking each corner like a personal slight. I sat wedged in the passenger seat with one hand casually braced against the dashboard. The top was still down, and the wind whipped her already tangled hair into a froth, so she had to keep fanning the strands from her eyes as if they were wisps of smoke. Overhead twilight was settling, and the first stars were pricking through the gloom.

"Where exactly are we going?" I asked.

"We're visiting a friend."

"Whose friend?" But she just grimaced against the wind, brushing away the question with the tangle of hair. I had the sudden vision of Henry, laughing wildly as the car tore away, looking more than a little foolish and out of his depth, and I strove for a tone of casual aplomb as she changed lanes without a blink, careening north out of town. "Do you always drive like this?"

"Like what?"

I slipped my hand onto the armrest and tightened my grip. We were in rush hour, such as it was, but she gunned it down the long slope toward the river as if the other cars were mere figments of her imagination and no stop light waited at the bottom. "So, what about that fifty bucks?" I casually asked.

"Afterwards."

"After what?"

"You'll see."

"Am I going to have to ask this friend for it?"

"What's the matter? You want to see it now?"

"No, that's okay. I trust you. But tell me about this frie-- Red light! Red light!" I shouted. "That's a red light!"

She braked to a shivering stop and then turned in her seat, a sudden look of worry on her face, as if the quality of our conversation was undermining her confidence. "You do know how to use a camera, don't you?"

My throat was dry and my chest felt too small for the rabbity pounding of my heart. "That depends," I croaked. "Use it for what?"

"In the bag. There's a pack of film."

"Who uses film these days?"

"Load it up, why don't you?"

The camera lay in the bottom of the grocery bag beneath a copy of the morning's paper, a sealed manila envelope, and a blue box of Polaroid film. She was still watching me doubtfully. "Think you can handle it?"

"It's all coming back to me."

"If you're not sure, you'd better tell me now."

I peeled open the box without a word, and tore off the foil. She shrugged and, an instant before the light changed to green, sent us lurching forward.

The camera was folded flat, like some threatened animal protecting itself. I turned it over looking for a switch, found one, and pressed it. Nothing happened. I found another, and the flat box popped open into something more resembling a camera, with a lens, a view finder, and everything else you might expect.

"It's that little button on the end there," Mona said, turning from the onrushing roar of a garbage truck to flick one finger in my direction.

"I've got it."

"The button on the end."

"Watch the road."

"It slides right in the front."

"That's a truck!"

"I've got it," she said irritably, swinging the car out of the way. "It's that switch right there."

"I see it!"

With a touch of the switch a little trap door flipped open. The film pack refused to go in, but I was only giving it half my attention. The garbage truck roared past in a huge tornado of noise.

"That blue tag sticks out," Mona explained.

"I see it."

"Are you sure you can do this?"

"Will you watch the goddam road!"

I shoved the film in and shut the camera. It started buzzing angrily and spat out a photograph which began life as a solid, midnight black and stayed that way. "Ready," I said, a little breathlessly.

But she looked only half convinced.

We drove in silence for a while, then turned onto a wide road and immediately again onto a narrow lane. The surface had clearly been paved against its will and had spent the last few years struggling back to gravel. The few asphalt patches were cracked and crumbled, and a dense wall of trees crowded in on either side as if they planned eventually to meet in the middle. The only good thing about the road was that it slowed us down. The Mustang crawled along, weaving from shoulder to shoulder, trying to avoid the deeper ruts, and with every bump Mona winced and peered ahead through the gathering darkness.

"You could use your headlights."

"Uh-uh."

"Is this some kind of surprise?"

"Something like that."

"And what exactly is going on?"

"I'll explain it all afterwards."

"I've got time now."

She frowned, but whether at me or the potholes I couldn't tell. "It's not complicated. Are you listening? Be ready with the camera. When I say snap the picture, snap the picture. Okay?"

"Okay," I said. "What picture?"

"Here we are."

The road curved past an old and weathered sign: Pine Knoll Estates and then widened and split into three tracks, now frankly gravel, separating three rows of trailer homes. The trailers looked older than the sign but not quite as bad as the road. They

had started out white with an occasional lick of black trim clinging stubbornly to the window frames, but in the deepening twilight they glowed a faint and sooty gray. Mona pulled up at the
end of a row, and after a moment's consideration backed the car
and turned it to face the way we had come.

"This is it," she said.

"How long has your friend lived here?"

"Not long."

I considered the car, arranged for a speedy getaway. "But
you're still on good terms?"

Mona leaned down, reaching between my feet, and drew the
newspaper and the envelope from the bag. Then she opened the
glove compartment and took out a hair brush and a lipstick case.

"I was wondering, when you were going to brush your hair."

"Have you got the camera?"

"Are you kidding? I am so on top of this."

She was peering up into the rear view mirror, working impatiently at her hair in short, choppy strokes. When she finally
finished, it was so light and lively with static that it floated like a
frizzy halo around her neck and face. "Shit," she muttered.

"That is one heck of a perm."

"Just shut up, okay?" She dropped the brush and tried to
smooth the hair back with her hands as if calming a Persian kit-
ten. Then she had the lipstick out. Her mouth was pursed. There
wasn't much light, but her face was so pale against the cloudy
black of her hair that the dark red lipstick stood out. The glasses
were dark as a burglar's mask.

"This isn't some sort of singing telegram, is it?" I was whispering now in the face of all this mystery.

"Something like that."

"Are you going to jump out of a cake and yell surprise?"

"Probably not." She climbed out of the car. The engine was
still running, and she left the door open. "Come on," she said.

"Tell me you've done this before."

We crept toward the first row of trailers. As we got further from the low panting of the Mustang's engine a noise like the sound of a distant crowd arose, and through the line of trees beyond the last gravel track the Interstate appeared, sudden and broad as a river, with headlights sweeping along on the current. In the constant pressure of the noise the whole scene turned dark and uncertain, as if at any moment it might dissolve into something even less reassuring.

"Is your name really Mona?"

"What?"

"Mona?"

"Yeah, Mona. Okay?"

"I've got some messages from your mother."

"Will you concentrate?" she hissed.

It was almost eight. I should be at the bar now, but I had wandered clear of my routine. The air was getting cool. I tried to imagine Henry here in my place, but I couldn't at first. Not old Henry. But then I remembered him laughing wildly in the careening car as if he couldn't believe what he'd gotten himself into. His life had suddenly opened to include the most unexpected things: romantic meetings, open cars speeding down the road, evenings spent lurking in the twilight with a woman he'd be kissing later that night. That was his life now. And the fact that I'd slipped into it, temporarily and by accident, just made it all the more startling. I thought of the old Henry, boring and familiar, who had opened himself so effortlessly into a life of such adventure. How exactly had he managed it?

I had been trying to do just that for so long. I'd found work in the toughest bar I knew, as a kind of offering to the rough hands of chance, letting myself in for whatever might come. But in the end I'd only fallen from one routine into another. The last six years had been as uneventful as a long car ride, and at some point along the way an awareness of nothing changing had given way to the certainty that nothing would.

But now my stomach was churning, though with fear or excitement I couldn't be sure. We crept past trailers that looked all but abandoned except for the muffled sounds of their televisions seeping out past the shades. Mona carried the manila envelope in one hand and the newspaper rolled like a club in the other. She was checking numbers on the mailboxes, and at the corner of the third she stopped, glancing back. "You're going to need the flash," she whispered.

I held the camera in both hands. There was a car parked on a little patch of dirt beside the trailer, a gray and boxy Jeep. Mona drew a tiny flashlight from her pocket, and in the sudden spot of light the gray paint turned to red and rust. As she bent to peer at the license plate the glare splashed back over her face beneath the nimbus of dark hair. The silver ring glinted in her nose. She wore the intent expression of a young girl on the first day of school.

"Tell me again what we're doing," I hissed.

"It's simple." Over her shoulder the venetian blinds in the nearest window flickered as figures moved across the TV screen and sounds of a pitched gun battle seeped through the wall. "Just take the picture when I say."

"Whose picture?"

"Whoever answers the door."

"That's it?"

"That's it. Think you can manage?"

What was I going to say? Cautiously she stepped up onto the tiny porch, then hesitated and slipped down again. She leaned so close I thought for a moment she was going to kiss me for luck, but instead she said, very quietly, "I need you to yell when I knock."

"Yell what?"

"Millie, it's me. Johnny."

"You're kidding."

"Millie, it's--"

"I heard."

"As loud as you can." And she gave a lame little shrug. "It's part of the joke. And make sure you've got the flash on."

"It's automatic. It's always on."

Mona patted me on the arm. "You're doing great." And she stepped up onto the porch.

Shaking out the newspaper, she folded the front page into a banner. I could see the gray smear of a headline, though the words were indistinct. With the envelope tucked beneath one arm she eased the screen door open and, raising her fist, loud in the darkness, offered up three sharp knocks.

I took a deep breath. "Millie!" My voice croaked like a rusted box. "It's me. I'm Johnny!"

Jesus Christ, I thought. One line for the night, and I blow it. But it didn't seem to matter. Mona gestured, and hurriedly I raised the camera, though when I looked into the viewfinder all I saw was darkness and the tiny, pale blur of her face.

"Again," she hissed. And again the three sharp knocks.

"Millie!" I called, louder this time. "It's me, Johnny!" Then, caught up in the thespian spirit of the moment, "Come on, baby! Aren't you going to open the door?"

That seemed to do it. There was the sudden scrape of a chair and a deep, hollow thud of something hitting the trailer floor, then the sound of footsteps. I barely had time to wonder just how big a woman this Millie was before the door burst open, and a man in boxers and a very clean white undershirt stepped into the sudden rectangle of light.

Nothing very distinct registered in that moment, though afterwards the photo turned out pretty well, all things considered, and looking at it I could see all I needed to. But at that moment I was aware only of the crash of the door, the strong, frat-party aroma of warm beer, and a loud, if blurred, voice shouting: "Tough shit, Johnny! Millie's not here!"

Mona slapped the newspaper across the front of that bright white shirt. "Now!"

He was just a pale silhouette in the dark of the viewfinder, and all I could do was try hurriedly to center it as I pressed the shutter. The bulb flashed, picking out every crack and peel in the door frame and, frozen within it, the sudden startled face: pale, wide-eyed, short blonde hair. An instant of surprise, then darkness. Mona tossed the envelope like a Frisbee in through the open door and vaulted off the porch. I snatched the photograph from the lip of the camera and was already turning when she grabbed my arm and jerked me into motion.

The man just stood there. In the face of all this activity he seemed immobilized by the beer and the flash. We raced back toward the car, but even as we reached it he still hadn't moved. In that moment as we piled in, just before Mona floored it and the Mustang fish-tailed over the gravel and down around the bend, I looked back and saw him standing in the light of the doorway, dim and indistinct. Only later did I have any sense at all of how the man looked. What stayed with me now as we drove away , as the tires ripped through the gravel and the car tore off round the curve, was his voice. In the distance behind us I heard the anger give way to a thin and puzzled tone as he called out almost shyly: "Hey. What's going on?"

6

We sat in a booth near the back of the Blue Diner. Alive with adrenaline and fighting to keep a manic grin from taking over my face, I had no idea what I'd just accomplished. But that didn't matter. I was buzzing like a fluorescent light. And across from me sat Mona with an answering look of electric satisfaction.

"That was good," she said. "You did good."

"Good? I did great. And what about you? Cool and confident. Grace under pressure."

"You think?"

"The way you jumped off that porch. It was poetry in motion. And look at that." I held up my hand, still faintly quivering with all that had happened. "Steady as a rock."

Mona grinned. "He never knew what hit him."

"Hell. I never knew what hit him." I pressed my hand flat against the table, feeling the vibration only now starting to leak away. After a moment, I looked up again. "So, what is it exactly that we just did?"

"Well, you just made fifty bucks and a free dinner."

"And you?"

"A little more than that," she conceded. "But, I'm buying dinner."

Rusty appeared with two menus in one hand and a collection of pink message slips in the other. She gave me a quick, frowning glance of recognition, divided the menus between us, and placed the slips in a little pile in the middle. "He give you the others?" she asked.

"Oh, right." I dug the tangle of messages out of my pocket and added them to the pile. "She asked me to give you these."

With a mournful shake of the head Rusty drew out her pad.

"Know what you want?"

"Something special," said Mona. "We're celebrating."

"Pork roast is as special as we got tonight. And Carlisle called. He said no hard feelings."

Mona frowned. "If he calls again, tell him to go screw himself."

Rusty made a couple of little marks on the pad, as if to make sure she got the wording right, and headed back toward the kitchen. Mona picked up the messages and started leafing through them.

"Who's Carlisle?" I asked.

"Just some guy. So what do you want? I hear the pork roast is pretty good. I think we're probably getting it anyway."

"That sounds fine."

With the excitement subsiding I began to feel oddly uneasy as the dubiousness of my situation had a chance to settle in. My father had never seemed like a man who might have a secret life, and yet here I was, sitting snugly in the middle of it. I wondered if it might not be a little difficult to explain. I had, after all, been invited—hired in fact. And it seemed unlikely that what I was doing could actually constitute stalking in any strictly legal and indictable sense. But I couldn't shake the feeling that I had somehow wandered in a little out of my depth. I said, "You've done this sort of thing how many times exactly?"

Mona shrugged. "That depends what you mean by this sort of thing."

"Well, buying dinner for some stranger off the street, say?"

"Technically you weren't off the street. You were at my office. Besides, your name's Harry, right? And you work at the hardware store." She stuck out her hand, pale and protruding from the heavy cuff of her jacket like some little sea creature stirring from its cave. "I'm Mona. Pleased to meet you." And she smiled.

Don't ask me why, I mean I'd known her for almost twenty-four hours, but it was only then that it hit me. Something in the smile. Before this there had been the candlelight and the dancing, of course, and the champagne. I hadn't forgotten about those. And that short, pink dress. But she was so obviously irritating; so slouchingly thin and resolutely unlikable. But then she smiled, and it was embarrassing. Like discovering your father's secret vice—the Penthouse under the mattress or the Ecstasy in his sock drawer. Here suddenly was more insight than I wanted about that new spring in his step.

"Likewise," I said, half-expecting something, a little shock, a small bolt of lightning, as we touched. But her handshake was firm and quick. It seemed suddenly important that I not smile back. "And what about the rest of it?" I said. "Driving up to some drunken guy and taking his picture? How often does that happen?"

"See, that's a little more often."

"And people pay you for that?"

"Not as much as they should. But that reminds me." She reached into her green plaid pants and drew out a thin roll of bills. Peeling off two twenties and a ten she laid them, curling and grubby, on the table. "Nice job."

"I'd settle for an explanation."

"Really?" She started to reach for the money.

"As well."

She laughed. A nice laugh. How had Henry managed to get himself a laugh like that? A nice smile, a nice laugh. Everything about her seemed to make Henry a little less clear to me. Her hair looked softly crazy. Her eyes gleamed. The ring in her nose glinted like the promise of some submerged exotic prurience.

"It's really not that complicated," she said. "Take our friend Biff."

"Biff?"

"Tonight."

"His name's Biff?"

"His wife hired me to find him."

"Millie," I said.

"No. Someone else. Her name's Jean. She's a nice enough

woman. A total flake, but she's had a lot to deal with."

"And she wanted you to take his picture?"

"She wanted me to find him and give him a letter. The picture was just the proof that I did what I'm going to tell her I did. In case she never sees him again."

"So who's Millie?"

Mona shrugged. "One of the reasons she'll probably never see him again."

"And you do this a lot?"

"More or less."

I digested that for a moment. Mona was nodding to herself, tapping her foot against the base of the table as if the adrenaline that had already faded from my bloodstream was still playing jumpily in hers. She pulled off the jacket and piled it on the bench beside her. Unveiled like that, the orange t-shirt looked even more garish, clinging to the shallow suggestion of her breasts. What was Henry thinking? What had he gotten himself into? Though even as I wondered, I had a vision of the short pink dress riding high on her thighs and the sound of her voice, a low teasing chuckle, as she swayed along beside him.

"He didn't seem too happy, did he?"

"What?" I looked up, startled.

"Biff." Mona was tapping out a rhythm on the table top.

"He did seem a mite confused."

"That's always my favorite part. Just that last bit. They have no idea you're on their trail until… Knock, knock. This is your conscience speaking."

"I don't suppose they're ever pleased to see you."

"Not so much. They tend to be kind of annoyed. But you get used to that."

I nodded with at least the appearance of understanding. "So, this makes you. . . what? Some sort of private detective?"

Mona glanced up in surprise. "Of course. What did you think?"

"Me? How would I know?"

"You came to my office."

"Oh," I said slowly. "That's right. But it wasn't exactly like that. I was just looking for someone."

"Then you came to the right place." She was leaning forward now, elbows on the table, suddenly all business. "What can I do for you?"

I considered that for a moment. "Now that you mention it, I'm not really sure."

"Just relax," she said. "Take your time." And she gazed at me through those heavy black frames with an air of kindly, professional encouragement that was completely at odds with the frazzled disorder of her hair.

"It's a little personal," I said.

"It always is."

"How long have you been doing this?"

"A few years. Why? You want to see some references?" "Do you have any?"

"Up in my office."

"Satisfied customers?"

"Most of them."

"It's really nothing," I said.

"You wouldn't have come to my office over nothing."

And that was true enough.

"There's just something I need to know about. Something I need to find out. About what's going on with someone."

"Girlfriend?"

"Not exactly."

"Boyfriend?"

"No. I'm not…. No. It's just this situation I've got. There's this friend who's acting a little strange."

"How strange?"

"Pretty strange."

"Have you tried asking her about it?"

I hesitated. "I don't think that would help. We're not all that good at communicating. We've been together for a while, and I thought everything was fine. I mean, not great. But still…. We've sort of gotten used to each other."

"Sometimes that can be enough," said Mona doubtfully. "It works for some people."

"Well, I thought it was working for us, but now I'm not so sure."

"So, what is it you want? You want me to follow her? Tell you what she's up to?"

"Could you do that? I mean, you do that sort thing?"

"All the time."

"Does it work?"

"Depends. I can tail someone, trace their movements, tell you where they've been, what they're doing. But that doesn't always help. I had one woman come in. She hired me to follow her husband. She was sure he was cheating on her. He kept making excuses, slipping away at night. Getting up early. Sometimes never coming home."

"Did she try asking him?" I said.

"He said he was working late at the office."

"What did he do?

"He was an accountant."

"And he was working late?"

Mona smiled wryly. "That's what she thought. She was certain there was another woman, and she wanted me to find out who it was. I checked his bank accounts, credit cards, his whole credit history. I checked his insurance records for some new beneficiary, driving records, even the police. And then I followed him. For three weeks."

I found I was leaning forward. "What did you find?"

"He was working late. That's all. I asked him about it later. He said he loved his job."

"An accountant?"

"He loved it. He loved the peace and quiet."

"His wife must have been relieved."

"She was furious. She divorced him. Took everything he

had." Mona shrugged. "That's the thing. You start messing with love, you never know which way it's going to go."

I managed another weak smile, but I realized that wasn't my problem. I hadn't started messing with love. Not me. And maybe that, in itself, was the problem. Oh, there had been occasional awkward episodes over drinks at the bar. Desperate fumblings here and there. But nothing really. Nothing that, even from a distance, could be mistaken for love. In all this time, I'd never even brought anyone home. Somehow I just hadn't felt up to it. And despite Edith Mullins, I'd always believed that Henry felt the same. I was sure of it. Until now.

Mona was gazing at me encouragingly, looking wild and disarrayed and oddly businesslike, and I offered up a bleak little smile. But what I was thinking was how the night before, with one hand on Henry's shoulder, she had swayed in the candlelight, coaxing a dance out of a man who, I was prepared to bet, had never thought it possible.

For the last six years, in spite of everything, there had always been one part I could count on. Despite the ups and downs, the hurt and anger and sadness, I could always be sure. No matter how I was dealing with it, no matter how I was feeling, no matter how badly I knew I was managing, it didn't matter, because at the end of the day when I lay down to sleep I could close my eyes on the grudging certainty that, whatever else I was doing, I was doing better than Henry.

"It would help," said Mona, "if you could give me more information. If you could just tell me what the problem is."

But it was all I could do just to shake my head. I had only just realized what the problem was. I had the same choked and panicky feeling that all her clients must come to her with: that sense of impending loss and abandonment, of looming disaster. And what could I tell her? What was I going to say? You've got to help me? It's my father? I think he's cheating on me?

7

If someone had asked me, growing up, if we were a happy family what would I have said? Doesn't everybody just say yes? I remember us laughing together. I remember playing little family games, going on picnics, having fun. At least I think I do. But after a while doesn't it get hard to differentiate between what you remember and what actually occurred? Every family has its problems, those little disagreements, those small moments of friction. And don't you have to take those in stride? You don't dwell on them. That's not the important part. The important part is that you love each other, that you count on each other. Isn't that right?

Maybe the problem is just that happiness is so hard to recognize. It arrives as a lifting of the spirits, a modest adjustment in your level of well-being, while sadness changes your life. It falls on you like a new way of being, fierce and clear the moment it arrives, while happiness can be clearly seen only in retrospect or in the bright potential of all that might be. And you find yourself trapped in the conditional mood. *It would have been different if. It's bound to be different when.* And every step forward becomes a step back, until you realize all you're doing is living in place, and the changes you're waiting for are all in the past.

When I came down to the smell of coffee the next Saturday morning I found my father kneeling in the middle of the back yard. He was dressed in old khakis and a tired plaid shirt and he was whistling cheerfully under his breath as he dug up a broad patch of tulips. Their buds were just beginning to show a faint promise of red and yellow, and as he pried them out of the soil he arranged them in a little crowd on the narrow concrete path where they looked startled and forlorn. I poured a cup of coffee and stepped outside, still in my bathrobe, taking in the scene with the day's first stirrings of unease.

Henry glanced up and wiped the sweat on his forehead, leaving a dark smear of earth. "Hey, there," he said cheerfully. "You're up early."

"It's ten o'clock."

"Really?" He glanced at his watch and shook it, then climbed to his feet. "How's the coffee?"

"Could be a little stronger."

"Is there any left?"

"A little," I said. "What are you doing?"

He paused for a moment, gazing sheepishly down at the uprooted plants as if at something embarrassing he'd only just noticed. "Nothing much. Mona said she might like some flowers."

"Did she say how many she wanted?"

There were maybe fifteen tulips sprawled across the walk. The hole in the garden looked like a bomb crater.

Henry shrugged. "I thought, since I was here, it wouldn't hurt to open the place up a bit."

"Open it up?"

"Just a bit. It's getting a little crowded. I thought I'd give them a little room to breathe."

Before Elizabeth left, and before he embraced the power of sleep, my father had always gardened. It was his one hobby. Perhaps, after the third generation, the pressure of ignoring the soil had started to tell, though he continued to hold out against anything practical. No fruits or vegetables. No herbs. He grew nasturtiums until someone explained you could actually eat them, and then he abandoned them completely. All he asked of his plants was that they grow, flower, die, and provide him with some steady occupation away from the store.

The yard wasn't a large one. It had started out as two grass rectangles flanking a concrete path and bounded by two modest flower beds. Barely a garden at all. But over the years, under the lowering threat of potential free time, Henry had gradually expanded his plantings, opening new beds in the middle of the lawn, paring away the sod in wider and wider arcs, until he'd whittled it down to a series of narrow grass paths dividing a landscape of earth and flowers. And then finally, succumbing to the inevitable pressure, the paths themselves thinned to vanishing, and the garden beds merged into a seamless expanse of floral sprawl.

There were a few things my mother hated about the garden, quite apart from the time it consumed. There was, for instance, no good way to look at it, no proper vantage point. The garden turned its back on its audience. From every spot beyond its boundaries it looked cramped and inscrutable, a pointless tangle of leaves and color. The only way to make sense of it was to be in the middle, edging carefully among plantings or kneeling precariously on the thin boundaries of vacant soil. It was a garden for Henry alone.

My mother had gone so far as to suggest a little clearing, perhaps even a patio with a table and chairs. A little spot where we could all sit and enjoy the fruits of his work. She had seen it in a magazine and cut out the picture. A latticework iron table and chairs, painted a bright and cheerful red, beneath a broad wooden pergola woven with ivy. The whole arrangement was pictured beside an enormous yew hedge and looked like something out of some ancient English estate. Certainly much too grand for our little garden. And maybe that was what Henry objected to. Or maybe he thought it was just too practical. He agreed immediately whenever the subject came up, but in the end did nothing about it. Even when Elizabeth went out and bought a red table and chairs, he kept coming up with reasons not to put them in, until finally, after more than a month, she simply returned them to the garden store.

Shortly after they were gone, so was she.

When she left, the garden had nowhere to expand, so, like Henry, it turned in on itself. Plants lived, bloomed, and died in such tangled proximity it was impossible to tell them apart unless you knelt among the leaves and followed each stem to the ground. There was barely room to stand. And still, when he wasn't planting or weeding, Henry was browsing through gardening catalogs, looking for that new addition that would somehow make sense of it all.

And now here he was, digging a big hole in the middle of everything.

It was maybe eight feet across when Henry finally stopped. He stood gazing at the earth for a moment, measuring the effect, then he picked up a rake and began smoothing the blank vacancy. As I watched I clung in vague desperation to the hope that my father was simply deranged. That the pressure of the last six years had finally been too much, and he had come unhinged. And when he paused, leaning on the rake, he did glance around in something like surprise, as if startled to realize all that he had done.

"Henry?"

"Almost there," he said.

"What are those?" I pointed to the edge of the driveway where an uneven stack of gray paving stones stood, looking new and out of place.

"They came this morning."

"Are you planning on putting them anywhere in particular?"

"I'm thinking about it."

"A little patio or something?" I said.

"Maybe." He glanced up. "What do you think?"

I felt a thin, hot wire of anger in my chest, sudden and yet somehow unsurprising, as if it had been wrapped unnoticed around my heart all these years. "Why?"

"I don't know. Some place to sit? Enjoy the garden?"

"I mean, why now? Is this Mona, too? Did she decide you needed a patio?"

My father shrugged. "It doesn't seem like such a bad idea, does it?"

"A bad idea? No. Good heavens, no. It's a great idea. It's fabulous. It's just a little late, don't you think?"

He stood there puzzled and nonplussed, as if he hadn't thought of it in just that way before. "Better late than never, wouldn't you say?"

"No," I said. "No, I wouldn't. Actually, I wouldn't say that at all."

He stood tapping the handle of the rake against his leg as if considering it all or maybe just waiting for me to finish, because after a moment, when I said nothing more, he glanced back at the pile of paving stones. "You want to give me a hand?"

I thought of the picture my mother had torn from the magazine. I thought of her bright red patio furniture, stacked in the garage for all those weeks, waiting for nothing more than to be carried back to the store. "I don't think so."

"It'll only take a little--."

It's your idea, Henry. You take care of it."

My father glanced down at the empty dirt and smoothed a little patch with the rake. They he let the handle drop and walked over to the pile of stones. They looked impossibly heavy, each one as broad as a manhole cover. My father nudged one with his boot. Then he bent and grasped the edge, hunching his shoulders, straining. The rock slid a little with a dry scraping sound. Henry braced his feet again, rocking the stone to the edge of the stack, and with a final effort he heaved it up so that it slid down the pile, hit the gravel with a crunch, and toppled slowly forward. After a hunched and panting moment he stepped over and reached down for it again.

"Jesus Christ! Will you cut it out? What? Are you *trying* to hurt yourself?

"Go have your breakfast," he said.

"I'm not going to have my breakfast!" I started forward, clutching my coffee mug as if I might pound Henry over the head with it.

He straightened up and wiped his forehead. Then he glanced

down at my bathrobe. "You want a pair of gloves?"

"Forget it."

I set the mug down and squatted by the stone, cramming my fingers under the edge. "Watch your back," my father said. "Lift with your legs."

"I've lifted a rock before."

We hoisted it up. The weight was like a sudden, terrible shock between us. We stood there, teetering and appalled. Then, staggering together, we steered it over to the hole. I started to lower it.

"Just drop it," Henry grunted. "Ready? One, tw--. Look out!"

I lurched forward as the rock slipped from my father's grip and I managed to let go as it flopped with a muffled thump onto the earth.

"Good," said Henry breathlessly. He was bent half forward, hands on his knees. "That's perfect."

I was panting hard. "Could you maybe not drop it like that?"

"It slipped."

"Well, could you maybe not let it slip? I'd just as soon not be crippled for the rest of my life just so you can show off for your ridiculous girlfriend."

He straightened up and regarded me for a moment without a word.

"Forget it," I said. I turned back to the pile

After a moment he followed wearily and stood, staring down at the gathered stones, each one as heavy as the first. "You know," he said. "You don't have to worry about Mona."

"I'm not worried."

"She doesn't have anything to do with us. I mean, she won't affect us."

"I am so relieved."

"I mean it." He glanced up, hesitating. He appeared about to say something more but in the end just seemed to lose track.

We'd never been much on talking. There hadn't been that much to say. Over the years the only thing on both our minds was my mother—what exactly had driven her away—and no answer to that could possibly be anything but terrible. So by an unspoken agreement we left it alone. And if gradually our silence came to include anything awkward or uncertain or simply too complex, that only meant that the larger subject of Elizabeth Drew Bailey had grown so vast as to encompass almost everything. Now with a shrug Henry bent and laced his fingers under the edge of the next rock, waiting for me, frowning over the task at hand.

As a boy I'd always believed that Henry and I were two versions of the same person. Two Henry Baileys, one junior, one senior, bound by a common substance. We were the ones my mother was angry with, or irritated with, or even occasionally pleased by. We were her two men, joined by her common feelings. And even after she'd left I held onto this notion. We ate together, worried together, grew sad and lonely together.

But now I glared down at him with what might have been simple anger, except for the sick, unraveling feeling that was so much a part of it. It wasn't just that he was moving on with his life, or that he was offering this new girlfriend one of the few things my mother had ever actually asked him for. It was that I began to realize how illusory any similarity had been, like the false attraction a magnet will lend to a fragment of iron. The only thing we had in common, it turned out, was Elizabeth. So when Henry reassured me that there was nothing to worry about with Mona, that she wouldn't affect us, all I could think as I stared down at him waiting patiently by the heavy, implacable stone, was how little of us there seemed to be.

When we were done, and the last rock was in place, my father scraped the toe of his work boot across one rough stone. "Not too shabby."

But I felt like an accessory to a crime. I turned and started toward the house.

"Harry?" he said. "Just one more thing?"

He led the way to the garage, and there they were: four ancient steel chairs, chipped and flaking into two or three different shades of green, and a round, grillwork table in a terrible, muddy brown.

"God damn it," I muttered. "Where did you find them? Some dumpster?"

"I bought them. Used."

"Oh, Henry."

"I was thinking maybe I'd paint them."

"How about blue?" I said bitterly. "Blue's a good color. How does Mona feel about blue?"

My father nodded thoughtfully. "Maybe," he said. "Blue's an idea."

It's a tricky thing losing your mother if you're a man. Nowadays you can't throw a rock through a bookstore without hitting a section on Motherless Daughters or Sisters Without Moms or My Mother, My Self. As a daughter it's somehow expected that you grieve, that you feel bereft and broken, not just privately, but publicly and for a very long time. For the time it takes to write a book, say. Or even longer. But as a man you notice that after a while people don't want to hear it any more. You see it in their eyes, in the quick, perfunctory sympathy. And if you mention it, you begin to seem mopey and pathetic.

But it's hard sometimes, the emptiness, the longing and the ache. The shock that comes out of the blue, long after it should.

I took up cooking.

From the ancient collection of my mother's cookbooks I created a whole nostalgia of dinners. It was like cooking in the fifties. Every meal had a kind of folk art grandeur that was its own comfort and reward. The recipes involved condensed soup or gravy mix or ketchup or four different kinds of canned vegetables. There were recipes that called for Velveeta or Spam or frozen peas. The Midwest is the land of the hot dish. The comfort meal. And so from my mother's recipes I made meatloaf and macaroni and "Hungarian goulash" with two different kinds of canned tomatoes. I made tuna casserole and beef stroganoff and three varieties of hash. I made dishes that hadn't been seen since Eisenhower was president, and each night I set them on the table with a kind of hopeful sheepishness, and my father ate them gratefully with a look of mild surprise, as if he'd tasted something like this long ago but couldn't quite remember when.

My favorite book on the whole crowded shelf was an old loose-leaf binder with gingham-red covers and all the old standards for the average homemaker. Mixed in were a series of recipes my mother had torn from the newspaper or peeled from the backs of cans over the years. As far as I could remember she had never tried any of them. She had tended to fall back on a few recurring themes: casseroles, meatloaf, an occasional pot roast. But these scattered fragments from the earliest years of her marriage stood as a kind of evidence that there was a time, at least, when she was trying. When she wasn't yet ready to give up and leave.

And sometimes I just paged through the book, from recipe to recipe, not looking so much for the evening meal as for some hidden insight into my mother's mind. She had collected all these scraps, stored them against some need; it was a gesture of the greatest optimism. And reading through them I was free to imagine the sort of happy, contented, and cozy domesticity that was permanently preserved in directions for Marshmallow-Jello Salad, Ham & Cheese Casserole, or Persian Army Chicken.

That evening I had the cookbook open on the counter, and I was just cracking a can of condensed mushroom soup when I heard Henry coming down the stairs. "How does chicken casserole sound?" I called. I had the breasts laid out on their grainy bed of breadcrumbs with the buttered Pyrex dish beside them. But as I turned to toss the lid of the soup can away I saw that Henry was wearing another tuxedo jacket, the black one this time, over the usual blue work shirt and khakis. He looked vaguely uneasy, as if he'd been dressed for a while but had only just noticed that nothing went together.

The tuxedos had been my mother's idea. She'd bought them

for Henry over the years, sometimes for his birthday, sometimes for no occasion at all, when he'd been wearing the same thing for five days in a row and she was desperate for a change. She bought them in thrift shops or vintage clothing stores and presented them, elegantly wrapped and boxed. Henry's reaction was always the same. He looked delighted, and immediately tried it on. Then it disappeared into his closet never to be seen again. When Elizabeth suggested he wear one, when they were going out or she just wanted to get dressed up at home, he always lifted one down on its hanger, looked it over, and inevitably came downstairs without it, smiling apologetically. "It seems too nice to wear."

After she left I took them from my father's closet. It seemed important that somebody wear them. There were six in a range of colors: burgundy, navy, black, white, brown, and a royal-blue number that even I saved for special occasions. When I'd first started wearing them my father said nothing. He smiled, though whether in silent appreciation or simply over the vagaries of human taste, I couldn't be sure. But he'd certainly never given any sign of wanting them back until now.

He fingered the black lapel. "What do you think? Is this too much?"

"Too much what?"

He smiled and with a glance at the ingredients on the counter said, "Is that for us?"

"Why would you think that? Didn't you hear? I've started cooking for the people across the street."

"You didn't need to," he said gently.

I felt a sudden blur of irritation, and something else: that low, hot fibrillation of hurt feelings. *But I thought you liked my cooking.* "Okay," I said. "So, what do you want to do? You want to order out?"

"The thing is," he said, "I was going to mention it earlier. I thought I might put together something. A little pasta or something."

"You're going to make dinner?"

"Just a little something."

"But I already bought the chicken."

"It'll keep."

"Not chicken. Besides, look. It's almost finished. Why don't I just--"

The doorbell rang. Henry frowned like a magician who's rushed the timing on a trick. "The thing is, son...."

Mona wore a sky blue rayon shirt covered with little cross-hatchings of gold and red, and a bright lilac skirt that would have gone well with just about any other top. Her hair, as wild and fluffy as the night before, was newly tinted a deep, cobalt blue. She stepped into the kitchen, looking bright and changeable as a mood ring, and abruptly she stopped. She stood there staring.

"Surprise," I said.

"What the hell are you doing here?"

"Actually, I'm just leaving."

"What do you mean you're just leaving?"

Henry glanced back and forth with an almost comic perplexity. "Have you two met?"

"No," I said. "What did you do to your hair this time?"

"Hey. It goes with the outfit, okay? And anyway, what the hell is going on? Are you following me?"

"Hello? I was here first. Remember?"

"And what?" she said peevishly with a glance at the counter. "You're making dinner?"

"You should be so lucky. Henry's cooking. I think you're having pasta."

"But what...?" she started, and then just petered out.

At which point Henry, tuxedo-clad and rising to the occasion, stepped smoothly between us like a half-dapper head waiter. "Harry," he said. "This is Mona. Mona, this is Harry." And he spread a shy and eager smile like a little rug between us, as if he couldn't be more pleased to have finally brought us together.

8.

Mom's Saloon and Fine Foods wasn't a large bar, but it managed to concentrate an impressive amount of bad taste within its narrow confines. It was an old and crooked shotgun shack, arranged like a badly joined pair of plywood shoe boxes painted three shades of camouflage brown. During daylight hours it was just one more shabby building in a shantytown of tire stores, muffler shops, and abandoned parking lots crowded together against the silty edge of the river. But at night it was an oasis of noise and smoke. It stood leaning above the bank as if washed up by an unexpected tide, as if any two men might put their shoulders to the front and send it sliding into the sluggish current. The fact that people had actually tried this—that after a particularly lively evening, disenchanted customers had been known to exhaust themselves shoving and cursing and falling down—could be taken as just one more proof of the bar's principal charms: the beer was cheap, the drinks were strong, and the customers were, by and large, unswayed by common sense.

I had been working there almost five years, ever since I'd first staggered in at the end of a particularly long and unproductive night. I'd been walking for hours at random, less and less inclined as the evening wore on to return home, where the fact that Henry was sleeping so soundly, after all that had happened, was more than I could bear. I paused at a corner to consider my options and saw the small square sign, glowing like a shabby beacon in the darkness. With a name like that, how could it be anything but an omen?

I stepped in through the door. The smoke and noise were exactly what I needed after all the lonely silence. I sat down on a stool. Mom, himself, was there, presiding behind the bar. He was

tall, maybe a shade over six feet, with thinning black hair plas-
tered back over a round, pale scalp and a pair of long sideburns
curved and sharpened to points. But it wasn't the hair or even
the sideburns that caught the eye and made that all–important
first impression. His whole body looked inflated. He wore a
black leather vest over a belly round and hard as a boulder. His
arms, as if in contrast, looked fleshy and soft, but each one was
only slightly narrower than my thigh. On one bicep he wore a
tattoo: a banner with the word Mom, looking like something out
of an old Popeye cartoon, except that instead of surrounding it
with a son's loving heart, there was a grinning death's head with
a dagger through its skull, making it clear that while Mom may
be a shortened form of mother, mother itself was, in this case,
meant only as an abbreviation.

He stood there, regarding me like stout Cortez on the peak
in Darian or Columbus with the New World rising into view. Or
maybe he was just bored. It was a slow night, there hadn't been
a fight yet, and Mom was feeling kindly. He said, "Got some ID,
kid?"

I took out the driver's license I'd bought from a guy at the
moving company where I was working. Mom glanced at it, then
he drew a beer and set it down in its own little puddle.

"Nice place you've got here," I said.

"That's a buck fifty."

I sat and drank my beer and looked around. It was crowded
and noisy, with the edgy laughter of a riot just about to break
out. No one paid me any attention, and that in itself was a comfort. With my next beer I asked for a job.

"Huh?"

"Job," I repeated. "Work? You need anybody?"

"You got any experience?"

"Hell, yes."

He regarded me for a moment. Then he laid my change delicately on the bar. "I don't think so."

I asked again with the next beer, and the next. "Have you

changed your mind about that job, yet?"

I can't imagine it now; he must have been in a very good mood. Or perhaps there's simply a shadow of unexpected luck that falls over the hapless and broken-hearted. All he said was, "What is it with you?"

"I need a job."

"Not here, you don't."

"Why not? I'd be great. Come on. Give me one good reason."

And very slowly he leaned forward and in a very gentle voice replied, "Because I said so. Okay?"

Maybe it was the beer, maybe the banked unhappiness of all that long, last year, or maybe just that, even through such giddy fatigue, I could recognize an unexpected kindness on the wing. But with the sudden pressure of tears behind my eyes I could only manage a whisper. "Please? "

He stared at me for a moment, then shook his head. "You've had enough." And with a hand the size of a baseball mitt he lifted away my half-consumed beer. But as if he could read my heart in the way that only mothers can, he set down in its place a mug of ginger ale. "Shut up," he said. "Drink this."

I sat propped there against the bar and drank the ginger ale as if it were medicine and I was under a doctor's care.

Across the room the noise was turning jagged. A voice rose out of the muffled confusion. "You did not!"

"I sure as hell did!"

"You sure as fucking hell did not!"

A silence fell like the little, turning moment just before the wind blows. Then a man in a black watch cap and a ragged denim jacket stood up and raised his voice in a tone of sudden, epiphanic illumination. "Why you motherfucking cocksucker!"

I glanced up to find Mom leaning over the counter again. That near-smile was on his face. "Hey, kid. You still want that job?"

I nodded.

"I imagine you got a lot of bouncing experience, right?"

"God, yes."

The man in the denim jacket was standing in a little ring of empty space, glaring out into the crowd like an angry badger. Together we regarded him for a moment.

"Try not to hurt him."

I climbed off the stool and approached the table slowly with a strange and disembodied absence of concern. I wasn't sure what I'd say when I got there, but after too much beer and a year's worth of unrelinquished anger I was curious to find out. What it turned out to be was: "Listen up, all you mouseketeers. I think the time has come to say goodbye."

The man in the watch cap turned and stared. "Who the hell are you?"

But there was no stopping me now. I was sliding forward on a slick of beer and rage and a kind of antic glossolalia. "The management asked me to come over and clarify for you the most convenient route of egress, which is to say the exit, which is to say the front door, just on the off chance that you've forgotten where it is."

"You... what?" The man glanced back at the crowd as if they might have a clue. The watch cap was screwed down tight on his head. His cheeks were prickly with whiskers.

"Please take a moment to gather your belongings. Don't forget to check the overhead compartments, but open them carefully. Some baggage may have shifted in flight."

"Get lost," the man said uncertainly, and gave me a tentative shove. I shoved back, and without further preamble he knocked me down.

I still don't remember hitting the ground. It felt more like a bounce or a sort of scrambling leap from a sprawled position, something with quite a high degree of difficulty but which I must have accomplished without much thought since the next thing I knew, I was gripping the front of the denim jacket in one clenched fist while furiously punching with the other. I'm not sure where I was hitting him, but even at the time I had the image of one of those old Popeye cartoons with a little cloud in the center of the frame and an array of fists flailing out in all directions. The man hit me again, and this time I felt the floor.

There was a chair next to me, tipped over on its side. I dragged myself up and stood. My nose was a huge, softball-sized ache in the middle of my face. "Go home," I said.

The man just stared. He looked untouched. His cap was pulled low over his eyes, and his jacket had a little smudge of my blood over one pocket. "Are you crazy?" He didn't sound belligerent now. He just seemed genuinely curious.

I swung at him again, and he hit me, low in the ribs. I went down, but I was up again as if on a spring. My fury was like cold air on an open nerve. It cleared my head and brought tears to my eyes. I leapt at the man. He knocked me down.

More slowly this time I climbed to my feet, clawing my way up the back of the chair. Each breath brought a little flower of pain in my side, and my lips were slick. When I was upright I held tight to the chair and stared for a moment. Then, grasping the back, I hoisted it into the air and held it there, balanced high over my head. The man just stared, wide-eyed and unbelieving, as if this were a trick he'd never seen before. The chair wavered a moment, alive with possibility. Then with a bellow, I smashed it down onto the wooden floor, and smashed it again and again until it came apart in my hands, until it fell to pieces. Then I raised the only fragments I still held, a part of the seat and one of the spindles, and I said, "Get out."

The bar was absolutely silent. The man in the watch cap stared at me with his mouth hanging open and his hands half raised. He started edging away. "You're nuts," he said, as if it had only just occurred to him and he thought it was something I should know. "You're fucking nuts." He seemed to consider this for a moment, as if grasping after some fuller statement of things, but he reached the door without further insight and let it slam behind him.

I stared at the roomful of people. They were very quiet. I

turned and trudged back to the bar and climbed up onto my stool. Mom considered me for a moment without expression. Then he dropped a damp cloth, grimy and beer-stained, onto the bar in front of me and told me to wipe my face. He set a shot of bourbon beside it. "Okay," he said finally. "You can stay. But keep your hands off the furniture."

My nose was broken, my rib was bruised, my left eye stayed shut for two days. But that was okay. Even the next morning, when Henry stared with open-mouthed shock and drove me straight to the hospital, it seemed in some strange way to be just right. Because, for the next couple of weeks at least, I felt a kind of balance, a kind of harmony between the inner and outer man. For the first time since my mother had left I finally looked the way I felt.

Tonight as I stepped in I tried to recapture that earlier sense of bruised and forlorn satisfaction, but it was nothing I could lay my hands on. The burgundy jacket hung limply against me. Henry seemed to have used up all the magic. I waded through the noise and smoke to the bar: a long, heavy oak counter crouching in the back. In the midst of all those plywood walls it was the only solid assurance in a ramshackle world, so that you could imagine a tornado ripping the roof off, and everyone still hugging the heavy oak for safety as the rest of the building fluttered up into the wind.

Mom was working alone tonight so service was slow, but no one complained. He was a man who always brought out the best in people. He glanced up. "You're supposed to be off tonight."

"I know. I was in the neighborhood. You need any help?"

"No. Take your day off. Get a life."

"I can't. I've been kicked out." I leaned forward, raising my voice into the hubbub. "My father's dating a girl half his age with blue hair. She has a ring in her nose. I've decided I'm running away from home."

Mom considered that for a moment. He said, "In that case

you'd better have a beer."

Across the room on the tiny dance floor couples were moving slowly to Muddy Waters. It wasn't a slow tune, but by some unspoken agreement the dancers were only listening to every third beat like Henry on the front porch by candlelight, following Benny Goodman's clarinet but slowly and at a distance. I sipped my beer. How did something like this sneak up on you?

I thought of Henry on the way to the hospital... when? Three months ago? With his arm numb as a stone. I was driving as fast as I could, and trying desperately to reassure us both. It's nothing. Your feet, your hands, they fall asleep all the time. It isn't serious. It doesn't mean anything. But Henry sat slumped, staring bleakly out at the ordinary houses going past, as if he'd never see them again.

"I can't feel anything."

"It's okay. It's nothing. It's just temporary." I was hunched over the wheel, trying to outrun the range of terrible possibilities suddenly looming over us both.

"No, it isn't! It's not okay!" His voice was almost a cry. "I can't go on like this."

His voice was like a needle in my chest. "You're doing fine," I said. "We're both doing fine."

But my father raised his arm, and the way it moved, stiffly and slowly, as if from a great distance.... "This isn't fine," he said.

"It won't last. We're managing."

"This has got to change. I'm going to die like this."

"You're not going to die."

"I'm dying now."

"No, you're not!"

And he wasn't. Not then. It was just nerves, stress. It was just all the usual things. But he had looked over with a face of blank and terrible wonder. "What are we going to do?"

I didn't know. How could I know? "We're doing the best we can," I said. But even then I heard the note of pleading in my voice. Aren't we? Tell me we are.

He didn't reply. Doing the best we can. It wasn't turning out to be much of a plan, and I guess he knew it. Maybe he realized, even then, how little help I was likely to be, and that any steps he was going to take, he'd have to take on his own.

And now he had. I should have been pleased for him. I tried to remember the desperation of that drive to the hospital. This was better, wasn't it? Anything was better than that. But that's the thing about emergencies. At the time you can't quite believe it's all happening. The only thing you want is to get through. You just want to drag yourself to that moment afterwards when you can look back on it all with relief.

But even relief is never quite what you expect. Because in those moments when your nerves are wild with fear, when everything is so clearly at stake, then at least you know what to do. It's all frantic and lucid and strangely automatic.

Afterwards, nothing is ever so clear again.

"Hey! What's with you? You call that working?"

I turned, a little unsteady on my stool. "Not tonight. Tonight I'm just drinking."

"Now, that sounds friendly. How many have you had?"

"More than is probably good for me."

"In that case, maybe I'll join you."

Alice Mulroney—Tiny Alice to her friends—claimed, in a rare display of ladylike modesty, to be only five-eleven, though it was generally agreed among the other regulars that she was six-two if she was an inch. She had huge, Pre-Raphaelite hair and a body of heroic proportions, which she encased in jeans, tight as a tourniquet around her soft waist, and plaid flannel shirts. She worked construction for the city and drank beer with the slow and steady pacing of an endurance athlete. In the course of an evening the rosy cheerfulness of her face would darken, shade by shade, to a deep, burnished crimson so that with some practice you could gauge the rate of her progress by the steadily deepening glow. At the moment her cheeks were at the hot pink stage, well past the evening's first blush but still far short of all they would eventually become.

"My father's dating a teen-ager," I said.

"Really?"

I shook my head. "No. I'm just trying to maintain a little perspective."

She slid in beside my stool and stood leaning against the bar. It put her roughly at eye level. "You know what your problem is?" she asked.

"Yes. I think I do."

"Your mug is almost empty." She raised her hand and flagged down Mom as if he were a wide and tattooed beer taxi. He set them down without expression, though with a quick, assessing glance at Alice's hue.

"I was making us dinner. Can you believe it? Persian Army Chicken. And she just walks right in, happy as you please. What kind of a person does that?"

Tiny Alice looked intrigued. "You never told me you were in the Persian Army."

"That's just what it's called. The point is, I went to a lot of trouble. You know, it's not that easy to make. You want to know what goes into it?"

She considered for a moment. "Sure. Why not? You never know when you might get to Persia someday."

"You take chicken breasts, and lay them in the bottom of a casserole. Then you cover them with rice. But you've got to dredge them in bread crumbs first. Did I say that already?"

"No. You didn't mention the breadcrumbs."

"Then you cover them with a secret sauce. You want to know what's in it?"

"I sure as hell do," she said.

"Campbell's condensed Cream of Mushroom soup. And you know what else?"

"What?"

"Nothing," I said. "Just the soup. That's the secret."

She smiled. Then she leaned ponderously close until I wasn't sure what she was going to do. "Don't worry," she whispered. Her breath was warm and humid on my neck. "I won't tell a soul."

9

I sat up straighter on the stool, peering over at her as if she might be something I had only just imagined. But there she was, still smiling. "Thanks," I said. "I'd hate for word to get out. You know, in cooking circles."

"It'll just be our secret."

"And thanks for the beer," I said.

"No problem. You can get the next round."

She was still leaning in. I was aware of the soft expanse of red plaid flannel and the extravagance of curly hair. There was a dusting of freckles across her nose that I had never noticed before. "So," I said carefully. "What are you doing here tonight? I mean, is there anything special you're doing? Here, I mean. With anybody?"

Her smile turned a little uncertain. "What do you mean?"

By this point, of course, I had no idea. But the vision came to me of Henry, standing gamely on the candlelit porch without a clue to call his own. "Would you like to dance?" I said.

She looked startled as if, of all things, this was the least expected. She peered toward the dance floor. "I'm not sure there's room."

"We'll make room."

"I've still got some beer."

She had maybe half a pint left. Without a word I took her glass and drained it before her startled eyes. When I set it down on the bar my eyes were watering and there was a dull ache in my forehead from the cold. "Okay," I gasped.

We made our way to the dance floor. There was a crowd milling around the edges, but once you eased past there was room to move. My brain was already swaying slowly to the music when

I turned and reached out tentatively. She was smiling half-quizzically as if trying to decide whether she was ticklish.

It had been a while since I'd been dancing, but this wasn't Arthur Murray. There was, I told myself, nothing to it. Her hair tickled my cheek. My hands felt humid and warm. We moved in a crowd of sleepwalkers, each milling around in his own little dream.

After a moment I said, "You know, he isn't even wearing his own clothes."

Alice opened her eyes and glanced around uncertainly. "Who?"

"Henry. He's wearing my jacket tonight. Though it's not like she'd even notice. You should see what she wears. Still, it makes you mad. Don't you think?"

"Hell, yes. Someone else wearing your clothes like that."

"I mean, can't he even dress himself?"

She nodded agreeably. "You know what I always say." And, leaning forward until her lips grazed my ear, "If they can't take a joke, fuck 'em."

I swallowed. "That's what I say, too."

She was maybe three inches taller, but that didn't matter up close. I had started out with a hand on her back and one in her right hand—some vestigial remnant of childhood dance class—but in this crowd that seemed nothing but affectation, and after a while I just dropped both hands to her waist. We leaned against one another and moved very slowly, as if we were trying to stand perfectly still but couldn't quite keep our balance. I was aware of the warmth of the room and the soft pressure through the thin cotton flannel. Her hands were on my back, rubbing slowly up and down, in time to the music. I tried to concentrate on it, but my mind kept wandering. I wondered what Henry was up to right now. Perhaps a little after-dinner dancing? A little candlelight?

Alice felt unwieldy in my arms, and I suddenly wasn't sure what was supposed to come next. I'd like to think I never really asked myself what Henry would have done. But as if by accident Alice and I started kissing. It had a surprised, though oddly untentative, quality like sledding at night when you know you're moving but don't know where or how fast. And as we kissed I became aware that it had been a very long time since I'd tried this with anyone. Alice's mouth was soft and nerveless, but she kissed as if she didn't have any plans to stop soon. She leaned against me, her breasts heavy and warm beneath the flannel shirt, her back broad under my hands. We swayed together. Slowly at first, in time to the music, then a little too heavily, distractedly, misjudging the angle until, clinging together, we found ourselves slipping from the vertical and toppling in luxurious slow-motion to the ground, where we lay in a dazed tangle amid the slowly moving feet.

"Oops a daisy," I said. I have no idea why. Then, "Are you okay?"

It was a very understanding crowd. The other dancers ignored us as we climbed to our feet, and the music seemed to have waited. We started in again. "I'm really sorry," I said. "I'm a little out of practice."

"That's okay," replied Alice, and she might have meant it, but she was brushing irritably at the dust on her jeans and peering around now as if contemplating her escape.

I wanted some way to keep her attention. I said, "I was here once when a knife fight broke out."

She glanced over. "No shit."

"There were a bunch of bikers in the corner arm-wrestling. There was a lot of shouting and cheering. And I guess one of the girlfriends got a little impatient. She was sitting across the room with some other guy. Word was they were actually, you know, doing the deed."

"You mean they were fucking?"

I felt myself blush. "Apparently. While across the room her poor boyfriend was getting trashed by the reigning champion."

"What do you mean apparently? You said you were there."

"It was hard to tell. I was concentrating on the arm wrestling."

She laughed. "You're kidding."

But that's the thing; everybody was, at the time. And then it broke up, and while the champion led the way to the bar, the challenger, rubbing his arm and feeling a little grumpy, started looking around, his thoughts turning to a more comforting presence. And just at that moment the more comforting presence climbed out of the booth, tugged her skirt down over her thighs, and smiled triumphantly.

A knife fight isn't what you'd expect from the movies. Not a lot of circling around, none of that dramatic slashing and waving. The two men approached each other slowly, hands almost at their sides, the short blades undramatic and workmanlike in their hands. They were shouting, cursing each other, and the greatest contrast was between the slow, pedestrian movements of their bodies and the grandiose exaggeration of voices leaping through the air, climbing all over each other.

People backed away, but not wildly. It's not like a gun fight, with the chance of a stray bullet. There was no panic. It was more like courteous interest, giving them room to work. The bar was suddenly quiet, except for the two voices. The dense background noise had died away. Someone had pulled the plug on the juke box.

Then the two men came in slowly, feinting in hesitant little jabs, shoving or blocking or grabbing with their free hands. It was hard to see. By the end they were so close together they looked as if they were dancing or struggling in some slower and more important version of one of those schoolyard shoving matches. I hadn't been close enough to see much, though that was as close as I'd wanted to be. The shouting grew wilder, more extravagant, all focused on the close, compact space between them.

Then they stopped. Stopped shouting, stopped jostling. They stepped back. One step, two. Then the boyfriend seemed to trip on something though the floor was uncluttered, and one leg just gave way. He collapsed as if folding up along unexpected joints and lay half on his side with his forearm crooked hard against his stomach. The girlfriend knelt beside him, though not close. An arm's length away. He still held the knife. And she stared at him with a shocked and angry expression, as if furious with him for all his bad luck. He was trying to speak but no sound came out. He might have been trying to blow out the candles of a birthday cake. He was wearing a black t-shirt, and the only change at first was that the patch of fabric under his arm began to glint darkly in the low lights. But then, after a moment, a thin line trickled onto the floor and turned suddenly bright red. As Mom picked up the phone and dialed for an ambulance, the older hands were already moving toward the door. No shoving, no dawdling: orderly as a fire drill.

The next thing I remember I was walking home, but I had stopped midway on the bridge over the river and was gazing back at the parking lot, waiting. When the ambulance arrived they brought the guy out on a stretcher, with a blood bag dangling over him. They slipped him into the back like a bread pan into the oven. The police came, but they didn't stay. And in the end there were just two people standing in the parking lot when the bar's small sign went dark. The woman looked cold in her halter top. She stood there hugging herself. But the man in the old army jacket made no attempt to warm her up.

This was what I'd stayed for. Not for the police or the excitement, but to see this. To see how this part ended. But at the last there was nothing to see. They didn't move. They just stood there, not even looking at each other. And then a police car stopped on the bridge and asked me what I was doing, and I turned and started home, though after a few steps, looking back, I saw they were still there, hesitant and cold, as if they couldn't make up there minds what had been decided.

"Did he die?" asked Alice.

"Not as far as I know."

"And nobody was arrested?"

"Nobody saw anything."

She smiled and leaned into me. "Sounds scary," she said, but she didn't sound scared.

For that, I suppose, you had to have been there. I could still recall the coldness in my stomach watching the fight unfold without a pause or the chance to rewind: the slow movements, each one clear and almost ordinary but leading to that sudden hush and the thin trickle of blood. And finally in the parking lot, those two all alone, who seemed to have done it for no reason at all, not even love.

"I'd like to see a knife fight," Alice murmured.

In retrospect, it may not have mattered what she said. I was pretty sure the guy couldn't have heard her. It was so noisy I barely heard her myself. But in that first instant when the man stepped up and stood there with a fistful of my shirt in one hand, the hem of Alice's flannel in the other, and his face pressed close between us, my first thought was that I wished she had just kept quiet.

"You wanna dance?" the man said.

I was so startled at first I didn't know what he meant. His face was narrow and clenched like a fist. He had short hair, and a taut smile directed evenly between us.

"She's already dancing," I said.

"That is one sexy outfit." He pulled the end of Alice's flannel shirt free, and abruptly he bent and rubbed the fabric all over his face, as if drying off on one of those awkward looped hand towels in a public restroom.

I snatched at his collar and jerked him away, but his fist was stilled twisted in Alice's shirt, and he dragged her half a step before letting go. Then he straightened up and smiled, his eyes small and bright as glass. "Oh, man. Don't you just hate it when people do that?"

"Maybe you should go dance with somebody else," I said, but I was thinking about the knife fight. All that yelling as the two men approached had made it seem as if that might be enough, as if all the anger might be used up in the shouting back and forth. But this guy wasn't shouting. He was wound up tight and all ready to go off.

"Maybe I'll dance with you," he said. "How'd you like that?"

"I'm not much of a dancer."

"That's too bad."

Alice was standing there, her face for once no longer pink, drained of any color except what the lights gave it, and she was staring, appalled, as if this were somehow my fault. I might have said something else then, something brave, to Alice. Afterwards I thought that would have been good, a really impressive thing to do. But my throat was dry, which was odd, I remembered thinking at the time, because my hands were as damp as they could be.

He wore a dark shirt just a shade too small as if he'd gained some weight in the shoulders since he'd bought it. It looked tight and under pressure like everything else about him. He leaned back toward the bar. The counter looked about a mile away, but he managed to reach back and touch it. People were edging away, forming a little band of onlookers like the audience at a golf match gathered around the tee.

The man's hand came back from the bar with a bottle of beer, and I thought, just for an instant, that it was all going to be all right, because if he was in the mood for a drink, then how pissed off could he be? But he was holding it all wrong, and with a quick flick he smashed it against an empty bar stool and held up a short, jagged corsage of brown glass.

With a glance at Alice he said, "What's with that hair?"

"What?"

"Has it always been that color?"

"I don't know," I said. "I think so." I was looking at the broken bottle. "I'll ask."

He smiled. "You'll ask."

He took a step forward. He was wearing brown cowboy

boots, looking shiny and new against the scuffed floor, and they made little scraping sounds as he walked. And that was the only noise. The room was quiet. Someone had pulled the plug on the jukebox.

He stepped forward, and I stepped back. Alice seemed to have turned to stone. She was clutching the untucked tail of her shirt in both hands and staring, her face pale and hollow. I stepped back again, and bumped into an empty table.

"Feels bad, doesn't it?" the man said.

"What?"

"Shoe's on the other foot."

I thought of his cowboy boots, but that didn't make sense. "You're making a mistake," I said.

"Yeah. I'm shakin'."

"You've got the wrong guy."

"Is that right?"

The only thing in my mind was the memory of how the knife fight had ended: the thin trickle of blood running onto the floor. My hand closed on something, the back of a chair, and I swung it up and held it out in front of me. It was quivering. It must have been heavy, but I don't know that for a fact. Somewhere I'd read you're not supposed to rush a man with a knife. A gun, yes. For some ungodly reason you're supposed to rush a gun. But not a knife. Or a broken bottle. And it didn't say anything about a chair. Perhaps no one had bothered to think how a chair might figure in. But suddenly I realized the man was just too far away. My eyes were blurring, and I seemed about to lose sight of him. He looked maybe fifty yards away, and I just started running straight at him.

He may have looked a little surprised at that, though I couldn't be sure. I was seeing him as if through a fishbowl. Besides, he couldn't have had time to get too surprised because no sooner did I start running than I hit him. I stretched out the chair like a lion tamer down to his last prop and drove him back against the bar in among the empty stools. And the bottle in his hand was somewhere off to the side for a moment, but just for a moment, caught in the legs of the chair. He looked startled as it came free. Then suddenly there was a huge shape behind him, and Mom reached over and did something quick and unclear, and the man's startled expression opened up into something even less certain as he sank down onto the floor.

10

I drove home slowly as if the truck were wired to a bomb and the slightest bump might set it off, stopping at each inter-section, peering up the dark and empty roads, checking the mirrors every few seconds to see if something more than the night itself might be following. Every few minutes a little cold front of shaking passed through me, and my muscles flickered like a neon sign at the end of its life.

Alice sat beside me. "Jesus Christ," she muttered.

"Alice?"

"Jesus Christ."

"Alice? Could you please not say that anymore?"

"Jesus Christ."

I stopped for the light at the corner of Prentiss, though there wasn't another car to be seen. It was after midnight. The clenched knot in the pit of my stomach was relaxing into a vague hollow feeling, and I sat in the particulate darkness trying to collect myself, trying to keep from scattering like so much pollen on a windy day. The red glow of the traffic light seemed unnaturally bright, and when it changed, the green had a fluid, molten quality that made me queasy.

"Technically, you're not supposed to rush a man with a knife," I said. At least I meant to say it, but my throat felt so dry that I may not actually have spoken. I tried again. "Where to?"

"Straight," said Alice, "and then over on Brown."

She'd been worried about driving home. "Look," she'd said. "My hands are shaking," as we stood outside the bar like a couple of strangers, like those two star-crossed lovers all those years ago. She had asked me if I wouldn't mind. It wasn't far, she'd said.

But now it seemed to be taking forever. My concentration kept dispersing with the breeze, and when we finally pulled up in front of her apartment I had to sit there for a moment to remember where we were.

Alice smiled imploringly. "Do you mind? I'm still kinda shaky."

I climbed slowly out of the truck, stepping down as if from an enormous height, balanced like a tightrope walker as I went around and opened her door. She held my arm all the way up the walk. "You could have been killed," she said.

Her tone wasn't what I'd expected. Not after I'd tipped us over on the dance floor. She sounded almost impressed. I wasn't thinking clearly, but still it occurred to me that maybe this wasn't going as badly as I'd thought. My arm felt warm where Alice held it and cold everywhere else, with a silvery chill creeping through my skin. I said, "I had a chair," though my voice sounded vague even to me.

"You're more dangerous than I thought." She turned in the darkened doorway. "I was terrified," she murmured. But she didn't sound terrified. She pulled out her keys and showed them to me. "I've got some beer in the fridge."

For a long moment I tried to want a beer. " Thanks," I said finally. "I'm not very thirsty."

"You could come in anyway." She was leaning in close, her voice down to whisper. "It's got me kind of excited."

I tried to feel excited. I thought of the warmth of her lips on the dance floor, the close swell of her breasts, but the night chill was seeping right through me. I was starting to shiver. "I'm sorry. But I'm a little out of it."

She leaned into me, voice low, her breath in my ear. "I was so scared I was creaming in my pants."

I hesitated, unsure if I'd heard her right. "Pardon?"

She was smiling now, her broad face rosy pink and painted with shadows. She kissed me. Her lips parted. My head felt light as a balloon, and I tried to concentrate all my attention on her mouth so I wouldn't faint or float away. "Can you tell what I'm thinking now?" she said.

I was still trying to formulate an answer when, with a smile, she closed the door.

I drove home. The night was an empty box. I felt the old sadness creeping into me though I told himself it was just fatigue. I wondered what kind of a loser I was that I couldn't even take an opportunity when it was offered. As I trudged up the back walk, there was the new stone patio with the huddled arrangement of table and chairs. On the table lay a crumpled napkin and an empty wine bottle. Another night, another party. Where did Henry find the energy? I thought of Alice, so scared she was creaming in her pants. It seemed as strange and distant as everything else.

I stepped into the kitchen. The aroma of Persian Army Chicken hung on the air, and there were dishes piled in the sink as a kind of silent confirmation of all that I was doing wrong. Dirty plates, wine glasses, silverware. And the fact that nothing had been washed, dried, and put away was added evidence that, for Henry at least, another evening had gone well. Was still going well. From the living room came the glow of candlelight and the low sound of voices.

They were sitting on the sofa, poring together over something, a book, an album, but at the scrape of my step they looked up. Hurriedly Henry reached over and turned on a lamp. "Harry?" He made it sound like a question, as if it could have been anybody else.

I waved the light away. "You don't have to. I'm sorry. I didn't realize you were still up."

My father was grinning sheepishly, squinting in the sudden glare. "Sorry about the mess. I'll get to that. How was your evening?"

Mona sat close beside him, her knees draw tightly together as if she'd been surprised in a different, more flagrant posture and had hurriedly moved. She didn't look particularly interested in how my evening had gone. "Fine," I said. "Same old same old."

"You want a glass of wine?" Henry held up a second nearly empty bottle.

"No. Thanks. I thought you were going to have pasta."

"The chicken seemed too good to waste. Besides, Mona wanted to try it."

"So, what'd you think?" I asked.

"Not bad. A little dry."

"You must have overcooked it."

"But there was lots of wine," said Henry.

"That didn't hurt," she agreed, and they giggled like a pair of kids on their first sleep-over.

It made me very tired. "I'll get out of your way then."

"Did you eat?"

"No. I'm just going to bed. I think if I just lie down...."

But as I moved toward the stairs Mona said, "Are you okay?"

"Why does everybody keep asking me that?"

She was staring at me now through those heavy black frames. "What's with your arm?"

I glanced down at the burgundy jacket. In the lamp light there was a darker burgundy blotching the left forearm. I hadn't noticed it before, and even now it didn't make any sense. "What is that?"

Mona was standing now, reaching for my arm. She tried to push back the cuff, but it wouldn't go any further than the beginning of the damp spot, even though there seemed to be a rip in the fabric now.

"It's okay," I said. " I must have spilled something."

"Take it off," she said.

"Really. I'll just--"

"Shut up." And something grim in her voice was starting to make an impression. She was already pulling the jacket off my shoulders, but removing it turned out to be a terrible idea. I was wearing a white shirt, and from the elbow to the cuff it was soaked with blood, wet and clingy, turning icy cold in the air. I plucked vaguely at it, but Mona slapped my hand. "Don't touch."

I was having trouble concentrating. It didn't hurt, but the sight of all that blood soaking into my shirt, as if I had so much to spare, was starting to go to my head. Hadn't she just said Don't touch? And here she was unbuttoning the cuff and peeling it back like wet paper.

"Careful," I said. "It's red."

It wasn't quite what I meant. Something about her bright blue shirt and the possibility of stains. She peered sharply up at me. "Take his arm," she snapped to Henry. Then, more soothingly, "You're doing fine. Just sit down."

I settled onto the sofa as Henry stepped up beside me. Beyond him the edges of the room were getting darker, and the walls themselves seemed vague.

"Put your head between your knees," Mona said.

"I'm all right...."

But the hand that wasn't holding my wrist was on my neck, pressing my head down firmly. I thought of Alice's fingers, stroking my back as we danced. "That's nice," I murmured. Then I was gazing down between a pair of spread knees only dimly recognizable as my own.

"Deep breaths," she said. "That's it. Breathe."

"Okay. I'm okay." My voice echoed between my knees. I was breathing as deeply as I could with my body bent double. The darkening edges began to recede. The walls steadied.

"Slowly," said Mona, as I straightened up. She had the sleeve peeled back from my forearm. "Good. It's not too bad. No, don't look. Look at your father."

But my eye was caught by a vivid, red smear on her blouse, like a damp apostrophe across the shallow swell of blue fabric. "Your breast," I said, though I meant to say blouse, and maybe that's what came out because she said, "It's all right. Don't worry."

I looked up. My father, unaccustomedly dapper in his tux, was staring down with a look of concern. "Sorry to ruin your evening," I said.

"What happened?"

But I couldn't think of what to say. The smear of blood tinged my skin an oily pink, and a darker crimson was welling up along a thin, jagged line that curved down across the forearm and out of sight. Mona was dabbing at it with a clump of tissues that already looked like a little rose of blood. Maybe it wasn't so bad. Maybe it would all be just fine. But as she dabbed I saw the whole jagged line move as if incompletely attached to the rest of my skin. "Oh my."

"Don't look!" she said. "Everything's going to be fine."

"Did I just say that?"

"Look at your father."

I looked at Henry: very neat, very tidy, looking elegant in black. He was handing Mona his handkerchief, and I felt a broad pressure on my arm. Now it was starting to hurt. "Is it bad?"

"Nothing to it. You just need a few stitches. Can you stand up? I think we should go to the emergency room." She spoke in such an unaccustomedly calm and comforting voice it made me want to smile, though I couldn't seem to manage that either.

"I'm fine," I said.

"Shut up."

Her Mustang was parked out front. I rode in back with Henry so he could keep the pressure on the handkerchief while Mona drove like someone deranged, as if the person driving and the person who had spoken so calmly about everything being fine were two different people.

In the ER there were magazines, a television, a bank of vending machines, and a dozen uncomfortable chairs scattered around, with never more than two side by side, as if all emergencies occurred singly or in pairs. I wondered what the receptionist made of our little parade: the well-dressed couple of disparate ages and the younger man looking like someone who'd injured himself dumpster-diving. They might have run into me on the way home from a party or picked me out of a gutter somewhere, two Samaritans doing their good deed for the night.

The receptionist looked me over as if she could estimate at a glance how far I was from actually passing out and then sent me to sit in the corner beneath the TV. Mona sat beside me, her hand clamped on my arm, while Henry conducted a tense and angry discussion at the desk. It didn't seem like Henry at all. I was touched.

"Open your eyes," Mona said sharply.

"I'm okay."

"Just keep 'em open."

"I like your skirt."

"I'll let you wear it when this is over."

The doctor was a very pink man with thinning blonde hair. He frowned over the arm, and after peppering the area with Novocaine, installed thirty-seven neat and workmanlike stitches.

"Is it okay if I close my eyes?"

He glanced at Mona. "How much blood did he lose?"

She held up the jacket with the sleeve soaked purple.

"Better keep them open."

We drove home more slowly than we'd come, and Mona let me sit in front as Henry crouched behind, leaning between the seats. "How are you doing?" he kept asking, and I kept saying, "Fine. I'm fine." I glanced a little shyly over at Mona. "Sorry to interrupt your evening."

"Yeah. Well, don't make it a habit."

The doctor had given me a couple of Percodan, but I probably shouldn't have taken both at once, and not before I got home. The trip from the car to the house unrolled at half-speed, and I drifted up the stairs like one of those big helium balloons in the Thanksgiving Day parade, dipping and riding on the breeze. My father tucked me into bed like a five-year-old and as he turned off the light I said, "Henry?"

"Go to sleep."

"It's okay, Henry. Really. She's nice. I like her."

11.

The next morning Henry looked in on me before he left for work, smiling with a fixed and determined cheerfulness. "How's the patient? How are you feeling?"

My head felt hollow from the Percodan, and beneath the gauze each individual suture was like a little claw in my skin. I gazed down at the thick white bandage with the vague embarrassment of having done something foolish and uncalled for. "Tell me this isn't a tattoo."

"Don't worry," he said. "It's okay. It's fine. The doctor said to take it easy. No heavy lifting for a couple of days. He said the stitches should come out in a week. Clean it with peroxide once a day, keep it covered, and it should be good as new." His voice was unflagging and bright with reassurance. He seemed determined to ignore by sheer force of will the possibility that this might have been a serious incident, that this could have been the end of me, that it had resolved itself so benignly through the very slimmest of chances.

"Is that what he said? Good as new?"

He hesitated, suddenly awkward, as if he'd meant to offer me something more substantial but had left it somewhere by mistake. "Are you okay?"

"Yeah," I said. "Thanks."

"I'm heading into work. You want some breakfast or anything before I go?"

"I'll get up in a bit."

"No rush. You should probably just spend the day in bed. Rest up."

"I'm not sick, Henry. I'm just hideously disfigured."

He looked momentarily disconcerted, as if he weren't quite

sure I was joking. "I don't want you to worry about this. It's nothing. It'll be just fine."

But it didn't feel like nothing, and I realized suddenly that I didn't want it to be just fine. I glanced up at him. "I'm sorry to break things up last night. It looked cozy."

"It's okay. Don't worry about it."

"It wasn't anything I planned. Just a little unexpected excitement at the bar."

"Forget it. "

"This guy attacked me with a broken beer bottle. He cut me on the arm--"

"It doesn't matter..."

"--then I hit him with a chair--

"Honestly..."

"--and my boss knocked him out with a baseball ba--"

"Harry! It doesn't matter!" my father snapped. He stood there speechless for a moment, his face ragged with worry. "The important thing is that you're okay." His voice was desperate. His eyes were pleading with me to agree. "We should be grateful it's no worse."

And I lay there staring up at him. All I could think was, Grateful? We should? Is that what we'd come to?

Years ago, in those earliest days alone, before we'd learned the delicate, light-footed way you needed to walk when you were living on such thin ice, I began drifting out in the evening like a boat someone had forgotten to tie up. While Henry slept, I crept around the darkened streets examining the evidence of other people's lives, the cars in the driveways, the toys forgotten on the lawns, looking for whatever light they might shed on what had become of us. And when that had made me more angry that I could stand, I wandered through the irregular no-man's land that even a town this size accumulated in the odd cracks and crannies of cheerful, Midwestern living—down along the river, past the old brick castle of the power station, and through the desert of quonset huts and parking lots crowding the narrow crescent between the railroad yard and the water plant. Sometimes I'd find a few hard figures, drinking or getting high or arguing among themselves in low, angry tones. I used to trace their voices in the dark like some lost settler looking for the light of a campfire, and then I'd walk right through the middle of them, hoping they'd try something, hoping they'd make a move.

But they never did. In retrospect I'm not sure why. Maybe I was just lucky. Or maybe there was something in the way I was walking that made it too clear I was looking for a fight. But for whatever reason, I never found one. The closest I came was one night when, for no reason I can remember, I discovered myself with a can of lighter fluid and a book of matches in a shelter in City Park. The police found me before I had anything more than the picnic table alight, and they managed to put it out. I was determined to offer a struggle, but when they finally arrested me I was crying too hard to resist.

The next morning Henry was waiting outside the jail. He had a cup of coffee for me and a blueberry muffin, and he drove me to the store without a harsh word or a demand for explanations. He told me it wasn't serious, that everything would be okay. He had explained it all to the police, and they were very understanding. There would only be a fine and some damages. It wouldn't even go on my record. We could just put it behind us; forget about it all.

I said nothing. He was doing the best he could, I know. And I was grateful. But at the same time there was something in his ceaseless attempts at equanimity that made me furious. As if, no matter what occurred, as long as we survived, it could be as if nothing had happened.

Now he brushed a fingertip over the gauze bandage with a kind of urgent reassurance, as if having a well-bandaged wound were the same as having no wound at all. As if escaping some worse disaster was its own sort of victory. "The doctor doesn't expect any complications. I don't want you to worry about this."

But I wasn't worried. I appreciated the concern and the sympathy and the desire to put it behind us. But sometimes it wasn't enough that things weren't so bad. And after last night I wanted to explain it to him. I wanted to offer the danger and the shock of it all in my own defense, as some sign that it wasn't just an accident. I wanted to hold up the whole terrifying pageant as something if not praiseworthy then at least remarkable, something out of the ordinary. Some sign that things could change.

It was mid-morning when I got out of bed and walked into town. I was no longer looking for a fight exactly, but I was looking for someone who wouldn't blame me if I did. I should have gone to Alice. That would have made more sense, if for no other reason than that she would likely have been pleased to see me. But I didn't think of her. Not then. Even though she'd been standing right there when the fight took place, looking on, pale and appalled through it all, I didn't associate her with the danger. And that should have told me something, even then. Because when I felt the pain of the stitches beneath the bandage and the lingering wonder at such a close call, all I thought of was the pressure on my neck forcing my head down between my knees and a low voice telling me to breathe.

I tried her office first. I climbed the stairs and knocked on the door, but there was no sound. So I tried the diner and found her sitting in a corner booth with her back to the door, a cup of coffee and a small notebook open on the table. The blue hair seemed even brighter and more of a mistake in the light of day. It gave her a pinched and peevish expression, as if it fit her head too tightly. "Look at you," she said. "You're still alive."

"As far as I can tell. Mind if I sit down? I promise not to bleed on anything."

She waved at the empty bench, and I slid in across from her, careful of my arm. She nodded at me. "How does it feel?"

"Better. It only hurts when I do this." I flexed my hand. "Or this." I twisted it around, feeling the stitches bite into my skin.

Mona frowned. "Maybe you shouldn't."

"How about this?"

"Cut it out! Just leave it alone."

I lay the arm gently on the table, as if it were something I'd brought along for show and tell, and pressed the bandage to quiet the dark throbbing. I felt awkward and self-conscious. But something else as well. I hadn't just fallen in the play-ground. It had been a knife fight, or the next best thing, and sitting across from Mona like that, I was feeling a little proud.

"I should have known," she said, "when you came into my office."

"Known what?"

"You look just like him."

"It must be the light," I said. "In real life we're not anything alike. Actually we're not even related."

"Henry tells it differently."

"You know Henry. You can't trust what he says." I hesitated. "What did he say?"

But before she could answer Rusty came over with a pot of coffee growing out of her left hand. She gave me a prim, disparaging glance. "There's room at the counter."

I was about to tell her that we were very nearly related, after all, and that just the night before her daughter had all but saved my life, when Mona said, "That's okay. I don't mind."

Rusty shrugged. "So, you want a menu?"

"No need," I said. "What's particularly good today?"

Rusty frowned. "Don't you just hate it when people ask that?"

"You're supposed to say it's all good."

"Yeah? You should think about working here."

"But is it all particularly good?" I said.

"The huevos rancheros were new last week," Rusty said grimly, "but they're starting to calm down."

I glanced at Mona. "Have you tried them?"

"I'm not a big breakfast fan."

Rusty lifted the coffee pot in the direction of the door. "Table over there had 'em. They're still okay."

"They sound too good to refuse."

"I'll tell the chef," she said and headed toward the kitchen to spread the welcome news. Mona returned to her notebook. I sat there fiddling with my knife and fork, feeling awkward again and shy. I remembered the cold, blurry feeling from the night before, the sense that all the world's edges were softening before my eyes and the only thing to hold onto was the firm sound of Mona's voice and the pressure of her hand on my arm. I flexed my fingers, just to feel the stitches bite. "I wanted to thank you," I said slowly.

"You're welcome."

"And to apologize. For barging in like that. And getting blood on your blouse."

She glanced up with the barest hint of a smile. "Is that what you meant to say? Blouse?"

I could feel the blush creeping up my cheeks. "I was a little out of it."

"I'll bet. What were you doing last night?"

"I was just minding my own business. But this other guy had a broken bottle he wanted to show me."

She looked, I thought, a little impressed. "Just like that?"

"It surprised me, too."

"And what were you doing, to make him want to show it to you?"

"Actually, I was dancing with this woman."

She shook her head. "It's bad luck to steal other people's girl-friends."

"Strangely enough, she was with me. Sort of."

"Sort of?"

I shrugged.

"And how did she react to it all?" asked Mona.

I remembered that warm and breathy whisper in the dark-ened doorway and felt a quick flush of surprise and desire, but at a distance, as if in someone else's dream. "She thinks I'm dangerous."

"Maybe you are. You're sitting there with thirty-seven stitches. Any more dangerous and you'd be dead."

I considered that for a moment. "Have you ever been in a knife fight?"

Mona shook her head. "Someone shot at me once. And one guy tried to run me over with a car."

"It scared the shit out of me," I said.

"Yeah. I know what you mean. I almost wet my pants. They say your life's supposed to flash before your eyes. I just remember looking at my watch and thinking it must have stopped. This guy was shooting, and I couldn't see the second hand moving."

"How did you feel afterwards?"

She laughed and shook her head. "That's the thing, isn't it? I felt great. Everything just a little bit brighter and louder. For some reason I kept singing 'Everything's Up to Date in Cincinnati' all the way home. How about you?"

I thought for a moment. I thought of Henry's determined efforts to muffle the whole night into a kind of half-remembered accident. It had been the single most frightening thing I'd ever gone through. But for the longest time I hadn't been feeling anything at all, and now I was beginning to realize that a riot of terror and rage were a fair exchange for six years of sadness.

"Actually," I said, "I'm feeling pretty good."

Rusty hurried over and thumped a large plate onto the table, then backed away, rubbing her hand on her apron. "That sucker is hot. You want Tabasco or ketchup?"

I gazed down at the sprawling train wreck of scrambled eggs and home fries in a bright massacre of red salsa. For some reason the whole vivid and extravagant mess made me smile. "No, thanks," I said. "This should do me fine."

Rusty shrugged and wandered off. It surprised me that even with the eggs right in front of me swimming in runny salsa I was hungry. I took a bite. "You know, these could be a lot worse."

Mona looked doubtful. But the eggs were spicy and bright

with flavor. I smiled and took another bite, and I was about to offer her a taste when I noticed, over her shoulder, a woman out on the sidewalk. She had just paid a taxi and was coming inside. She was short and baby-doll plump with fluffy hair like brown smoke trapped in a curly perm around her face. She wore the jeans of a much younger girl, and a white satin blouse with a froth of ruffles down the front, but what I noticed most was the expression of pettish determination as she headed straight for our table.

Mona glanced up at me. "What's wrong?"

"I could be mistaken, but I think someone--"

"I have been looking all over for you!" The woman glared at me just long enough to provoke the sudden, panicky feeling that I had somehow forgotten both her and our appointment, then she turned on Mona. "I checked your office. There was no one there."

I was already preparing some sort of apology, but Mona was made of sterner stuff. "I'm in the middle of a meeting," she said. "Can't this wait?"

"But I have an appointment."

"Not until tomorrow."

"But it's important!"

Mona sighed like a woman who would have protected me if she could. "Jean Tipton, this is Harry Bailey. Harry helped me locate your husband."

She glanced from me to the salsa-red carnage of the huevos rancheros with apparent concern, as if the state of one cast considerable doubt on the state of the other. "You're a private detective, too?"

"More a friend of the family," I said.

She blinked uncertainly. "Which family?"

"He works free-lance," said Mona. "I bring him in on the important cases."

Jean nodded as if that made perfect sense, but her plump fingers kept fluttering at the edge of the table until, after a moment,

I moved my plate and made room for her to sit. She slid in beside me with a quick, grateful smile. "He wasn't there," she said.

"Yes, he was," said Mona patiently. "I showed you the photograph. It's a Polaroid. You can't tamper with a Polaroid."

"I went over the next day." She glanced mournfully at me. "I had to leave work early. Take a taxi all the way out there."

"Jean's car was stolen," Mona explained. "She's been having a bad few weeks."

"I'm sorry."

"It's been just awful," she agreed. "And now this. I got all the way out there, I knocked on the door. I waited. He wasn't there. *She* was there. I didn't know what to do. I had to threaten to call the police before she let me in. And then I looked everywhere. There was no sign of him. Or not much. A dirty undershirt at the bottom of the laundry hamper. That's all."

She seemed to expect some response. I said, "You looked through the laundry hamper?"

"I was furious. Like a crazy person. I said some terrible things. Terrible."

I nodded sympathetically. "I'm sure you didn't mean them. You were just upset."

"Oh, I meant them, all right. She's a two-timing, white trash slut-ass bitch, and I told her so. " She smiled gratefully. "But, thank you. I was very upset."

Mona was shaking her head. "I warned you about that, Jean. I told you, you should have come the other day."

"I didn't want to force him to meet me. Don't you see? I wanted him to want to. I wanted him to come to me." She gave her a long pleading look, then turned back to me, searching for a softer touch. "You can't force someone to love you," she said. "Can you?"

"No. I suppose not."

"You can't. You try and you try. But there's no way you can." She offered me a thin, sad smile. "You think I'm being silly, don't you?"

I started to offer up some bland reply, but then I thought of my mother, not dead in a car crash or a terrorist shooting or a plane wreck. Just not wanting to come home no matter what I wished. "No. I don't think you're silly."

"The problem," said Mona, "is that now he could be any-where."

But Jean was shaking her head. "He couldn't have gone far. He wouldn't leave. Not really. He's going to come back to me."

"Then maybe you should just wait."

"I can't wait. I need you to find him now."

And she seemed so intent and certain I found myself lean-ing toward her unconsciously. "And then what will you do?" I asked.

"Talk to him. Just talk. He needs to listen to me."

"But what if he doesn't want to? What if there's nothing you can say?"

"He will. He loves me. He just doesn't understand. He's been gone for a while. We really haven't had a chance to talk." She hesitated. "That's all. If I could just see him. Just to talk."

I thought about that. Just to talk. I thought of the weeks and months of waiting for the phone to ring, for a letter to arrive, for the doorbell to announce that it was all just a mistake. Just a few words to prove... what? That after all this time, we hadn't been forgotten completely?

I said, "How long has he been gone, Mrs. Tipton?"

"It's Miss, actually." She offered a sad little smile. "We're not really very traditional. But we've been together so long. You un-derstand. Please call me Jean. About three years."

"Three years?" Mona was staring in disbelief. "What do you mean three years? Why didn't you tell me that?"

Jean looked a little sheepish. "We've been going through a sort of a trial separation. It hasn't been easy."

"And you haven't talked in all that time?" I said.

"Sometimes. On the phone. He's been out of town. "

"Where?"

"I don't know."

Mona looked dubious.

"I asked him, but he wouldn't say. He wouldn't tell me where." She smiled sadly, blinking back tears. "Isn't that pathetic?"

Mona took a deep breath. "Jean," she said, and then seemed to run out of inspiration. She shrugged. "We'll look for him. But it's not going to be easy. He's going to be more careful. And, frankly, if he's only been in town a few weeks after so long away, there's not going to be much of a trail."

"I understand. But you'll find him, I know you will. Won't you, Mr. Bailey?"

"Harry," I said.

"Harry."

What could I say? "I'm sure we will."

"Thank you." Her smile was so eager and grateful, it was its own sort of heartbreak. "It's been so nice meeting you. If only the circumstances...." She gave a forlorn little shrug, as if she couldn't quite think how to finish the thought, and stood up.

"We'll be in touch," said Mona drily, as Jean, with a vague, unhappy nod, turned and hurried out, looking like nothing so much as a plump and woebegone pigeon with important places to go.

12

Mona sat gazing after her for a moment, glowering to herself, then she picked up a fork and stabbed a piece of potato off my plate. "Please find my husband. But, oh. He's not really my husband. And, oh, by the way, it's been three years." She chewed irritably. "After a while you should maybe think about cutting your losses, don't you think?"

I thought about the last six years spent with nothing but my losses to console me. "You can't just ask her to give up."

"He's given up on her," said Mona. "I can guarantee it."

"You can't be sure."

"I'm sure." She forked up a little clump of eggs and chewed.

"Help yourself," I said. "There's plenty."

She drew the plate toward her, frowning with annoyance. "Besides, what's she going to do? Track down this guy so he can tell her to his face he doesn't want to see her again?"

"You never think it's going to come to that. You always think there's going to be something. A reconciliation. Something to make up for it all," I said.

But Mona just shook her head. She flicked aside a shred of fried onion, then reached across for my knife and cut one of the angled potatoes in two and ate both halves. She didn't seem to be enjoying it. She ate the way she drove, with a kind of grim indignation, as if the foolishness of the world were a personal affront.

"You think he's still in town?" I asked.

"You heard her. He wouldn't leave without saying good bye." She picked up a piece of toast and bit off its head.

"I thought that was kind of sad."

"Yeah, well. I've got news for you. They're always kind of

sad. But that's just the way it is. You're not doing them any fa-
vors by building their hopes up."

"Just a little sympathy--"

"The fact is," Mona said sharply, "most people who leave
don't come back. It's as simple as that. They just don't. If they
wanted to come back they wouldn't have left in the first place."

"You don't know that. Not for sure."

She shrugged. "In this business you see a lot of different reasons why people leave. Sometimes they're looking for love, or
better sex, or more excitement. Or they're running out on money worries or a bad marriage or domestic violence. Or maybe
they're just bored. Sometimes they just want a change. Or maybe
not. Maybe there's no reason at all. They just want to leave. And
usually none of that changes. People move on."

I felt my heart twist in the cage of my ribs. "So what do you
want her to do? Just give up hope?"

"No," said Mona with a grim expression. "That's the thing.
The people who leave, they move on. That's the whole point.
But nobody who's left behind ever gives up hope. And there's
no starting over under the weight of all that."

I thought about that. Surely it's not true. What about us? Henry and me. We've picked our lives up, haven't we? We've made a
new start. I mean, if there's one thing you could say about Henry
now, he was no longer pining. He was no longer lost in hope. He
had clearly moved on.

"Is there anything you can do?" I said. "About Jean, I mean."

"Probably not. If he'd been around for a while there's some
stuff we could do. Credit search. Check for parking tickets. Trace
old friends or contacts. That's how I found him the first time.
Millie was an old friend. But it was just dumb luck. And if it's
only a few weeks…." She shook her head.

"So what do you do?"

"I don't know. There are a couple of things." She hesitated,
then glanced up. "There is something we could try. Maybe. Are
you busy?"

"I think I've got a few more minutes."

"It doesn't always work."

"Might as well try anything, if you think it'll help."

"The thing is," said Mona darkly, "I don't want you laughing."

"What do you mean?"

"Just don't." Then she turned toward the counter. "Hey, mom! Got your cards?"

"We're going to play cards?" I asked doubtfully.

Mona ate another potato by way of answer, but a few minutes later Rusty wandered over, wiping her hands on a dish towel, and slid in beside her. She drew from the pocket of her apron a little packet wrapped in a red silk scarf and, undoing it, laid an oversized deck on the table. Then, with a look of studied concentration, she shook out the scarf, folded it diagonally, and tied it gypsy-fashion around her head. She gazed unsmilingly at me. "The silk protects the cards from stray energy and vibrations. When I put it on, it sets this time apart from all other times."

I nodded cautiously. "I can see that."

She turned to Mona, "Now, what is it you want to ask?"

A tarot deck has seventy-six cards, four suits and a range of scenes and figures—the wheel of fortune, the devil, the hanged man, the fool—that lay out before the discerning reader each pilgrim's journey through this world. I didn't know all this at the time, of course. There are some things you only learn in spite of yourself. At the time all I knew was that there must be some Rule of Antitheticals operating in the realm of love in order for Henry, the most unexceptional of men, to have gotten himself involved in what was clearly some sort of witch's coven.

Rusty, even more dour than usual in her silk scarf and apron, slid the deck to the middle of the table. "Move your plate," she told me. "And wipe the table. Make sure it's clean."

"I thought you were kidding when you said I should work here."

"Will you just wipe it off?" said Mona irritably. "She needs to concentrate."

I ran my napkin over the scuffed wood. Then Rusty leaned forward and swirled the cards around in a great confusion, mixing them up as if stirring a cauldron. And as she swirled, she chanted. "Events of the day are both random and not. Chosen and not. Free and not. Ordered by chance, the spirits, and destiny. We pick and choose, and find our way, with the help of the cards and the fates and the luck of the draw."

With a little nod to herself, she gathered them together and straightened the pile, then squinted up at me. "You got something you're dying to say?"

"No, ma'am."

"Good." She looked over at Mona. "So?"

"There's a guy--," Mona started.

"This isn't about Carlisle again?"

"No. And will you shut up about Carlisle? It's that guy I told you about. The one who's disappeared. He's the husband of the woman who just left. Or at least, as close as she's likely to get."

"You said you found him."

"We need to find him again."

Rusty shrugged, as if it were all the same to the forces of darkness. "Who's going to draw?"

"I am."

But Rusty regarded her for a moment consideringly. Then she turned. "You."

"Harry," I said.

"You choose."

"Choose what?"

"Do you have a photograph?" Rusty asked.

"I've got a driver's license."

"Of the husband," she said patiently.

Mona was checking the pockets of her leather jacket. "I've got one here somewhere, if I haven't.... Here it is." She pulled out the Polaroid we'd taken at the trailer park and held it out by one corner as if careful of prints.

"Give it to him."

Reluctantly I took it.

"Don't look!" said Rusty sharply. "Turn it to face the cards. Hold it by the corners. Both hands."

"It's not that heavy."

"You've got to form a complete energy circuit between you and the image."

I peered at her. "Please tell me you're kidding."

"Just look at the picture and concentrate."

"But I can't see the picture."

"Please shut up," said Mona. "Please? And concentrate? This is important."

Obediently I gazed down at the black and shiny back of the photo. "How's this?"

"No negative thoughts," said Rusty sternly. "You'll disrupt the flow."

So I held the photograph by the two bottom corners as if it were a small divining rod and shut my eyes so that the full flow of psychic energy captured in the picture could travel unperturbedly up one arm and down the other. I sat perfectly still for a long, long time. "Is something supposed to happen?"

"Lift it up," said Rusty. "Against your forehead."

"Pardon?"

"And keep it there." The stitches tugged at my arm as I raised it. "Now, concentrate."

"On what?"

"On that night," said Mona. "The sight of him by the trailer. Standing on the porch. Just picture him in your mind."

"It might help if I could look at the photo."

"No. Keep your eyes on the cards and concentrate." Rusty stroked the deck in her hands, as if lightly coating it with something. "Think of his name. Think of....?" She glanced over.

"Biff," said Mona. She checked her notebook. "Biff Jackson. Full name Brian Patrick. Birthday: November 11, 1982."

"Think of Biff," Rusty said, "and concentrate. What are his habits? What are his routines? What does he do? Where does he go? Where is he?"

"I have no idea," I said.

"Now." Rusty laid the deck down and with one smooth stroke spread it out into a broad fan. "Choose ten. No. Don't let go of the picture."

And so, holding the photograph between pinched fingers, I pointed one by one to ten cards, which Rusty drew from the deck and arranged in their own much thinner pile. Then, setting aside the remainder, she began to deal out the ten. She laid them face down, four in a row, then three above it, then two, then a single card at the top. "This is your past," she intoned, her hand drifting slowly over the bottom row.

"Whose past? Mine?"

"You're being Biff," said Mona. "Think like Biff."

"I don't even know Biff. And what's with that name anyway?"

Rusty reached out and turned the bottom row over one by one. "Ten of Swords. Ace of Swords. Six of Wands. Two of Cups." She pointed to the first two. "There's danger here. Or violence. Possibly anger. A lot. But it's just taking shape. This is the first and second step of the path. You and someone else."

"Me who? Me, Biff?"

"I don't know. I can't tell. First there's just one of you, and then two. Bound together by anger and by something else. Or maybe it's just that the danger is growing. Doubling."

"You keep saying danger. What do you mean danger?"

Rusty was frowning. "I can't be sure. He's been in some sort of trouble or risk. Some dangerous situation. Or you have."

"What do you mean I have? I'm being Biff, right?"

"Maybe. I can't be sure. But it's recent. Trouble. Violence, maybe. Something."

My arm was throbbing, as if on cue. I smoothed the sleeve over the cushion of gauze and adhesive tape. "I cut myself. Last night."

"That's right," said Mona. "Is that interfering? Maybe it's causing static or something."

"Maybe." Rusty tapped the Six of Wands. "Here's wisdom, or at least craftiness."

"The Wands are wisdom?" I asked.

"Or experience. Or illness."

"That's kind of a lot of leeway, isn't it?"

"So you decide. What do you think?" She was looking at me earnestly, the red silk scarf riding up over thin, plucked eyebrows the color of ground cinnamon.

I tried to remember the man in the trailer park, illuminated so briefly by the flash of the camera. The stunned look, the surprise, the face no more than a blur in the darkness. I'd been so concerned with taking the shot, with not screwing it up, and then with just getting the hell out of there, that I didn't notice very much at the time. What I remembered was the man's voice, plaintive and uncertain. What's going on here?

"I wouldn't have thought wisdom," I said. "And he didn't look sick."

"Crafty?"

"Maybe."

Rusty pointed. "And the two of Cups."

"What about them?"

"Love. Young lovers, or young love. Passion."

"Millie?" Mona asked.

"Or the other woman. The wife."

"Jean."

"Maybe. Or maybe just love in general. But it's only a two. It's not clear how important it is to him. Maybe it's too little, or too late."

And I thought about that. Too little, too late. I wondered what my own cards would look like, if I weren't holding Biff's picture, if I weren't standing in for him. Violence, anger, love. It could be my life summed up with such daunting succinctness, though where my own cards would rank love I couldn't guess. I'd grown so out of practice I couldn't even remember what it felt like. The closest I got was Tiny Alice's hoarse and promising whisper, and even that was overlaid in my mind by the faint dreamlike queasiness of shock and loss of blood.

Rusty reached out to the second row of cards. "This is your present," she intoned. She turned over the ten of Hearts, the five of Wands, the three of Wands.

"More wisdom," I said. "Does this mean he's getting smarter?"

"It could also mean seclusion," Rusty said. "Or privacy."

"He's hiding from her," Mona explained.

"That would fit. Or loneliness."

I hesitated. "What do you mean loneliness? This is Biff, right? We're talking about Biff? Because I don't want my fortune told."

But neither of them seemed to hear. They were staring down at the cards. "So, loneliness maybe, but definitely seclusion," said Mona. "Does it tell you where?"

"The ten of hearts."

"Millie again?"

"Maybe," Rusty said. "It could also be another woman. Another girlfriend. Or it could be his mother." She glanced up at me. "Does he have a mother?"

"I have no idea."

"Is anything at all ringing a bell?"

"No. I'm sorry. Not yet."

She shrugged and tapped the row of two cards. "This is your future."

I was surprised how unsettling the words sounded. "I'm not sure I want to see it."

"Concentrate." She turned the two cards over. The first was a dark figure, face cloaked beneath a hood, skeletal fingers grasping a scythe.

I gazed at it for a moment. "That doesn't look good."

Rusty nodded thoughtfully. "Death. Or danger."

"Whose?"

"It's in the future."

"But his future, right?"

"Yes. Probably." She turned the second card over. The Queen of Cups. "It's a good card. A sign of love, nourishment. But next to Death like that...." She shook her head. "His wife maybe. Maybe a girlfriend. Maybe his mother. Maybe she's lost, maybe she's gone. Maybe she's dead."

I felt a twist of something almost like panic. His mother lost, or gone, or dead. "These are his cards, right? I'm being him."

"I think so," said Rusty hesitantly. "At least...." She was brushing her fingertips over the faces of the cards as if there were more to be read than could be seen. And I remembered all the times I'd imagined my mother dead, half-hoping for it. I found myself thinking, *I didn't mean it, I didn't mean it*, like someone whispering in the dark.

"And that last card?" said Mona. "What's that for?"

"That's the answer. Past, present, future, and the answer lying above them all. Now, this is the tricky part," Rusty said. "We have to know the question."

"Where is he?" said Mona. "Where do we look? That's the question."

Rusty nodded and, leaning forward, slowly intoned, "Where is Biff? Where is Biff? Where is Biff?" She reached for the card, and hesitated. Then, to me, "You do it. Turn it over."

I reached down and with the edge of the photograph flipped the card over. It was the King of Swords.

"Shit," muttered Mona.

"What?" I was looking from one to the other. "What is it? What's wrong?"

Rusty looked grim. "Danger. Power. A threat. Somebody important. Somebody powerful, potentially dangerous, but not necessarily. And with the queen like that. I don't know. Nourishment, home, health, love. But, the King. Somebody important. Nourishment, danger, and strength, all tied together."

I was staring bleakly up at her. "Could you possibly be less precise?"

"What about you, Harry?" Mona said. "Are you getting anything?"

I shook my head. "Of course not. Nobody tells me anything." I felt oddly let down by it all, though what I had expected I couldn't be sure.

Now Rusty was leaning forward, puzzling over the cards. "That King of Swords. So close to Death and the queen there. It's odd. You don't usually see them together like that, back to back. His mother and some powerful threatening man. But so close they're almost touching. You're sure you're not getting anything? Comfort of some sort, but mixed with a threat? Violence, sadness? A mother? But a dangerous mother?"

I just shook my head. I wasn't a good person to ask about mothers. So close they're almost touching. My mother was a long way from close, and a long way from comforting. Love and sadness. Here and gone. I'd been thinking about it for six years now, and hadn't come close to understanding. "Sorry," I said. "I'm not getting anything. The only mother I know now is a bartender, and he's not that much of a comfort. Are we through with this?"

I flipped the photograph onto the table. It lay among the cards like another portent. Though, of what? Surprise? Annoyance? Incomprehension? I peered down at it. Poor old Biff. Standing framed in the doorway, his face pale and vague but his voice plaintive. *What's going on?* I had been wondering the same thing myself as we were driving away, and in retrospect my memory of Biff was colored by the mild and reasonable tone of his question. I could imagine him, puzzled and even a little hurt to be left standing there in the dark.

But as I turned the picture around I noticed something else, as well. This was the first chance I'd had to see it under the light. It was darker than I'd expected, given all the flash; the night crowded in around the edges. But every detail was sharp. And as I looked down at it now, it put to rest any memory I had of some shy and hesitant voice in the dark. "Oh, shit."

I had glimpsed the picture before, of course, but now I saw it clearly. Pale face, bleached out by the flash, standing sharply against the black of night. The expression was less hapless than I remembered. Biff stood there, hunched in the doorway, blonde hair bristling above a clenched face. He looked pissed. And his eyes weren't puzzled. They looked narrow and mean and familiar.

In the photograph he was holding a beer bottle. I hadn't noticed it at the time. He was holding it down at his side, but not as if he were planning to offer us a drink. He held it as if at any moment he might smash it against the railing and raise it up like a brown glass bouquet.

Part Two:

No Truth But In Things

13

It should have been more of a comfort that *Mom's*, like the very best things of this world, never changed. When I showed up at work the next night Muddy Waters was again on the jukebox, the air was smoky and loud, and Mom wore an expression of patient exasperation that might have been lifted intact from that very first night when I'd appeared and was beaten into one enormous bruise. He had a damp beer rag adorning his shoulder and a full case of Southern Comfort tucked purposefully under one arm, but at the sight of me he set the case down on the bar and leaned companionably against it. "Man, don't you look like shit."

It was barely seven o'clock and the place hadn't even begun to fill up. The only one at the bar was a slouching figure in matted gray hair and greasy plaid who glanced up from his beer with distant interest, like a man who knew so many people who might match the description he could barely be bothered to check.

"I was just telling Frankie here you probably weren't dead," said Mom.

"Hey, I'm on time. What are you complaining about?"

"I'm not complaining." He nodded at me. "How's the arm?"

I glanced down at the taped edge of the bandage peeping out from under my cuff. "It smarts a bit." In fact it ached like crazy, as if some deranged chihuahua were hanging by his teeth from my forearm. "How did you know? I didn't notice, myself, until someone pointed it out."

Mom laughed, a sudden, wet whoosh of amusement, like opening a can of warm beer. "Guess I was paying more attention. So you're not going to die on me?"

"Seems not," I said.

"Anything permanently rearranged?"

"The doctor said I can live a healthy and productive life."

"How many stitches?"

"A few. Thirty-seven."

"Attaboy. Ever had 'em before?"

I shook my head.

"First few days you got to take it easy or you tear 'em right out." He scooped up the case of Southern Comfort again as if it weighed nothing at all. "I'll do the lifting, next couple of days. You keep an eye on things up here. Okay? You think you can handle that?"

"Yeah. Thanks."

"And take it easy on the rough stuff. You get in any more fights, you gotta throw yourself out." Another little whoosh of laughter, then he turned and started toward the basement.

"Mom?"

He glanced back.

"You know that guy? From last night?"

"What about him?"

"You know where I can find him?"

He turned back, frowning, the heavy case of liquor all but forgotten under his arm. "You don't want to do that."

"Yes, I do."

"Listen, kid. Just forget it. There's nothing in it for you. Some things you just wanna let go."

"It's not like that. A friend of mine just needs to talk to him, that's all."

He shook his head in the half-admiring, half-annoyed tone of a little league coach with one of his less promising players. "You got balls, kid. I'll say that for you. But you tell this 'friend' of yours he's gonna cut you up, he sees you again."

I thought of the face clenched like a fist and the hard, eager eyes, and I remembered that cold molasses feeling as the whole room seemed to suffer a slow leak. For my part, I'd be perfectly happy if I never saw him again. But I couldn't very well tell Mona that. Somehow, without knowing it, I had slipped into that awkward and undefined stage of actually caring what she thought. "Has he been in here before?"

"Are you listening?"

"Please?"

Mom shrugged resignedly. "Not lately. And not that often. But you keep your eyes open and you leave him alone. There's nothing you want to talk to him about, except you do it long distance. You hear me?"

"Yeah."

"I'm serious. Don't piss me off here. I'm just getting you trained good. I don't want you fucking up on me." And with a sorry shake of his head he turned and headed down the stairs.

The crowd began to pick up after eight and almost immediately the place was packed. The noise was so loud it didn't have room to echo, so like a gas under pressure it just liquefied. I used to love this time of night, balanced against the sound. It was like being in a crowd so dense you couldn't fall down. But tonight it felt different. The noise itself seemed threatening. Between pouring drinks I searched the crowd, trying to get a good look at every man before he got too close, wondering if I'd spot the blonde crew cut in time. Below the counter on a shelf Mom kept half a baseball bat, the thin end of an old Louisville Slugger wrapped in electrician's tape. As I moved up and down the bar I took it with me, and every time I brushed the counter or lifted a rack of mugs out of the washer, the stitches throbbed in my arm like a sharp reminder of what any given moment could bring.

I thought of Rusty laying the tarot cards down. Each one defining the hapless course of my life. Violence, illness, and loneliness. Love, she'd said, but not very much and no particular object. Maybe just love in general, but too little too late. I looked around at the crowd, raucously unraveling with a kind of wild, untuned inevitability amid all that smoke and noise. I tried to feel comforted by it, by the routine of it. I tried to recover the sense of protection it used to provide—the reassurance that no bad luck, no further tragedy would stoop low enough to find me here. But tonight it was like a wake-up call in a motel so seedy and depressing you knew, even as you opened your eyes, that you'd regret it.

"Is this seat taken?"

Pink-faced and cheerful, Tiny Alice slid onto an empty stool and sat there, grinning expectantly. There should have been nothing surprising about seeing her there. She perched comfortably on the barstool as if she'd ridden it all the way from home. But I had somehow managed to suppress large portions of the night before. It had come to seem a long time ago and safely sheltered by the vagaries of strong drink. And now here it was again gazing roguishly back at me, and the sight of it caught me off guard. "Hi," I stammered, and then blushed like a debutante, glancing around to see if anyone had heard.

At a place like Mom's they don't teach you much as a bartender, but the first rule is inviolable: never greet your customers. A bar is the one place in the world where people want to be taken for granted. It provides the regulars, who spend too much time here as it is, the reassurance that no one's really keeping track, while conferring even on newcomers the warm and spurious comfort of belonging. In the edgy clamor of the day-to-day, a measure of smooth indifference is the grease that keeps things running.

But something in Alice's grin suggested there was no longer need for such formality. "You're looking bright-eyed and bushy-tailed," she purred.

I managed a weak smile and hurriedly set a beer down before her. "I wasn't sure you were coming in tonight."

"Why?" she said. "Did you miss me?"

"I was just thinking, after all the excitement…."

"Yeah," she said. "That was something, wasn't it?" And she leaned close over the bar. "You should have come in last night.

It took me an hour just to get myself calmed down. You could have given me a hand." She leaned back, grinning, and hoisted the beer. "So, how about you? How'd you sleep?"

"Actually, I decided to get a few stitches." She smiled uncertainly, waiting for the joke. I peeled back my cuff and showed her the bandage. "Thirty-seven, to be exact. It turns out I got cut in the fight last night."

She peered down at the broad, white bandage. "Jeeze Louise."

"I guess that's why I was feeling light-headed. At your place, I mean." I could feel myself blushing again. I might as well have been back in high school.

She laughed. "I wondered about that. I thought you were getting a little shy all of a sudden." And she gazed at me archly. "So, how are you feeling now?"

I wasn't sure. She looked so large and substantial, so red-faced and hearty, that I felt strangely embarrassed. I suddenly couldn't remember whether I'd actually touched her breasts last night or only wanted to. I thought of dancing with her: the soft back with the deep furrow of her bra strap under my hands and the half-remembered lushness of her lips. Sober, now, it seemed vivid and mortifying, like kissing your boss's wife at the office party. Though lurking behind everything were those last few words, glowing warmly in a darker corner of my mind. Creaming in my pants.

"Fine," I said. "I'm fine. Pretty good, really. I seem to have a full range of movement, though the doctor told me no heavy lifting."

"Good to know. We wouldn't want you straining anything. Does that include dancing?"

I smiled nervously. "I think the management might frown on it. I'm working tonight."

"Too bad." With her beer in hand she slid off the stool. "So, how late are you working?"

I hesitated. "Pretty much until closing."

"I'll be around," she said, and winked. "Just think of me as the American Express card. Don't leave for home without me."

As the evening progressed, Alice drifted back every so often to pick up another beer and say hello. Her grin grew broader and her face redder, as if the temperature were rising and she was the only one who could feel it. At the same time, her expression, though growing blurry, continued to offer the same tacit promise. It reminded me of a piano recital I'd given in the fifth grade, the last year before I convinced my mother to let me give up the instrument. I'd spent almost two hours in a back room of my piano teacher's house, rifling through her collection of Readers Digests and waiting for my turn. Though I had practiced my pieces until I was sure of every note, I spent the afternoon in a small low-pressure system of anxiety, a handkerchief growing soggy in my clutched, perspiring hands. And now I felt just like that, and once again I recognized my problem. It wasn't that I was afraid I wouldn't know what to do. It was just, I told myself, a little stage fright.

Time passed, if anything, too quickly. Between serving drinks, keeping an eye on Alice, keeping track of the baseball bat, and watching for the first trace of a blonde crew cut in the shifting crowd, I didn't notice Mona until she was standing right in front of me. I glanced up and saw a shaggy burst of dull magenta hair around a pale raccoon face, and I was already reaching for an empty beer mug before I realized who it was.

"Can't this place afford a real bartender?" she asked.

Her lips, dark and painted to match her hair, seemed to float a few inches in front of the pale white skin, giving her a slightly indefinite look, as if she weren't fully committed to her present appearance. She wore red plaid cargo pants, baggy and low on her hips, and a bright yellow tank top beneath the leather jacket. All together she seemed just too bright for the place, but there was something so fierce and boisterous about her outfit that despite myself I smiled. In those first moments, before caution, good manners or sense could kick in, when you're exposed to the darkest and most mysterious truths of your character, I discovered I was very pleased to see her.

"I was in the neighborhood," she said. "Thought I might stop in for a beer."

"You're in luck. I happen to have one left."

She slipped up onto a stool. There was a relaxed air about her that I hadn't noticed before. Maybe it was just that after-hours familiarity that any bar brings out, or perhaps nearly saving a person's life creates its own sort of intimacy. For whatever reason, if she wasn't exactly smiling, she was at least frowning in a friendlier way. "Quite a place you've got here."

"Just a little bit of heaven," I agreed. "Is this your first time in?"

"I'm not that big on bars. I mean I don't hate them or anything. But after a while they start to depress me. Just a few too many lost souls."

At the time I just nodded. But ever since I've spent more time than I should have wondering if she meant me, if she could tell that much in just that first glance. But I only set the mug down and glanced at her hair. "What happened to the blue?"

"I decided I needed a change."

"It's been what? Three days?"

She looked up, a thin vein of doubt glinting in her eyes. "What's the matter? Don't you like it?"

The dye seemed to have calmed the perm's wild derangement into a stiff, wind-blown disarray, but the color, unlinked to anything in nature, looked too much like something out of Ringling Brothers. "It's nice," I said.

"You think so? Really?" Her hand crept up to one feathery edge. "You don't think it makes me look too pale?"

"You know what they say: you can never be too thin or too pale.

She straightened with a frown. "Now you're saying I'm too thin?"

"No," I said hurriedly. "I didn't say that."

"This is a cool color!"

"I can see that."

"A lot of magazines are showing this color. It's very hip right now."

"It looks great. Fabulous." I was grasping a little wildly now. "It's got a kind of bright, wild, cheerful thing going on."

"Cheerful?" She looked disgusted. "It's supposed to look sexy."

"I meant sexy."

"Cheerful!" she muttered. "What am I, a clown?"

And she had come so close to my most hidden thoughts that I had to fight to keep my smile inanely in place until, with a shake of her head, she turned to glower out at the crowd. So much, I thought, for easy familiarity. Even saving someone's life only goes so far.

"I'm not," I said finally, "a good person to ask about fashion."

"No kidding."

"You shouldn't listen to what I say."

"Don't worry."

"What about Henry? That's what matters. I'll bet Henry loves it."

"I'll bet he does."

"What did he say?" I asked encouragingly.

"What do I look like? The Post Office? Ask him yourself."

Only then did I recognize the man who stood a few paces behind her, looking sheepish but game and hopelessly out of place in a crisp blue shirt and beige slacks. My father waved.

"What's he doing here?" I demanded.

"He wanted to come. He said he'd never been before."

Henry raised his voice against the noise. "You realize that? All these years, and I've never seen where you work?"

"This may not--" I started, and raised my voice. "This may not be such a good night." But he just cupped his hand to his ear and smiled weakly.

I glanced at Mona, "Is this such a hot idea? Does he know why you're here?"

"I told him I was doing a little scouting." She shrugged. "I thought he could use a night out."

"See, I'd have thought it was better if only one member of the family gets cut up in a bar fight."

"Don't go all girlie," she said irritably. "He'll be fine."

I glanced around at all the usual clientele. They were quite a bunch. There was a great deal of skin showing, though not much of it attractive. A lot of denim and leather, vests and sleeveless jackets, short skirts and halter tops. Outside, the weather was chilly for mid-June, but at Mom's people tended to dress for the bar, and inside it was always high summer: rowdy, overheated, and balanced on the verge of a fight. And in the midst of it Henry was peering around with a kind of cheerful and wide-eyed uneasiness. I felt a little twist of irritation. What was he doing here? He didn't belong. He had his own life, which was obviously going so well. Why couldn't he at least leave me mine?

But Henry didn't seem to notice. He sidled up to the bar and squeezed in beside Mona. "What a crowd," he said grinning, then he nodded at Mona. "Did you see the new hair? Great color, don't you think?"

"He hates it," she said.

I shook my head. "I didn't say that. I said it looked nice."

But Mona was having none of it. Her hand crept up again, pinching the stiff hair.

I leaned toward her. "Didn't you think about just leaving it black?"

"Black is boring. Tell him, Henry."

My father shrugged philosophically. "A girl's got to do what a girl's got to do."

I ignored him. "I liked it black. I thought it looked great black."

But she just looked at me as if that, in itself, were part of a much larger problem that she couldn't even begin to address.

"You've got to keep it exciting," she said, leaning closer, almost shouting in my ear. "You've got to keep people on their toes."

I glanced over at Henry. What could I say? It seemed to be working. I'd never seen him looking more cheerfully on toe. He noticed my attention. Leaning in he said, "I think what we need under these circumstances is a beer. What do you think?"

I sighed. "Better let me see some I.D."

While I filled a mug he stood gazing around, managing to look both out of place and proprietary, as if his obvious abundance of good cheer had somehow made the bar his own. He seemed to be enjoying everything—the noise, the crowd—as if each detail were new and enchanting. He raised his beer and took a timid sip, then suddenly said, "Hey! Is that a dance floor?"

"Possibly," I said.

"Come on." He was grinning at Mona. "Feel like practicing?"

"I just got a seat."

"Harry'll save it for you. Won't you, son?"

"Probably not," I said.

"Well, it doesn't matter. We'll get another. Come on. It'll be fun."

He was holding out his hand. I'd always thought of him as such a shy man, quiet and reluctant, but now all of that was clearly a thing of the past. I marveled at this suddenly masterful Henry, and marveled even more when, with the first reluctant hint of a smile, Mona slid off the stool and took his hand.

"That's the spirit," said Henry, and he grinned at me, my mild and mousy father. "Let this be a lesson to you, son. Sometimes you just have to take what you want." And Mona laughed.

Together they made their way toward the dance floor. Their clothes stood out, bright and neat against the shabby background. They could not have looked more out of place, like some middle-aged accountant and his moll. But what annoyed me most was not that Henry couldn't have looked more foolish, but that he didn't even begin to realize it. He had no clue.

There was an old Elmore James song on the jukebox now,

slow and cranky. They started dancing. Not well. They looked stiff, and even from a distance I could see Mona giving instructions. That annoyed me as well, but Henry didn't seem to mind. He was laughing, trying to lead and follow at the same time. They turned and rebounded off another couple, and Henry apologized quickly, but he was laughing still. He danced her around. That one sip of beer had gone straight to his head and he was cutting loose, painting the town red. And now Mona was grinning, too. She was saying something. Laughing. I tried to remember if I had ever actually seen her so cheerful before. She looked like she was having fun. They both did.

I picked up the rag and gave the bar an irritable wipe. How could I ever have thought he needed my help? Here I was, having spent so much of the last six years worrying for both of us that I had settled into a constant twilight of sadness, while Henry seemed to have hopped a freight train to Funville without a second thought.

And all of a sudden, I recalled a moment, clear as could be. I hadn't thought about it in years. I'd been maybe ten at the time, upstairs doing my homework, and I heard all this laughter suddenly rising from the living room. I went down to see what was going on. Because it was that unusual. I heard the laughter, I went down the stairs, and there were my parents watching TV. At least, the TV was on, but they weren't paying attention. They were curled up in the easy chair, both of them, sitting sideways across the arms, as if they'd fallen accidentally and gotten tangled up. They were laughing. That's all. They weren't doing anything. It wasn't one of those terrible Freudian moments of childhood awakening. They were just sitting there together, fully clothed and laughing. But at the time they looked up at me as if I'd caught them at something, and I felt a stab of sudden, anguished jealousy, sharp as a knife, that somehow they could be having so much fun without me.

When Henry wandered back a couple of songs later he was pink-cheeked and breathless. He reached for his beer and took a long, thirsty drink. "Did you see that?" he demanded. "A regular Fred Astaire." Then he tilted his mug up again, gulping manfully until the last of the foam glided down his throat.

"Careful," I said. "You're not used to it."

But he just set the mug down, watery-eyed and grinning. "Well, I've got a lot of making up for lost time. Better set me up another one, son. I've got a man-sized thirst."

"Where's Mona?"

"She said she wanted to wander around a little, check the place out."

I spotted her, a bright head of hair floating through the smoke. She was easing her way through the crowd, moving cautiously as if the floor were sticky and she didn't want to think about what might be on it. He was smiling as he watched her. "She's a treat, don't you think?"

I didn't bother to reply. He had that bright, overeager look you might see in one of the nerdier high school boys—the math team president, say, or the head of the chess club—gazing at his first girlfriend. You could tell it had been a long time coming and he didn't want to waste a minute.

14

Henry settled cheerfully at the bar as if he'd taken root. He sipped his beer and shyly ogled the poster of two women in leather chaps, entangled on the saddle of a new Heritage Softail. He peered with sidelong fascination at the passing crowd: the panoply of tattoos and the wincing weight of silver jewelry crowding lips, noses, and cheeks. I kept waiting for his expression to change, for his eyes to turn bleak and uneasy, for the smoke or the noise to gnaw away at him, but Henry beamed like a man secure in his happiness. One citizen in a black mohawk with silver-embroidered eyebrows and a row of chrome spikes protruding like tusks from beneath his lower lip, sidled past Henry's khaki and oxford cloth with a glance of wary unease, but my father just smiled with the easy good cheer of a greeter in a fifties department store. "How you doin'?" he said.

What had he done to deserve such confidence? Where had it come from? It was like another sign of all I'd done wrong that after half an hour my father felt more at home in the bar than I did.

So when Alice drifted back with an empty beer mug, and he gave her a smile like the mayor of the place greeting one of his constituents, it annoyed me so much that I kissed her. She stepped up onto the brass rail and slid the mug across the bar, overbalancing in her enthusiasm, and on impulse, with a glance at Henry, I leaned forward with dry lips. She was too drunk to be startled. In that state when everything is equally unexpected, her mouth bloomed warmly under mine with a kind of mild and equable surprise. But when she settled back onto her seat she was smiling, if a little blearily. "Whoa. Can I get a beer chaser with that?"

I turned to Henry, whose expression had turned wide-eyed and startled. "I'd like you to meet somebody," I said. "Henry, this is Alice. Alice is one of our most valued customers. Henry, as you can see, is here on an inter-office exchange program from L.L. Bean."

"Well," said Alice, with a look of grave politeness, "that must be very interesting."

"He's just kidding," said Henry with his easy smile. "I'm his father. I'm here visiting." He said it as if he had come from a long way off. And with an air of beer-heightened formality he stood up and shook her hand.

"This is Henry's first trip to the bar," I said.

Alice looked startled. "A virgin. That is so sweet." And I watched with something between embarrassment and satisfaction as she shifted over onto the stool beside him. "Well," she said. "You're in good hands, Henry. Your son is a great bartender. One of the best I've met."

"He knows," I said. "He's very proud."

"And not a bad kisser," she added, in the spirit of full disclosure.

"Alice was here for my little adventure last night."

"Really?"

"God, yes." She leaned close with the air of one revealing a deep secret. "He almost got killed. This guy came at him with a bottle?" She shook her head, marveling. "I was so scared...." I braced myself. But that's all there was. Alice just shook her head in wonder, and Henry nodded sympathetically.

"Alice and I were cutting a rug at the time," I said.

"That's right." She smiled as if it were all coming back to her now. "We were dancing. He's a pretty great dancer, too," she confided.

Henry smiled benignly. "It runs in the family."

Once having settled onto the barstool, Alice seemed reluctant to rise. She and Henry were laughing quietly, nodding together, subsiding gently into a cheerful haze of conversation. I went back to work, trying to keep an eye on everything: the crowd, the customers, Alice, my father, and the constant possibility of Biff turning up with a broken bottle in his hand. But, in the middle of it all my eye was continually drawn to the bright distraction of magenta hair floating through the smoky room. I kept glancing around to find it. I would wash the glassware, drift over to top up my father's beer, work my way down the bar, and every few minutes glance out into the room after Mona.

She had the Polaroid of Biff in her hand, and she was stopping at little knots of men, showing them the picture. Occasionally Henry would glance up at her, and he'd get that funny little smile on his face again, but he didn't have enough sense to be worried. He thought it was all fun; he thought this was the life. So I kept half an eye on her for him, and half an eye for me. It was like watching television with the sound turned down, but I could see the body language and read the little jokes and leering suggestions from across the room. She managed to keep shaking them off, but she looked thin and overmatched in the rowdy crowd.

Then at one group she stopped and held up the photo, but no one seemed interested, at least not in Biff. Mona shook her head, then shook it again. The three men shifted, easing in on either side. She peered around, and then smiled thinly as one man laid his hand heavily on her shoulder. I glanced back at my father, but he was oblivious. "Henry!" I hissed, but he didn't hear me. Across the room Mona turned and tried to slide away, but the men were all around her now, blocking her path. She glanced around from face to face with a tight, determined expression.

"You plannin' to pull that?" said a deep voice.

I looked up, startled. Mom stood there with four empty mugs in one large fist and a frown on his face. I had my hand on the beer tap, but nothing was coming out.

"You got to pull it toward you," he said.

I flipped the lever and started to fill the mug. "I thought you were downstairs."

"I'm here now. "

"Good." I picked up a tray and set the fresh beer in the middle of it. "I'll be back."

I moved quickly through the crowd. As I slid up beside Mona she was saying, "Yeah, that's real nice. But I'm looking for this guy."

The man with his hand on her shoulder eased in a little closer. His hair was swept up in a huge black pompadour that might have been sculpted out of shoe polish. "Honey, he's not going to show you anything I can't."

I shoved the tray into the middle of the group. "Empties?"

"We're busy," said the man.

"Just doing my job." I glanced at Mona. "Everything okay?"

"Everything's fine," she said, but she looked, I thought, just a little relieved.

"Yeah," said the man under the pompadour. "Everything's fine. Now get the fuck lost."

I turned to him. "Did you look at the picture?"

"What the hell do you care?" This was a thin, vole-like man in an old fatigue jacket.

"I took it. I like to see my work appreciated."

Mona held out the Polaroid. The man in the pompadour glanced at it. "Pretty shitty job. He looks kinda pissed off."

"He was pissed off when we got there."

"He's been in town maybe a few weeks," said Mona. "He ran off and left his wife. Without a word. She's worried sick."

"Bastard," muttered the third man. He had a five o'clock shadow of salt and pepper spread evenly over his cheeks, his chin, and his narrow-domed head. His black t-shirt strained over an impressive paunch. "How about I buy you a beer, darlin'? You can tell me all about it."

Mona set her empty down on my tray and lifted the one full mug. "Looks like I've got one, thanks."

The man looked down at the empty tray, then up at me. I braced myself. Under the bandage my forearm was throbbing, but I tried to ignore it. "He was in a couple of nights ago," I said. "There was a fight."

"Oh, yeah. I heard about that," said the pompadour. "Some big dyke and her candy-ass boyfriend." He ran two testing fingers over the slick hair at his temple and looked sly. "You a dyke, honey?"

"No," said Mona. "But for you I'd make an exception."

He nodded at me. "Your boy-friend a candy-ass?"

"Ask him yourself. Do I look like a matchmaker?" And she turned, "Come on, Harry," and strode away without a backward glance.

I hesitated a moment, then followed with a vaguely disappointed feeling running like a slow leak. "You're right at home, aren't you?" I said.

Mona's glance was not altogether unkind. "Did you think I needed rescuing?"

"I thought maybe you could use a hand."

Across the room there was a sudden flurry of action, the thump of a beer mug on a table, then a very thin man in a cowboy shirt stood up and sprayed fragments of half-chewed popcorn out into the room as the whole table roared. Mona took a sip of her beer and shook her head doubtfully. "I can't believe you brought a woman here."

"She was here already. I just asked her to dance."

She looked around from the bar to the tables to the slow and crowded chaos of the dance floor. "Is this where it happened?"

"This very spot."

"You didn't think maybe you should just run away?"

"It occurred to me afterwards."

She nodded. After a moment, "It was a nice thought, coming over like that. But I can take care of myself."

"I can see that," I said. But I didn't move.

She took another pull on her beer and glanced quizzically over the tops of her glasses. "Don't you have to go back to work?"

Back at the bar Mom was standing over the flowing beer tap. "If you run into anyone'd like a job," he said, "tell 'em we could use a bartender back here."

I didn't bother to reply. I started washing mugs with a grim determination that left two of them cracked and sent a large chip skipping out of a third. Mom watched for a moment, but even he seemed to think better of it. Without another word he filled a beer mug and headed down to the basement.

I was buzzing with a low current of embarrassment, like a man who'd ridden to the rescue and fallen off his horse. Down the bar Henry and Alice were still leaning together companionably. Alice's complexion had brightened to the deep red of a sunburn and she was offering up a wide, wet laugh at something my father had said. But Henry was still bright-eyed and smiling. Despite all that early talk of a man-sized thirst, he'd spend most of the evening sipping delicately at the top half-inch of his beer, and now his expression was clear and unmuddled. He was pacing himself, like a young man already thinking ahead to who was waiting for him at the end of the evening. And I was overcome by a sense of irritation surprising in its fierceness. I thought of all the efforts I'd made over the years to protect Henry from his own unhappiness, to save him from the effects of a marriage, whose wreck was largely his fault. And clearly he needed no one's help but his own.

I was at a loss. But what was I supposed to do? I needed to take some steps. As Henry himself had said: Sometimes you just have to take what you want.

When I walked over Alice grinned blearily up at me. "Getting close to closing," she said meaningfully. Henry, nodded companionably, smiling like a man who, however little he deserved his good fortune, was going home with Mona.

"In that case," I said, "you'd better have another drink," and I topped up both their beers. "On the house. And there's a special tonight. Tequila shooters. Two for a buck. In honor of Henry's visit."

Alice laughed. "Did you hear that, Henry? You're a celebrity."

I laid the two pairs of shot glasses before them, and filled them quivering to the lip. Henry eyed them doubtfully. "I don't know, son. I'm not sure--"

"They're in your honor, Henry. It's like drinking a toast. You're pretty much obliged."

"Come on, Henry," Alice said. "There's nothing to it." And she raised one shot, tipped it back, and chased it with half her beer in one long breath. She set the mug back on the bar, grinning.

With a hesitant smile Henry raised the first shot, holding it awkwardly, careful not to spill. He took a cautious sip.

"You don't sip it, Henry," Alice said. "Down the hatch." Reluctantly he drained it like a capful of Nyquil, and then took a fractured, gasping sip of beer to put out the fire.

"That's the spirit," I said. "You're a natural."

He lowered his mug, wide-eyed and breathless. "Actually, I'm not much of a drinker."

I was already refilling both their glasses. "Well, I can see that's going to change."

15

Mom's was usually jumping until closing time, but tonight things started to taper off about eleven and by half past, the bar was becalmed like a sailboat in the tropics. Men sat stunned, nursing their beers, while out on the dance floor the crowd seemed to be waiting for its second wind. Henry and Alice sat hunched together like a couple of old army buddies, mired in a sodden conversation about the relative merits of mescal and tequila. I cautiously watched over them, topping up their beers like a good host. When Mona finally wandered back Henry glanced up to greet her, befogged with good cheer. "Welcome, senorita. Don' say a wor'. I know jus' wha' you need." He raised a finger in my direction. "Bartender? Another *cervesa* for the lady, por favor."

Alice was grinning blurrily. "Your dad is such a peach." And then, to Mona, "His dad is such a peach. Did anyone ever tell him that?" And she turned to Henry. "How do you say peach in Spanish?"

"I ha' no idea."

Mona hesitated, regarding Henry with a look of pale disappointment. There were no seats to be had, and he made no move to stand up. The Tequila had taken the edge off his gentlemanly instincts. Reluctantly she squeezed in beside him, but after giving her a cheery little wave he turned back to Alice.

"Henry's having fun," said Mona.

"He's just had a little too much to drink."

"Who's his friend?"

"That's Alice," I said. "I'll introduce you."

"Don't bother." Up close she looked weary and glum. "I'm pretty tired. Can you make sure he gets back okay? I'm going to head home."

I felt the disappointment like a twinge. "You can't just dessert us."

"I don't want to spoil his fun, and I'm beat."

"But things are just starting to warm up."

She glanced around wearily at the dispirited crowd. "You think?"

"No question," I said. "What you need is a beer."

"No, thanks. I've been on my feet all day."

But with the brisk and pleading tone of the truly desperate, I said, "Don't move."

I sidled down in front of a small, wiry man with watery eyes and a sagging face. He sat swaying on his stool like a palm tree on a breezy day, gazing forlornly at the empty beer mug in front of him.

I said, "You look like you could use a walk. Just to clear your head."

With an effort he raised his head. "What?"

"How about letting the lady sit down?"

"Hey," he said belligerently. "This's my seat." He poked a finger at the bar. "Tha's my beer. See? My beer, my seat. Get it?"

I picked up the mug. "It's empty."

"So?"

I filled it up and set it down. "Drink it somewhere else."

He regarded the beer for a long, unsteady moment, as if clarifying all the details of the transaction. Then he picked up the mug, "Okey dokey," and carefully climbing down, he wandered away.

Mona smiled, too tired even to be cranky. She slid onto the stool. "Thanks." In the low light of the bar the ring glinted in her nostril like a little, silver apostrophe.

"Why did you pierce your nose?"

The smile faded. "Why do you keep doing that?"

"Doing what?"

"Because it looks cool," she said.

"I wasn't being critical."

"Sure, you weren't."

"It does look cool. You have a cool nose."

"I do have a cool nose," Mona replied. "And you're kind of a jerk sometimes."

I felt a sudden flush of awkwardness heating my face. "I don't mean to be."

"Yeah? Well, that's not so clear."

"I'm sorry."

"Just shut up."

"I like your nose."

"Like I care."

She sat slumped against the counter, hunched and deflated. Even under the leather jacket her shoulders looked thin and drooping. I poured a beer and set it down like a little offering before her. "So. Any luck?"

"Not a whisper."

"You talk to everybody?"

"At least twice."

"Mom said he hadn't been in for a while. Maybe he doesn't come that often."

"Well, duh," she said, but she seemed too tired even to be derisive.

A few seats down, Henry leaned forward. "Tell her about the special," he called. Then he grinned. "Tequila for all my friends."

That caused a faint flurry of interest along the bar, but the night was too far gone even for that, and it just died away. Mona was looking up expectantly.

"It's a little family special," I said. "Cuervo shooters. Two for a buck."

"You think that'll help?"

And despite the obvious evidence to the contrary hunched and laughing down the bar, I said, "Couldn't hurt."

I set the shot glass on the counter and filled it. Too tired even to pick it up, Mona lowered her head and sipped. Her glasses had slipped down the bridge of her nose, but she seemed not to notice. I reached out and pressed them back into place. She looked startled, but less annoyed than usual. She took another sip, and gazed thoughtfully down at the golden liquid catching the dim light of the bar like a lens. "Tell me about your mom," she said suddenly.

"What?"

"Your mom," she said. "If it's not a problem."

I glanced worriedly over at Henry, but he was deep in his conversation with Alice, nodding over his beer with a blurred and oblivious smile. "Why?" I asked.

"I just wanted to hear about her. Know what she was like."

I hesitated. What did it matter? She was long, long gone. Though, of course, that was just the point. "Has Henry talked about her?"

"A little."

I shook my head. Oh, Henry, I thought. It seemed the saddest thing in the world. That he could be doing so well, starting over again—dating again, for God's sake—and this is what he'd talk about. I could just imagine it, in the middle of an evening, an awkward silence. Or maybe suddenly something reminded him, and he just couldn't help it. I felt it, myself, sometimes, like a rut carved into your memory. You just kept slipping back in.

"I don't think I can help you. I don't really remember her."

"Nothing?" said Mona. "What she liked? What her hobbies were? That sort of thing. What she enjoyed doing? You must remember something."

And as she spoke I felt a sick and sinking feeling, because even as I said I didn't remember, I realized it was true. I tried to think of what my mother had done for fun, and nothing came to mind. As an only child you're supposed to notice things, you're supposed to be tuned more sharply to the world, but in retrospect, clearly, I hadn't noticed nearly enough. My skills had all been devoted to *not* knowing. After all, these were my parents, going about their own mysterious lives, and I had taken them on faith. I just assumed that everything was going as it should, that the little arguments, the tensions, the unspoken rifts, were just part of the usual landscape. Like any child I assumed there were things I just wasn't going to know, and that somehow what I did know would be enough. That things would take care of themselves.

And they don't, of course. How could they? And all you've done is to gather together everything that's most important into one big bundle of hope. When it goes, everything goes. If Elizabeth could leave—in the face of every hope and expectation— then what did I know that was true? Nothing that came before was certain. Nothing that came afterwards made sense.

And now, thinking back, I felt like someone recalling a test he'd failed. If only I had studied. If only I'd been paying more attention. But at the time I hadn't realized just how much our family was an act of pure hope. Like a flying carpet out of the Arabian Nights, it needed all our attention, all our concentration just to stay aloft.

"What did Henry say?" I asked.

Mona gave a sad little smile. "He said she was beautiful."

Funny, I thought, but after so many years that was the least clear thing about her. She was tall, dark-haired. But even now, when I remembered so much else, I could barely recall what she looked like. "I'd have to take his word for that."

"For what?" said Henry abruptly.

In the sudden silence he was leaning forward, smiling at us with drunken good cheer. I felt the dread suddenly hot in my chest. It wasn't my fault. He'd been the one to bring it up. But now he sat there, relaxed and unwary, and I wanted nothing more than just to protect him. "We were just talking," I said.

"About Elizabeth?" His voice seemed suddenly too clear. Even after all that tequila he had no trouble with the name, though it had been years since I'd heard him say it. He was smiling wistfully. "Do you remember her, son?" His eyes were bright, drooping a little from the beer but otherwise undimmed by sadness. "It's been so long, do you remember anything about her?"

"No," I said. "A little bit. Not much."

He looked troubled at that. And I felt it myself—that sharp tug of loss. "What about you?" I asked. "Do you still remember what she looked like?"

"Oh, yes," he said, as if it were still against all his better judgment.

I glanced at Mona. She wasn't shocked or angry. Not even annoyed that her date was once again drifting back over such old ground. She looked thin and deflated and a little sad, though it might have been just the fatigue, or that terrible hair. She was holding the empty shot glass, turning it in the light, as if it were a jewel someone had given her which was proving less beautiful than she had expected. Hurriedly I reached out and lifted it from her fingers. "Ready for another?"

Quickly I filled it up. I poured one for Henry, too, and for Alice. A drink for all my friends. But Henry wasn't distracted. He was still marveling at all that he recalled. "You must remember something," he said to me. "Anything at all?"

Mona was pouring her tequila through her lips with such measured concentration you might almost imagine she wasn't listening. I thought, Come on, Henry. Give it a rest. But I considered the question. And as I did I caught brief glimpses of her, little shards of memory coming to me now, sharp and glinting.

My mother refinished furniture, for a while. She painted for a while, she did needlepoint. When she took up tennis I used to throw her balls so she could practice. I wasn't good enough to hit with her; she became too impatient; so I stood at the net with a bushel of old tennis balls at my feet and threw them to her, forehand, backhand and a long, drifting lob. We'd do this for hours, until my arm was sore, and my throws were wild and unreliable. She never complained, but when she missed a shot, which happened increasingly often as we both got tired, she would bark out brief and explosive curses at the empty space just before her so it was difficult to tell who she was angry with, herself or me. And in the same spirit, later, when she took a life drawing class at the local art gallery, she asked me to pose for her. I sat there in my bathing suit for hours, struggling not to move, as she became increasingly frustrated, tearing off one sheet after another from her easel and crumpling them up. She never said a word until the end, when she threw down her pencil and told me to go away. She never blamed me, of course, but it was clear. Even in the simplest matter of throwing a ball or just sitting still, I was utterly insufficient for her needs.

"What I remember," I said, glancing up, "is that she kept burning cookies."

"She baked cookies?" said Mona.

"Well. She burned them. Technically I suppose it's not the same thing."

"Boy," said Alice, chiming in, "I wouldn't mind a cookie right now."

"Do you remember that?"

"No." And I watched my father's smile fade slightly, like a cloud over the sun. I wished I hadn't spoken, but he looked at me so expectantly I had to go on. "For a while there, she was baking every week. "

"That's right. I'd forgotten." Henry shook his head, marveling. "That was a long time ago."

"She tried a new recipe each time, but she couldn't get them right. They'd be too dry, or too moist. They'd fall apart, or they wouldn't taste quite right. And then she'd burn them. Just to be sure."

"She didn't burn them," Henry protested.

"Every time."

"Are you sure?"

"She couldn't have burned them all," said Mona.

"Every last one. She'd put them in the oven, set the timer, and then forget all about them. Next thing you know, the house was full of smoke. That's what I remember most. The smell of smoke and burned sugar, and the taste of charcoal."

"You'd eat them?" said Mona.

"How could we not?"

"I thought they were good," said my father wanly. He'd never looked so fragile, the smile barely floating on his lips.

My heart ached, but I was tangled in the story and didn't know how to stop. "I was afraid she'd feel bad if I didn't, so I always ate three. I thought if I only ate one she'd know I was just pretending. And if I ate two, she'd think I was just eating the second to prove I wasn't pretending with the first. But that third one, I knew, would convince her."

Mona considered that for a moment. "And did it?"

"No," I said slowly. "In the end, I guess not."

Henry was peering down into the froth of his beer, his lips moving ever so slightly, as if he were doing sums in his head. Then he gave his head a little shake.

"You okay, Henry?" I asked.

"Yeah." He conjured up that fragile smile. "I'm fine."

"You want to dance?" asked Mona. "You know what you said. We've got to practice."

But he just shook his head. "I don't think so. I'm a little tired."

She smiled encouragingly. "You know what they say. If you can walk, you can dance."

"I think I'll just sit this one out," he said.

Mona sat back looking glum and subdued.

"He's just had a little too much to drink," I said.

She shrugged and gave her empty shot glass a little push. "Did you say those things were two for one, or three for one?"

"Are you sure that's a good idea?"

She looked thin and pale in all those bright colors, like one of those paper dolls that almost disappears behind her clothes. She nodded and tapped the bar. "Line it up." But when it was poured she just looked at it with a thin, bemused expression.

"Do you want to dance?" I asked suddenly.

She glanced up, startled. "What?"

"Dance," I said.

The music had changed. There was something slow on the jukebox, though nothing I recognized. She listened to it for a moment, undecided. "Aren't you working?"

"I'm taking a break. Come on. I hear you're such a smooth dancer."

It was, I knew, a mistake. As she sat there, considering, the heavy shell of her jacket hung open like a pair of gates she'd forgotten to lock, and the yellow tank top, bright as a beacon, snugly defined the shallow curve of her breasts. I should just let her sit there, let them all sit there, and in another hour just drive them all home. I'd done enough to Henry for one night. But what I said was, "Come on. It's just a dance." And I picked up her untouched tequila and tossed it back. It burned all the way down and then rose like smoke through my brain.

16.

We walked across the bar like strangers and when we got to the dance floor Mona turned uncertainly. As she stepped in, I raised my arms and draped them loosely around her shoulders. She was swaying a little from the drinks, but as far as I was concerned, that one shot of tequila wasn't nearly enough. I was thinking way too much about where my hands should go and what my feet were meant to do. Her body was thin and solid beneath the stiff leather, and as I moved she bumped against me. Our knees collided. She said, "You dance like your father."

"I'm not asking for lessons.

"Slow down. That's too fast."

"Did you hear me?"

"Listen to the rhythm."

"Will you be quiet?"

She was moving more and more slowly. Beneath the baggy drape of the plaid cargo pants her hips were swaying as if in direct contradiction to my own. I thought of Henry, moving happily just off the beat, bumping cheerfully around the dance floor without enough sense to know how foolish he looked. But not me. Oh, no. Whatever else I knew, I knew that much. But if I was so smart, what exactly did I think I was doing? I felt Mona's hand settle on my waist, pressing firmly, forcing me to slow down even more. I lost any shred of concentration. My feet slowed to a shuffle. And at that moment, as if to confirm that I had, indeed, finally found the proper rhythm, Mona took a half a step closer, briefly pressing her hips against me like the docking of two space craft that had finally synchronized orbits. "See?" she said. "Isn't that better?"

I swallowed hard. "I said I didn't want any lessons."

She wasn't as tall as I'd thought. For some reason I hadn't been able to tell until then, but as we danced her feathery hair barely brushed my chin. An acrid chemical smell of magenta dye wafted up beneath the secondhand smoke and a faint, lingering hint of almond shampoo. "You've got nice hair," I said.

"Liar."

"No, it is. Really."

"I hate my hair. I'm thinking about going blonde. I think that might help."

"Help what?"

But she just shook her head.

We danced for a while in silence. I glanced up once and saw Henry leaning back against the bar, watching us with a slightly puzzled expression, and I quickly looked away. I concentrated instead on the couple dancing beside us. The man wore a denim jacket with the sleeves torn raggedly off and a pale, lavender bandanna tied buccaneer-style over his head. He had a dark red mustache with a little tuft beneath his lower lip, and the rusty shadow of a three-day beard. His girlfriend wore a leather halter-top and a mass of white-blonde hair so frizzy it looked more taunted than teased. She had wedged herself into her jeans, and the waist band cut into the meat of her hips, raising a soft, pale bulge over the curling lip of denim. Yet despite the snugness, her partner had managed to squeeze his left hand beneath the waistband all the way up to the knuckles while his right hung twisted in the string of her top. Her own hands were tucked into the front pockets of his jeans and were moving slowly as if searching for change that had slipped to the very bottom.

I watched without a word. The song gave way to something slow from Sonny Boy Williamson, and after a moment I felt my hands glide of their own accord down the smooth shell of Mona's jacket until they came to the stiff hem and slipped beneath. I waited, breathless and appalled, but she didn't seem to notice. Her body felt solid under the thin membrane of the tank top. The warmth of the room seemed to concentrate in the space between us. I thought of Alice and the broad feel of her back, my arms reaching wide to encompass her, but beneath the jacket Mona was sleek as a seal.

As if I might draw her attention from my hands I said, "What kind of a name is Mona?"

"It's a beautiful name. It's sophisticated and unusual." She didn't look up. She might have been talking to herself, whispering angrily into the pocket of warmth between us. "Harry?" she said. "You think that's any better?"

"I didn't say it was better."

"I mean, come on...."

"I didn't say it was better."

But she just shrugged.

"Is it some kind of family name?" I asked.

"Will you stop it?"

"I'm just asking."

"No. It's not. Okay?"

"So, how'd your mother come up with it?"

"She didn't. All right? I did."

"You named yourself?"

"What's wrong with that?"

"Nothing," I said. "It's fine. It's a beautiful name."

"You're damn right," she said. We swayed to the languid rhythm as she chewed on her thoughts. "Jane?" she demanded. "Is that any better? What kind of a name is Jane? Jane Ann Biederman. What kind of a parent gives her kid a name like that?"

"Who's Jane Ann Biederman?" I asked.

"Nobody."

The music died away and reluctantly, after a moment, we lowered our arms and stood there waiting. I said, "You want to sit down?"

"No."

I glanced back guiltily, half-expecting Henry to be frowning intently, with all his reluctant suspicious confirmed, but he was all vague good cheer while, beside him, Alice peered blearily around as if she'd been transported to this place miraculously without her knowledge or consent. Neither of them waved. After a moment B.B. King came on, singing something slow and dirty. I hesitated. "People are watching."

"So? It's just a dance."

I told myself she was right. It didn't mean anything. Complete strangers did this all the time. But I could feel the warmth between us seeping through my chest like some spreading poison. I'd read once if you were bitten by a rattlesnake you were supposed to stay very still, or if you had to move, do it slowly so the poison took as long as possible to reach your heart. I concentrated on moving very slowly. "So your real name is Jane Ann Biederman?"

"It's not my real name. My real name is Mona Brown."

"Jane?"

"Don't call me that. I don't answer to that."

"Jane Ann?"

"You tell anybody, and I'll kill you."

"You've got pretty hair, Jane."

"Will you shut up?"

My hand slipped more or less of its own accord down to the small of her back, where the fabric of the tank top ended well before the pants began. The smooth ridge of her spine curved down, damp with perspiration, and I slowly traced the vertebrae as if memorizing a passage in braille.

"What's the difference," I asked, "between a Mona and a Jane?"

"A Mona makes her own mind up. Nobody tells a Mona what to do."

"Do people tell Janes what to do?"

"People don't pay attention to Janes; they don't bother with them. They forget all about them. You can say goodbye to a Jane without a second thought."

"But not a Mona?"

"No way. Janes, they let you walk all over them, but a

Mona...?" She shook her head. "Nobody walks over a Mona. You know what I mean?" She was peering up at me.

I said I thought maybe I did.

She nodded. "You realize you've got your hand on my ass."

My throat was dry. I had trouble swallowing. "Do I? Maybe I should move it."

Mona gave me an owlish stare. "You do what you want. It doesn't make any difference to me."

At the end of the night we stood, the four of us, out in the parking lot as if waiting for a sign of what was to come. Mona was weaving slightly, but it might have been the music still drifting faintly through her head. Henry was standing perfectly still, but he had a tendency to settle. Alice stood with a thoughtful expression on her face, and I thought for a moment she was going to be sick, but then she turned to me. In the glare of the streetlights she was smiling almost coyly. She leaned in close, and I thought she was going to kiss me. "I'm going home now," she whispered and left the words hanging there.

I hesitated, then glanced over to where Henry and Mona had come to rest at the head of Mona's red Mustang. She was reaching into a pocket for the keys but seemed to be having trouble finding them. Henry was smiling and nodding, as if he he'd seen this movie before, but couldn't quite remember how it ended. I turned back to Alice. "I've got to take my father home."

"Are you sure?"

"Are you going to be all right driving?"

"You're kidding. This is nothing. You should see me when I'm drunk."

I didn't know whether to kiss her or not. I couldn't tell if she expected it. So in the end I leaned forward just as she turned toward her car and bumped a little kiss onto her cheek. She settled into the driver's seat and shut the door, though after a moment's thought she rolled the window down. "Do you remember where I live?"

I thought she was asking directions at first and I started to explain, but she gave me a meaningful look.

"Yes," I said.

And with a nod she started up the car and drove off.

I trudged back to the Mustang. Against all odds, Henry had developed something of a second wind. He had slipped his arm through Mona's and they were now gazing down together at the bright red hood. "It's a great car," he said. And then, by way of explanation, "It's so shiny."

She patted his arm companionably. "And that's just the outside." They both dissolved into giggles.

I looked from one to the other. "I think maybe I should drive."

But Mona shook her head. "That's another thing about Monas. They always drive."

"You sure?"

"Monas are always sure."

She managed to get her keys out this time and walked around to the driver's side, but as she approached the door she slowed to a halt. Henry peered over in friendly concern. "Is it broken?"

"How about some coffee?" I asked.

"Forget it," she said. "No coffee. You think I need coffee?"

Henry shook his head supportively. "I don't think so. I find it keeps me up."

I eased in beside Mona, but she saw me coming and turned, holding the keys away. "Don't...." But once she started turning she couldn't stop, and she continued all the way around in a graceful pirouette and sank slowly to the ground.

Henry gazed down at her for a moment in mild perplexity, then companionably followed suit. "Down's a daisy," he said and, settling onto the gravel, leaned comfortably back against the front fender.

Mona frowned. "It's not down's a daisy."

"It can be."

"Henry?"

"I'll have to get back to you," he murmured, closing his eyes, leaving Mona with the startled expression of someone who's just discovered she's been talking on a dead phone.

I eased down onto the gravel beside her. "Are you okay?"

"Henry's asleep."

"I think you're right."

"It's me, isn't it? I'm boring, aren't I?"

"You're not boring."

But she just shook her head. She looked so forlorn I said, "You want to try pushing the bar into the river?"

She looked up with vague interest. "Could we do that?"

"That's what I hear."

She turned, squinting doubtfully at the narrow, crooked building. "It doesn't look too heavy to you?"

"Are you kidding? A little shack like that?"

"Monas are very strong," she whispered.

"I know."

"I'm just a little tired."

"Are you hungry? We could get some pancakes at the Country Kitchen."

She shook her head. "I don't want to."

"How about an omelet? You know, breakfast is the most important meal of the day."

"People just fall asleep when I'm talking to them."

"I don't."

"Or worse," she said bleakly. "Do you know what that asshole Carlisle said to me?"

"Who?"

"He told me I was like a man, only with tits. Not even big tits." She was staring glumly down at the shallow curve of the tank top, glowing between sprawled halves of her jacket. "He said it was like fucking a man. I mean... Shit. How was I supposed to feel about that?"

I glanced over at Henry, but he was fast asleep. "What did he mean?"

"How should I know?"

"Maybe it was a compliment."

She scowled. "Are you even listening?"

"I'm just trying to think. I mean, it's not like you look like a man," I said.

"Who the hell knows what he meant."

"You know, he's probably just threatened by you."

She shook her head listlessly. "I don't think so."

"He could be."

"No."

"It's possible."

"You don't know Carlisle." And she sighed so wistfully that I raised my arm and very cautiously laid it along her shoulders against the side of the car. I felt her stiffen for a moment, but in the end she leaned back against it.

"You know what I think?" I said. "I think you were just too good for him."

"Really?"

"Definitely. I mean, Henry would never say anything like that, would he?"

She chuckled. "No. Not good old Henry."

"There you are, then. The thing is, this Carlisle probably thought he was getting a Jane, and didn't know what to do with a Mona."

"You think?"

"Absolutely."

"Well then," she said. "It's his loss. I'm tired of losers anyway."

"Don't let Henry hear you say that."

"Henry?" She giggled. Then, turning, she called, "You're not a loser, are you, Henry?"

He shifted in his sleep but didn't reply.

She smiled. "Henry's the nicest guy I've met in a long time."

"That's right. No question. He's a very nice guy. That's not exactly what I meant." But I was having trouble deciding what exactly I did mean. All I thought was, if he's so nice, why was he so easy to leave? What were we doing by ourselves in that house for six years?

"We should go," I said. "We'll drive you home."

"I drive. Monas always drive." But she seemed to be talking about something distant and hypothetical. When I reached out for the keys she released them slowly as if they were the string of a balloon. "Whoops," she said softly.

I helped her up and into the passenger seat. She slouched low, leaning her head back. "You can come if you like," she said.

I turned. "Henry?"

"Are we leaving?"

I helped him into the back seat, then climbed in and started the engine.

"We need the top down," announced Mona, and she reached out to the console. With a whine the roof folded back from the midnight sky. "Now we're talking. Let's glide, Clyde."

I drove slowly, enjoying the breeze and the sight of her leaning back staring up at the sky. It felt like an undeserved moment, mine only by mistake. I knew that, in the morning, when everybody sobered up, there'd be no trace of it left.

"Great stars tonight," said Mona. "You know any constellations?"

"Just Orion," I said.

"That's my favorite, too. Henry?" she called back over her shoulder. "What's your favorite?"

After a moment his voice rose, "I like Orion, too."

I parked in front of her apartment and turned off the engine. After a moment in which nobody moved, I said, "Henry?" There was no answer. A low snuffling snore rose from the back. "He's a little tired," I said. And then, "Maybe I'd better walk you up."

Mona led the way upstairs, heavy on her feet, climbing the railing hand over hand. "I don't remember it being so far." At her apartment she unlocked the door, then turning, leaned unsteadily in the doorway. "You can't come in."

"Okay."

She peered up at me. "Don't you want to?"

"I'd better not."

"Well, you can't." Then she hesitated. "I'm glad you came along tonight."

I wondered how drunk she was, how bad the lights were. "I'm Harry," I said. "Henry's in the car."

She shook her head fondly. "Good old Henry." And she leaned her cheek forlornly against the edge of the door. "Am I boring?"

"No."

"Then why don't you want to kiss me?"

I just stood there for a moment. I should have told her again that I wasn't Henry, I should have made sure that she knew, but I hesitated, suddenly dry-mouthed and uncertain. Then I leaned ever so slightly forward, more a drift than a movement.

"Too late," she said and, stepping back unsteadily, closed the door behind her.

17

With my father curled daintily in the back seat of the Mustang I drove home through the thin chill of one a.m. letting the cool air leach the hot amalgam of doubt, embarrassment, and desire from my blood. I thought of Mona, closing the door almost regretfully, and I had my first fleeting glimpse of that most human of truths: the humiliations we remember most as we grow older are not the foolish things we do, but the foolish things we fail to do.

I parked in the alley beside our truck. Henry stirred. "Mmm?"

"We're home."

He sat up slowly, balancing with care. "You know, son. I think I might be a little drunk."

"Don't worry," I said. "I'm a trained professional."

I helped him up the stairs and eased him down onto the edge of his bed. He hunched there tentatively, gazing around as if maybe he'd meant to make other plans and just couldn't remember what they were.

"Are you going to be sick?"

He gave a little murmuring laugh. "Isn't it funny how things work out?"

"How bad is it? Do you want some help?"

But he just shook his head. "God damn it, Harry. We should have done this years ago. I don't know what we were thinking." And he started humming to himself. Something jaunty and fun from earlier in the night.

I knelt and started to unlace his shoes.

"I can do that," he said.

"I've got 'em." I pulled off one and then the other. "You feeling dizzy? Anything spinning?" But he just shook his head. "Are you planning to get undressed?"

"Maybe later." He dragged the bed covers down, tugging them out from beneath him and climbing in—work shirt, khakis and all. Then with a low and peaceful sigh he closed his eyes, "Thanks, son. I'll take it from here."

"I'm going to put some aspirin on the beside table."

He didn't reply.

"Dad? If you wake up in the night you want to drink lots of water."

He smiled sleepily. "What time is it?"

I glanced at the bedside clock over on what was once my mother's side. "One fifteen."

"Where's Mona?"

"She's okay. She's home. We took her home."

"Out on the town," he murmured happily and drifted off to sleep.

This couldn't have been the way he'd expected the evening to end, all alone in that broad and empty bed, but still he was smiling. Thinking about Mona and being out on the town. There was something so effortless about it. He reminded me of one of those cartoon characters who sleepwalks through a construction site—up on the girders, over the machinery, high above the rubble—without a false step, without a hitch, while everyone trying to save him crashes to the ground.

I stepped out quietly and closed the door, feeling suddenly alone in the darkness, as if every sweet dream my father had, drew him further away. I felt the silence reaching out its long thin fingers, binding me to that empty old house.

Sleep was out of the question. Narrow as it was, my own bed was emptier than I could bear. I thought of Alice. You remember where I live? Red-faced and cheerful, wrapped in a friendly cloud of warmth and beer. I could go over there, just knock on her door. Just to see if she got home safely. What was the harm? Henry had his sweet dreams. What about me?

I wandered downstairs and out into the yard to stand, lonely in the darkness. And there was the red Mustang still sitting in the driveway like a bad idea I'd never quite gotten out of my mind.

I knocked on her office door and waited, thinking about that one, lonely shot of tequila and wishing I'd had a whole lot more. At the other end of the hallway the light had burned out. The whole building was silent and shadowy. She must be asleep; how could she not be? It was two o'clock in the morning, and every sensible corner of my brain was telling me to turn around and go. But good sense was a tramp and a vagabond, and no fit companion on a night like tonight, and having knocked once there seemed no reason at all not to knock again. A moment later came the sound of footsteps.

"Go away," she yelled. "I'm not going to tell you again."

After a moment I said, "You didn't tell me the first time."

The door opened. Mona peered out warily as if she'd never seen me before. "What do you want?"

And I lost my nerve. I held up her car keys, dangling lamely from one finger, and managed what I hoped was a smile. "I just came by to return these."

She had taken off the leather jacket, and had changed out of the yellow tank top into a loose, white t-shirt. But as if feeling insufficiently accessorized, she wore a large, white towel like a turban around her head. Her face was doughy and pale without her glasses, and even the silver ring in her nostril looked tired. She squinted up at me, still wreathed in tequila fumes, and her voice softened with dawning familiarity. "What are you doing with my keys?"

"Returning them."

"How did you get them?"

"I drove Henry--."

"Shit!" In the distance behind her a timer start buzzing, and she turned without another word and fled like a vampire at dawn, leaving the door ajar.

After a moment's silence I stepped inside, and stood there in the tidy severity of the living room, without a clue. "Mona? Hello? I should probably just be going now." I crossed to the bedroom door and peered in. It was a shambles. The jumble of clothing on the floor might have exploded out of a trunk, and her leather jacket lay stiffly over a chair as if it had passed out some time ago. "Is everything okay?"

"God damn it!" Her voice erupted out through the open bathroom door, and when I got there she was standing at the sink with her glasses in place and the towel in her hands, staring in furious despair at the mirror. "Would you look at that! Would you look what it's done?" Her hair hung wet and limp almost to her shoulders, and in the fluorescent light it seemed to have wilted from magenta to a mottled brown like some unwise attempt at camouflage.

And suddenly aware of how far in I had wandered, I glanced around. The bathroom was large and old-fashioned with an old grainy tub crouching in the corner with a rounded edge and claw feet. By the sink next to a paper pharmacy bag stood an open box of Clairol Nice'n'Easy with the face of a very pretty blonde woman on the front. Next to it was a juice glass with a picture of Fred Flintstone on the side, standing up to his armpits in red wine.

"Will you look at this?" Mona wailed. "Look at it! You call this blonde? It looks awful."

"Maybe you didn't leave it in long enough."

"No kidding, Einstein. What are you? A licensed cosmetician all of a sudden?" She turned and thrust the box at me. "Twenty-five minutes. Right?"

Hurriedly I scanned the little chart of directions. "Do you have salon-damaged hair?"

"I sure as hell do now."

"Twenty-five minutes," I agreed.

She pinched a single lock of the now-brownish hair and sighed. Then picking up Fred Flintstone, she drained him to the dregs. "You want some wine?"

"Sure."

"It's in the kitchen. Bring the bottle why don't you."

The kitchen was like the bedroom, only with hard, breakable objects instead of clothes. There were dishes in the sink and a forest of glassware smeared with lipstick, fingerprints, and the lingering stains of more festive times. I found a second juice glass in the cupboard, this one with a picture of Wilma and Pebbles, and half a bottle of Cabernet in the fridge. When I got back to the bathroom Mona hadn't moved. She was staring into the mirror, still pinching at a strand of mottled hair as if trying to wake it from a deep sleep.

"You know, you don't have to refrigerate red wine," I said.

She shook her head wearily. "Do I look like a cocker spaniel?"

I hesitated a moment, taken aback. Then, uncorking the bottle, I topped up Fred to the eyeballs, and, as a safety precaution, filled my own. "That depends. How do you feel about cocker spaniels?"

"Fucking Carlisle. He said that. He told me I looked like a cocker spaniel."

"Did he tell you to put red wine in the fridge?" She turned, scowling impatiently, as if one of us wasn't following the conversation. Hurriedly I said, "He's a jerk. Obviously. Who cares what he says?"

But Mona looked unconvinced. "You think the perm was a mistake?"

"No. Definitely not." The perm was so long ago now it seemed like the height of common sense compared to all that had come after. I tried to remember it as it had been, fluffy and black. Now it looked like nothing so much as an old sweater left too long to soak.

"It's a mess," she said bleakly.

"It's supposed to look that way. It's windblown."

"You think?"

"Definitely."

She sighed and turned back to the mirror. The hair hung like rumpled brown curtains on either side of her glasses. She took another pull on the wine. "I'm thinking blonde."

"Really?"

"I think that's the answer."

"How blonde?" I said.

"Really blonde."

I glanced at the Clairol box, with the very blonde woman on the side looking so smug and self-satisfied. "Like that?"

Mona snorted. "That? That's this." She yanked spitefully on her hair. "How blonde is this?"

She snatched up the paper bag and dumped out a white cardboard box with serious red lettering like those warning signs outside a toxic dump. Advanced Color Stripper. And in plain black letters, Salon Use Only. From beneath the counter she brought out a brown plastic bottle of hydrogen peroxide and a white shower cap. And only then, when the full enormity of her evil experiment was upon her, did she hesitate. "Is this a mistake?"

It's almost impossible to answer correctly in these circumstances. I knew that even then. But I saw that wild glint of hope in her eye, and I had come all this way. "How bad can it be?"

"Carlisle said I'd look like Harpo Marx."

I looked at her. Between the flagging perm and the pale face, Harpo seemed a real possibility, but the pinched and hopeful look in her eyes caught me and carried me along. "Forget Carlisle. He probably can't even spell Harpo Marx. What about Henry? What would he say?"

"Oh, you know Henry. He'd probably just tell me I'd look nice either way." She seemed unconvinced by even so ringing an endorsement. She drained her wine, then looked up into the mirror again to see if that had made any difference. "What do you think?"

I should have kept quiet, almost certainly. But what I said

was: "If I have but one life, let me live it as a blonde."

With a resolute nod she reached for the box. "I need a bowl or something."

I returned to the kitchen. Mona had, as far as I could tell, no mixing bowls, no soup bowls, and only three cereal bowls, all of which were in the sink and had been for a while. But in the back of one cupboard I found a yellow plastic dog dish, and in the fridge there was another nearly full bottle of chilled merlot. By the time I got back she had the white plastic bag of color stripper out and was tearing it open with her teeth.

"Careful."

"I've got it." She emptied it into the bowl: a little anthill of what looked like kosher salt.

"Wait," I said, and she glanced up nervously. I held out the cabernet. "To kill the pain."

She peered into the mirror again, at the hair like wet and matted felt. As I filled her glass she opened the peroxide and poured it into the bowl. A rush of caustic fumes filled the air, burning my sinuses, making my eyes water. "You're going to put that on your head?"

"You might want to take that off," she said. I was wearing the brown tuxedo jacket with black lapels and pockets. I took it off and draped it over the back of the toilet. I wore a black t-shirt underneath, and on my bare forearm the white bandage looked huge and embarrassing. So bright and histrionic. But Mona didn't notice. She was peering down into the bowl. "We could probably use a spoon," she said, but without waiting she picked up a pink toothbrush from beside the sink and stirred the mixture to the consistency of white house paint.

The fumes coiled up, acrid and harsh, but Mona seemed undissuaded. She reached for the faucet and filled the sink with warm water. On the floor beside the tub was a small plastic bucket with a big red starfish on it, looking like a souvenir from someplace closer to the ocean. As she bent and picked it up, the fragile ridge of her spine showed tight beneath the thin fabric of the t-shirt, unmarred, as I noticed almost without meaning to, by the slightest hint of a bra strap.

I was aware suddenly that we were alone in a silent apartment. There was no candlelight, and no music, but there was wine and that nervous, freighted feeling of tension and high stakes that was my lingering recollection of high school. And I realized that, while this wasn't exactly a date, it wasn't entirely different from one, either. "This is fun," I said.

"What?"

"Never mind. Don't forget the glasses."

She pulled them off and shoved them blindly in my direction. Then, hunching over the sink, she dipped the plastic bucket and drained it cautiously over her head. The water flowed through the hair, darkening and smoothing it, opening a pale line of scalp down the back, then cascaded over her shoulders, soaking the t-shirt and splashing onto the floor.

"Wait!" I said. "Hold on."

She raised her head like a swimmer, eyes clenched tight, frowning against the water. In the mirror she looked six years old, except where the t-shirt clung wetly to the bones of her shoulders and the shallow, pink-tipped breasts. Hurriedly I grabbed a towel from the rack and draped it under her chin, then back over her shoulders like a bib, but the image of her nipples crinkling through the wet fabric glowed in the hidden darkness of my brain. "Do you have a safety pin?"

"Maybe in the cupboard."

"Come on."

In a stiff and synchronized lockstep we backed up three steps to the cupboard, and I found a pin and fastened the towel. Then she bent over the sink again and reached for the bucket.

I picked up the box. "It says your hair's supposed to be dry."

"It's okay. It goes on smoother this way."

"Are you sure you know what you're doing?"

But she was already reaching for the bowl. The mixture had thickened into cream of wheat, but the fumes still scalded the air. She dipped her fingers into the paste and started smearing it over the top of her head.

"Shouldn't you use rubber gloves?"

"If you see a pair let me know."

The paste went on stiffly, resisting the wet hair, refusing to spread smoothly. Mona squinted into the mirror, daubing awkwardly with cupped fingers, but unable both to tilt her head down and see at the same time. "Shit. I can't--. Look at that."

"Here. Stop. Wait! Let me." She relinquished the bowl and I cautiously scooped out a pasty handful. "Lean your head down. Now, don't move." I spread it over the little swirl of a cowlick at the crown of her head, then along the pale line of her part. "How much do I use?"

"All of it. Just all over."

"Are you sure?"

"What? We're going to save it for tomorrow?"

I smeared it on, then worked it into a gritty lather. The fumes burned my throat, and I thought I could feel it stripping the color from my fingers. "Tip back." I spread the paste over her scalp, massaging it in while trying to expose as little skin as possible, though by this time, of course, it was all over my hands. A trickle of water ran under the gauze on my forearm. The stitches were throbbing.

"You're supposed to rub it in," she said.

"What do you think I'm doing?

"Spread it around."

"This can't be good for your hair."

"Of course it is. What do you think it's for?"

The cream of wheat was thinning to the consistency of glue, turning the hair ropy and stiff. And despite the harsh chemical smell I was enjoying myself. I savored the smooth feel of her scalp under my fingers and the curve of her skull, delicate and sweet, narrowing to the softer give of muscle and tendons in her neck.

"Make sure you get it all the way out to the ends," she said.

"It is."

"And it's got to be even. Make sure it's not blotchy."

"Are you kidding? This is a work of art." I drew the lather out to the ends of her hair. "How do you suppose you'd look in pig tails?"

Her eyes were grimly shut. "Cut it out," she warned. "Don't do anything."

I gathered two handfuls, malleable as frosting, and twirled them into drooping towers.

"Will you stop it?" She squinted up into the mirror. "That looks stupid."

"Did you have pigtails as a girl?"

"Every kid had pigtails. Mothers think they're cute."

"Were they?"

"No."

"I bet they were. I bet you were a cute baby."

"God, yes. Can't you tell? Now cut it out. You'd better wash your hands."

And it was true, I could feel the chemicals creeping like ants' feet over my skin. I dipped my hands in the sinkful of warm water, and felt the paste slough off as if it were taking my fingerprints with it. I rubbed gently, wondering what it was doing to Mona's scalp. "How long are you supposed to keep that in?"

"I don't know. Forty-five minutes, I think."

"You think?" Shaking off my hands I picked up the little folded road map of instructions. They were finely printed and dense with warnings. "Did you read these?"

"What do they say?"

"It says you're supposed to do it in stages. Three steps. Twenty minutes each."

"So I'll leave it in for an hour."

"It says separate stages."

"The blonder the better." Mona was reaching, feeling along the counter for the shower cap. "Here. Give me a hand."

I stretched it open and helped ease it over the matted hair.

The elastic bit into her forehead. A thin smear of paste edged below the band, turning faintly blue as it dried. I unpinned the towel. With her hair gathered up, her face looked even more pinched and white. Her throat, unprotected, curved delicately into the damp and sagging neck of her t-shirt. She leaned forward, reaching up to ease the back of the shower cap, and the shirt gapped open over a sudden glimpse of one naked breast with its tight, rosy smudge of a nipple. She squinted up at me. "Do I look too stupid?"

I swallowed and hurriedly reached for my wine glass. "Uh-uh," I said.

18.

In high school I was what my mother, with great kindness, called a late bloomer. And late bloomers, she said, were the best sort of people. The whole idea of late blooming had grown in me, the implication that there was some beautiful blossom of an accomplishment stored away and biding its time until just the right moment. But as years passed I'd begun to worry that the right moment had long since come and gone, and I simply wasn't equipped to recognize it.

I thought about that as we drank the wine and waited. In the end Mona decided to give it an extra fifteen minutes, just to be sure, and we sat together on the edge of the tub watching the timer tick. I kept thinking I should put my arm around her. I should kiss her. Sometimes you just have to take what you want. But that's the downside of waiting to bloom. There are so many wrong moments for every occasional right one.

"What color was it before?" I asked, nodding at the shower cap.

"You saw it before."

"I mean before that."

Mona frowned thoughtfully. "Purple, I think. It didn't really go with anything. I just felt like it."

"And before that?"

"A kind of brownish-orange. I had a coat I really liked so I dyed my hair to match."

"And before that?"

"I keep thinking I'll find the perfect color."

"Perfect for what?"

She shrugged.

"What color was it originally?"

"No color at all," she said. "That was the problem."

"It must have been something. What color is no color?"

Mona considered for a moment, then she stood and walked into the bedroom and came back a moment later with a photograph in an old silver frame. I tilted it up to the light. "Who's this?"

"Who do you think?"

It was a young girl, five or six, with fine cinnamon hair in short, uneven bangs. She was smiling. A little nose, little teeth, eyes squinting cheerfully. "Is that you?"

"No. That's Young Jane."

"She's cute."

"Yeah, right. How do you like that hair? Is that awful, or what?"

"I like it."

"Nobody likes red hair."

"I do."

"It got sort of light and boring as I got older. It just hung there." She shook her head. "Completely forgettable."

"I doubt it. Who took the picture? Your mom?"

She hesitated. "My dad."

"Ah," I said.

"What do you mean, 'Ah'?"

"It's a good picture."

"What do you mean, 'Ah'?" she said more testily.

"So, what about your dad?"

She was leaning against the counter, shoulders hunched and her face closed into a frown. "What about him?"

"I heard a rumor he died."

"No shit," she said. "Died how?"

"That's the thing about rumors."

"Did you hear I killed him?"

"I didn't know you then."

"You don't know me now," she said. She held out her empty glass. "You mind?"

I laid the picture down on the floor and picked up the bottle. My own glass was nearly empty. I filled them both. Young Jane was smiling up at us with an unthinking recklessness of good cheer that reminded me of Henry. Over the years, all the disappointments had nearly squelched it, and I used to think I'd never see him happy again. But now here he was, on top of the world. And here I was, with the woman who had made him so happy.

"Sometimes I like to think I killed him," Mona said. "He left home when I was twelve. And thirteen. And fourteen. He left home a lot. But he always came back."

"Where'd he go?"

"Away. I never knew. No, that's not true. Sometimes he brought me back stuff. A little Mount Rushmore pencil sharpener. That was one thing."

"That's cool. Have you still got it?"

She shook her head. "I hammered a nail through George Washington's forehead after he left the next time."

We considered that for a moment together, gazing down at the photograph of Young Jane. I tried to imagine that sweet-faced girl splintering the head of our first president, but it was more than I could do.

"Was he some sort of traveling salesman?"

"Just the traveling part. I'm not sure what he did for the rest of it. He always claimed not to remember, and maybe he didn't. Remembering wasn't one of those things he was good at."

"What was he good at?"

"Nothing."

"Everybody's good at something."

Mona looked up at me, as if I'd actually said something interesting. "You think so?"

"I'd like to think so."

She seem unconvinced. "My mother was good at two things. She was good at throwing him out, and she was good at taking him back again. That was pretty much it."

"How about you?"

"I just watched for a long time. Then I decided it wasn't any of my business. One day... I was seventeen, I think. I think it might have been my birthday. He knocked on the door. He was drunk. It had been maybe five months. He could have been drunk for all of it, the way he looked. He gave me a big smile. He was always so happy to see me. My mom wasn't home. It was just me."

"A small, private party."

"Yeah. That's right. So I shut the door in his face. I didn't say anything. I opened the door, he smiled, and I shut the door. After a while he drove away. I think he ran into a tree or a truck or something."

"You think?"

"I think I read that. Or maybe someone ran into him. Or he just forgot where we lived, or how to get home. He was always forgetting how to get home."

I considered that for a while. "Have you got any pictures of him?"

"Nope." She nodded down at the frame. "Just that."

I gazed down at it for another moment, considering how little good a photograph does. If it's a picture of better times, then where's the comfort in that? If it's a picture of something worse, you might as well forget it.

"When my mother left," I said, "Henry threw away all her pictures. He didn't get wild or anything. You know Henry. He's not the wild kind. He just put them all in a box and stuck them in a closet. And later, when I went to look for them, they were gone. A whole boxful, out with the trash. I thought it was pretty impressive, getting rid of it all like that. A clean sweep."

Mona nodded. "Sometimes I think I should do that. Get rid of this."

"Definitely not. How could you get rid of a cutie like that?"

She shrugged sadly. "It's nobody I know."

When the timer went off Mona stood before the mirror and peeled the shower cap off her head like a surgeon removing the bandages. The bleach had dried into a thick, floury paste so that every curl and tendril might have been formed out of paper mache. I couldn't see any difference in color. I'd expected the brown dye to bleed out into the paste, but it was the same bluish white, and I felt that first, low rumble of dread.

"What do we do?" I said. "Chip it off?"

Mona filled the bucket, and leaning forward over the sink, poured it slowly down the back of her head. The water sluiced wildly off the hardened paste and ran over her neck, drenching the towel and soaking a wide path down her spine. "Shit!"

"Careful."

But the water was running into her eyes, and she was groping blindly. "Shit! That stings."

"Keep your eyes closed!" I grasped her shoulders and pulled her gently upright. "Come on. We'll use the tub."

Mona sank to her knees, feeling blindly for the curved edge, then leaned forward like a seasick passenger at the railing. I turned on the water. "Make it warm, okay?" She was shivering.

"You want a dry towel?"

"Just get this stuff off."

She bent down but the faucet was too short and she couldn't get more than her forehead beneath the flow. She bent her neck, as if trying to stand on her head against the side of the tub, and held her hands up to fold the running water around her hair. "God damn it--!"

"Here. Wait." I eased her back from the faucet and filled the little bucket. "Okay. Watch your eyes."

As I poured, the paste and then the hair beneath it began to soften and flow, but the water, running off and swirling down the drain, looked like some kind of optical illusion. There was no hint of brown. No trace of it. It looked bluish-white like the run-off from some arctic icecap, but as it flowed away it left the hair with a pale metallic finish and a sharp, damp, chemical smell.

"I think what we've got here is some serious blonde," I said.

"Really? Kind of Marilyn Monroe?"

I hesitated. "Maybe."

"Let me see."

"Not yet. Watch the eyes."

With one last rinse I turned off the water and set the empty bucket down. Mona hunched stiffly, the now-blonde hair hanging in two ragged sheets. I draped the towel over her head and shoulders. "Okay. Straighten up."

She climbed blindly to her feet, and I rose with her, tucking the towel around her throat. The t-shirt was hopelessly soaked. Her breasts glowed through the fabric, pale and pinkly tipped. I glanced up guiltily, but Mona, indifferent to the chill, was drying vigorously. After a moment she pulled off the towel, and stood, gazing into the mirror. "Holy shit."

I couldn't tell whether she was pleased or not.

Her hair, no longer frizzy, stuck out wildly in all directions like an explosion of feathers. Yellow feathers. Bright yellow feathers.

"Holy shit," she repeated more softly and held out her hand. "Give me my glasses, would you?"

She slipped them on. The heavy black frames stood out like a roadblock across the bridge of her nose. They were the most solid thing about her. The edge of her scalp was reddened, and the elastic of the cap had left a crooked indentation across her forehead, but her cheeks were pale, her eyes were pale, and her hair was the color of a newly hatched chick. "Oh," she said.

And still I couldn't tell. But then her shoulders sagged, and her breath leaked out in a long, heart-rending sigh. "Oh, no."

"It's okay," I said. "It's not so bad. Really. It looks nice." I reached up to smooth the hair back from her face, but it wouldn't smooth. It felt stiff and rubbery.

She moaned. "I look like a dandelion! I look like fucking Tweety Bird!"

"No, you don't."

She reached up and pinched a thin wild strand and, after an instant's hesitation, gently pulled. I immediately wished she hadn't. It stretched. Like a rubber band. A bright yellow rubber band. She stared in horror, and when she let it go, it just stayed there, bending like a swan's neck in the air. "Holy shit," she whispered.

There was, I noticed then, a pounding on the door. I didn't know how long it had been going on. I thought at first it might have been my pulse, but then the noise sharpened, sounding fierce and loud even two rooms away. A voice called, "Mona! I know you're in there!"

I glanced at my watch. It was three-fifteen. "Are you expecting company?"

But Mona, gazing bleakly into the mirror, didn't even turn. "Tell him to go away," she said bleakly.

The pounding came again. "Open the goddam door!"

She settled with a sigh onto the edge of the tub. Her shoulders drooped. The glasses gave her a calm and studious expression, even as the hair was screaming wildly. "If you could just go and beat the shit out of him," she whispered, "and come right back, I'd really appreciate it."

I approached the door cautiously, but as I drew nearer the pounding stopped, and for a moment I stood there, wondering if that was that. But then the voice, startling even through the heavy oak, yelled, "Come on, Mona! I know you're in there. Open the goddam door!"

I turned the deadbolt and stepped back. There was silence. Then after a moment the knob turned almost hesitantly and the door eased open. The voice was lower now, gruff and almost gentle. "For god's sake, baby. You don't need to lock me out like some--" Then he saw me. "Who the hell are you!?"

He was shorter than I'd expected and much, much wider. He had thick brown hair and a full beard, like one of those drawings that can be turned upside down and looks like a smiling face one way and a frown the other. He was frowning now. In his left hand he carried most of a six-pack of Rolling Rock, hanging like a pocketbook from those little plastic loops, while his right hand made a fist the size of a grapefruit.

"She really doesn't want to see you now," I said.

But he just glared at me, and his voice rose on a mist of anger and beer. "Mona!"

She stepped into the room, gripping the rolled towel like a club in one hand. She had put on her leather jacket for moral support. "What do I have to do, Carlisle? Do I have to call the police?"

Carlisle turned ponderously and stared. "Jesus! What the hell did you do?"

I knew what he meant. Even in that short time away I'd forgotten how bright it was. It looked otherworldly. Carlisle was shaking his head. "Oh, man," he muttered. "Oh, man." And he was glancing back and forth between Mona and his six pack of beer as if one of them might offer an explanation.

I took a step closer and lowered my voice. "For God's sake, don't be a jerk. Say something nice." And I turned back toward Mona. "You look nice. He thinks it looks nice."

"I told you," said Carlisle. "Didn't I tell you? You look like fucking Harpo Marx."

"No, you don't," I said hurriedly. "Not at all. Nothing like him."

"Harpo fucking Marx," he repeated, shaking his head. "What're you thinking?"

"I'm thinking," said Mona, "that you are the biggest asshole I have ever met. And I'm thinking if you ever set foot in my house again I'm going to call the police."

"Oh, baby..."

But she turned away. "Harry? Please?" And there was something in her tone, something fragile and pleading beneath the anger, that made me step forward even as I wondered just what I was planning to do. Throw him out, I suppose. Punch his lights out. Something from the standard repertoire of high school heroics. But, I was saved the trouble. Dropping the six-pack, Carlisle grabbed two fistfuls of my t-shirt and thumped me hard against the door.

"Is this the guy?" he demanded.

I felt a little cricket of pain in my arm and, glancing down, saw a tiny red feather seeping through the bandage. "Hey."

"I'm calling the police," said Mona. "I'm picking up the phone."

He thumped me again. "Is your name Henry?"

"Call me Harry, please."

"Oh, man," he said. "Oh, man. This is the guy? You dumped me for this?"

"That's right," said Mona. "This is the guy. You got a problem with that?"

Carlisle turned with an expression of hurt and outrage, and even with the neck of my shirt stretched taut against my throat, I felt a little pang of sympathy. I said, "Sorry you had to hear this way."

"Man. I ought to break your face..."

"Got the police on the line!" Mona yelled. "I'm dialing." She had the phone in her hand.

"Jesus." He let go of my shirt, and I settled to the ground. He made a show of wiping his hands. Then he bent and snatched up his beer. "I see you again," he said, "I'm gonna spread your nose all over your face." He glanced back at Mona. "Harpo fucking Marx," he muttered and stalked out the door.

It took me a moment to catch my breath. My arm was throbbing and the little red stain was spreading into a bloody shamrock. I said, "He was shorter than I expected." Mona, I noticed, was still holding the phone, but more as if she were about to pound nails with it. Her face was tight. She seemed to be chewing on a small and bitter thought. "Forget it," I said. "He's a jerk. What does he know? It looks great."

But she just shook her head. "You're bleeding."

"It's okay. It's fine."

"I've got some antiseptic."

She turned and trudged back to the bathroom, but when I got there she was staring into the mirror again, mesmerized by the sight. Abruptly she grabbed a handful of hair so that it splintered out like straw between the clenched knuckles. She pulled on it fiercely, yanking at it for a long furious moment, then let it go.

"Jesus," she whispered. "Look at me. I look awful. I look just awful." Her cheeks were blotching pink against the white, and tears were pooling in her eyes.

"No," I said, hurrying forward. "No, you don't."

"He's right."

"He's a jerk."

"Harpo Marx."

"No." I reached up and fluffed the hair. It felt dry and raspy. "It's like any haircut. It just takes a little getting used to. Maybe if you brushed it?"

It was more hope than suggestion, but in times of trial you grapple onto any possibility. She glanced up. "You think?"

"Absolutely."

But when she picked up the brush and tried to drag it through the garish tangle, it wouldn't go. She pulled. It wouldn't budge. She set her teeth, applied more pressure, and the brush came free. But when she held it up, there was a handful of frayed yellow hair embedded in the bristles.

"Oh my god." Her voice was thin and desperate, rising in a little crescendo. "Oh Jesus, Mary, and Joseph!"

"It's okay."

"Look at it!"

"It's fine."

"It's not!"

"Here! Give it to me!" I pried the brush out of her hand and pulled the clumped hair free, dropping it onto the floor. Then, cautiously as I could, I tried to ease the bristles through the tangle, shallowly at first, then a little deeper. The hair was stiff and resistant. I could feel individual strands coming free with separate little pings.

"It's breaking," she whispered.

"Just a little."

"Oh, no."

"It's just the ends. They're just a little snagged." But as I looked I saw that thick strands of hair had actually melted together like some kind of plastic. "Okay. We might have to cut a little off. "

"How much?"

"Just a little. Close your eyes."

I found a comb and a pair of scissors under the sink. I eased the comb down through the hair until it wouldn't budge any further, then I snipped. The knots came at different places. I tried to save as much as I could. The scissors cut with a hard, slicing sound, and Mona winced each time, her face puckered against the tears. When I was done I picked up the brush and tried to smooth the remainder, but it was all abrupt cuts and ragged edges. So I picked up the scissors again.

"Can I open my eyes?"

"Just a sec."

A few more minutes and I gave up. I set down the scissors and ran my fingers through the hair. Stiff and short, it jutted out at all angles, a bristling yellow array. "All right."

Mona opened her eyes. She stared bleakly into the mirror. Her glasses had slipped down her nose, and her eyes, pale and unprotected, were welling with tears. I reached out and gently pressed the heavy frames back into place. Clumps of hair had tumbled into the empty sink and were sticking like feathers to the damp porcelain. Mona sighed and reached up to wipe her eyes. It was too much. Even her powers of language failed. "Shoot," she whispered.

"Actually, I think it looks kind of cool."

"You don't have to say that."

"It does. Honest."

But she turned, hunched and bleak. Hesitantly I reached out and eased my arms around her. With a sigh she settled against my chest. "I look so bad," she sighed.

"No, you don't. It's just the nighttime. Things always look better in the morning." But as I said it I realized that was just something my mother used to say. It wasn't anything you could count on. And suddenly the undependability of it all—the mistakes and the bad luck and the lurking unhappiness—was more than I could stand. I leaned down and kissed her. I had to. It was suddenly the only thing I had to do.

She looked startled. Her hands crept up my chest, hesitantly at first, then more forcefully, then finally with a panicky fervor. She was shoving at my chest. "Wait! Stop!"

I let her go. Her face was drawn and ashen. I thought, god oh god oh god, what have I done? "Mona? Are you okay?"

"Please."

"I'm sorry," I said desperately. "I would never have--"

"Oh no." And suddenly, standing in the close and acrid air, she seemed to remember all that she had drunk that night. The beer, the tequila, the wine. It all came back to her. She turned, and I managed to get the toilet seat up just as she knelt and brought up the entire night's worth of fun and nourishment with a fierce and startled urgency that convulsed her for a long, long moment, and finally left her, dazed and exhausted, clinging to the rim of the bowl.

I brushed the hair back from her forehead and helped her to her feet. I flushed the toilet, then filled a glass and let her rinse her mouth. Then, dousing the bathroom lights, I led her into the bedroom and eased her down onto the edge of the bed. I helped her off with her jacket. "You'll feel better if you sleep."

She sat there, making a silent inventory of her resources. After a moment she leaned forward to unlace her shoes, but the movement carried her in a slow, smooth roll until she was suddenly kneeling on the floor again, wide-eyed and startled. "Whoa."

I lifted her up again, and knelt to remove her shoes. I peeled off her socks. She had a thin, silver ring around the second toe on her left foot. "Does this mean you're engaged?"

She didn't smile. She reached down tentatively and unbuckled her belt, then stood. The plaid pants billowed down like a curtain falling. She wore a pair of plain panties, only slightly whiter than her skin, with pink scalloped trim and a thin wispy hint of cinnamon hair escaping the elastic. With her feet still wrapped in the muddle of fabric, she sank back down on the bed. I thought of Henry, laughing off any help, drifting into cheerful sleep with thoughts of the evening dancing in his head. Mona sighed. She stared down at her naked legs, pale and puckered in the cool air. "I look so awful."

"No, you don't. You look really nice."

But she just shook her head, forlorn. She lay back as I lifted her feet up onto the bed. I draped the sheet over her. She closed her eyes.

I leaned down, brushing the fringe of bright hair back from her face. "Are you going to be okay?"

She nodded without a word.

"Is there anything I can do?"

Her voice was low and humid. "Please go away."

"Good night, Jane," I said, but she gave no sign of having heard.

I stepped out onto the sidewalk. The night was cool and still. Beneath the street lamps the Mustang looked shiny as red plastic. I suddenly realized I still had the car keys in my pocket, and I thought about going back. But the night had caught up with me. The wine and tequila and fatigue were all mixing together into a thick cloud behind my eyes. I thought of the innocent cotton panties, with their tiny scalloped edge and the wispy hint of undyed hair, and I wondered if it was simply a measure of my just desserts that the image would always be linked in my mind to the acrid smell of peroxide and the sounds of Mona throwing up.

"Hey, buddy," said a low voice. "Nice car."

In the back of my mind the memory of Carlisle's threat to do something mean-spirited to the arrangement of my face was still fresh enough that I wasn't altogether startled when someone grabbed my jacket, but when I turned I found myself eyeball to eyeball with the one face I had, at some point late in the evening, completely forgotten to look for.

Biff was smiling. "I'm not going to beat the shit out of you," he said.

"Good." I swallowed. "That sounds good to me."

"I'm just going to tell you something, and I want you to listen. You keep away from me."

"I'm trying," I said. "I am so trying."

"I'm not going to tell you again. You keep away from me. You keep away from Jean. And you keep that big, pushy girlfriend of yours away, too."

"Okay. That seems fair. I'm sure she'll agree."

"Shut up," he hissed. "If I see you again..." He hesitated, as if he hadn't even considered that possibility yet.

"I understand," I said. "You couldn't be clearer." But apparently he thought he could.

He hit me once in the stomach, and I folded up like a circus leaving town. I lay on the ground, gasping so hard, that I didn't even hear him start his car, but the headlights came on, and the square, boxy darkness of a rusty red jeep pulled out of the parking lot. And frantically I had to think for a moment where I'd seen that car before, because that was a clue, I knew. Even in the ponderously slow, wine-soaked centers of my brain I knew that this was an important bit of information that Mona would want to know. But then I remembered when I'd last seen the car. It was when I'd last seen Biff. It was Biff's car. That's whose it was. And even given the circumstances it seemed a disappointing piece of detective work.

It turned onto the street, looking suddenly too gaudy for the darkness: the red brake lights glowing, a row of yellow lights gleaming in a flat line across the back of the roof, and like a name tag shining out in its own halo of light, the license plate. The license plate, I thought. I should at least remember the numbers. But there weren't any numbers. Just a little taunting word: Genie. A little magical apparition that, with a cheerful beep of its horn and a little puff of exhaust, vanished into the night.

19.

At seven the next morning I woke from a hunched and anxious dream to the distant sounds of my father bumping around downstairs. My head ached and a churning, desperate feeling had centered itself in the vicinity of my stomach. I tried not to move. One shot of tequila, half a bottle of wine. It seemed just one more sign of how pitiful I'd become that this was enough to do me in. But that wasn't all. I had made my father's girlfriend throw up simply by kissing her, and that, as much as the alcohol, left me feeling unprepared for the day.

I listened to Henry moving heavily around the kitchen. He seemed to be dropping pots and pans. Each thump and muffled clatter reminded me of all the beer he'd drunk, all the shots, and I thought about how cheerfully he'd drifted off to sleep without the slightest suspicion of all that awaited him in the morning. That was the only thing that got me out of bed. Poor Henry. I'd laid him low as surely as if I'd hit him with a rock. Now I managed to trudge to the top of the stairs. "Henry? You okay? You need to take some aspirin. And water. Lots of water. And just go back to bed, okay? Henry?"

But when my father appeared at the bottom of the stairs he looked so chipper and cheerful, with a wide smile on his face and a look of such obvious anticipation of the day to come, that I sank onto the top step and just stared. He was dressed and pressed in a new shirt and slacks, with the newspaper in one hand and a loaf of bread in the other, and he called up cheerfully, "Morning. How did you sleep?"

"Are you okay?" I asked.

"Never better."

"You're not hungover?"

He tapped the loaf of bread against his chest. "Fit as a fiddle, and ready for adventure. You want some breakfast? I'm making eggs."

I struggled back to bed, and stayed there for the rest of the morning, as Henry sauntered off to work. At twelve-thirty the doorbell rang, and then rang again. Then it started up and continued uninterrupted for three full minutes as I lay watching the numbers change on the face of the clock. I finally sat up and pulled on my clothes and washed my face and brushed my teeth as the painful buzz gradually dulled into the background haze of discomfort. I was chewing three aspirin and a pair of Tums as I opened the front door and peered out through the screen.

Mona stood on the porch, head down, arm out, leaning all her weight against the button. When the door opened she glanced up and almost reluctantly let it go. She looked as bad as I felt. Her face was pasty behind those heavy black frames. Her lips, bare of lipstick, looked bleached and thin. And the hair.... I had almost forgotten the hair. She wore a lime green headband that smoothed the yellow feathers back from her forehead, leaving a faint gleam of perspiration untouched along the hairline. She was frowning, scowling at me, as if it were all my fault and if she only had her superpowers back for one brief moment she'd make me pay.

"Henry's not here," I said.

"Where is he?"

"He's gone to work. He feels fine. He's fit as a fiddle and ready for adventure."

We stood there wordlessly for a moment like the survivors of some terrible train wreck from which only the engineer had escaped scot-free. "Tell me you're lying," she said.

"God protects the innocent."

Grimly she digested the notion. "What happened last night?" And then hurriedly, as if the full implications of the question were too much to consider at once, she said, "I can't find my car keys."

"Oh, sorry." I patted my pockets. "I've got them here some-where. Don't worry."

She frowned. "I wasn't wearing any pants this morning."

"Maybe you left them at the bar."

She looked momentarily daunted by the possibilities. Then she peered up at me, and I could see her calling upon all her reserves of courage. "Did anything happen?"

"How much do you remember?"

She was scowling again. "If I knew that I wouldn't be asking, would I?"

I pushed open the screen door. "Have you eaten anything?"

"What about Henry?"

"He went to work, remember?"

Reluctantly, she stepped inside. "I mean, how much does he remember?"

"I don't know. You'd have to ask him. Come on."

Cautiously we made our way to the kitchen, moving like a pair of medieval pilgrims trudging through the pain of this world with the faint but dogged hope of a life to come. "We have eggs and bacon..."

"Oh, please."

"...and toast. We have oatmeal. I could make huevos ranche-ros...."

"Will you stop it?!"

There was nothing so comforting as the knowledge that one person, at least, was as foolish and uncomfortable as you. I drew out a chair, and Mona subsided wordlessly into it. "Have you taken any aspirin?"

She nodded gingerly.

"How about Tums?"

I set a pair of bowls on the table, a box of cornflakes, and the milk. Then I handed her two spoons and went up to get the Tums. When I returned she was still holding the spoons, staring down into her empty bowl.

"You'll feel better if you eat."

I shook out the cornflakes and poured the milk. Mona sat hunched and silent, her usual annoyed expression muffled by an air of banked unease. "Did you take me home last night?"

You'd have thought there weren't that many answers to such a question, but I spent a long moment studying her expression. "Now that you mention it, I believe I might have."

"Did I ask you to?"

"I think we all sort of agreed on it together. You, me, and Henry."

"Henry was there?"

I considered that. "At first. More or less. But then he went home."

She gave the cereal a stir, then reluctantly took a bite. The milk dribbled down her chin, and she wiped it off with her fingers. "Was Carlisle there?"

"He stopped by. He's a fun guy, isn't he?"

"He didn't do anything, did he? I mean, he didn't stay?"

"Well, he yelled a lot. He seemed a little upset. But then he left."

"Did he try to kiss me?"

I hesitated. "I don't know. I don't think so."

"I think he did." She was scowling again. "It'd be just like him to try it when he could see how drunk I was. He can be such a jerk sometimes."

I could feel myself blushing. "I take it you told him about Henry."

"Sort of. I thought he'd take the hint and leave me alone." She stared glumly down at her cereal, doubtless thinking about what jerks some people could be who wouldn't just leave her alone. She glanced up again. "We didn't do anything, did we?"

"No," I said carefully. "He left--"

"Not Carlisle." She poked at her cereal, the faintest dawn of pink rising in her face. "I mean, I know we didn't. So, don't tell me we did. I'd remember. Right?"

"No."

She frowned nervously. "No, I wouldn't remember?"

"No, we didn't do anything." I hesitated. "What do you mean by anything?"

"Did you take my pants off?"

"Not exactly. Not the way you mean."

"I got sick, didn't I?"

I nodded.

"When?"

I hesitated. "Sometime after the hair, but before the pants."

"Terrific." She stared gloomily down at her cornflakes. They were growing soggy, but the color remained undimmed. She gave them another stir.

"Could you maybe just eat them, and not mix them around like that?"

"I can't believe it," she said abruptly. "What a jerk I am!"

I winced. I hadn't expected her to be altogether pleased, but still... "It wasn't that bad. I mean, I thought parts of it were fun."

"It wasn't supposed to be fun. I was working. I should know better than to drink on the job."

"The job?"

"I'm not usually like that."

"I believe you," I said.

"I take my job seriously."

"I know.

She stopped and seemed to realize she was seeking reassurance from the wrong quarter. "Where was Henry all this time?"

"He was in the car at first. I took him home."

"So he didn't come upstairs?"

"He was a little tired."

She looked as if she'd found a pit in her cornflakes. "Is he mad?"

"He didn't seem mad."

"You didn't tell him anything? About last night?"

And once again I tried to read in her expression all that she might mean by that. "I think he's going to notice the hair."

She shook her head. "I mean the other stuff. My pants and getting sick. And everything."

I peered at her. I wasn't sure how many of my own bad intentions she suspected, but my guilty conscience seemed to expand to fill the silence. "No," I said finally. "I didn't tell him."

"I don't want him to know," she said. "Does he?"

"I don't think so."

"Because I don't want him to."

"Okay."

Mona ate her cereal staring grimly down at the table top, and there was something strangely comforting in her peevishness. Hunched as she was, lapsing into her own stew of annoyance and regret, she seemed to give off a kind of warmth, the way someone with a bad sunburn radiates a sort of second hand glow. We sat together in a companionable silence punctuated by the clink of spoons.

"You know," she said after a while, "I don't think he's coming back to the bar."

"Henry?"

"No."

And that reminded me so suddenly that I was amazed I could ever have forgotten. "He was there last night."

"I'm not talking about Henry."

"Biff," I said. "Biff was there. What kind of name is Biff, anyway?"

Mona stopped in mid-chew, a glaze of milk moistening her lips. "Why didn't you--?"

"Not at the bar. At your place. He was waiting outside. I was just standing there, thinking maybe I should check up on you one more time, and there he was."

"Did you find out where he was staying? Did you tell him Jean wanted to see him?"

"No. He asked me to please stop bothering him. And to stop bothering Jean as well. Then he left."

"We're not bothering Jean."

"I know. I didn't get a chance to tell him."

"Why not? You found him, couldn't you at least--"

"No!" I said. "All right? It was a very short conversation."

She hesitated, peering at me with a sudden and unexpected bloom of concern. "Are you okay?"

"Fine. I'm fine. He just scares the shit out of me, that's all."

Mona considered that for a while, long enough for me to wish I hadn't mentioned that last part about the limits of my courage. But in the end what she said was, "You were going to check up on me?"

I shrugged. "I just wanted to make sure you were okay."

"That's nice. Thanks." She ran her hand through her hair. "Did you ever go to bed drunk and wake up with a tattoo?"

"No."

"It's like that."

"You said you wanted it blonde." But she just shook her head fretfully. "Does this mean you've got a tattoo?" I asked.

"Just a little one."

"Where?"

"None of your business."

I nodded. It was true, of course. None of my business at all. But that seemed to matter less and less. "Does Henry know about Carlisle?"

"Henry doesn't need to know."

"He's going to find out."

"No, he's not."

Does he know about me? I almost asked. But then, even I wasn't sure about me.

I considered all our efforts to protect Henry when, in spite of everything, he was the one going so cheerfully about his day. "Don't you think Henry can take care of himself?"

"I don't want him to know," she said fiercely. "Any of this. I don't want you to tell him."

I shrugged. But that was okay with me. And surely it was a sign of just how lame I was, how needy and aching, that it pleased me to keep the secret. After all, we hadn't even done anything, and we were already agreeing not to tell Henry. And what was that, if not a bond of some sort?

Even if you're doing it for completely different reasons, even if one of you is only mildly embarrassed by her lack of professional dignity, you're tied together by the lies you tell as surely as by the bonds of love.

20

Consider the Prisoner's Dilemma. You're asked to imagine what you would do if you and your partner-in-crime—your father, say—were thrown into jail awaiting trial. The evidence is slim, but each of you is given the chance to turn against the other, to buy your freedom at the cost of his. If neither breaks, you might both go free, but how can you be sure? So you have a choice. Do you betray him, or wait for him to betray you? Do you count on his moral principles or your lack of them? It's a thorny question.

But here's what's worse. It isn't the act of making the choice that alters things. It's the realization that a choice is possible. That your interests, once identical, have so appallingly diverged, and the betrayal that once would have seemed unthinkable is not.

Mona called the next evening while Henry was out in the garden, painting his patio furniture. "Hi," she said.

I gripped the phone tightly, but kept my voice level. "Hi. How are you feeling?"

"Fine. I was just calling..."

"Henry's in the back yard. I think he's working on a surprise for you. Hold on. I'll get him."

"No." She hesitated. "I don't actually need to talk to Henry. The thing is... I'm going over to see Jean Tipton. I just thought you might want to come."

"When? Tonight?"

"I know, it's kind of last minute."

My watch said ten to seven. "I was just heading out to work."

"Never mind, then. Sorry. It was a bad idea." She started to hang up.

"Wait! Mona?" I heard her breathing on the line. There were,

I thought, so many reasons not to do it. Not least because I knew for a fact that Henry would never have done it to me. "What time?" I said.

I didn't ask why she wanted me along. I told myself there were probably lots of reasons. Maybe she thought I had a stake in the matter, since I was the one Biff kept beating up. Or maybe she just wanted company in case he showed up again. Or maybe, in the last, lingering grip of yesterday's hangover, she was still irritated with my father's cheerful good health. Ultimately as much as you may love someone, you can't really trust a man who doesn't suffer for his sins.

In any case, for whatever reason, when I heard Mona pull up in front of the house I poked my head out the back. "See you, Henry. I'm just headed out for the evening. I might be late."

"Don't work too hard," he called. "And give my regards to the regulars."

I nodded and turned, but some lingering flicker of honesty drew me back. "I'm not exactly going to work," I said. "I called in sick. Something else has come up."

"Really?" He turned, the red-stained paintbrush poised in one hand. "Where are you going?"

There was no reason not to tell him. After all, it was perfectly innocent. "Just out."

"Alone?"

"Not exactly."

"Good," he said. "You need a break. Take the truck if you want."

"That's okay. I've got a ride. She's waiting now."

"She?" My father smiled teasingly.

"I've got to go."

"Don't forget to have fun," he called.

Jean Tipton's neighborhood had a haphazard feel, as if the houses were not so much built as stored temporarily, like Mardi

Gras floats in the off season. They perched on a shallow hillside, each in a different style: a white saltbox beside a cedar contemporary beside a small yellow cape with dormers like a frog's eyeballs. Jean lived in a blue alpine chalet with red scalloped trim and a gingerbread balcony, and as we pulled into the driveway its dark, blank-faced windows peered mournfully down at us.

Mona cut the engine and sat frowning at the darkened house with the tight-lipped embarrassment of a tour guide who's forgotten to call ahead. "She said she's always home in the evening."

"Maybe she's hiding."

"She's not hiding."

"Maybe she's asleep."

"It's eight o'clock. Who goes to sleep at eight?"

Then suddenly, as if to answer *Not Jean Tipton, that's who*, the back door beside the garage opened, and out she stepped wearing a short, pink raincoat clutched at the throat and an expression of pale anxiety. She hurried down the driveway to the car, stepping awkwardly through the darkness in a pair of yellow rubber boots like a woman escaping a flooded building. "Thank God," she gasped. "I'm so glad it's you. I saw the headlights. I didn't know what to think. I was just getting ready for bed and I heard a noise." She stopped abruptly and stared down at Mona's yellow hair. "What in the world--?"

I felt her tense beside me, and I leaned forward hurriedly. "What kind of noise?"

Jean jumped like a startled pigeon, then bent and peered more deeply into the car. "Mister Bailey? Is that you? I didn't see you there." Her hand fluttered up to her hair, as if momentarily distracted, but she turned back to Mona with a frown. "I think there's someone inside. In the house."

"Now?"

"I think I heard someone."

The image of a clenched and angry face came clearly to my

mind. "Maybe you should call the police."

"But, what if it's nothing?"

What if it's not, I thought.

Jean was frowning worriedly. "Couldn't you come in? Just for a minute? Just to look around?"

Mona wore the annoyed expression of one whose sense of style had almost been insulted by a woman in a pink raincoat, but I'd been on enough cub scout camping trips to remember what it was like when every noise was a bear and every rustle might be the last sound you'd ever hear. Besides, I was a private detective, at least for tonight, and sitting beside Mona in the cool darkness of what was, on some level at least, a night out, I felt the sudden, first reckless need to show off.

With half-held breath Jean led us in through the back door, down a hallway dark as a closet, until we emerged finally into one of those truly comforting kitchens, too cozy and old-fashioned to allow anything untoward. The light above the range glowed like a campfire, the cupboards were varnished plywood, and there were a pair of steel ovens that must have looked sleek and faintly nautical forty years ago, but which now only seemed quaint and self-deprecating, like someone's eccentric aunt.

Her rubber boots squeaking on the linoleum, Jean ventured nervously around the room peering into every corner until she came to a reluctant halt in the far doorway, at a loss to deal with the sudden and unexpected reassurance. She smiled weakly. "Can I get you anything? I may have some wine somewhere. I think there's cheese in the fridge. I could make us a snack...." Her voice faded off in a thin little puff of embarrassment. "I get a little nervous sometimes. You know. When you're alone you hear all sorts of things. And living on the park like this, you sometimes get people wandering past. You didn't see anybody when you pulled in, did you?"

I glanced at Mona. She looked grimly disapproving of any such feminine weakness, though she was keeping an uneasy eye on the deep shadows encroaching from the corners. "No," I said reassuringly. "There was nobody."

But Jean stood there, poised and uncertain in the raincoat and boots, as if the house had sprung a leak and she didn't know what to do next. I felt a welling up of that sudden reassurance and kindness that other people's fears always bring out. "We could take a quick look around," I said. "If that would make you feel better."

"Could you? " Her face pinkened with gratitude. "That would be so nice. It would just take a moment. Is that okay?"

"Fine," said Mona. "Whatever. But let's just turn on some lights, okay?"

Jean led the way on a slow tour of inspection through the darkened house. There was a small dining room, then another hallway to the living room, and a low carpeted den like a ply-wood hunting lodge nestled off the back. At each room she shuffled nervously, cleared her throat, then poked her head in with a hesitant, "Anyone here?" I followed and Mona brought up the rear, switching on every light as she went. She seemed to be picking up on some of our hostess's nervous energy. "There's no one," she said impatiently. "You don't have to be frightened."

But Jean just returned a sheepish smile. "I'm such a scaredy cat. Do you live alone?"

"Yes."

"I don't suppose you get nervous."

"No."

She looked disconcerted at that, but then glanced over at me. "I don't suppose you live alone, Mr. Bailey?"

I tried to think of a response that didn't involve the words, No, I still live at home with my father. "Please call me Harry," I said.

"It's just… I imagine all sorts of things."

"Then, don't!" said Mona sharply, though she was definitely looking a little skittish herself. "Just tell yourself there's nothing to be afraid of. That's all. You're alone in the house. There's nobody here. And for God's sake, keep some more lights on!"

"You're right," she said doubtfully. "It's just me, I know. But still.... Would you mind checking the upstairs? Just for a second?"

She looked so anxious, how could we possibly say no? Though with a glance up the darkened stairway Mona looked as if she'd like to. "I'll go," I said.

Jean smiled gratefully. "I'd be such a scaredy cat without you."

"Yeah," said Mona sourly. "He's a real comfort, isn't he?"

With a nervous glance Jean led the way to the foot of the stairs. The light in the hallway washed partway up the steps, but the top was locked in shadow. She hesitated, then marshaling her courage, began climbing like Edmund Hillary on that last, difficult face. I started to follow, then turned. Mona stood anchored to the bottom step. "Do you want to wait here?" I asked.

"Where's the light switch?"

"It's up at the top," Jean called apologetically. "It's kind of a funny old house. Would you rather wait until I turn it on?"

"No. That's all right," said Mona, but she didn't budge.

"It's just up here. I'll get it." And after a moment there came the click of a switch. There was a single, bright, unreassuring flash, and then the night descended again, but this time over the entire house. After a moment Jean's voice drifted down, mild and regretful. "I was afraid of that."

Nobody moved. Light was leaking in from the living room windows, and I could make out Mona's silhouette, hunched stiffly on the stairs.

"Don't worry," Jean called brightly. "It's just a fuse."

"Can you fix it?" Mona's voice sounded tight in the darkness.

"I'm not sure I have any extras. They'd be down in the basement."

"Do you have a flashlight?"

"There might be one in the bedroom."

I felt my way back down the stairs. "Are you all right?" I

whispered.

"Of course I am!" she hissed.

"You're sure?"

"Just shut up, okay?"

I reached out, feeling for her hand, and found it locked in a death grip around the banister. "We just need to go down to the basement--."

"Forget it!" She transferred her grip to my hand as if trying to strangle it. "Let's just hurry this up."

Jean called worriedly from the darkness above. "What are you doing down there?"

"We're coming," I called, and as Mona maintained an iron grip on my hand, I led the way slowly up.

"It's a little spooky, isn't it?" said Jean sympathetically. Mona muttered something indistinct. We crept down the hall, feeling our way.

The darkness was full of sounds. The stairway creaked, the walls themselves shifted and sighed. Outside, the breeze rattled the branches. "Did you hear that?" Jean's sudden voice, disembodied, floated in the dark. "Kind of a thump or something? Did it sound like a footstep?"

"It wasn't a footstep," muttered Mona. I could almost hear her teeth grinding. "It was just a shutter or something. One of the screens."

"Sometimes," Jean whispered, "I think there's someone out there. I can almost feel them watching."

"There's nobody out there!" snapped Mona, but she was kneading the knuckles of my hand like so many worry beads, and at the sound of a faint, muffled creak she jumped. "What was that? It came from downstairs."

"Wasn't it up ahead?" said Jean.

But already the sound had turned vague and general in the darkness. I leaned into Mona's ear. "It's nothing," I whispered. "Don't worry."

"I'm not worried! I'm just not that crazy about the dark."

Meanwhile Jean was edging forward again, a vague blur of movement. "Here's the bedroom. It's an awful mess. I should clean it up..."

"Is there a flashlight?"

"In the bedside table."

"Then," said Mona, "I don't care how messy it is."

"Just give me a moment." There was the sound of a door opening, and with a whispered, "Anybody there?" she crept into the darkened room.

"Jesus Christ," muttered Mona.

"She's just a little nervous."

"No shit. She's making me crazy." Her grip was a steady pressure on my hand. "And would you stop flirting with her, for God's sake?"

"What? I'm not flirting."

"Well give it rest, why don't you?"

There was the low scrape of a drawer opening, and a moment later the jittery glow of a flashlight came on, bouncing across the floor. "Got it," Jean called.

"Well, come on, then!"

"Just a second."

The light danced over the walls and across the shadowy tangle of an unmade bed. Highlighted in the darkness it looked as wanton and disheveled as an out-of-the-way motel. And among the rumpled pillows, as if for that added touch of prurience, sat an enormous brown teddy bear with a blue jacket and a floppy yellow hat. "There you are," Jean cried and hugged it close. "Mommy was so worried about you."

Standing in the pink raincoat, clutching the bear in her arms, she looked sad and desperate, like a lifeboat passenger saving what she could. But she managed a brave smile. "Say hello to Harry and Mona, sweetie. They rescued us." I half-thought she might start moving its arms in accompaniment, but she just gave a weak little shrug. "Would either of you like a glass of wine? Paddington thinks I'd better have some, and he doesn't like me to drink alone."

Mona led the way with the flashlight. Jean carried the bear, hugging it under her chin and whispering to it, gaining courage by the moment. By the time we got to the kitchen her nervousness seemed to have given way before the obligations of company. "I have candles somewhere. And there's cheese in the fridge. Please sit down."

She propped Paddington on a chair and went rummaging through drawers until she found what looked like old Christmas candles, bright red and bayberry-scented. She arranged them on the Formica table like a cluster of little tree stumps. The flames dipped and flickered, casting a glimmer of light that reached no further than the edge of the table and set the shadows, darker now and oddly shaped, throbbing against the walls. "Isn't this cozy?"

"Where's the basement?" Mona demanded tightly.

"I'm not sure you'll like it. It's a little gloomy. We could just let it go until morning," said Jean.

"Please. Just tell me where it is."

The door was in the hall under the stairs. But when Mona pulled it open, the scent of old stone and mildew rose out of a darkness so complete it took only a moment's hesitation for her to close it again. We returned to the kitchen.

The duties of hospitality seemed to transform Jean. She set the table with a jar of pickles, half a bag of Doritos decanted into a bowl, a plate of saltines, and a little brown crock of cheese spread. "And I've got Riunite." She opened the fridge, dark as a cupboard, and pulled out the remains of a large box of wine. "Might as well drink it up. It's not getting any colder."

Mona was clearly a woman in need of a drink, and for my part I realized, whether it was the darkness, the candlelight, or Jean Tipton hovering like a hostess in foul weather gear, even Riunite sounded good. I held up two glasses and watched her fill them to the brim with wine that, even in the candlelight, looked pink as cough syrup. I held one out to Mona. She took it gratefully and without preamble, tipped it back. The level sank like a barometer with a storm coming in.

"There you go," said Jean approvingly. She was smiling, as if at last we were entering into the spirit of things.

Mona lowered her glass with a little gasping breath. "We just need to ask you a few questions," she said, "and then we can get going."

"There's no rush. Here." Jean handed me the wine box. "There's plenty more. I have another in the fridge."

As I refilled her glass I realized unexpectedly how much I was enjoying myself. The wine, the cozy glimmer of candlelight in a strange house. I raised my glass and clinked it against Mona's. She glanced up, startled, then reluctantly smiled.

"That is so sweet," said Jean. "You make such a sweet couple."

"We're not exactly a couple," I said.

"Not at all," said Mona.

"We just work together. That's all."

Jean smiled waggishly. "You don't need to worry. Your secret's safe with me."

I thought about that one kiss in the bathroom, all those nights before, and the moment's hurried glimpse of pale breasts. "There's no secret," I said.

But Jean just shrugged cheerfully. "Nobody here but us chickens." Then, to me, she said, "You're married, aren't you, honey?"

"No."

But she was nodding wisely. "I can always tell. The really nice ones... they're always married. It's tough, isn't it? All the sneaking around. Finding little hideaways. Stealing time when you can."

I glanced at Mona. The dark didn't seem to be bothering her as much—maybe she was getting used to the candlelight, or maybe the Riunite was taking the edge off things—but as she sipped she was watching me with inscrutable interest. I could feel myself beginning to blush. "It's really not like that."

"I know, honey," said Jean. "It never is. But what can you do? When it's love, it's love." She drained her glass in one long sympathetic go.

In the silence that followed I gazed down at the plate of crackers, the Doritos, the red and orange swirl of port wine cheese in its dewy-sided crock. A small, forlorn mirage of an evening out. I picked up a knife, spread some cheese on a cracker, and held it out to Mona. "It's a party," I said.

"You are so sweet. Isn't he sweet?"

"Every so often," Mona agreed.

"It just takes me back. Biff and me…Talk about sweet. It was love at first sight. That's what it was. He was crazy about me, and I just couldn't get enough of him."

"How did you two meet?" asked Mona, the softness of the wine slipping into her voice.

"Oh." Jean shrugged. "In a bar somewhere. You know how it is. You're a little lonely, a little down, and then this sexy man walks in, and you think: Honey, your luck is about to change."

I thought about that. I wondered if you always recognized a change in your luck. I wondered if you always knew. "And did it?" I said. "Change, I mean."

"Oh, sure. A couple of times." She wrapped one arm around the bear in her lap. "That's the thing about luck. It changes, then it changes again. It's nothing you can count on. But we had fun. One night, we broke into one of those miniature golf courses. You know the one up the highway? After midnight sometime, and we played all night, laughing and drinking. He could be such a scream. There was a time, we were together every minute. We just couldn't be apart. And the sex…." She sighed and shook her head.

"Pretty good?" said Mona.

"Honey, that man could squeeze you dry. There were days we never got out of bed except to eat. That's the thing about love, it does make you forget your troubles. It makes you think there's nothing else matters." She sighed and raised her glass, startled to find it empty.

"I don't know," said Mona. Her voice sounded wistful and hesitant. "Don't you think it's over-rated?"

"Sex?" said Jean.

"Love." She shrugged uneasily. "I'm not even sure what it means any more."

"Oh, honey. That's just so sad."

"Is it? I mean you put so much into it, you just get your hopes up. Then you get to the end and think, well, that was pretty terrible. What was the point?"

"It's give and take," Jean agreed. "I'll give you that much, and then some. You think Biff hasn't let me down? You think he hasn't made some bad mistakes? But, honey, I'd take him back in a minute."

"So, you still haven't heard from him?" Mona asked.

"He's not what you'd call a great communicator."

"But nothing at all?"

Jean glanced up. "Why? What do you mean?"

"It's just Harry ran into him the other night. I thought he might have gotten in touch."

Jean looked worried. "You saw him?"

"We talked," I said. "He told us to stay away from you."

"Did he?" She smiled sadly. "He was always kind of protective. That's what makes it so sad. You love each other, but there's so much against you. You try and try. But they just can't leave you alone."

"They?" I asked. "Who's they?"

"Oh, my family, his family, the police."

"Police?"

"Just everyone." She was filling her glass again, frowning as the empty box trickled to a halt. "Everybody's trying to keep us apart. I mean, it's none of their damn business, is it? It's nothing we want. Can't they just leave us alone? It's our life." She started to raise her glass. "Look. It's just like this. Is the glass half-full or half empty. It's all in how you look at it." A little vaguely now, she looked at it again, trying hard to see it half full.

Mona was frowning. "Why the police?"

Jean shrugged blearily. "How the hell should I know? Spite. Maybe they just can't stand to see us happy." She held out her glass. "Can you help me out, honey? There's another in the fridge."

I stood up a little unsteadily and retrieved it. There was almost nothing else in the refrigerator. Even in the warmth of the candlelight it looked hollow and bereft. I had the sudden image of what it would mean to come home every day to an empty house, with the silence so intimidating that you peopled it with footsteps and imagined intruders, if only because on some scale of things it was better to be frightened than lonely. Better even to be sad, angry, resentful. Anything but lonely. I held up the box.

"You are so nice," said Jean as I filled her glass. "Why is it the nice ones are always taken?"

"Jean...?" said Mona.

She took an appreciative sip. "You know, I'm not sure it isn't better warm."

"Jean!"

She shook her head impatiently. "It's nothing we want! It's their problem, not ours. They're just doing it to keep us apart. You know? It's like that, what's it's name....Romeo and Juliet."

I nodded sympathetically. "Star-crossed lovers. "

"Is it? Well," she said. "They might have changed the name. The point is, it's just the same. They're spiting our love. I mean, why should we suffer just because the police have a bug up their ass?"

"It does sound unfair," I conceded faintly.

"See, I knew you'd understand. I could tell right away." She gave a teary and alcoholic little sigh and hugged the bear more tightly on her lap. "You can't fight love."

"Jean," said Mona carefully. "What bug exactly do the police have up their ass?"

Jean hesitated, as if slowly recollecting something. "I don't want to talk about it. I didn't mean to mention it. Besides, it's not fair. It's not Biff's fault. I mean, it's not like he didn't do his time. At least, most of it. I mean, what do they want?"

Mona sat very still, frowning a little uncertainly. She glanced up at me, and more from reflex than anything I topped up her glass. Then I refilled mine. "Jean?" she said. "When he was out of town all those years? Where was he exactly?"

Even as drunk as she was she managed to look sheepish. "He moved around a little."

"How little?"

She fluffed up the bear's little yellow hat. "Anamosa, mostly. Till he got out."

"Got out?"

"Left." She shrugged. "I mean, you can't blame him. Have you seen it?"

"No."

"It's so depressing."

Mona opened and closed her mouth. "He was in prison?" she said.

"I told you that."

"No. You didn't."

Jean waved that away. "It was just bad luck. A misunderstanding more than anything."

"And then he left?"

"A little earlier than I thought. It caught me by surprise."

"And he hasn't contacted you?"

Jean's tone was confidential. "I think he might be a little embarrassed."

We sat there for a moment in silence. And as I considered how embarrassing it must be to find yourself out of prison earlier than anyone expected, I heard the sound of a door slam. After all the creaking and whispering, all the worries about screens and footsteps, it stood out, sharp and startling.

Mona froze. "What was that?"

"It must be the wind," said Jean. "Or a shutter. Didn't you say it was a shutter?"

"That wasn't a shutter." Mona set down her glass and stood up. Her hand, I suddenly realized, had crept back into mine. "Did you hear where it came from?"

But Jean was on her feet now, too, clutching the bear. "Wait. Where are you going?"

"We'll go take a look," I said. "Why don't you stay here and call the police."

"I can't," she said. "What if it's nothing?"

But then a terrible rattling sound echoed through the walls, as far from nothing as it was possible to be.

Mona turned. "Is that the garage?"

"No!" Jean shook her head desperately. "I didn't hear anything."

And in that instant came the grumble of an engine rising quickly to a roar, then the skid of tires and a crunching crash.

"Jesus!" cried Mona. "My car!"

We reached the door in time to see the rusted red Jeep, having exploded out of the garage into the now-crumpled nose of the Mustang, wheel around and plunge headlong across the sloping lawn. It fishtailed once as it hit the asphalt and then vanished down the street. As Mona stared after it, mouth agape, I turned toward Jean and met a look of the most profound embarrassment.

21

As might be expected, the evening went downhill from there. Jean burst into tears and locked the door behind us. Mona, in a grinding rage, managed finally to coax the Mustang into life, wreathed in ominous black fumes. I suggested a drink, but she just glared at me. I suggested dinner. But she dropped me at the house and roared off down the road, wearing the wisps of burning oil like a thundercloud over her head and leaving me with strange, remembered images of candlelight and bad wine.

I spent the next morning searching for her. I stopped at the Blue Diner, but the only familiar sight was the roast pork dinner making its reappearance as an open-faced sandwich under a layer of beige gravy. There was no sign of her at the apartment. But I had learned a thing or two. I checked the town clerk, the police station, the Ford dealership, and every Body Shop and collision service in the phone book, and just a little before noon I walked into the public library and found her hunched at a table in the back. She was peering into the darkened cave of a microfilm reader as if her concentration alone were lighting the screen. Images of old newspapers slid like reflections across the bottom of a swimming pool.

"Well," I said. "You're the last person I expected to run into."

She glanced up, scowling, but despite the fierce expression, her tone was surprisingly mild. "What are you doing here?"

"Hank's Auto Body said they dropped you off here around eight."

"So?"

"So, it's almost noon. I was getting a little worried."

"Shouldn't you be at work?"

"I told Henry I needed another day to recuperate. How's the

car?"

She just shook her head. "The front end's smashed, the radiator's shot. Even the chassis's bent. They said it was going to be at least a couple of weeks. That stupid cow!"

"Are you sure you're supposed to talk about your clients that way?"

"She was laughing at us. Leading us around like a couple of girl scouts doing our good deed for the day."

"Were you ever a girl scout?"

"I don't like people lying to me. I don't like people laughing at me."

"She wasn't laughing."

"It pisses me off."

"How could you know?"

She glared. "It's what I do. That's pretty much the job description. I'm supposed to find out what people aren't honest enough to tell me."

"So what are you doing here?"

"Looking for Biff."

"And you think he's in there?" I nodded at the pile of little boxes. "His fifteen minutes of fame?"

"Somewhere."

"You're not planning to look through all those papers?"

"Page by page. I'm starting with the locals, but it could have been anywhere in the state. So I'm checking the police blotter, the news section, any little highlights or human interest stuff. And the pictures."

"That sounds," I said, "like just about the most boring thing I could imagine."

She peered up at me. "So, now that you're here, are you going to give me a hand, or what?"

"Isn't there someone we could just ask?"

"Sure," said Mona. "When I find out, you can just ask me."

We spent the afternoon at the library. There was only one ma-

jor paper in the state. But a dozen smaller ones divided the slow
and ordinary news of the hinterland among them. The pages
rolled through my machine like one of those long slide shows
of someone's Hawaiian vacation where every shot has a palm
tree, and every palm tree looks the same. I kept glancing over
at Mona, but she was deep in concentration, and after a while,
having spent so much effort pretending to read, I found I actually was. There were stories on prize-winning pigs, and road
repairs, and hog confinement lots and water quality scares and
prize-winning heifers and Four-H contests and grade-school
field trips to the state fair, all jumbled together like so many answers just waiting for the proper question.

I did as she suggested. I checked the front page, the back,
the human interest stories, the police blotter, working my way
through the years. At some point I began to develop the uneasy
certainty that I had missed it, that I had just passed it by, and it
was lurking somewhere at the bottom of the take-up reel. But
Mona showed no sign of stopping, so I kept looking until something caught my eye. It was in the local paper, a thin, amiable
daily that came out each afternoon after all the most important
news had already broken. It was under the Police Blotter, a tiny
item only a few sentences long. *Charged with Disturbing the Peace.
Elizabeth Bailey, 42, of 416 Pontiac Drive, following a disturbance at
her home.* I stared at it for a long time.

Mona looked up. "Something?"

"No."

I read it through again. I'd forgotten all about the episode. It
had been so long ago it had slipped right out of my mind. I'd
been upstairs doing my homework when the argument started
in the living room. I had no idea what it was about. I kept turning up the radio, and though her voice continued to rise through
the floor, the words were unclear, and eventually the argument
passed. But when my mother's voice faded, it was because of the
blue lights flashing in through the front window and the knock
of the policeman on the door. I had gone to the top of the stairs

and peered down at the officer, a middle-aged man with a tired expression, asking what the problem was. And I remembered feeling so embarrassed that I slipped quickly back to my room, and when I came out later the policeman was gone, and all was quiet. Henry and Elizabeth were reading at opposite ends of the sofa, having apparently put the whole matter out of their minds.

Now I sat up a little straighter and turned the crank of the machine, scrolling back through the days and weeks with a kind of grim fascination. Now that I knew what to look for I found the stories more easily: other charges of disturbing the peace, complaints by the neighbors, police called to break up arguments. Usually they were under the Police Blotter, but sometimes they stood on their own in short, inconspicuous paragraphs. Officers responding to a neighbor's concern that the house was being robbed arrived to find a pile of broken crockery in the back yard and the lady of the house calmly sweeping the steps. She had slipped, she said, and dropped all thirty-two pieces: dinner plates, salad plates, cups and saucers. Her husband,. Henry Bailey, Sr. of 416 Pontiac Drive was not at home. He had just now gone out for a walk, she said, but he would be back soon.

He had turned up, I remembered, a couple of hours later, and no one had mentioned the dishes, though we ate off paper plates for a month.

I kept reading. Every story reminded me of something I'd forgotten, and I lingered over each as if it were a clue in need of decoding. They stretched back ten years and more. Some I remembered, others I didn't, even after reading. They might have happened to somebody else. One appeared as a small, human interest story under *News About Town*. A humorous item about a man, his name unreleased by police, who had called for help in getting back into his house. He'd returned home one evening to find the locks changed. The police broke a small window in the back, through which the man's son, 10, was lifted. The young boy, proud and excited, had hurried through the house to open the front door. The father, still blessedly unidentified, cited "a domestic squabble" as the cause of the problem. His wife was unavailable for comment. She had gone out to a movie for the evening.

At the time I had thought it was thrilling. Boosted up by the policeman, I had crawled through the kitchen window and over the counter, then snuck like a burglar through the empty house. The policemen were laughing when I emerged; Henry was grinning sheepishly among them. I'd always thought he'd simply forgotten his keys. And though I knew he kept a spare hidden in the garage, I was just as pleased to have the excitement. Though it had been followed by yet another argument that evening, this one not attended by the police.

I felt my eyes blurring with fatigue. I was amazed by how many occasions there had been. How could I have forgotten them all? Somehow I'd simply erased whole portions of my life, and as I read the scattered accounts it was as if I were uncovering someone else's past. It must be someone else's; I remembered a happier childhood than these stories allowed. I remembered my parents, fond and loving. I remembered them laughing. We were happy, weren't we? A happy family? How could there be so many discrepancies? As if I'd confused two different lives, the one I remembered, and this other one, enacted by these named and unnamed sources in a whole series of fights and fragments.

I glanced down through the pile of boxes, searching until I found the date I wanted. I threaded it on. The front page was centered in the view screen with the date at the top: six years ago almost to the day. I'd forgotten it was a Thursday. I read the whole paper, page by page. There was nothing of real importance, nothing that stood out. A Planning and Zoning meeting. A drop in the stock market. The plans for an expansion of the library. It was a perfectly ordinary day, all but indistinguishable from the one before or after. This is, after all, not so small a town that the departure of a single person could be counted as news.

All the rest of the day we read, Mona and I. We were both stiff and glassy-eyed, when she leaned over and tapped my shoulder. "You're going to like this."

It was a small story in the Decorah section of a three-year-old Dubuque *Herald-Republican*. It should have been bigger, but it was pushed off the front page by a summer of heavy rains that had raised every river in the state over its banks. The story appeared instead in a little boxed sidebar with the headline *Ten Years for State Bank Gunmen*.

The suspects, Brian Patrick Jackson and Delbert Harris Clancy, had entered the Decorah Branch of the State Bank and Trust in the late afternoon of Thursday, March 12, wearing ski masks and carrying what would turn out to be non-firing replicas of Civil War era cap-and-ball revolvers, which Clancy collected. These two particular weapons were copies of the pistols Wild Bill Hickok was said to favor, and perhaps that accounted for some of the things Biff and his partner had said. *Reach for the sky. Nobody move. Put your hands where I can see them.* They seemed to be enjoying themselves, caught up in the spirit of the moment. The bank clerks were also caught up, as was the only bank officer remaining late on that day, a vice-president in charge of trusts and estates who oversaw the gathering together of the cash and the safe departure of the two gunmen, and only then, with a certain peevish dignity, pressed the alarm button.

It's likely the police would have tracked down the two robbers eventually. Certainly the state prosecutor testified it was only speeding up the inevitable when Clancy was found, minus the ski mask but with both genuine, non-firing, full-scale replicas, sitting on the ground beside his car in the parking lot of a Quik Trip with a broken nose and a fracture rib, but without the money. He wouldn't describe the nature of the disagreement that had left him so battered, nor would he reveal Biff's last known address, though under the effects of painkillers he eventually let slip Biff's name. They found him, a week later, across the state in Mason City. He was alone, with forty-seven dollars and change in his pockets. He denied knowing Clancy, denied ever owning a ski mask, and said if they found a hundred and twenty thousand dollars on him he would eat it. Clancy's last request before sentencing, his ribs wrapped in tape, much of his face obscured by bandages, was to be assigned separate prisons.

Mona was nodding with weary satisfaction. "A hundred and twenty thousand dollars."

"Imagine that," I said.

I tried to sound impressed, tried to recognize the importance of what she'd found, but my mind was on other things. I was thinking about the happy family life I'd spent the last six years grieving for, but which we now seemed never to have had. And I was trying to figure out why it felt as if Henry had lied to me all these years, when in fact he had simply not said a word. I marveled at all that was unknown, all that was hidden and awaiting discovery, as if your life were a dark road. As if all you could do was drive along, careful as you could, and wait for the pothole, the drop-off, the sudden deer in the headlights that was all the warning you were going to get.

22.

"People never tell you the truth," said Mona. "It's always a last resort. In the moment, people will say anything. 'I love you. I won't leave you. I'd never hurt you.' It's easy. Maybe they even believe it. But in the end it's only words. What matters is what they do. The decision they make when they absolutely have to. Do they lie or not. Do they cheat or not. Do they leave or not. It's when no one's watching that the truth comes out. Nobody tells it to you. It's the one thing you have to find out for yourself."

"But how do you know it's the truth," I said, "if no one is watching?"

"No one but us."

We were sitting in a car in the dark at the edge of the park. The air was a gentle whisper, and the moonlight sifted like clouds of pollen between patches of deeper shadow. It was getting late. Mona sat slouched behind the wheel, her eyes on the alpine chalet across the street. Occasionally a car drove slowly into sight, looking for a dark and romantic place to pull over, and as the headlights filled the windshield she leaned over, resting her head against my shoulder, tickling my cheek with her hair for a moment until the car had passed and we were in darkness again. Then she straightened up and resumed her surveillance.

She had picked me up that evening, the rental car smelling of cigarette smoke and oil. "Now just to get this straight," I said. "You're not actually going to charge her for the time you spend spying on her? I think you might be on some shady ethical ground there."

"I don't like being lied to," she said grimly. "I'm going to see what she's up to. You don't have to come if you don't want."

But of course I came. Who was I, if not someone with an interest in the truth?

I had always imagined a stake-out as something Bogart might do for five minutes in the middle of *The Big Sleep*. But this went on and on. Jean came home by cab, hurried inside, turned on every light in the place, and that was pretty much that. As the evening lengthened, the bright and unremarkable house seemed to have less and less to do with us. We waited, but there was no sign of the Jeep, or Biff. No sign of a gas man, cable man, Jehovah's Witness, panhandler. I got so used to nothing moving, it seemed impossible anything ever would. And as I continued to stare dutifully at the house, I found myself increasingly aware of Mona sitting beside me, and the time seemed to stretch out like that moment at the end of a blind date when you pull in front of her house and both sit, unmoving, waiting to see what will happen next.

"I didn't mention anything to Henry," I said.

Mona stared at the house without a word.

"About this stake-out, I mean. I don't know whether you're one of those ogres for honesty, but I didn't think there was any point in telling him."

"Okay by me." We were whispering, both of us, though there was no one around.

"He was smiling all afternoon," I said. "I think he was singing to himself."

"Good for Henry."

"You've made a big change in him."

"Glad I could help."

"There have been some real losers in the past. You can't imagine. Ironing in the living room. Standing around in their slips. You are such an improvement."

Mona said, "Please stop talking."

She was dressed for the occasion entirely in black. It was the only time I'd seen her in matching colors. Her face was pale in the soft darkness with the glasses like a racoon's mask and her hair a glowing apparition. Now would be the time to dye it black, I thought, though I didn't mention that. Truth be told, I was beginning to like it. Even in the darkness it looked jagged and fierce.

"Tell me again how you got started on this."

"I didn't tell you the first time," she said.

"So, tell me now."

She shifted in the darkness; it might have been a shrug. "I read a book. A few books, actually. You can get a license pretty easily in this state, as long as you don't want to carry a gun."

"And you don't?"

"You don't really need one. Most of the job is just looking stuff up. Birth certificates, licenses, insurance, credit cards. It's all out there. You just need to know where."

"And you thought that would be exciting?"

"Not exciting, exactly. Reassuring. Knowing that whatever you need to know is out there, just waiting for you to find it." She shrugged again, as if that were that. The silence settled in. We sat side by side like passengers on a cruise ship watching the distant horizon. Her voice, when it came again, was a whisper in the breathing dark.

"I used to go looking for my father when I was young. Ten or eleven." She spoke slowly, her eyes still on the house. "This was before he started serious traveling, but when he still had trouble finding his way home. It'd start to get late, and my mom would start to get mad. Sitting there, glaring at the TV. And I'd sneak out and get on my bike, and I'd go looking for him. "

She would pedal hard through the cool night, trying to read her father's mind, trying to decide if there'd been anything to suggest one bar more than another. She grew very observant. What had he been wearing? What had he been talking about? Had he seen an ad on TV for hot dogs or barbecue or country music? Did he mention any friends or stories? Anything might be a clue, and Mona tried to sort it out as she pedaled, bar to bar. George's had the cheap burgers, but the Shamrock had better beer, and The Naugahyde Lounge had karaoke on Monday, Wednesday, and Thursday. To decide where he'd gone was to decide what he was feeling that night. And when she finally walked into the right place and found him, she loved him more than any other time, because in that moment she understood him in the only way that mattered.

And in that first moment he always looked pleased to see her. As if he'd been hoping she would find him. As if it had all been a complicated game, and he had only come out so that she would come looking. He'd laugh and say, "That's my girl. She's a regular bloodhound." And he'd lift her onto his knee, or onto the bench beside him, and she'd eat peanuts or pretzels, and maybe get a sip or two of beer before he'd finally agree to go home.

He always agreed. And that was part of the game, too. Her reward at the end of the search. She had found him, and he would go quietly. That's what he always said. "Just one more, and I'll go quietly." But the real reward was that fifteen or twenty minutes while they sat together and he finished that last drink. While she ate peanuts and got sleepy in the dim and raucous air, and felt him next to her on the bench, warm and solid and there because she had found him.

"You always found him?" I asked.

Mona shrugged. "It wasn't that hard. He always went to the same spots. At least at first."

But then he started driving further away, further out of range.

The first time she couldn't find him she spent the night riding everywhere, all the usual bars, even checking the yellow pages for the ones she didn't know. But in the end she pedaled home alone, feeling hopeless and undone. When he finally did come stumbling home, it was Mona who came down to yell at him, while her mother slept. "Where have you been?"

He shrugged peevishly. "I went up to Shueyville. So?"

"Don't," she said furiously. She was what? Twelve years old. And sounding even to her own ears more like her mother than she'd have wished. And that look on his face, neither proud nor welcoming. The look of harried annoyance that until then he had reserved for Rusty alone. "You should just stay in town! Why can't you just stay in town?" she said.

But she knew why. Because she'd gotten too good; she could find him too easily. And so she drove him away, out beyond the local haunts, out onto the road. And once he was there, she had lost him.

And now Mona sat, slouching grimly. Her glasses had drifted down her nose, and I wanted to reach out and press them back into place. I wanted to tell her she didn't have to worry, now. That Henry wasn't going anywhere.

In fact, that had always been the problem as much as anything—Henry so settled and set in his ways. But maybe that was the comfort as well. And for the first time I wondered if maybe my father really could make Mona happy. It hadn't occurred to me before, but maybe they were just what each other needed. And I felt a little twinge of desperation.

There was once upon a time a particular species of pigeon, *Raphus cucullatus*, that lived on the island of Mauritius for thousands of years. It had no predators. It grew huge, as if to fill the empty space. Strong legs, a powerful beak. The wings wasted away, but so what? There was nowhere to fly, and no point in trying. It flourished all alone there. Isolation made it strong. It was perfectly suited for the life it led. But then men came to the island. They brought rats and pigs, they brought clubs and guns. And they killed off every one. Strong as they were. Perfectly adapted.

For all these years I'd thought Henry and I were doing all right. We'd adjusted to the loneliness. And it might be that we could have managed, left alone to our own devices, our own little ecosystem. After all, we had adapted. We'd evolved. Perfectly suited to being alone. But who wanted to be alone? Not my father, that's for sure. And how could I blame him? It was the law of evolution. One man's *Raphus cucullatus* was another man's dodo.

We sat staring at the lighted house, car windows open, all the sounds of the night around us. A warm breeze carried a little charge of static like the air before a storm. "Yosemite Sam," said Mona drowsily.

"What?"

"The tattoo. It's just a little picture of Yosemite Sam. You know, the cartoon character?"

I glanced over. "Why him?"

"I don't know. I always liked him. Something about the mustache. And the hat; I liked his hat. And he was always so angry. I guess I kind of identified."

"Yeah," I said. "You remind me of him. So, where is this tattoo?"

"None of your business. What's the time?"

I checked my watch. "Quarter after twelve. How long are we staying?"

"Long as it takes," she said. Another long moment. "I'm thinking about getting my eyebrow pierced. Or maybe my tongue."

"Does Henry know?"

"It's my tongue. I'm not going to ask Henry."

"Doesn't it hurt?"

"I suppose. It'd be kind of cool, don't you think?"

"Wouldn't it bump against things?"

"That's the idea."

"Oh," I said. "I guess I don't completely get it."

She turned her head on the headrest, as if too tired to lift it. "You don't think it'd be cool?"

"It's just the whole piercing thing …."

"I think it'd be fun." She shifted drowsily. "And it's supposed to be great for oral sex."

I sat very still. I tried to resist the sudden, unwelcome vision of Henry discovering one night without being told that his girlfriend had a new accessory.

Beside me Mona laughed softly. "Carlisle used to go on about it. Talking it up. How great it'd be." She snorted. "Course it's not his tongue."

"Good point," I said. I wondered if maybe I should mention Carlisle to my father. Just to keep him apprised and up to date. "What else does Carlisle say?"

But Mona didn't reply. After a moment, as an afterthought, "What a jerk," she muttered, leaving me to wonder which of us she was thinking about now.

"Heads up," said Mona. A car swung past. Hastily she edged over, and I draped a dutiful arm across her shoulders. The head-lights rose and faded. She started to relax, but then the front door opened and Jean stood there, peering out. We continued to sit perfectly still.

"Think she can see us?"

"Don't move," said Mona.

I leaned my cheek stiffly against her hair. After a moment, in its own pursuit of verisimilitude, my right hand settled hesitant-ly onto the curve of her stomach, where the hem of the t-shirt didn't quite reach as far as her jeans. Mona appeared not to no-tice. She seemed to be giving all her attention to the house. But as I sat, dutifully unmoving, my fingertips drifted of their own accord along the narrow strip of exposed skin. "You are unbe-lievably smooth," I murmured.

"Yeah. Everybody tells me that." Her eyes were still on Jean, but her voice seemed to have grown a little thin and breathy in the darkness. When, after one last look around, the figure in the doorway withdrew, Mona continued to sit perfectly still, watch-ing the house as if afraid to turn her head.

My throat had gone dry. It was all I could do to whisper. "We should be careful. She might be looking out the window."

"Do you think?"

"Just to be safe. We don't want to take any chances." My fin-gers slipped beneath the hem, drifting across the silken skin.

"I've wanted to touch you for so long."

"Well, you can't," she said.

"If I wanted to kiss you, would that make me a terrible person?"

Mona turned. We were barely a breath apart. "Will you shut up? I'm working here."

And there wasn't anything else in the world I could do. Beneath the pressure of my lips her mouth parted. My hand burrowed beneath the t-shirt, tracing its way up over the shell-like delicacy of ribs to the sudden, smooth fabric of her bra. But as I tried to reach further the black t-shirt bound my arm.

"Careful," she whispered. "It's my favorite shirt."

"Mine, too."

"Don't rip it."

I was pulling at it gently, stretching the hem beyond repair, unveiling in the darkness the pale expanse of skin and the white cotton hindrance of her bra. No lace. No decoration. Plain and utilitarian, it made my heart skip. I fumbled beneath her for the clasp. She arched and turned. ""Let me," she hissed.

"Wait."

The clasp gave way. The smooth bra loosened and let the shallow, succinct weight of her breasts slip free. Her flesh, pale and cool at first, warmed under my hand. The sound of her breathing filled the car. It must have been hers, because my heart was pounding from the lack of air. Or just the reverse. Too much suddenly after so many years. My fingers curved around the perfect delicate heft of her.

"You're touching me," she whispered, as if it were nothing I might have noticed. She was frowning. Her expression would have looked tense and alert if her eyes had been open.

From somewhere high above I watched my fingers follow the drift of gravity from the dip of her breast to her ribs to the narrow waistband of her jeans. They fumbled at the button, the zipper. Two dark leaves of denim opened, curling back. My fingers slipped beneath, to where the softly matted hair was growing humid and warm.

"Close your eyes," she whispered.

"I can't. You are so beautiful."

"You don't think I'm too thin? You don't think I feel like a boy?" I tried to reply, but my chest was too small for the breath I needed. "Do you feel it?" she whispered. "Do you feel how wet I am?" Her fingers, urgent on the buttons of my shirt, slipped in cool patterns over my chest. "Do you really like my hair?"

The bright blonde was unruly even in the darkness, but under my hand a wispier coat of indeterminate color and immeasurable softness, was growing slick and richly fragrant. "I do," I said. "I love it."

"Oh god," she murmured breathlessly. "What are we going to tell Henry?"

I felt the words lodge themselves like an icy knot in the pit of my stomach. But my hand, wedged hotly between her thighs, paid no attention at all. I felt despicable. What kind of a man steals his own father's girlfriend? But even as the thought emerged, it held a thin silver glint of satisfaction.

The slamming of a car door came to me from a long way off, a different world altogether. I glanced up with a kind of vague bewilderment and noticed a yellow cab at the foot of the drive way.

"Wait," I whispered. "Wait!" And even I didn't know if I was talking to Mona or the cab driver or to the whole wildly unspooling set of circumstances. But it had no effect. And before my horrified eyes the taxi eased from the curb and sped away down the street with Jean Tipton nestled in the back.

Mona drove home cursing and seething in the darkness, as I sat marveling at how innocence is protected and how the forces of the world continue to look out for Henry Bailey.

"God damn it!" she shouted. "Are you sure it was her?"

"I caught a glimpse."

"Was she laughing?"

"She wasn't laughing," I said. "She didn't even see us."

"Jesus Christ! What the hell were you doing? You were supposed to be watching. It was a goddam stake-out! You were supposed to keep your eyes open!"

"My eyes were open!"

"Jesus Christ!" Her cheeks were flushed with a mixture of fury, embarrassment, and the hot, banked wattage of those long moments come to nothing. We jerked to a stop in front of her apartment, and she cut the ignition as if twisting off its little head. "I should know not to work with a goddam amateur!"

"Well, at least I saw her!"

"Oh, great," Mona snorted. "And then what? Wait, wait? No shit, Sherlock. Did you think she was just going to pull over and give you a chance to pull your pants up."

"My pants were up," I said grimly.

"Well, fuck you, too!"

She scrambled out of the car, slamming the door as if she wanted to weld it shut, and stalked into the building, leaving me fuming, enraged. And something else.

I thought of Henry at home lying peacefully in bed, and I was aware, beneath the rush of anger and desire, of a little whisper of relief. Cool and gleaming, it startled me, but there it was. I'd been saved from despicability, drawn back from the edge. And sitting there in the wake of Mona's swirling departure, I thought about my choices—even then I had choices. This would be the time to leave, when I could still look my father, if not exactly in the eye, then at least in the general direction of his face.

But once, when I was in junior high, I stole a roll of magnesium from a science class, and lit one end, just to see what would happen. It burned like a white-hot fuse until the flame reached the roll itself, and then it rose to something else altogether. The glare and the heat were like some localized disaster, burning as if about to set the air itself on fire, while I stared in fascination at something so far out of control. Mona's anger was like that. I had felt so muted for so long, when what I wanted to do was

kick something, break something. I wanted to howl like a ban-
shee. But I'd done nothing at all. And now here was Mona, burning furiously. I wanted to warm my hands against it. But more
than that. In that one moment she seemed the spark I needed to
set my life alight.

I climbed the stairs and found her pacing the living room,
looking for just the right thing to smash. But there was nothing
sufficiently fragile. She snatched a big square cushion from the
sofa and threw it against the base of the easy chair and started
kicking it furiously, her face clenched and fierce. "God damn it.
God damn it! She was laughing at us!"

"She wasn't laughing."

"She was jerking us around!"

"She didn't even know we were there," I said.

"You don't know that."

"Yes, I do."

She snatched up the pillow and turned, glaring at me,
hunched and fervid. "What are you smiling at?"

"I'm not smiling."

"It's your goddam fault! You think this ever happened to me
before?"

"You tell me."

"Never. Not one goddam time!"

"You never got distracted before?"

"No! I do my goddam job--"

"Not even with Carlisle?"

"No! Jesus Christ--""

"Did you ever take Henry on something like this?"

"Of course not!"

"Good." I grabbed the pillow and yanked it out of her hands.
She stared, startled for an instant, then she rushed me, swinging
her fists, punching furiously at the pillow in my hands. Even
through the foam it hurt. "Hey! Cut it out!"

"Make me!" She punched me again.

I swung the pillow, huge and unwieldy. It bounced off her

shoulder, knocking her back against the chair. She wrestled herself upright, glaring fiercely, her glasses balanced crookedly near the end of her nose. "You want to fight? Is that it? You want to fight me?"

I dropped the cushion and grabbed her. She was hot and squirming, all sharp bones and muscles, but I held her tight, as she glared up at me over the crooked rims of her glasses. "What?" she panted. "You're chicken now? You had enough?"

I kissed her, feeling the hard surprise of her teeth give way to a furious struggle of lips and tongues. I was snatching at the hem of her shirt, dragging it up until her arms were momentarily pinned above her head. Then the shirt swept off, taking her glasses with it. It caught around her head, sweeping her hair back for a sudden, frozen instant, before releasing it in an angry tangle. Then her face was pinched and breathless, and my hands were climbing the narrow fret board of her ribs to the startling softness of her breasts. She shoved me away, then reached down and tugged at her waistband, fumbling the zipper down, as I snatched at my own clothes, trying to keep pace. Her pants wilted away from thin, pale legs. Then she bent and peeled down her panties, a dark and surprising shade of green, until they stretched like a cat's cradle around her ankles. But when she tried to step out, her shoes caught in the tangle and she started to fall.

I caught at her waist, not steadying so much as following her down, and we toppled onto the sofa. Somehow she kicked free of her shoes, wrapping her legs fiercely around me, and I clutched at her, as if all either of us could do now was just hold on.

23

The sun was rising as I walked home. The carpet burns on my knees chafed against the rough fabric of my jeans, and the spot at the base of my spine, where I had rubbed a patch of skin the size of a quarter down to blood without noticing, throbbed faintly. Though later, when I took a shower it would feel as if my skin were on fire, as if it had been sanded off, so that Mona's scent rising through the steam, still clinging despite the soap, would be tied in my mind not to the silky feel of her, which was even then starting to fade from my most immediate memory, but to those little flowers of pain, and all I'd be left with in the end, as I stood drying myself alone in the silent house, would be the smell of Dial soap and the ache of scraped skin that together seemed an apt correlative of my hot, encroaching guilt.

But now as I walked through the early morning, the scent of her on my hands was the only thing real. The gray light was fluid and insubstantial, and the darkness itself couldn't hold its shape. Even the events of an hour earlier were only a melting impression, though as I walked I tried to hold onto the physical sensations: her skin, the velvety, yielding warmth. The sound of her breath, caught in a moment's surprise at the back of her throat, then released with the added freight of a low and raspy moan. I tried to hold onto it all even as it slipped away with every step until, when I started up the walk to the house, with the sky already awash with silver and pink, I might have been returning from a dream.

The truck was there, stolid and white, with the squat box of the cargo cover like an abandoned cabin on the back. I slipped past, smooth as a burglar, and started down the walk, then stuttered to a stop. The lights of the kitchen burned bright. My late

night had rolled right over into Henry's early morning. And as
I stood there, appalled, I thought, Turn around. Retreat! Get the
hell out of here! But I couldn't seem to move, and an instant later I was still poised like a deer in the headlights when the back
door opened and there stood Henry in a red-and-white striped
apron, raising his coffee mug in cheerful salute.

"So you finally decided to come home. Where have you been?
I was worried sick."

He didn't look worried sick. He was grinning and holding
the door open, welcoming home the prodigal son. I tried to recall the biblical story, wondering what exactly the prodigal had
returned from. Something disappointing, no doubt. Didn't he
squander all his money, shame himself, disgrace himself in the
eyes of the world, and yet still his father killed the fatted calf? I
wondered what the father in the bible would have done under
these circumstances. Squandering your money and disgracing
yourself in the eyes of the world seemed small change, considering. I stepped reluctantly into the kitchen. The aroma of fresh
coffee filled the house, the smell of bacon. But still Mona's scent
was so strong on my skin it didn't seem possible he'd miss it. As
casually as I could I slipped my hands into my pockets. "I hope
you didn't wait up."

"Sorry," Henry said cheerfully. "I thought you were in bed
till I saw you coming up the walk. Does that make me a terrible
father?"

"Maybe not terrible."

"How about some breakfast?" he said. "You must have
worked up an appetite." He let the screen door close and turned
back to the stove. "Got some bacon. Some scrambled eggs. A
little toast. What do you say?"

"You go ahead."

"Don't tell me you're not hungry?"

And I realized with a kind of appalled fascination that despite everything, despite the guilt and the gnawing realization
of the depths of my betrayal, I was starving. "Actually…."

"That's the spirit." Henry opened the fridge, removed the foil-wrapped bacon, and laid three more strips into the pan. "How many eggs?"

"How many are left?"

"Three it is," said Henry. He cracked them into a bowl that already held a swirl of beaten eggs. "You really worked up an appetite."

I swallowed. "Long night at the bar."

"Did I ask? I did not. I'm certainly not one to pry." He began to beat the eggs into a frazzle, then glanced up, smiling impishly.

"Well," I said, "maybe not all at the bar."

"Who was she?"

"Just a friend. Well, a friend of a friend, actually."

"A little more than a friend," Henry laughed, "judging from the look of you."

I blushed, suddenly breathless at the thought of what might be written across my face, and with a weak smile I sidled over to the sink. There was no hand soap so I squirted a generous pool of Joy onto my hands and scrubbed them until they were raw and lemon-scented.

"So," Henry asked, "where'd you go?"

"We ended up back at her place...." I hesitated, disconcerted by a twinge of something that was almost satisfaction, even a little glimmer of pride. I must, I realized, be a truly terrible person, but in some strange way, this was the closest thing to a genuine father-son talk we had ever had. A sort of My Three Sons moment: coming home from a date and checking in with the old man for a little paternal advice. I'd never done it before, and I realized now that despite the guilt and the queasy, expanding awareness of all that I had done, I was pleased after all these years to have something to tell. "It was nice. A little unexpected. It wasn't something I had planned."

Henry's face puckered into a gruff approximation of parental concern. "I hope... you know... you used sensible... precautions."

I smiled bleakly, touched by the awkwardness and concern.

"I'm nothing if not sensible."

"Is she nice?"

Nice? I thought.

In our slow progress from sofa to bed, conducted like a desert caravan pausing to drink at oases along the way, she stood bent over the end of the desk, over the clutter of papers and folders and a few cold, scattered paper clips, as I smoothed my palms over the curve of her ass, and letting my thumbs glide down the narrow cleft as if shaping it from clay, I eased her thighs apart. She was tensed like a runner in the blocks, knees bent, her cheek pressed to the cool steel surface as I traced my way down to the hot and yielding revelation of her, and with infinite slowness eased myself in, feeling her flesh give way, then enfold me, all enveloping warmth and velvet, as her voice rose up to me on the silence, a low suspiring breath of half-surprise.

"Yes," I said, my chest tight even at the memory. "She's nice. I think you'd like her." And I marveled that some raging thunderbolt didn't simply strike me dead.

Henry busied himself with breakfast as I dried my hands and took an empty mug from the cupboard. In the warmth of the kitchen the night's fatigue was catching up. I lifted the coffee pot. "You want some?"

"I'm good."

I poured myself a cup. I was trying to act normally, but it took all my concentration to remember what that was. You pour the coffee. You put the pot back. You drink it. You smile. You say, "So, what did you do last night?"

My father shrugged. "Just stayed home. I tried to give Mona a call. Just a last minute thing. I thought it might be fun. Practice a few of those dance steps. But she wasn't home. She said she might be working." He offered me a confiding smile. "That's the thing with these private detectives. Always sneaking around."

I drank my coffee, without milk or sugar, bitter and black because that's what I deserved.

We ate at the table in our usual places. Henry seemed pleased to have me there, and he ate slowly, lingering over each bite. I couldn't really taste anything, but I tried to match his pace. I didn't want to seem too rushed or too slow. I tried to remember what a clear conscience felt like. "This is nice," he said.

"Yeah."

"I'm glad. About last night, I mean." He was suddenly shy. "It's none of my business. I know that. And I want you to know that I know that."

"I get it, Henry. Thanks."

"I've been a little worried about you. Oh," he laughed self-consciously. "Not worried, exactly. I know what a good kid you are. Strong and solid. Dependable. But you've been through a lot. And you've been looking out for me. Don't think I don't know that, too."

I was having trouble with the eggs. They were perfectly cooked, tender and moist, but I found suddenly that my throat felt too tight to swallow. "It's okay," I said. "No charge."

"Anyway, I just wanted you to know that I know…." Henry laughed again at his awkwardness and shrugged it away. "That you deserved better."

All I could manage was a gruesome smile. I was wondering what it was exactly I did deserve, and hoping I never got it. I took another bite and forced myself to chew.

"It's funny, isn't it?" Henry was smiling more faintly now.

"Funny?"

"All of this stuff. Dating. The whole business. You sort of forget how to do it."

"Yeah."

"I just want you to know," he said, "if you ever want to talk about it, about anything, I'm here. "

"Good to know."

"After all, we're sort of in the same boat." And with sudden cheer he raised his mug in salute. "Here's to it. A little romance never hurt anyone."

Could that possibly be true? I thought. I raised my mug in

reply. "Here's hoping."

When my father went off to work I went to bed and slept uneasily. I kept having terrible dreams about how happy Henry was to see me. I woke around ten when the telephone rang and then again about noon and two. Each time I let it ring. At three-thirty I got up, showered, daubed ointment on my knees and back, and dressed. There were three messages from Mona on the answering machine. Hurriedly I erased them like a criminal disposing of the evidence.

I was making dinner when the doorbell rang. I tried not to jump. I'd spent the afternoon out of the house, trying to keep busy, to keep moving, trying to figure out what I was going to do. It seemed impossible to see Mona again. How could I? I was having trouble even imagining what it would do to Henry. Here he was, happier than I'd seen him in six years, happier than I ever thought I'd see him again. And I was going to destroy that? I had to do something to make it up to him, without ever, ever letting him know what had happened. I was thinking about the old days, when you could simply join the Foreign Legion and die nobly in the desert. But there were no options like that now. Nothing so simple. And when the doorbell rang, all I could do was stand with my hands in a bowl of cold hamburger and nowhere to run.

I called, "You want to get that?" But Henry didn't reply. He'd gone up to take a shower half an hour earlier and had vanished completely. The doorbell rang again. I washed my hands and dried them carefully, praying all the while, please let it be a Jehovah's Witness.

It was Mona. She wore black tights, a short blue skirt, and a green polyester blouse decorated in what looked like little exclamation marks. It hung open over a leopard print tank top. Her hair was smoothed back under a bright green hair band, and her glasses looked like a burglar's mask. She regarded me coolly, though there was a hint of what, in someone else, might have been shyness in her eyes. "I wasn't sure you'd be home," she said. And, glancing at the apron, "Isn't it supposed to say Kiss the Chef?"

I smiled weakly. "I'm making meatloaf."

"I've heard of that." Her tone was cool now. "Is Henry around?"

"Somewhere. I think he's taking a shower, but he may have fallen asleep."

"Busy day?"

"Oh, you know Henry."

"I meant you." She lowered her voice. "Where did you go last night?"

"It was this morning."

"So?"

"I thought I should be getting home."

"Just like that?"

I shrugged awkwardly, my face burning.

"I thought you might call," she said. "Sometime. Did you get my messages?"

"I did. I was going to. But things got kind of hectic…and I had a lot on my mind."

Her expression grew even cooler. "Yeah. Whatever."

I hesitated, then slowly leaned forward. "Don't get anything on my shirt," she warned. And then she stood with a distant and speculative expression as I kissed her very softly on the lips. "And that was what, exactly?" she asked.

"I don't know. I could do it again."

"You do what you want," she said indifferently.

I leaned in again. Her lips were soft and dry as a flower, stirring a little under mine. Upstairs the floor creaked, and I drew back guiltily, aware of Henry just a step and a gasp away.

"I read somewhere that there are men who even send flowers the next day," said Mona.

"I'm sorry. I should have."

She shrugged and looked bored. "I'm thinking about getting

my eyebrow pierced."

"Don't do that."

"I'm not asking."

I eased her glasses down and kissed the pale and delicate arch of the unpierced eyebrow, feeling the narrow apostrophe of hair smooth beneath my lips.

Mona started to speak, but swallowed instead. "Cut it out."

I kissed the other one. "I'd have thought your eyebrows were perfect just the way they are."

"And what did that cost you?" She scowled up at me. "You couldn't even call?"

There was another creak overhead and Henry's voice drifted down. "Who's there? Is that Mona?"

I turned hurriedly. "It's just the gas man."

But Mona leaned forward and yelled up the stairs, "Hey, Henry. Shake a leg. I've got the meter running."

He bent at the top of the stairs, peering down. "You're early," he called.

"I'm ten minutes late. But you're nice not to notice."

"I'll just be a sec," he said, and vanished back into the bathroom.

I stared down at Mona with sagging surprise. "You're going out with Henry?"

"Yeah. Didn't he tell you? A little dinner. A little dancing."

"He didn't mention it."

"Well, you know," she said drily. "He probably had a busy day."

I stood there for a long and speechless moment, then shook my head. "Why?"

"Why what?"

"You're going out with him."

"Is that a question?"

"Mona...?"

"Because he called and asked me, that's why."

She was gazing coolly up at me, as if there were nothing in

the least complicated or unexpected about the news, and I felt a sort of slipping uncertainty, like that first instant of a banana peel beneath your shoe when you feel it begin to move. "That's why you came over?"

"Henry wanted me to drive. He said he wanted to leave you the truck. He seemed to think you might have big plans tonight."

"I thought I might, too."

"Then maybe you should have called."

"Maybe I should have."

"He said you've been getting out a little. Having some fun. He said it was good for you."

"Is that what he said?"

She was smiling grimly. "I told him, if you were making any plans, you hadn't told me about them."

"I said I was sorry."

"No, you didn't."

Actually, I couldn't remember whether I had or not, but I was starting to get angry now, with a bitter blossoming mixture of guilt and disappointment. Mona gazed at me without expression. "I don't know how late we're going to be," she said.

"Yeah, well. You wouldn't want to keep Henry up past his bedtime."

She frowned. "Don't be a jerk," she whispered. "Please?"

I tried to swallow, but my mouth was dry. "I'm sorry. It's just... I've been trying to figure things out. I should have called, but I didn't."

"I was just thinking." Her voice was still a whisper. She threw a quick glance past me up the stairs, but there was no sign of Henry. "If we're back early, I could maybe give you a call."

I stared. "If you're back ...?"

"It was just a thought."

The faint, mortifying glimpse of her pity struck a hot spark of cruelty from my heart. "A twofer? You are energetic."

"Don't."

"Thanks anyway," I said. "I'm going to be busy. Didn't Henry tell you? I've got plans."

With a clatter of footsteps and a cheerful little whistle under his breath Henry bustled down the stairs. He wore a black t-shirt, black chinos, and the white dinner jacket.

"Jesus Christ," I said. "You look like Ricky Ricardo."

"Thank you, thank you. I'll be here all week."

"Is that my t-shirt?"

My father grinned. "And your pants. But the shoes," he said, "are mine. Ready to roll, toots?"

He extended his arm to Mona, and she took it stiffly, with a glance at me that would have taken paint off a wall.

"We're leaving you the truck," said Henry.

"You make it sound like a bequest."

He smiled, "Have fun tonight. As I'm sure you will." And with a little bow he shepherded Mona down the steps to her rented car. They looked completely mismatched, one elegant in black and white, the other colorfully discordant, but the way Henry walked, leaning in and whispering, it was clear he hadn't the slightest idea how little they belonged together.

24

The next morning my father was standing in the garden as a couple of deliverymen unloaded a wooden pergola he'd bought as a kit from the Pleasant Valley Garden Shop. He looked pleased and excited. The kit arrived in neat bundles of two-by-fours, orderly and self-explanatory, but as the men departed and Henry set to work, the boards gave up any sense of logic. He laid them out in a complex acrostic of joints and angles, trying to line up the pre-drilled holes, trying to arrange the whole structure flat on the ground as if he could build it in two dimensions and then just inflate it. But every time he moved one piece he shifted another, knocking it all out of kilter, so he ended up rushing from board to board like a man demented, trying to work both ends of a see-saw.

What did he think he was doing? Couldn't he lay his hand to something even as simple as this without letting it billow out of control? Everything he touched grew more complicated, and he didn't even know it. He went cheerfully about his business, tugging at one board, shimmying another, blithely unaware of the splayed and appalling tangle that surrounded him. I tried to feel angry. I wanted only to feel angry. But there was something about his earnest and feckless fumbling that left me mired in confusion, as if I were implicated in every fault and mis-step. Every error he made drew me in. The scattered lumber was like an emblem of our lives, tangled beyond recovery, and it tied me with a knot of guilt and despair that Henry had no clue.

"Almost got it," he said. But the boards slipped again, and with a shake of his head he straightened, wiping the sweat from his face. "You feel like giving me a hand?"

"No, thanks."

"It'd be a whole lot easier with two."

"You're doing fine on your own."

"It'll just take a minute."

"It's your goddam pergola, Henry! You build it!"

A startled look blossomed on his face, the look of a puppy who'd expected something better. "What's going on? Are you okay?"

"I'm fine. I'm great. I'm sorry. I just don't want to build your damn kit, that's all."

My father considered that for a moment, peering up at me as if looking for something in particular. "How was your date last night?" he asked finally.

"I didn't have a date, okay? I decided to stay home. Some people just stay home, sometimes."

"I thought--"

"She canceled, all right?"

"Just like that?"

"Yeah," I said. "Just like that."

Henry was shaking his head with comradely sympathy. "I'm sorry. Did she give a reason?"

"As a matter of fact, she's seeing someone else."

"Oh, jeeze. I'm sorry."

He kept saying that. It made me furious. But here's the thing. It was oddly comforting, as well. And there was nothing I could say. He had no clue what was going on. He looked so concerned, so sympathetic. And I tried to hold onto the straight simplicity of my anger, as if it were something I'd earned, as if it were something I had a right to, but it was all growing cluttered and confused.

"So what are you going to do?" he asked.

"I don't know."

"You know what they say. Lots of other fish in the sea."

"Is that right?" I said tightly. "Is that what you've found?"

Henry stood for a moment in the middle of the lumber's hieroglyphic disarray. "As it happens," he said, "I may have something that could help. I've been saving it for a rainy day, but this'll do. Hold on." And with a shy, mysterious glance he hurried into the house and emerged a moment later holding a large, fat joint as if it were a discovery he'd been meaning to show me for some time.

"What the hell is that?"

He looked both proud and a little sheepish. "Don't tell me you've never seen one before."

"I've never seen you with one. Where'd you get it? Did Mona give it to you?"

"Ask me no questions, and I'll tell you no lies. But this should help what ails you."

I thought of all that ailed me in that moment. And I caught a sudden, unwelcome glimpse of Mona stoned with my father, draping herself across her desk or burrowing fiercely into the sofa. "I don't think that's going to help."

"Can't hurt. Come on." Henry drew a lighter cheerfully from his pocket. "Let's fire it up."

"What? Now? Here?" And before I could stop myself I cast a nervous glance around the empty yard. "You can't just light up a joint in the middle of the day."

"Who's going to see? Come on. Live dangerously."

But I couldn't. And I realized in that moment, with appalling clarity, that all my tangled feelings of guilt and anger were only the least of my problems, and that everything I'd been most afraid of had finally come to pass. Beneath the shifting, alchemical forces of personality and circumstance I had somehow become my father. But what had happened to Henry?

In the bright, ordinary sunlight, with the faint sounds of some distant marching band floating on the breeze, he set fire to the jumbo doobie and, frowning down at the glowing tip, sucked up smoke as if breathing through a narrow straw. "You've got to hold onto it," he gasped, and patted his chest. "Deep as you can."

I had stopped getting high a few years ago when I realized

all it produced was an uncertain mixture of paranoia, sadness, and inexpressible rage that left me wound up like one of those little string toys, rushing to the edge of the table just to stop there seething at the brink. But my father was grinning, holding out the joint like a dare. I shook my head.

"Come on. It'll help."

"How long has this been going on?"

He laughed ruefully, picking a stray bit of stem from his tongue. "Not all that long. I decided I needed to branch out a little. Expand my horizons." He drew in another lungful of smoke, squinting in concentration. "How about this? Did you ever think we'd be sitting around getting high together?"

"I can honestly say I never did."

He took another drag, then held the joint at arm's length, gazing meditatively at the rising thread of smoke. "See? Don't things look less complicated now?"

"Less complicated than what?"

"Wait," he said. "You have to see this." And he drew from beneath a two-by-four the single sheet of directions that had come with the kit. "Here. Take a look at this. Isn't it a riot?"

There were no words. There was only an exploded diagram of boards and bolts, with little dotted trajectories and an implicit assurance that it was all so simple it didn't even need to be broken into steps. But the more I looked the less stable the lines became, moving like synchronized swimmers across the page.

But Henry seemed unfazed. "Let's start here...." He pointed at random to a juncture of lines suggesting a particularly fiendish freeway intersection. "...and work our way out."

"That's the top," I said peevishly. "What do we do? Just hope it floats in the air until we find the uprights?"

"Okay," he said reasonably enough. "We'll start at the bottom." He knelt amid the tangled boards and pulled two ends together. "Hand me a bolt, why don't you?"

I scowled down at him. "What? You just choose any two? Just like that?" I could hear the anger in my voice, out of all proportion.

"You've got to start somewhere."

"You've got two cross pieces! You need an upright."

"This is an upright."

"God damn it! This is an upright." I kicked at another board, knocking it against his leg.

"Easy, there."

"Jesus Christ, Henry!" I snapped. "You don't know what the hell you're doing!"

I stopped, frozen and chagrined. Some clearer part of my brain knew it wasn't fair. But what did I want? To see my father as angry as I was, or just to coax enough of an argument out of him to justify all I'd done?

Henry knelt there on the stone patio staring down at the boards in his hands, joined now by nothing more than the empty holes lined up between them. "What's this about?" he asked. "It's not about this girl, is it? Or about Mona?"

"It's not about anything."

He let the boards drop and after a moment's indecision picked the remainder of the joint up from the table edge. He got the lighter going and took a deep, rough lungful of smoke, but it didn't seem to be doing as much for him this time, and he blew it out like so much gray despair. "How long," he said, "does a man have to drag his mistakes around, do you think?"

I hesitated, taken aback. "What do you mean?"

"How long before you can just put them behind you?"

The years of sadness lay in every word, but I couldn't bear to sympathize. I hadn't asked for this. I hadn't asked for any of it. I clutched the anger to my heart. "It depends," I said, "on the mistake."

"A really big mistake."

"I don't know. A long time."

My father nodded slowly, not so much in agreement but as if it were the answer he'd expected. "Do you believe in second chances?"

What was he asking me for? What did it matter what I believed?

"I didn't," he said. "I used to think we were made by our mistakes. That's who we were. There was no getting away from it,
and all the wishing in the world wouldn't change a thing." He
spoke as if he were all alone, a man trapped in his garden with
his thoughts. But after a moment he looked up. "What's your
worst mistake?"

I didn't even have to think, but all I said was, "I don't know."

"You're lucky." He flicked the roach out into the tangle of
plants. "Did you ever wonder if maybe there was just one person out there for you? Just one chance? Out of all those people
out there, just one? I used to think about that. One person, one
chance. It's hard enough actually finding her. I mean, you're
lucky enough if your paths even cross. But then, to find that person and screw it all up. What then?"

I thought about that. About how easy mistakes were to make.
How they snuck up on you with their own rough inevitability. "I
don't know," I said. "Maybe you're just screwed."

"But for how long?"

And I thought of the two of us, so tangled in each other's
mistakes it seemed we would never get clear. Forever, I thought.
Maybe you're screwed forever.

"But then what if you get a second chance?" he said. "Just out
of the blue? It isn't anything you do. It's not about deserving it.
But what if you get one? What if it just falls into your lap? Don't
you think you should take it? Don't you think you owe yourself
that much?"

But what about me? I thought. What do you owe me, after all
this time? What about my second chance? What about my first?

I swallowed hard. "I take it you had fun last night?"

"Oh, yeah." He smiled wanly.

"And Mona? Did she have fun?"

"She certainly seemed to."

"Did she say anything?"

"Mona? About what?"

"Just anything. About me?"

"She said you were a good dancer."

"Really?"

"Well. She said you weren't bad. You know Mona."

"Nothing more?"

"What should she say?"

"And you had fun?"

"Hell, yes. I'm turning into a social butterfly. Who'd have thought it?"

"Are you going out again?"

"Tonight. You want me to leave you the truck?"

"Where are you going?"

"A little dinner, a little dancing."

"You'll be going steady next."

I thought he'd smile again, but he just shook his head, marveling. "I think about all this. About Mona, about second chances. All of it. And I am so grateful. I can't tell you how much."

I watched him bleakly, the anger and sadness fused into a little nugget in my chest. "I guess maybe you should be," I said.

I grabbed my jacket from the house and hurried away down the alley. There wasn't anywhere I needed to be; just away from there. But after a few minutes I found myself doubling back, working my way down Lawrence Street, a block back from the alley, peering between the houses and the trees until I caught sight of Henry, standing on the patio, laying the boards around him. From a distance he looked small and unfamiliar, absorbed in his work. I watched him, and as I did I realized I had never looked at Henry from so far away before. In all these years, in my whole life with him, distant was the one thing I'd never felt.

What if there were only one person for each of us? What if we only got one chance? Or two? Was I screwed, then, forever? Did I owe Henry his happiness just because it could have been mine?

I could hear him whistling, hear the thump and scrape of

boards. He had made some progress. The kit was taking shape. It leaned like a crooked and vacant frame propped against the patio table. I thought of that picture Elizabeth had clipped out all those years ago: the beautiful iron pergola rising elegantly over that perfect English garden. Did Henry imagine this was anything like that? Did he even remember? It was hard to tell. But whether he remembered or not, there he was, working away in his own little world, bolting together the pieces of his own second chance.

What had Mona said? It's only when no one's watching that the truth comes out? The phone rang. He picked it up from the table. "Hello? Oh, hi." I could hear his voice warming, molding itself to Mona's voice on the other end. "Great," he said. "Of course I'm ready. It's going to be fun. A little dinner, a little dancing. That's right." He laughed. "Yeah, me, too. Seven o'clock. That's right. I'll see you tonight. I can't wait," he said. "What? Oh, I told him. Well, not exactly. But I'm sure he'll be fine with it. He's having a little girl trouble now, but he'll be fine. He's a big boy, he can look out for himself."

I watched him as he turned off the phone and set it down.

25

I knocked on her door and then, without waiting, knocked again. I held a bouquet of spring flowers clenched in a hot and clammy hand.

"Okay, okay." The door opened, and there she was. She wore a dark purple shirt and a short orange skirt that seemed to be having trouble getting along. She looked pale and serious, but when she saw me the tight knot of her expression loosened into something cool and wary. She glanced curiously at the flowers. "Well," she said.

"I've got to talk to you. I wanted to ask you something. I should have called, I know, but it was kind of last minute." As the nervous tone carried me in through the doorway I noticed the woman sitting in one of the easy chairs before the desk. It was no one I knew. Thick and middle-aged, with dark, graying hair and a drawn face, she looked angry and uncomfortable.

"I'm with a client," said Mona.

"I'm sorry. I didn't realize." I turned to the woman. "I'm sorry. I just need to interrupt. Just for a minute." I glanced back at Mona. "Please?"

She hesitated, weighing the magnitude of my anxiety against the more official worries of the woman inside, recalling as well, perhaps, the uneven tenor of our last encounter, but in the end, with a glance at the bouquet, she relented. "I'll just be a moment, Mrs. Grace." And she stepped out into the hall. "So?"

I clutched the flowers. "How did it go last night? With Henry?"

She looked startled. "That's what you wanted to ask?"

"No," I said. "Yes. Did you have fun?"

"What?"

"Last night."

"Yes."

"How much fun?"

She was frowning impatiently. "What's going on?"

My throat felt tight. My voice sounded breathless and foolish, even to myself, but I couldn't stop. "What did you do?"

"With Henry? We had dinner, I told you. What's wrong with you?"

I wasn't sure, but I'd have given a lot to know. "These are for you," I said and handed her the bouquet. The paper around the stems was damp and crumpled.

She took them with the first, faint beginnings of comprehension in her smile. "They're beautiful." She sniffed the flowers. They hadn't, as far as I could tell, any scent, but I may just not have noticed. "What's the occasion?"

"I wanted to apologize. About yesterday. I was a jerk."

"That's true," she said.

"I'm sorry. I'd like to make it up to you."

"What did you have in mind?"

I swallowed hard. "Have dinner with me. Tonight. Dinner and dancing."

"I can't. Not tonight."

"Please?" I said. "I have to see you."

She looked up at me, caught between warmth and curiosity, touched by my obvious derangement. "What if I've got things to do?"

"I don't care."

"What if I have other plans?"

"Cancel them. I want to make you dinner. Right here. We'll have dinner. We'll dance."

"Here?"

"Right here. Tonight. Seven o'clock."

"Not at seven," she said. "I can't."

"Please," I begged. "Here. Tonight. At seven."

She hesitated, then gently smiled, relenting in the face of my desperation. "Okay." She reached up and kissed me lightly on the lips. "Don't get your panties in a bunch. I'll change my plans."

"Good," I said. "That's good." I felt oddly breathless. "But just one thing," I added. "Don't tell Henry."

I didn't go home. I didn't want to see my father, and I didn't want to be there when she called him to cancel. I walked to the Eagle Market and bought pasta and cheese and tomatoes and mushrooms and parsley and wine, and carried them around. I felt homeless, locked out of the day's ordinary events. I kept thinking about Henry, how it would seem to him. And as I wandered around waiting for the time to pass, everything looked foreign and unfamiliar. I noticed the cracks in high brick walls mended with mortar, back alleys crowded with dumpsters and the odds and ends of displaced moments: a bent shopping cart, the wheel of a bicycle, a length of garden hose curled and flattened like roadkill against the stained concrete.

When I presented myself at her door just a little before seven, she let me in with a quick, wan smile. It looked as if she might have had some words with Henry, but I didn't ask. She was dressed in black, t-shirt and skirt, as if we were setting out to spy on someone. It gave the night a sly, clandestine feel, as if to demonstrate that even here behind closed doors we were sneaking around.

She had lit candles on her desk and on the coffee table, and the quivering light gave the office a prickly air of nervous expectation. "I don't really have a lot of pots and pans," she said.

"It's just pasta."

"I like pasta."

I had planned to saute the mushrooms and tomatoes, then add the cheese to melt before tossing the pasta. I'd planned to make a nice dinner. But my heart was pounding. Her glasses looked heavy and black; her hair too bright. With her pale face she seemed to stand behind them both, behind her clothes, like one of those thin paper dolls on which a variety of outfits could be hung or removed. "You look like a paper doll," I said.

"Is that good?"

I set down the groceries and removed her glasses. Then I grasped the hem of her shirt, and as she lifted her arms it slipped up and off like a cloud from the face of the moon. I felt powerful and slow. My hands were large against the meager curves of her body, the sharp shoulders, the springy declaration of her breasts. I could almost span her waist with my fingers. I wanted to ask her what she'd said to Henry, how she'd put him off. I wanted to ask if he'd ever had his hands just there, if this was something they had done. But as her fingers settled on the back of my neck, and the open skirt slipped down her alabaster hips, Henry slipped just as smoothly from my mind.

She lay back on the desktop, her body impossibly long, but slender now rather than thin. Shallow breasts, grown shallower still, lay crowned with pale pink. Her belly offered a slope of unblemished ivory except at the gentle, boney prominence of one hip, where a small dark blotch sharpened on closer examination into the cheerful likeness of Yosemite Sam, his thick mustache flowing, six-guns raised. I brushed my lips over the unsmearable ink, and the warm sound of her chuckle rose and then caught in her throat. In the candlelight a wedge of pale cinnamon hair glowed, so at odds with the shock of wild yellow above that it brought to mind the photograph of the young, red-haired girl who had long ago given way to Mona in all ways but this. "Young Jane," I whispered.

"What?" she said vaguely. "What was that?"

The mossy hair tickled my nose, and my tongue traced the hidden intricacies of flesh more pink than pale and growing pinker still. "You're so wet, Jane."

"I don't know who you mean." Her whisper was thin, breathless. "You must be talking to somebody else."

"Jane."

"Stop it."

"Jane Ann Biederman."

"Cut it out."

"You are so beautiful, Jane."

"Come up here and say that."

As I crept up the slope of her body, my stiff, unruly flesh found its own way, and the velvety warmth engulfed me like a thick and humid whisper.

"Oh!"

"Do you like that, Jane?"

"Slow," she breathed. "Go slow." Her hands were on my hips. "Like that," she said, in a voice like a feather. "Just like that."

My lips brushed her ear. "Is that what you like, Jane? Tell me what you want." I longed for her to cry out, but her voice dropped even lower. She was writhing silently beneath me, a graceful struggle, grinding herself urgently against me, if you could call it grinding when the flesh involved was so meltingly soft.

"Tell me, Jane," I whispered hoarsely. "Tell me you want me." I thrust harder, trying to surprise a gasp of pleasure. I needed to hear her voice, hear her whisper. I needed to hear my name on her lips, but she was swallowing her cries. "Do you want me to stop? Is that what you want?"

"No."

"Then tell me. Tell me you don't want me to stop."

But her voice hung the barest hint of a smile on the air. "You do what you want," she whispered. But her hands were gripping my hips. "Oh!" she gasped. "Like that. Yes! Just like that! Oh!" And she clutched me hard against her, legs clamped tight, as her voice caught me, dragging me along, emptying me, leaving me breathless and panting and conscious of our bodies so sweat-slick and hot there seemed no boundary between them.

I left just after one-thirty. I slipped out of bed, leaving her curled delicately like a shrimp who's slipped her shell for the night. For a moment I held the covers up, seeing, in the faint light from the bathroom door, the thin shoulder and the dip of her waist. I felt the pressure of a soft and woolly tenderness, and

I wondered if this could be what Henry felt, though I knew my father's feelings were simpler, more pure. Henry loved her for herself, while I, in some dark, unadmirable corner of my heart, loved her, not just for what she gave to me, but for what she didn't give to Henry.

Silently I dressed. Then I bent and tucked the covers around her. Even in sleep her face was pinched, as if her dreams annoyed her. I slipped out the door, closing it quietly, and hurried down the stairs, not wanting to run into anybody, not even a stranger. I walked home through the cool and empty evening, thinking about Henry, about his never finding out, never knowing. It would kill him to find out. We would just have to continue like this. It was the only thing to do. But he was bound to figure it out. And what if he did? I remembered his voice: He's a big boy, he can look out for himself.

At the sight of the kitchen lights still burning I slowed. The prospect of my father, having spent another night alone without knowing why, brushed its cold finger through my chest. Reluctantly I stepped inside. "Henry?" But there was no sound. The house was asleep, and the thought that Henry had headed off to bed, leaving the lights on to once more welcome the prodigal son was almost more than I could bear.

But in the dining room, I found the note and realized it wasn't consideration that had left the lights burning. I read it, standing at the table, then slowly and quietly, as if it might be a mistake, I climbed the stairs to my father's bedroom door and eased it open. In the darkness the bed was flat and undisturbed. The room was empty.

Numbly I re-read the note. It wasn't complicated. I don't know why I was having so much trouble. All it said was: *Out with Mona. Back late.*

26

The first rule of surveillance is to learn to think like your subject. You have to watch him so closely you can anticipate his every move—when he's going to turn or glance back, when he's about to stop. You need to take note of every detail so you can get inside his head, so you can figure out not only what he's doing but why. Which brings us to the second rule. You must never let him know he's being followed.

The next day after work I stood upstairs in the open door of the bathroom and watched my father shave. He frowned into the mirror, turning his face this way and that as he ran his fingertips over his jaw, pinching critically at the first soft suggestion of a double chin. Then he filled his fingers with a modest cream puff of foam and spread it in eager little dabs across his cheeks. He picked up the razor, then hesitated. "You need to use the bathroom?"

"No. That's okay."

"Is there something you want?"

"I'm just watching. You don't mind, do you?"

That morning I'd arrived at the store and found Henry whistling while he worked. He was waiting on a customer, a pretty, middle-aged woman with short brown hair and a wide mouth, and smiling as he totaled up her purchase. I had seen her around. She ran the jewelry store in the downtown mall, and she had stopped in any number of times for batteries, stamps, extension cords. I'd barely even noticed her. But she was chuckling now at something Henry had just said, and as she turned she gave her head a little flirtatious toss and sauntered out wearing a lingering smile that could have meant almost anything.

Who was it who said: There is no way to speak of things as they are; only things as we perceive them to be? For the rest of the day I would watch as women came and went, all ages and all shapes. Some of them familiar customers, others not. It was nothing unusual, just an average day.

It's only that I had never really paid them much attention before. I'd always known Henry was charming, but I had never considered where that charm might lead. But now I watched as a whole parade of women bought light bulbs and padlocks and envelopes and key chains and little bottles of whiteout: a series of small purchases they could surely have done without. I couldn't help myself. Each one seemed a study in ulterior motives. They joked and laughed and flirted, and as they left I searched their faces, looking for a hint of something wilder beneath the friendly smile. It could, I realized, be any one of them.

I set two coffees and a paper bag of muffins on the counter. Henry glanced up. "Two cups? You must have gotten in late last night."

"One's for you. Just in case you need it. "

He laughed. "You have no idea." His hand hovered over the two cups. "Cream, two sugars?"

"That one."

He picked it up gratefully and pealed off the cover. "I don't know how I ever gave this stuff up." He took a cheerful, noisy sip.

"You had a late night, yourself," I said.

"Too late." He shook his head ruefully. "Too late, too busy, and too much fun. I am way too old for this."

Though in fact he didn't look way too old. He looked healthy as a baby, all pink and relaxed. He opened the bag I'd brought. "One of these for me, too?"

"Blueberry or pumpkin."

"Pumpkin," he announced. "Definitely pumpkin." And he laughed. "Can you imagine? All of this?" He seemed to include everything: the coffee, the muffin, the night before. "It's like being a kid again. You know what I mean?"

"Yes," I said. "I think I do."

He grinned and took a bite, shaking his head at how unbelievable it all was. I'd never seen him quite this way. But I took in the little smile playing on his mouth, the bounce in his step as if a weight had been removed, and it all seemed perfectly clear. No doubt about it. Someone had gotten lucky last night.

So now I stood, leaning in the door frame of the bathroom. "This is the second time you're shaving today."

"Really?" Moving within a cloud of genial preoccupation, he ran one experimental finger over his cheek. "I must have lost count."

"You going out tonight?"

"Thought I might." He shaved in quick strokes along the underside of his chin, pulling the skin taut. The razor whispered little scraping sounds to itself, then it splashed like a small duckling when he rinsed it in the sink. I tried to notice it all, as if any one of these tiny details might offer some clue.

"A little dinner?" I asked. "A little dancing?"

"Maybe just dinner tonight."

"That should be fun. Is Mona picking you up?"

My father hesitated. "No," he said. "Not exactly."

My first reaction in the earliest hours of the morning had been a strange little blossoming of relief, like a fist loosening in my chest. I felt rescued, off the hook. Because if Henry was seeing someone else, if he was sleeping with someone else, then I was clearly not in danger of breaking his heart.

But then I felt a little rustle of irritation. In that innermost chamber of the heart, unswayed by reason or guilt or commonsense, his little note made me angry. I mean, what did he think he was doing? What if Mona found out? Here he had this second chance. With a woman younger, hipper, and way cooler than he deserved. And he was cheating on her? I wanted to tell him, you can't treat people that way. You're going to hurt her feelings. You're going to lose her. You're going to screw up all over again.

I know. It wasn't as if I didn't recognize the moral flaws in my own position. But God damn it! Henry didn't know that. As far as he knew, he had a second chance with Mona, and he was blowing it all because he wanted to sow some wild oats.

Now he rinsed off the last of the lather and patted his chin dry. "So," I said, "will you be taking the truck?"

"I thought I might. If you don't have any plans for it."

"No. That's okay. Thanks. Are you leaving soon?"

"Pretty soon."

"Well," I said. "I'm going to head off then. Don't do anything I wouldn't do."

He glanced up into the mirror at me. "Are you going to work?"

"Not tonight."

My father grinned. "Attaboy. Big plans?"

"Hell, yes."

The truck was an old model Ford with a square cargo cover like a little shanty on its back. It was always fairly messy, full of old tools and boxes of nails and racks of copper tubing, but tonight it was as crowded as the inside of a watch. I raised the back hatch and squeezed in between a high, red tool chest and a cardboard spool of television cable. Half-hunched, trying to remove the handle of a wrench from the small of my back, I heard a distant slam from the kitchen. I sat very still. There was a long silence into which the rising sound of whistling gradually intruded, then the squeak of the driver's door was sudden and loud. Henry climbed in. He started the engine, slammed his door. And with a lurch that set the whole truck rattling, we took off.

I crouched, bracing myself awkwardly against the creaking sway. Above the noise and syncopated rattle of everything around me I could just make out, like the flightpath of a butterfly, the thin whistling tune that ran through Henry's head and spilled out onto the air. I tried to track our route by the turns we made and the passing glow of stop lights through the dusty windows, but there was no order to the movement, and after a few minutes I just gave up.

Instead, as I rode, I tried to imagine what Henry was thinking, what was going through his mind as he rattled along. Maybe it wasn't that much of a mystery. The nature of love remained that one incommunicable puzzle that we all held in common. And even as I crouched there, one more piece of the random baggage he was dragging to his rendezvous, I was aware, beneath my irritation and curiosity, of a warm companionable feeling. After all, how different were we? Just two more men bound together by hope and desperation. And huddled within the creak and sway of Henry's hurtling momentum, I saw how little love resembled anything but itself. You conjured it up from the depths of pure longing, but somehow, despite the best intentions, it ended up feeling like a crime you carried out against your own heart or someone else's.

When we finally lurched to a stop, the whole truck gathered itself into stillness. Henry's door opened. He climbed out and slammed it shut. I waited in silence for the space of one long breath, then crept to a window and peered out. The glass was caked with dust, and I could barely make out a little line of shops under the glare of the streetlights. But as I pressed close to peer out, there came the sudden scrape of a key in the lock, and I flung myself back, landing crookedly against half a roll of carpet, as Henry climbed into the driver's seat. He started up the engine. Craning my neck I could make out the back of his head about four feet away and the green paper cone of flowers that he sniffed appreciatively then set down on the passenger seat.

He began singing. It was low and under his breath, but the voice carried back to me above the enveloping creak and rattle. "Dum da da mood for love. Simply because you're near me. Dum da da dum you're near me…," until the truck hit a series of potholes that drowned out all the rest.

This time when we pulled to stop I stayed right where I was. Henry was pulling himself together, smoothing his hair, brushing at his jacket. Then he reached for the flowers like a nervous conductor for his baton and climbed out of the truck.

I waited. I heard low murmurous voices, distant and indistinct. After a moment they wandered away, and there was only the steady sound of traffic. I counted to thirty. And again. Then, easing forward, I crept to the window and peered out. I was in a nearly empty parking lot in a little u-shaped courtyard below a lurid pink sign that said Tiki Motel. The building itself looked anything but tropical. It was low and dark, like a short train of brown boxcars abandoned on a siding. There was no movement. The traffic noise came from an overpass, spanning the road like an aqueduct half a block away. I crept to the back and climbed out.

There was not a sign of anyone. It was maybe eight o'clock. All but three of the units were dark. I glanced around. There was a gas station across the street, a used car lot on the other side, and darkness in between. I thought, how do you lose someone so quickly?

Hesitantly I crossed the courtyard. The curtain on the first lighted window was drawn, and the air conditioner was wheezing away at full gallop, but over the noise I could make out the sound of some game show on the television, the rising murmur of laughter and applause. I didn't suppose even Henry would have come all this way to watch TV, so I sidled up to the second. Through a narrow gap in the curtains, I could see a man in a rumpled suit perched on the end of his bed beside a white plastic ice bucket, sipping something from a motel cup. What might have been the same soundtrack rose indistinctly. Perhaps they only got the one station. The third unit was empty and silent.

I stood for a long moment, stiff and uneasy, trying to imagine what Mona would do. I turned back toward the first building.

The motel office was more cheerful than anyone had any right to expect. The walls were bright orange, and an inflatable palm tree hung from the ceiling. A plump young man sat at the counter with a college textbook open before him, while in the background Wheel of Fortune was playing on the television.

"I wonder if you could help me," I said. "I'm looking for a man named Bailey. He's run away from home again. He really shouldn't be out on his own. Sometimes he checks into a motel and just drinks himself into a stupor. It's very hard on the family."

The young man looked up unmoved, as if it were a story he'd heard before. "Are you the cops?"

"In a manner of speaking. I'm a private detective."

"Yeah?" He looked me over with momentary interest, but in the end seemed disappointed. "I can't tell you anything."

"But I haven't asked, yet."

"We can't give out the names of our guests."

"No, see. I just told you his name."

"I can't help you."

"But what if he's in trouble? Think of his family."

"Sorry. It's a rule."

"Listen. I can appreciate that. God knows, we need rules. Where would...," I glanced a little wildly at his book, "Where would accountants be without rules? But this... It's really important. How about if I make it worth your while?" At that he glanced up with the first suggestion of genuine attention, but when I pulled out my wallet I realized I had only seven dollars to my name. "Actually. Would you take a check?"

He regarded me with the look of one whose plentiful store of God-given patience has been unfairly tried. "How about this?" he said. "If you want a room, rent one. Otherwise I'm calling the cops."

"Did you at least see him?" I said. "He was right out there. He pulled up in a truck. He was carrying flowers..."

"Hey," he said. "Do you know anything about double entry

bookkeeping?"

I hesitated. "No."

"Neither do I. And I have a mid-term tomorrow."

27

When I called, Mona sounded as pleased as could be expected. "What the hell is your problem?"

"Are you busy?"

"You know, you could call earlier. Many people do. It's called 'making a date'."

"Have you had dinner?"

"Yes. In fact I'm having it right now."

"Are you watching Wheel of Fortune?"

"No."

"What are you wearing?"

Her voice hung on the line for an uncertain moment. "Are you drunk?"

"Not yet. Can I come over?"

There were candles burning and jazz on the stereo. She wore the dress I'd first seen her in all those weeks ago, the pink uniform with the black campaign ribbons. It was even shorter than I remembered, and her thin legs descended to a pair of heavy black shoes that looked like some kind of podiatric bondage gear, but which, I had enough sense to realize, were brand new. Somehow the mass of them provided a reassuring balance to the heavy frames of her glasses, like two poles of a compass anchoring the pale slenderness of the body between. "Nice shoes."

She was frowning in concern. My clothes were rumpled and grimy from the truck. A bottle of merlot was clutched hopefully in my hand. "You look awful," she said.

"You don't."

It took a moment for her to weigh that, as if wanting to be sure she hadn't misunderstood. Then she stepped up in her heavy dominatrix shoes and kissed me. "What have you been doing? Cleaning out somebody's attic?" She brushed at my shoulder in a small, proprietary gesture that was a comfort all by itself.

"I should have called you," I said.

"That's okay. I'm getting used to it."

"What did you do today?"

She shrugged. "A few odds and ends. I stopped by Jean Tipton's house, but there was no sign of her. I left a few messages. Not a great day. How about you?"

"Not great," I agreed.

It seemed such a lackluster conversation, but somehow its very dullness, the slow quotidian kindness and familiarity, soothed me. We stood together, tired and still, as if this were the most natural thing in the world, lingering in the candlelight talking about the day, as if, despite ourselves, we had won through to this little bit of calm. I raised the bottle. "I brought some dinner."

"Let me open that." She lifted it from my hand. "You should sit down. You look beat."

But when she emerged with the wine, not Fred and Wilma this time, but two new and elegant wineglasses held carefully by their stems, I was still standing. She looked beautiful and thoughtful and somehow more serious, as if the thin and fragile goblets suggested some new stage between us that was itself no less delicate. It was comforting, but somehow—like all forms of comfort lately—it unnerved me. "Why do people hire you? I mean, when they want you to follow someone, what are they looking for? What do they expect?"

"I don't know. Different things. Reassurance, maybe. Sometimes they come with suspicion, and all they really want is to be proved wrong." She handed me a glass. "Other times, they just want to know that they're not being made a fool of."

"And when they find out they are? What do they do?"

She shrugged. "About what you'd expect. Divorce, most of the time. But sometimes not. Sometimes they don't do anything at all."

"Nothing?"

"That's the worst. They care too much to leave, and too much about what's happened to ignore it. They end up stuck between love and resentment. You want to tell them just to clear out. Cut their losses. But that's always easy to say. In the end, it just depends what they want."

I wondered about that, about reassurance and the bonds of resentment. And I wondered what it was, exactly, that I wanted. "Did you tell Henry about us?"

"No." She glanced up. "Did you want me to? I sort of thought you didn't."

Her calm surprised me. She seemed open and easy, untroubled by the lurking guilt that had woven its way into every twist and turn of my thoughts. "I don't know. How do you think he'd take it?"

"He's pretty understanding. I think he'd be all right."

I hesitated. "How about you?"

"Me?"

"If Henry were seeing someone else. Would you want to ignore it or would you want to know?"

I had expected a number of different reactions, but this one least among them all. She smiled. "That's a little hypothetical, isn't it?"

"What if it weren't?"

"Well," she said, "hypothetically speaking, in Henry's case, I'd be prepared to ignore it."

"Really? You wouldn't mind?"

"He's a big boy. I'm not going to tell him what to do."

And I realized that my ideas of love were woefully insufficient. I'd wandered into deep waters. Maybe I should have been reassured, but I expected something more—anger, fury, irritation, at least—some greater stake in the matter. And it bothered me, because if Mona could shrug Henry off so easily, with all his laughter and charm, where in the world did that leave me?

"I think he's seeing someone else," I said. "In fact, I'm sure of it. I followed him tonight. To a motel. The Tiki Motel. For God's sake, what kind of a name is that?"

Mona was staring in stunned surprise. "You followed him?"

"He's with another woman."

"Are you sure? Did you see her?"

And I felt a dull sliver of satisfaction as if, by the calculus of love, her jealousy of Henry might somehow say something about her feelings for me. "No," I said. "I lost him. I think they met and drove off in her car."

Mona considered that in silence. For a moment she looked on the verge of saying something more, but in the end she only shrugged. "Okay. So?"

"It doesn't bother you?"

"No. Does it bother you?"

"Yes."

"Why?" she asked.

Why?

And I realized I had no idea. Why should it bother me so much? Why did it follow me right here into this room? And why did it seem as if everything I felt, everything I wanted and did, somehow had its pivot set in the shaky foundation of Henry's heart?

Gently Mona laid a hand on my arm—where the stitches, gone for almost a week, still maintained their phantom pinch and ache. "Harry," she said softly. "He's entitled to his own life. And so are you."

And that was true. But I felt like some animal who'd lived so long in a narrow cage he could no longer remember how to move. She was gazing worriedly at me now. I swallowed. "What's wrong with me?"

"Nothing. You're fine."

"I'm not," I said. "I'm really not."

"Did you eat anything today?"

I thought of the blueberry muffin in the bag at the store. It was probably still there. "No."

"I've got some lasagna from downstairs."

"Thanks. But I'm not hungry." I became aware of the jazz drifting on the currents of the room. "Would you dance with me?"

"You should probably sit down."

"Please?"

We set our wine glasses on the desk, and she stepped in as if ministering to a patient. We moved slowly, following the music around the narrow space between the sofa and the desk. I leaned my cheek against the stiff whisper of her hair.

"I'm sorry," I said. "I'm kind of a mess."

"No, you're not. You're fine."

But I thought about Henry and me, huddled together all these years like two men in a leaky boat. He had all but ceased to be my father. My mother's departure had removed any difference between us. Whether I'd gotten older or Henry younger I couldn't tell, but as close as possible, we were the same age, and he had needed looking after. I thought of all the half-smothered irritations, the constant constraints, the effort. But at the same time I marveled at the satisfaction it had given me. And I wondered if I hadn't been secretly pleased, all this time, to have had him to myself. I wondered if it was simply true that I had always felt left out and alone, and with Henry, at least, I'd had some company. But now?

"I'm a little scared," I whispered.

"Of what? There's nothing to be scared of."

But that wasn't true. "I'm scared of being left behind."

"I won't leave you behind."

And Henry?

We moved for a while, swaying in the candlelight, and I wished that this was all the protection I needed. My voice was low. "You like me better, don't you?"

"Better than what?"

I gave her a shake.

"Yes," she said, and I heard the smile in her voice. "I like you better."

The knock on the door, when it came, shivered the silence: a thin, urgent rapping. It came again. And reluctantly I stepped over to answer it. Jean Tipton surged in with the opening door. No pink raincoat, this time, no rubber boots; she wore jeans and a dark sweater. But there was something about her expression—and about the large stuffed bear she carried clenched in her arms—that gave her a lingering air of stricken alarm. And more. She wore a bruised and swollen sunset beneath one eye.

"Jean?"

"You've been spying on me!"

"No," said Mona, "Not exactly." But her voice trailed off.

"You've been watching my house."

"Jean? What happened to your eye?"

"You're fired!" she said fiercely. "I don't want you around anymore."

She was clutching the bear in both arms as if it were the only thing keeping her afloat. She swayed, and as I reached for her arm she started to give way. Together we eased her onto the sofa, and she sank back nervelessly, with Paddington slouched beside her as if his strength, too, had abruptly given out. Only then did she notice the candlelight and the pink grandiloquence of Mona's dress.

"Oh!" She looked stricken. "I'm interrupting."

"It's all right."

"I should go."

"Just sit," I said. "Are you all right?"

She gazed around the room, wide-eyed and exhausted. "The candlelight's so pretty."

"How about some wine?" I said.

"You're having wine? Oh. In a bottle. That is so romantic."

I fetched my glass from the desk and held it out, blood red in the candlelight. "Just like old times," I said.

She glanced from Mona to me, wearing a weak coquettish smile. "I knew it was love. No matter what you said."

"Did Biff do that?" demanded Mona.

"No."

"He did, didn't he?"

"No, it was you," she said. "Both of you. You made him do it."

"You've got to get away from him," I said.

"It wasn't his fault. He was just upset. You made him upset. He saw you that night. It made him so angry. You're scaring him away."

"Jean," said Mona, "you came to me, remember? You wanted me to—"

"I didn't want you to spy on me! I wanted you to find him. I didn't want you to chase him away."

"We need to call the police," I said.

"No!" She looked frightened in a way that left the bruise under her eye glowing darkly. "He'd hate that. And what could they do?"

"They could protect you."

"I don't need protecting. Don't you see? I don't need help, I don't need protection...." She gave a little sob, as if all that she didn't need was just too much to bear. "I just need to know what to do, that's all."

Mona sank down onto the sofa beside her. "Look at yourself, Jean. Look what he's done." And she hesitated, considering for a moment all that he had done. "He's not going to give it to you, Jean."

"What?" She looked up, startled and anxious in a whole new way.

"We know about the money," Mona said gently. "He's not the sort of man to give it up."

"Give it up?" She looked bewildered. "What do you mean?"

"I think he's dangerous--."

"I don't care about the money!" Jean said hotly. "It isn't about the money. Is that what you think? It's him. That's all. I want him back!"

"Just him?" said Mona. "Not a hundred and twenty thousand dollars? That's a lot of money, Jean. But I don't think he's the kind to share."

"You don't know. He'd give it to me, if I wanted. I'm sure he would. If he had it."

Mona peered at her intently. "If he had it?"

But Jean was frowning now, looking peevish. "He doesn't know where it is."

"He lost it?"

"No."

"Jean…?"

"I hid it," she said defensively.

Mona was staring now, hunched into silence in that short pink dress. "You hid it?"

"I want him back. Don't you see? I want him to come back to me, and you're driving him away."

"Call the police," said Mona firmly.

"I can't--."

"This isn't safe. You've got his money. What do you think he's going to do?"

"I'll give him the money. He knows that. But he has to come back."

"Where has he been living?"

Jean looked stricken. "At the house. Of and on. We've been getting along so much better." She gazed wistfully down at the glass in her hands, thinking about how romantic it was that I would go to all the trouble to buy wine in a bottle. "I hate it when he's angry. He can be so loving. Is that too much to ask? Look at this. Candlelight. That beautiful dress." She shook her head sadly. "I just want him to be the way he *can* be. You don't know him. You don't know what he can be like. He's funny. He's gentle. Oh, not too gentle." She glanced up at me as if she might have given something away. "Nothing like that."

"No," I said. "Just gentle enough."

"Exactly." She wore a tired smile. "I have to go." She climbed to her feet and stood, gazing around at the room, warm and muffled in the candlelight. "Did you bring the wine?" she asked wistfully.

I nodded.

"Did you bring flowers?"

"No. I forgot."

"Are you having dinner?"

"Just lasagna," said Mona.

"Did you make it?"

"It's take-out."

Jean sighed is if that were an even greater sign of love. She held out her wine untouched. I took it. "If you'd all just leave us alone."

"You came to us, Jean."

"It was a mistake." She turned to the door. "You're putting him in danger."

"But what about you?"

She just shook her head sadly. I looked at the droop of her shoulders and the bleak hopeless gaze. "You can't make them stay," I said. Why had it taken me so long to realize? "No matter what you do. If they want to leave, they'll leave. You can't make them love you."

"But he already does. He loves me. I know. I just need him to understand. I need him to--"

"Jean!" said Mona. "That's not how it works. You've got his money."

"I don't care about the money! I hate the money. Don't you see? If there weren't any money he'd come back to me in a second! He'd be here right now."

"Jean…"

"It's love." She stood in the doorway, fists clenched but both arms dangling, as if even now she was ready to fight for him, if only she had the strength. "Go away," she whispered, though she was the one leaving. "Just go away."

"He's going to want that money," Mona said grimly. "Even I can tell you that."

"Well, he's not to going to get it," she said, and gently but firmly closed the door.

28

"I need a drink," said Mona.

I nodded vaguely and started to hold up Jean's untouched wine.

"Bigger," she said.

"Come with me. I know just where they live."

It was called the American Bistro, though there were no flags, no stars and stripes, and nothing more American on the menu than grilled Chilean sea bass in an orange pepper glaze. The food was ambitious rather than good, and the service was slow, but the drinks were large, and it was just down the street. We took a table before a large mullioned window, which promised a panoramic view but looked out only onto the sidewalk and the parking lot of the Quik Trip across the street, and we drank martinis in honor of Mona's beautiful dress and because there was nothing like gin to capture the mixture of girlish festiveness and sharp desperation that lingered in Jean Tipton's wake.

We started slowly, but after a while there were a number of empty glasses on the table, and Mona was gazing down with a ruminative frown as if wondering exactly how they'd gotten there. "You know," she said. "These don't taste so bad after a while."

"Isn't that the truth."

"Still ...." She gave a poke with one finger that set the two large olives rattling around the bottom of the glass. "I'm not a big fan of the olive."

"Give 'em here, then. Can't let 'em go to waste."

She scooped them out and transferred them with a careless splash. But then, returning to her now unadorned drink, she looked a little forlorn as if suddenly unsure about the new minimalist approach.

"What was it," she said, "that the partner didn't press charges on? What's his name? Clancy?"

"Delbert Clancy. Broken nose, broken arm. Something else. Ribs, I think. He claims he fell down."

Mona shook her head wearily. "What does she think she's going to do?"

"She thinks she's going to make him love her. She thinks he's going to realize how much he misses her, and what a fool he was to cheat on her, and how he wants more than anything else to be with her."

"Don't," said Mona. "Please? Don't make fun of her."

"I'm not. I think it's the saddest thing in the world."

I could hear how bleak my voice sounded. It was a tone that seemed to have seeped into my bones. "I used to think," I said, "if my mother just came home again, just for a few hours, if she just came through town on a bus and got off and walked around, that she'd realize what a mistake she'd made. Or if I could just find her and call her. If she could just hear our voices, that would do it. That it was all somehow a mistake. That she didn't really know what she was doing, or what it would be like, or maybe she just felt too proud to admit she'd made a mistake. And that used to drive me crazy, the thought that she might want to come back but just couldn't. I went through the phone books at the library alphabetically, looking up every Elizabeth Drew, E. Drew, E. Bailey. Starting with Albuquerque and working my way up. I got as far as Galveston before I quit. I'd spent maybe two hundred dollars on long-distance calls. And then one evening I was home from the store early, and the phone rang, and there she was."

"She called you?"

"Out of the blue."

Mona was watching carefully. "What did she say?"

I shrugged. Though I remembered, of course. She'd said, Henry? I'd recognized her voice immediately, even after more than a year.

Mom. It's me.

Harry? You sound just like your father.

Where are you?

I'm fine. I'm doing okay, she said. I'm working in real estate, now.

As if that were really what I was worried about. Was she making a good enough living.

But where are you? I asked.

I've got to go now, Harry. Don't tell your father I called.

Or maybe what she said was *do* tell your father. That seems more likely. But it all happened so quickly. And there I was holding the receiver, with nobody at all on the other end, and I'd never even asked her to come home.

"I hung up the phone," I said. "I didn't even think about star sixty-nine. And I asked Henry. He said she'd been calling, every now and then. She'd never say where she'd been. She never talked for long. Henry thought it would just upset me to know."

"And did it?"

"No kidding."

"Maybe she just needed to hear your voice," Mona said.

"But that's the thing. Don't you see? I'd always thought that would do it. Just hearing our voices. I thought that would bring her home. But it did just the opposite. That seemed to be enough for her, just to say hello. " I stopped, leaving my voice hanging in the air. I thought about Jean Tipton. *He loves me. I know. I just need him to understand.*

"Do you still miss her?" asked Mona.

"I used to. I used to miss her like crazy. But now?" I shrugged. "Now it's too late. She could come crawling back, all the way from Albuquerque on her hands and knees, and she'd still have been away six years because she wanted to."

Mona frowned. "You don't know that."

"Of course I do."

"Do you think Henry feels that way?"

I reached out and fished an olive from the glass with two damp fingers. It looked like a little green head, smooth and featureless, cored out and emptied—its pit and all its little green thoughts replaced by the soft, folded shock of red pimento. "I haven't the slightest idea what Henry feels. And that's God's truth."

"You don't think," said Mona, after a moment, "if you could find her...?"

"I don't want to find her, now. I don't want to see her. What good would it do? That's the thing. That's the whole problem." Whatever the martinis were doing to my verbal precision, in their own way they were making my thoughts much clearer. "Even if she came back ... even if she decided it was all a big mistake ... so what? What about all those years when she didn't think that? When she thought it was just exactly what she needed. When what she needed was to be away from us, and to talk, every now and then, without saying anything important, because all she needed was to hear our voices. And it wasn't even my voice. Henry's voice." I stopped and looked up bleakly. "I just realized that. She wasn't even calling me."

"I'm sure she asked Henry about you."

I shook my head. I felt empty, as if all this talk had just hollowed me out, with not even a pimento where my heart should be. "You make up little stories, without even realizing it. Without telling them to anyone but yourself. Just little explanations that let you get from day to day. I told myself it was Henry who drove her away. It was Henry who didn't love her enough, who didn't give her what she needed. He was too boring, too self-absorbed. He didn't do anything but work and garden and sleep." I smiled bleakly. "Now look at him. He's a changed man. Thanks to you. You made a whole new Henry."

She laughed, a little uncomfortably. "Yeah. How about that?"

"But, here's the thing," I said. "If Henry drove her away... if he was the reason, then why did she hang up on me? Why was he the one she called?"

Mona looked at me for a moment in warm and sudden concern, but even she couldn't think of a thing to say.

"You want another?" I asked.

"I think three's my limit."

"Quitter." Thoughts were slipping back and forth through my mind, with nothing in common but a sad sense of foreboding. "Do you think she'll be all right?"

"Who? Jean?"

"Maybe it'll work," I said. "Maybe he'll take one look at her and think, what a fool I've been. She'll give him the money and he'll toss it aside and say, you're the one I want. I'm sorry to have stayed away all these years. I'm sorry I left in the first place. I'm sorry I called you and never said more than hello. What do you think?"

I glanced over with something that wasn't utterly unlike hope, but she was frowning thoughtfully. And I realized I had no idea what she was thinking.

"Are you ready to leave?" asked Mona.

"Sure."

Out of the corner of my eye I caught a glimpse of something moving like a spirit in the darkness. A sudden inadvertent revelation, as if I'd called it up without meaning to. A large car driving past, glowing under the street lamps. A Lincoln, huge and absurdly white on the narrow street. It swept by like a great zeppelin swooping through a dream, drifting past on a little rush of tires. And in the glow of headlights it was lit up for an instant, just for a flicker of time. And I saw Henry.

Just like that. The slow drifting flight of the car interrupted, frozen, by that moment's illumination. And there was my father, laughing in the passenger seat beside a woman. I didn't need to see much. Even in that moment I could tell it wasn't the brunette from the store. She was blonde, and whatever else she might have been, she wasn't dressed for the Tiki Motel. She wore a pale blouse that caught the light in a shimmer. And then they were gone.

I might have imagined it. Even immediately afterwards it seemed like a trick of the light. But the look on Henry's face lingered. Turned in the passenger seat, laughing and eager, he was sailing away through the night. But whether leaving me behind or inviting me to come along, I couldn't be sure. It was an omen, of course. But that was the only thing that was clear.

"What?" said Mona. "What is it?"

"Do you want to come home with me?"

She was looking a little worried now. "We could go to my place. It's closer."

"No," I said. "Come to mine."

As a boy in high school, a late-bloomer, and always a coward at heart, I used to dream about sneaking a girl up to my room. I would lie there at night, with the breeze brushing the curtains, and imagine it as a sweet and secret triumph over all my parent's arguing. I imagined lying there, all wrapped together in a warm knot of arms and legs, with the noise of their raised voices fading into the background. A little cocoon of sex and self-sufficiency.

But, like the worst of late-bloomers, I had missed the boat again. No parents left to sneak Mona past, and even the dream of self-sufficiency was marred by the bright, recurring image of Henry swooping through the darkness on his own eager way. As I led her, not up the step-ladder onto the roof and through the window as I'd always planned, but in through the back door and up the stairs, I realized not for the last time that, while you sometimes get what you wish for, it is seldom what you hope.

It was a beautiful night. Outside the leaves of the walnut tree swam like a school of fish in the lights of the neighboring garage. They flickered and turned. And the breeze, little more than a sigh, leant the slightest of motions to the curtains. We undressed in silence and stood there pale as ghosts.

For such a long time the things I'd wanted most were always the hardest to hold. My mother, my own happiness, my plans for my future. The most precious things made themselves felt only by slipping away. Now I hesitated with Mona before me, suddenly feeling as if, were I to reach out even now, my hands might come back empty. I stood there, naked and uncertain. Then Mona stepped close and kissed me. Her lips were shadowy, but her body, pressing firmly against me, was solid and warm.

"It's like a tree house," she whispered.

We lay down on my narrow bed. What was a man of twenty-four doing with a bed so narrow? It was like a sign of all that hadn't changed, the proof of all the effort I'd spent trying to stand perfectly still. There was barely enough room to lie side by side. Mona peered up at me, still wearing her glasses. I tried to lift them off but she shook her head. Her eyes watched me closely.

"I need to tell you something," she whispered.

"What is it?"

She hesitated, then seemed about to change her mind. But her hand, much less tentative than her voice, traced its own path between us and was in the process of differentiating, by touch alone, where one body left off and the other began. Her fingers closed round me, guiding me in. "Tell me I look nice," she breathed.

"You look beautiful."

"Something else," she said.

"What?"

"It's about Henry and me."

"I know."

"No, you don't."

"I don't care." And I covered her mouth with mine. After a moment our breathing was the loudest thing in the large and vacant stillness of the house.

But gradually the very silence began to seem menacing. No voices raised. No voices at all. I thought of all the time I'd had over the last six years to grow accustomed to the silence, but now, suddenly it seemed more than I could bear. I opened my mouth. "I love you."

It slipped out. I hadn't meant to say exactly that. But it came to me as an accidental skip in my chest, a sudden and unexpected stutter against my ribs like a heart murmur, only breathed aloud. I hesitated, appalled, uncertain if she'd even heard.

Mona shook her head. She was gripping me hard, her arms around me. "Don't say that. Don't say it if you don't mean it."

But I didn't know what I meant. Only that the silence was so loud, and I needed some sound from her. "Tell me," I said. "Tell me something."

But she just clung to me, in a kind of slow struggle, her fingers digging into the hollow of my back, burying her face in my neck so that the hard edge of the glasses dug into my skin and her voice rose muffled and indistinct, not so much heard as felt.

29

I awoke into darkness from a dream as vivid as it was fleeting. It slipped away even as I opened my eyes, but I was aware of a bubble of sound, half-heard on my lips. "Mom?" It hung on the air, echoing faintly.

The word made me angry. It didn't mean anything. After so long, I couldn't put a face to it, or a voice. It was just a single syllable that stood for a certain kind of loneliness and the empty expanse of the darkness. Beside me Mona shifted noiselessly on the narrow bed. Her body was warm, her breathing as soothing as anything I could imagine. I burrowed in against her, creeping back into sleep, and when I opened my eyes again it was to the faint silver light of six o'clock filling the windows. She was still there curled against me, one hand under her cheek, the other pressed limply against my chest but whether to push me away or bring me closer I couldn't be sure. I listened, only half aware. The house was silent at first, and then I heard the muffled creak of footsteps. Sleepily I thought, Henry's up, bright and early as usual. Some things never change.

And then I was wide awake.

The sun was up. Henry was up. And I faced that one aspect of the situation that all of my teenage daydreaming had consistently overlooked. In my imaginings, it was always the creeping *in* through the darkness that had absorbed my thoughts. I never considered how difficult it might be to creep out. I glanced down at Mona. She looked unworried in sleep. I tried to remember what time my father went to work. If we could just wait him out. But even as I considered it I knew, with all the martinis from the night before, that there was no question of waiting.

Cautiously I slipped out of bed and pulled on a pair of shorts.

Then I crept to the door and peered out into the hall. There was no sign of Henry. His bedroom door was sealed and solid. The bathroom stood enticingly empty. I slipped out, mindful of the creak in the floor, and scurried to safety.

With every movement I was aware of the sound, the clink of the handle, the rush of water in the pipes. And as I reached for the doorknob again I realized I was holding my breath. I slipped out into the hall, like a burglar on tip toe, and at that moment exactly, with a little rattle of the knob, Henry's door opened, and there he stood. "Harry."

"Hi."

"I didn't think you'd be up yet."

"I'm not. Not for long. Headed back to bed even as we speak." I was aware of the thick and musky scent clinging to me like a broad, olfactory banner. I smiled weakly and took half a step back toward my door.

"Did you have a good time last night?" he asked.

"Yes, thanks. It was great. How about you? "

"It was nice."

"Good," I said. "Nice dinner and everything?"

"Oh, yeah. Great dinner."

"Good. Great. Well, I'll see you." And I turned toward my bedroom door with something like hope in my heart, only to see it open as if on cue, revealing Mona, thin and sleepy-eyed in one of my t-shirts.

I stood there frozen. Mona raised her hand in what might have started out as a wave but died away into a kind of startled shrug. "Morning, Henry."

I swallowed hard. "Henry," I said. "I think you know…"

"Mona? What are you doing here?"

"I just happened to be in the neighborhood."

"I can explain," I said.

But when I turned, Henry was looking cheerful as could be. A big smile, bright and indulgent. "Well," he said. "Isn't this a nice surprise. How about some breakfast?"

I wondered, for an instant, if my father was sleep-walking or maybe just drunk, but he stood there fresh-faced and ready for the day, smiling as if this woman in a stretched out t-shirt, puffy-eyed and smelling of sex, had just stopped by to say hello. I stared at him, wondering if something wasn't altogether clear, if maybe he was simply missing some crucial part of this.

"Mona spent the night," I explained.

"Well, I guess so."

"You guess so?"

Then, before he could reply, a brisk, amused voice, came drifting out from behind his half-open door. "Wouldn't you know it, I think I've lost my pantyhose."

I stood, staring at the doorway with the kind of dread a deer must feel when the headlights come on and it hears the sound of the engine behind them.

"I was going to tell you," Mona said.

But I barely heard.

The woman's voice was getting louder. "You don't suppose we left them outside, do you?" And she stepped into the doorway. She wore the same shiny blouse from the night before. Blonde hair brushed, face composed.

I was vaguely aware of being under dressed in the plaid boxer shorts, but that was the least of it. "Mom?"

She looked startled, but not shocked. Why should she be shocked? She knew who she was. She'd known all along. And there was nothing surprising about finding me here. I lived here. I'd always lived here.

I looked at Henry, then over at Mona, then back at Elizabeth Drew Bailey, returned from the dead, from the whole series of fatal accidents and kidnappings I had imagined for her over the years. Nobody looked surprised now. Henry looked a bit sheepish, perhaps. And Mona, laying a dry and icy hand on my arm, looked a little guilty, like someone who'd had a piece of awkward news rushed upon her when she was still planning on taking her time. But nobody looked shocked, except me.

"Harry?" said my mother. "Is that you?"

Who else would it be? Who else was exactly where he'd been for the last six years?

"How are you?" she said.

And there was something so breathtakingly simple and unexpected about the question after so many years away that all I could do, with the cold knot of shock in my stomach and Mona's cold fingers gripping my forearm, was to respond exactly as she'd taught me all those years ago. "I'm fine, thank you," I said. "How are you?"

Part Three:

Missing Persons

30

Over the years loneliness plays tricks on you. There comes a time when you begin to think that living without love is the same as protecting yourself against its loss. You think you're safe because for so long you've had nothing to lose. And then one morning you wake up and realize the possibilities for loss are more varied and arcane than anything you could have conceived.

Henry offered to make everyone an early breakfast. He had eggs, he said, and mushrooms and a piece of cheese. There might even be some bacon. He stood there in the hall as if all of this were according to plan, as if it could not have worked out better. And I said, no. Thank you. I wasn't that hungry. And Elizabeth said, sweetie, we should leave these young people alone. As if the two of them had just come home and found their son making out on the sofa and were being so thoughtful and sensitive and understanding because they didn't want to embarrass him or cause an awkward situation. So they turned, the two of them, and went down to breakfast, and I was startled by a sound I hadn't heard in years, something I hadn't even realized I'd missed or forgotten until I heard it again: that particular shifting creak of the stairs as two sets of footsteps descended together.

I walked into my bedroom and pulled on a pair of pants. Mona's fingers, when they touched my bare arm again, were cool and tentative. "Are you okay?"

"Okay?" I turned. "What do you mean, am I okay? Why shouldn't I be okay? Give me one goddam reason why I shouldn't be okay!"

"Please don't get mad," she said.

"You couldn't have told me?"

"I wanted to. I almost did."

"Almost? What the hell is that?"

"At first he asked me not to. And then, after a while, I was afraid you'd be upset."

"No shit."

"I had my responsibilities. I had a duty to Henry."

And what about me? I wanted to say. What about your responsibility to me? But it sounded too childish: *I thought you said you liked me best.*

"In a way," said Mona after a moment, "it's sort of funny, isn't it? I mean, it doesn't change anything."

Change anything? Of course it did. There seemed to be nothing in my life that it didn't change. "So you're saying... what?" I asked. "That you knew Henry was seeing her?"

"I found her for him. That's what I do. He hired me to find her."

"And all that stuff with Henry? All the dancing and dating. What was that? Just a little extra service?"

She was hugging the baggy t-shirt against her ribs as if she were suddenly cold. "Don't, Harry."

"No. Come on. I'm curious."

"He just needed a few hints. He wanted a little practice. Just to get ready for when he met her."

"And that was okay with you?"

"It was fun. I like Henry. He deserved a chance to be happy. And look on the bright side." She gave me a parched smile. "At least it must be a relief to know I wasn't sleeping with your father."

And I knew it should have been. I knew it should have been a huge load off my mind. But somehow, in the whole roiling mixture of emotions, relief seemed inextricable from the bitterest disappointment.

Mona sat down beside me. "Come on. Don't get mad."

"I'm not mad."

"Good."

And I wasn't. I was furious. For no good reason I could explain I was suddenly alive with anger. I looked at her, hunched and uneasy in my t-shirt, and thought about how different everything had looked just a few minutes before. It had all seemed so clear. How much I had wanted her. How much I'd been willing to do to get her. How much I'd been prepared to hurt Henry just to have my way. But if you get someone for all the wrong reasons, how can it still be the same? Would I have pursued Mona if I'd known the truth? Would I have gotten so jealous of Henry if I'd realized it was all just practice and that this was where he was heading? Gazing at Mona, I thought of the maze of misunderstandings, and I tried to imagine where we would have ended up without them. Not here, I thought. Definitely not here.

"Did you and Henry have a good laugh over me?" I asked.

"No. Of course not."

"You and Elizabeth?"

"No."

I tried to hold onto my anger, because without it I was afraid I'd be crying like a baby. "I thought you were on my side."

"I am."

But I just shook my head. "How could you be?" I said with awful bitterness. "I wasn't the one paying you."

"Well, you can just cut that out!" snapped Mona, straightening up. "Because I've got news for you. I don't need you mad at me. And here's a bulletin. I don't deserve it. I was doing my job."

"And a hell of a job it was."

"You're damn right! Your mom's been gone for six years, and you didn't do shit. And guess what? I found her in a month."

"Well, good for you."

She straightened up furiously, her fists clenched. And I thought for a moment she was going to hit me. But she only glared. "And what the hell were you doing?" she demanded. "Going after your father's girlfriend? How sick is that?"

"You weren't his girlfriend."

"You didn't know that. Jesus Christ! Cheating on your own father? That's disgusting."

"I wasn't cheating on him."

"You thought you were."

"Will you stop saying that?"

But, of course, it was true. And in the darkest, least admirable corner of my brain I felt deflated by it all. Let down. And worse. Now that I was no longer competing with Henry for Mona's attention, I had the terrible realization that I wasn't sure what I felt. I wasn't sure where that left us. I stared down at the bedroom floor, the twisted sheets, the tangle of Mona's clothes. Everything about me felt wrung out. "I'm going back to bed," I said.

"You just got dressed."

"So?"

She hesitated. "So, what does that mean? You're going back to bed."

"It means I'm going to bed. You can do whatever you want."

"No," she said, her voice compressed to a low, fierce whisper. "Because if I did whatever I wanted, I'd be punching you right in the nose."

"Oh, that's great," I said bitterly. "Now, suddenly, you're all communicative."

"Fuck you," she said.

"Fuck me? Fuck me?"

"She's back, isn't she? I found her for you."

"But that's just it," I said. "It wasn't for me. And I'll bet Henry's already paid you, hasn't he?"

She whirled and started snatching her clothes from the floor, then shoved past me into the bathroom. When she emerged a moment later she was back in the pink and black dress. The sight startled me; it seemed so long ago that I'd last seen it.

Even then, I suppose, I could have reached out to stop her, it would have only taken a word. But in the hot and tangled fury of the moment it already seemed impossible. She held up my t-shirt between thumb and forefinger like something funda-mentally distasteful. "You may want to wash this," she said and dropped it at my feet.

I shrugged tiredly. "I'll drive you home."

But Mona just looked at me and held up her apartment key in one tight fist. "I would rather stick this right in my eye."

She turned and stalked away down the stairs. And she might have slammed the door on her way out if she hadn't remem-bered at the last minute that my father was in the middle of breakfast. It closed instead with a muffled click.

She always did have soft spot for Henry.

31

After that I waited. I managed to be especially busy all the time—at the store, the bar, shopping, running errands—but all I was really doing was waiting. Waiting to see what this meant. Waiting for it to end. Waiting for my mother to vanish as if, having arrived so suddenly out of the blue, she was bound to disappear again just as mysteriously.

But there she was, living with us in a way both heart-breaking and ordinary. She brought with her a series of unimportant moments that I experienced as if I'd been waiting for nothing else all these years. The sight of her pouring coffee in the morning. Buttering her toast. Straightening a magazine on the table before her. I watched her constantly. But after all that I had thought to say to her, all I'd wanted to tell her over the last six years, I found myself with startlingly little to say. A few words in passing. Nothing more. I asked no questions at all. She moved into our daily lives with such assurance that she left no room for uncertainty, and all my feelings of memory, longing, and sadness were gradually distilled down to a single, bitter germ of love and blame.

On the first night I made tuna casserole. It had been my favorite growing up. Whenever I'd had a bad week in school or things weren't going well around the house my mother would make it as the embodiment of comfort. Tuna, egg noodles, cream of mushroom soup, frozen peas, canned pimentos, and a scattering of crushed potato chips on top. I followed her recipe exactly. In retrospect it might have been a little too reproachful. But she couldn't have been more charming.

She wore a pale silk dress, a silver necklace, and an unremembered suggestion of make up on her cheeks and lips. Her hair was carefully cut and colored with highlights that must have taken hours to apply. I tried to decide whether she looked familiar or not. There were a series of faint lines at the corners of eyes and mouth that looked new, but I couldn't be sure. There was about her the blurry indistinctness of two images inexactly superimposed. And after the shock of that first glimpse I could no longer tell the difference between what I remembered and what I was seeing now.

Henry wore the burgundy tuxedo jacket. I dressed in black. We ate like strangers. Henry talked about the store or the garden. Elizabeth told stories about real estate. Like a kid on a first date I tried desperately to think of things that would interest her, stories of my own life, things that I'd done, but they all seemed too seedy or too foolish for the silk blouse and the beautifully cut hair. Nothing I could think of from the past seemed to fit this woman sitting here now, and anything about the present seemed too large for the room.

But Henry rose to the occasion, and Elizabeth as well, as if it were a contest or some game they were playing. She laughed at his jokes, smiled at my stilted comments, and complimented me on the meal. "Are those tomatoes?" she asked.

"Pimentos."

"And peas?"

"And potato chips. Don't you recognize it? It's your recipe."

"You're kidding." She laughed. "Did I really make this?"

"This was my favorite. We used to have it on Friday nights. I used to love it. Don't you remember?"

"It rings a distant bell," she said with a doubtful smile.

"It was a long time ago," agreed Henry.

"Yeah. But tuna casserole. How could anyone forget that?" I was smiling, too, as if the dish represented merely a quaint and foolish phase we'd all gone through. As if it were nothing more than a kind of distant joke that had happened to somebody else. "And what about Persian Army Chicken? Do you remember that?"

"Army chicken?"

"Persian army. You found the recipe in the newspaper. You clipped it out and glued it to a three by five card. I've got it in the kitchen. You take the chicken breasts and lay them on the rice, then the special sauce. Do you remember it?"

"The sauce?"

"It's cream of mushroom soup."

"That's it?"

"And then you bake it. You remember what temperature?"

"I have no idea."

"Three-fifty. You used to make that for us all the time. And meatloaf? Do you remember what you used to put into your meatloaf? You called it your secret ingredient."

She was laughing now. "I don't know. Onions?"

"Oatmeal. A cup and a half of oatmeal." I was talking faster now, accelerating with a kind of grim determination: one detail after another. "And porcupine balls? Do you remember those? You used to laugh about the name, and I never knew why."

"I remember those," said Henry.

"You mix up the ground beef and egg and bread crumbs and shape them into little meatballs. Then you roll them in uncooked rice. Then you simmer them in tomato sauce until the rice cooks. They're supposed to look as if they're covered with little spines. We used to have them with frozen peas. Don't you remember that? And Uncle Ben's wild rice?"

Elizabeth was shaking her head helplessly, and I was trying not to let the note of desperation creep into my voice. But I was thinking how much those meals had meant to me, how much in the foolish and ordinary pattern of each day they'd embodied the comfort of my childhood. I was like a doctor reaching out to an amnesia victim, trying to recall her to her past, but Elizabeth just looked rueful.

"I was never," she said finally, "a very good cook."

The next night I made Persian Army Chicken. But while it was still cooking Henry came in to say Elizabeth felt like ordering Chinese, and wouldn't that be a nice change? So we sat around the table scooping rice and vegetables and hot, gummy sauce onto our plates, and drinking white wine that was meant to go with something much sweeter.

"Isn't this fun?" said Henry.

The third night Henry told me that Elizabeth wanted to take us out to dinner. "Both of us," he said with an unconvincing smile, and what was there to do?

"You have fun," I said, and tried not to notice the relief in his face.

After that I pretty much gave up on dinner. I lived on cold cereal and whatever leftovers I found in the fridge after one of their nights out. Picking through the foil-wrapped packages and white paper sacks huddled on the shelves I could trace their progress. Chinese, Indian, Thai, Mexican. It was a world tour.

Then finally, when I'd nearly forgotten what it was I'd been half-expecting, Elizabeth left. The airport limo picked her up, and she flew back to Chicago. And I waited for things to get back to normal.

But they didn't, of course. How could they? Things were different now. Henry was different. He was energized, considerate, full of jokes and good humor, as if he were practicing a new trick and didn't want to lose the knack.

And when she arrived again Friday night, I just stepped back the way someone waiting a long time at a bus stop steps back when he sees the bus is already full and isn't even slowing down.

I called in sick at the bar and took to walking in the evening again. And sometimes late at night I would swing past the Blue Diner for no particular reason except that, in a long, wandering route chosen more or less at random, it was not altogether out of my way. In the end, though, nobody ever called out to me to stop, and only once did I run into anybody I knew. I was wandering one evening down Linn Street when the narrow and inconspicuous door opened and Mona emerged with a sudden, startled look. We stood for a moment in silence. Then she said, "You coming to see me?"

"Just out for a walk."

She nodded, stiff-faced and uncertain. "I called. A couple of times. Did you get the messages?"

I wanted to tell her I'd had to fight the urge to call her. That I had to struggle to maintain my anger because increasingly it felt as if that was all I had to depend on. But the only thing I said was, "Yeah, thanks. I got them."

She shook her head angrily. "What do you want, Harry? You want me to say I'm sorry? I'm sorry. I'm sorry you're so pissed off. I'm sorry you're so fucked up. But you know what? I'll tell you a secret. This is not my fault. And you know what else? It's not my problem."

"Now, suddenly, you can't keep a secret?"

"Fuck you, Harry."

"Yeah," I said. "That's right."

She glared for a moment, then turned and stalked off, leaving me to wonder how, in all the evenings of anticipating this conversation, I could ever have imagined it would make me feel better. And I marveled at how it had come to be, that the only one I really wanted to talk to was the one person to whom I had nothing nice to say.

32

One night I came home from the bar to find my parents out in the garden. Elizabeth was sitting at the red patio table in the glow of candlelight sipping a glass of wine as Henry, balancing on a step ladder, struggled with something on the pergola over her head. She looked beautiful in the golden haze, and Henry looked handsome, if a little eccentric, in creased khakis and oxford shirt. If you'd never seen them before that night you might have taken them for a long-married couple comfortable in each other's company and enjoying their own little patch of the evening. It was a charming, even romantic scene, untouched by the past, untouched by anything. And standing there hesitantly at the foot of the walk, I realized this was exactly the scene I'd always longed for during the last six years. Except that somehow I'd always imagined a place for myself within it.

But tonight, clearly, it had nothing to do with me. I told myself to keep walking, to pretend I was just renting a room in the house and had to cut through a stranger's yard to get to my apartment. But as I came down the walk my mother smiled in greeting, and my father twisted around to glance back over his shoulder. "Here's the man," he said. And that's all it took.

I slowed to a halt. "You're up late."

Elizabeth waved her glass at the garden. "It's a beautiful night."

"I'm working on a little something here," said Henry, "but I could use an extra pair of hands."

"What exactly are you doing?"

"Just a little project," he said. "A little home-coming present for your mother."

He had found a long string of lights tangled in the alley behind the store. They were in a burly knot as if the wire had been wrestling with itself, and after a long struggle he had gotten them half-undone and was trying to wrap them around the wooden beams of the pergola. "It'll be like our own little constellation," he said.

I told myself it was a sweet idea. Romantic. Henry bustling around like some lovestruck twelve-year-old assembling this elaborate gesture of his affection. But I was aware of the glinting irritation running like a vein of silver through my heart. "Are you just watching?" I said to Elizabeth.

She laughed affectionately. "It's his idea. He's doing fine."

"Well, if he's doing fine..."

"Oh, come on," she said cheerfully. "Join the fun."

Your childhood is always lying in wait. It's like a pit you dig and then trick yourself into again and again. There was something in my mother's smile and my father's hearty good cheer that seemed to hold out to me an old chance once again, and I felt myself grasping at it the way a drowning man will make a grab even for an anchor if it's the only thing that's thrown. Maybe it's all a matter of degree. If you grow up smothered in signs of affection, it takes a lot to make an impression. If not, then even the smallest gesture stands out. And somewhere in what seemed like a lifetime of irritation and sullenness I knew that all I wanted was to see her laugh and tell me I was doing fine.

I stepped over to the ladder and peered up at Henry. The mass of wire in his hands looked as if it had been buried somewhere and only recently exhumed. "You sure they work?"

"They worked before."

"I told him to test them," said Elizabeth, "just to be sure."

My father was frowning in concentration. He had the string draped crookedly over one hand and a short piece of picture wire in the other, but he couldn't seem to make both work at the same time. He tried to wrap the lights around a protruding bolt at the juncture of two boards, but the ladder rocked on the patio stones. "Watch out!" cried Elizabeth, laughing as Henry flailed.

I could feel the first thin fingers of impatience, and I had the sudden image of Mona on the front porch all those weeks ago, arms crossed, tapping her foot as my father wrestled ineffectually with the champagne cork. "I don't suppose you have a plan?"

"Of course," he said cheerfully. "I'm going to wrap it over here, wire it up, and plug it in."

"Just like that?"

"It shouldn't be that hard."

I reached up peremptorily, climbing onto the bottom rung of the ladder and trying to take hold of the wire. I had visions of stepping in smoothly and, before Elizabeth's admiring gaze, untangling it with a flick of the wrist. But my father had a firm grip on it and he tugged it back.

"You just need to straighten it out," I said.

"That's what I'm doing."

"If you loosen it, you can work out the knots!"

"I'm loosening."

I snatched at it.

"Boys!" said Elizabeth. She was laughing. "Try to get along." Which irritated me to no end and made Henry laugh.

"You know what would make this easier?" He twisted around on the ladder and grinned. "I don't suppose you've got any more of that fine smoke, Betsy?"

Fine Smoke? I turned and stared. But as in so much else, my mother was unsurprised. She sat, legs elegantly crossed, a pair of slender-heeled sandals decorating her feet, and gazed up with a patient smile. "I might have some somewhere."

"Well, bring it on out," said my father jovially, like the frat boy he'd never been.

"You didn't really say fine smoke, did you?" I asked as Elizabeth stood and strolled into the house. My father just grinned, and after a moment she emerged carrying a precisely rolled joint like a tiny magic wand. She lit it carelessly and, without hesitation or self-consciousness, walked over to the ladder.

"Henry said you don't smoke?"

"Well," I said. "Not all the time."

"Good for you." And drawing in an impressive lungful, she handed the joint past me to my father.

Grinning down at us he took a quick toke, then another, catching at the smoke with sharp little breaths, and handed it to me. "Would you mind?" he gasped and nodded at Elizabeth.

I passed it on, and she took another drag and watched with narrowed eyes the thin gray cloud swirling in the candlelight. "This is nice," she said, but whether about the evening or the quality of the pot I couldn't be sure. In either case, Henry was nodding his agreement, grinning and exhaling as if he'd never had so much fun. What was I supposed to do? In the end I couldn't help it, and in the face of all experience and good sense I said, "I might try just a little."

"That a boy," said Henry, and Elizabeth, looking languidly amused, passed it over. I felt like a kid drinking a glass of wine with his parents for the first time and I drew in the smoke with that same combination of shyness, pride, and some vague feeling of momentousness. Elizabeth, though, seemed not to notice. As I passed the joint back she said, "It's a beautiful night," though to no one in particular.

In a sudden paroxysm of helpfulness I stepped off the ladder and dragged a chair over beside Henry. Climbing up I grabbed the tail end of wire dangling from his fist and stretched it up along the wooden beam.

"Wait," he said. "I've got it. I want to wrap it around the beam." And he made a little spiral gesture that rocked the ladder.

But I ignored him and, reaching awkwardly under the board, I passed the short stretch of untangled wire to myself, then looped it over the top, which brought me face to face with a big, ragged knot of twisted lights. I could feel the smoke creeping up under my nerves, spreading little barbs of impatience. "Jesus, Henry. I thought you untangled it."

"I was getting to it." He was humming to himself, untouched

by frustration. "Here. You hold this part." And he worked at it, tugging ineffectually at the tiny twists of wire, enjoying himself just to be fiddling. "So," he said after a moment. "How are you and Mona?"

"How are me and Mona what?"

"How's that working out?"

"It's not."

"What's not?" asked Elizabeth, growing suddenly bored with the sky and taking up an interest closer to earth. She set the joint down on the patio table and retrieved her wine glass.

"We're talking about Harry's love life."

"You're talking about it," I said. "I'm not that interested."

"Who is she?"

"You met her," said Henry. "Just briefly. The other night?"

"Oh, yes. This is that detective? She's a little odd looking, isn't she?" said Elizabeth.

I glanced over. "Odd?"

"She's so thin. And that hair. What has she done to that?"

The sight of my mother, looking so carelessly elegant in the candlelight, was in itself suddenly irritating. "She likes it that way," I said. "I think it's kind of cool."

"And those clothes? What was that dress?" She laughed.

"She's a little idiosyncratic," Henry agreed. "But she's a nice girl."

I turned at this suddenly tepid praise. "Excuse me?"

But Elizabeth was hurriedly agreeing. "I'm sure she is. But I don't think I could bring myself to put a ring in my nose." As if that, in the end, were the real issue.

Henry turned to me. "I was just thinking. We could always have her over, if you wanted to. We could have dinner together."

"You're kidding. We're going to double date now?" I turned to Elizabeth, ready for her amused demurral, but she was smiling thoughtfully.

"Maybe we should have her over," she agreed. "I'd like to meet her. More formally, I mean."

"Can we just do one thing at a time here?" I said, snatching at the wires.

"Easy," said Henry.

"Couldn't you maybe have straightened them first?"

"Sometimes you just have to jump in."

"Oh, stop it. When did you get so Zen all of a sudden?" I was prying at the general tangle, teasing it out, but as part of it relaxed into larger loops, the rest tightened down like a fist. "God damn it!"

"Here," he said.

But I batted his hands away. "Why couldn't you just buy a new one?" I snapped.

"This is better."

"And cheaper."

"And better," said Henry. He was grinning at the repetition. He tried to twist a length of wire around the first short section of the cross beam. He tugged on it to get a little more slack, and every time he tugged the tangle in my fingers tightened again.

"Will you cut it out!"

"I just need a little more."

"This is a rat's nest."

"Stop complaining. I untangled the first part."

"Well, the last part is a piece of shit!"

"You are such a baby." He was laughing.

The smoke, I realized, had been a big mistake. Instead of smoothing out all the rough angles of my thoughts it had drawn me to the edge of fury, and the thick, stoned self-consciousness was creeping in. Everything felt distant and unconnected: my father's good humor, my mother's cool amusement. None of it had anything to do with me.

"Look," said Henry. "You can't just tug on it. You've got to massage it."

"Jesus Christ, Henry. Massage it?"

"Now, look," he said, laughing. "You've got to smooth the tension out of its long, stringy body." And reaching out, he started to ease the big tangle of lights and green wire apart.

I'll do it!"

"Well, if you just—"

"Don't pull it!"

"You just have to--."

"Oh, for God's sake!" said Elizabeth. "Give me that!" She spoke with cool impatience, and as we glanced up, startled, she stepped over and waved me off the chair. "Get down." And slipping off her shoes, she climbed up in my place. "You are so pathetic, you two."

"It's not as easy as it looks," protested Henry, but he was grinning. My hands were clenched.

She had the joint again. She lit it, took one last, hard drag and flicked it out into the darkness. Then, smoke dribbling from her mouth, she grasped the dangling wire just above the plug, and gave it a sharp twitch for emphasis. The plug waggled lasciviously, and Henry smothered a giggle. "This is one end," she said.

"Well, duh."

"All you have to do is follow it."

"What do you think we've been doing?"

"I have no idea," she said, but her tone was suddenly all flirtatious amusement. "You just loosen it, and push this through." With carefully groomed fingernails Elizabeth teased at the first knot, coaxing it apart, dragging the plug through. "See?"

Henry started to applaud, then caught at the beam as the ladder rocked. "Bravo."

But she was already at work on the second knot, and I was watching her face, the little crease of a frown between her carefully shaped eyebrows, the determination in the set of her mouth. She had nothing else on her mind. Nothing that had happened, nothing she'd done. There was no awkwardness; no anxious awareness of having left and returned. She looked utterly unbothered. And I watched, feeling light and hollow.

Perched above the ground in the middle of the darkness they

stood, the two of them, buoyed by the candlelight. She worked faster now, and my father, ever the obedient helper, looped the unraveling wire like a skein of yarn between his hands. Elizabeth followed the plug through an intricate pattern of loops and corners until at last, with one final gesture, the wire relinquished itself into a single, long strand.

"Attaway, Betsy!" Henry cheered.

I stood there. After all that effort it was still just a crimped and ratty string of lights, so obviously junk that no one in his right mind would have bothered with it. Yet Henry had picked it up, twisted and useless, and Elizabeth had made it, if not good as new, at least as good as it was ever likely to be. And I had done nothing but make it all more complicated. How could you argue with a metaphor like that?

Elizabeth brushed off her fingers and, with a careless hand on my shoulder, stepped down from the chair. Then, slipping on her shoes, she strolled, without hurry or a glance, into the house.

Henry just gazed after her. "Isn't she something?"

I once read somewhere that, of all the sports, there is nothing as addictive as falconry. Once you've released the bird and then drawn it back to your wrist across a wide, clear sky, you can never give it up. Falconers will say it's the sense of power that comes from bending something so wild to your will. But I've never understood that. It seems less a matter of power than hopeful pleading, and the two are rarely the same. At the slightest irritation the falcon will simply fly off and never return, so you can't afford to discipline it or even pique its self-regard. You give it little bits of food, and you see to every aspect of its comfort, and you let it do whatever it wants, just so long as it comes back. And when you release it, you just hope that it's all been enough to make it want to return. But really. What kind of a sport is that? It's more like a long series of humiliating gestures, trying to win the affection of a slim thoughtless creature that is all but indifferent to you.

As I watched, Henry fastened the lights. He wrapped the wire back and forth, over and under the beam, spiraling it to the end. Then he climbed down. He had an extension cord spooled on the back steps, running from the outside socket by the basement hatch to the patio, and he stood there, with the two plugs in his hands, like some dignitary preparing to cut the ribbon on a brand new bridge.

"Well, go ahead," I said.

"In a minute. Why don't you blow out those candles, just for the effect."

So I blew out the candles and we stood there in the darkness, waiting.

"You should invite her to dinner," said Henry. "It would be fun."

"It wouldn't be fun, Henry. Trust me."

"It would give your mother a chance to meet her."

"We've broken up, Henry. Did I mention that? And since when was my mother so interested?"

But before he could answer, the back door opened and out she stepped, elegant and self-possessed. And as Henry eagerly jammed the two plugs together, the lights came on like a little constellation of white stars gathered over our heads, and Elizabeth smiled graciously, accepting the gesture as nothing more than her due.

33

I had assumed if I just ignored the idea, Henry would forget all about the double date, but he didn't. So on Saturday night I descended the stairs in a haze of candlelight and déjà vu to find Benny Goodman on the stereo and the living room ready for a party. The coffee table was laid with mixed nuts, a plate of celery and carrots cut into strips around a small bowl of dip, and four coasters marking our places the way those consoles on a television game show announced even before the game began where the contestants would be sitting.

My mother sailed out from the kitchen in an elegant red dress, pearl earrings, and an old, plaid apron that looked like a hand-me-down from her previous self. She wore a glance of satisfaction that drifted smoothly around the room until it seemed to catch on something as it passed over me. "Don't you look nice," she said, as if it really were a question.

I glanced down. Black pants, white t-shirt, brown tuxedo jacket. "What's wrong with it?"

"It looks fine. Never mind. Where are the crackers?"

"I have no idea."

She turned. "Henry?"

My father emerged from the kitchen bearing a butter knife like a silver baton tipped with sour cream.

"Where are the crackers, sweetie?"

"I told you. They're in the cupboard."

"I looked."

"The other cupboard. Hey." He pointed the cream-daubed knife at me. "Looking good."

"You, too," I said. "Nice outfit."

He wore a pair of black pants from my closet, a white tuxedo shirt he'd borrowed a week before, and the burgundy dinner jacket. He grinned. "You like it?"

"How could I not?"

The week had passed quickly enough. I didn't spend much time at home. On Wednesday Henry caught me on my way out the door. "We thought we'd have a little dinner party Saturday."

"We did?"

"Your mother and I. We thought it might be fun. Just the four of us."

"I only count three."

He smiled and, as if it had only just occurred to him, said, "You should bring someone. It'll be fun. Why don't you plan on coming around seven."

"Henry," I said gently. "I live here."

Now Henry grinned and stepped up beside me. "Hey, Betsy. Look. The Bailey twins."

But Elizabeth had her mind on other things. "We need to put the napkins out. And the glasses. And open the wine. Red and white."

"Already done," said Henry cheerfully.

"Then you can bring them out, and the artichoke hearts, but don't pour until we're all here."

Henry gave a wink and headed back toward the kitchen. Elizabeth turned. I could see her checking things off one last time. Nuts, crudités, glasses, napkins, music. She frowned. "Where's your date?"

"She's meeting me here."

"Soon?"

"Any time, now."

"Did you tell her it was at seven?"

"I told her."

"She's ten minutes late."

"I'll be sure and mention it when she gets here."

As my mother turned without another word and headed toward the kitchen I recollected Henry telling me how much fun it was going to be. I poured myself a glass of wine.

By the time the doorbell buzzed I was on my third.

"Finally," said Elizabeth. She had removed the apron and now took up her position in the middle of the room. My father joined her. He had punctuated the lapel of his jacket with the tiniest dab of sour cream. Together they stood like a very short receiving line as I crossed reluctantly to the door. Despite the wine, I was nervous. I hesitated, gathering my courage, then stepped forward and opened wide the door.

Tiny Alice had obviously made an effort for the evening. Her plaid flannel shirt was clean and bright, and she had brushed her hair into a wild snarling mass. She might even have washed her jeans. They looked tighter than usual, biting in beneath the soft swell of her stomach. She carried a thirty-pack of Rolling Rock like a little cardboard suitcase. "Just so we don't run out," she said cheerfully.

In that first moment, seeing Alice in the house, out of her usual context, looming so large in the carefully ordered living room, it occurred to me that I had gone too far, like the boy who, having shown the rubber mouse to the babysitter, stares aghast as she leaps onto the sofa screaming. But my mother was made of sterner stuff. She glanced at Henry with a bright, frozen smile, and stepped forward with the resolution of a proven soldier.

"Hello," she said. "I'm so glad you could come...," and she glanced peremptorily at me.

"Alice," I said, but then realized I had no idea what came next. "I'm sorry, Alice. What is your last name, anyway?"

She laughed good-naturedly. "It's Raeburn. With an R." And looming over our hostess, she reached out and enveloped her hand. "Most people call me Tiny Alice. Or just Alice."

"Just Alice," I said, "I'd like to present my mother, Elizabeth...," and found myself again in a wilderness of unknowing. I blushed. "I'm sorry. But I'm not sure about your last name, either."

"Drew," said my mother. "Elizabeth Drew." And she smiled

even more sternly.

Alice looked delighted. "Like in Nancy Drew?"

"Yes."

"I used to read those when I was a kid. The Mystery of the Hidden Staircase? Remember that one?"

"Yes."

"The Secret Diary?"

"I've read them," said my mother.

"Isn't that something?" Alice shook her head, marveling at the ways of chance as she turned to Henry.

He wore a look of dazed unease, but offered his hand gamely. "Alice."

"And of course you remember Henry," I said.

"Sure, I do. Good to see you, Henry. How's tricks?"

"His last name is Bailey," I explained. "And look, everyone. Alice brought beer."

You start off in this world with a family, at least two people tied to you by blood and good intentions. And you hold onto them, binding them to you with hoops of illusion and hope, so that, in a world of uncertainty, you're tied together by something besides chance and desire. You can stake a claim to them, to the flesh itself, the similarities of gesture and intonation and the clinging knowledge that at some level, even if it's only molecular, you are the same. But in the end, blood turns out to be a weak argument.

It wasn't just that I was angry. It wasn't that Elizabeth was so determined to make the evening just so. And it wasn't even that Henry embraced all of it with such absurd and whole-hearted pleasure. It was the obvious showmanship that bothered me most. The desire to make me both an audience and a willing participant in this impersonation of a family.

"Harry? Why don't you put Alice's beer in the fridge."

Alice laughed. "I guess you'd better. I can't drink 'em all at once." She held out the little suitcase out to me like a hotel guest checking in, but then she caught herself. "Wait. Guess you'd better leave me a few." She pried out four cans and gathered them in her hands. "Just so I don't get behind." Then, popping the first beer one-handed, she offered up a broad smile as if all were right with the world.

We sat on the sofa, Alice and I. Elizabeth took the chair. Henry dragged over a low ottoman and perched like a nervous shoe salesman. "Would you like to try the dip?"

"Nah. Thanks," said Alice. "Just the peanuts for now. I'm not really into all that frou-frou stuff." And gathering up a large fistful she leaned back, surveying her surroundings with pleasure. "You know, there's nothing," she said, "like a good party." And with a cheery salute she drained her beer.

For a moment I almost felt sorry for Elizabeth. She was smiling so fixedly, taking a series of delicate and fortifying sips of her wine. "I gather," she said, "you're not a detective."

Alice stared for a moment, startled, then the laughter bubbled out in a little cascade of peanut crumbs. "I guess I'm not!" She grinned, then turned to me. "What have you been telling these people?"

"Alice works construction for the city," I said.

"Technically I'm a Teamster. Construction is all those guys up to their butts in mud at the bottom of the hole. I'm the one in the backhoe. It may not make a lot of difference to you, but you can bet your ass it does to them." She gave Elizabeth a knowing glance, one woman of the world to another, then reached for a fresh can and popped it open.

Henry seemed to be wilting on the spot. He peered bleakly down at his watch, as if calculating his earliest possible bedtime. But years in commercial real estate had made their mark on my mother. "So, how did you two meet?"

I draped an arm over Alice's broad shoulders. "It was over cocktails, strangely enough. We struck up a conversation." I turned. "Am I remembering correctly?"

Alice laughed, waving away all the niggling details. "I

wouldn't be surprised, but you can't ask me. I don't always remember how much fun I've had."

"We were playing pool," I said.

"Were we?" She looked pleased. "That sounds like fun. I
can't remember the last time I played pool."

"We had the table to ourselves."

Alice gave my thigh a companionable pat and winked at
Henry. "This guy. You got to watch him all the time."

"We had a bet," I explained. "It was eight-ball."

Alice glanced over with the first glimmering of recall. "Didn't
you made some joke about balls? Was that you?"

"Well," I said, "if it wasn't, it should have been."

Henry was looking fascinated in spite of himself. "What was
the bet?"

Alice grinned. "Damned if I know. This wasn't about showing you my boobs, was it?"

"No," I said faintly, and caught myself. "That must have been
somebody else."

She laughed. "Well, whatever it was, you can be sure I paid
up. Some bets you don't mind losing, you know?" She hesitated,
a sudden startled look coming over her face. Then, she lowered
her chin in concentration and a moment later lifted from her
very diaphragm a profound and resonating belch. "God bless
me."

Henry looked startled, Elizabeth stunned. I could feel myself
blushing, but I spoke up gamely. "Gesundheit." No one else said
a word.

Then, like a reprieve, out of the silence, the doorbell rang.
Nobody moved at first as the sound faded into a lingering echo.
But after a moment Henry shifted. He half stood, then sat again,
and finally glanced up at me. "Maybe you should get that."

"What? I'm the butler, suddenly?" The last tendrils of embarrassment shaded quickly into irritation.

"I just thought..."

"It's your party."

But he looked so unhappy that, after another moment, I stood up. As I did, Henry stood as well. "What? Do you want me to get it, or not?"

My father hesitated, his face alive with indecision, but as I turned toward the door he turned as well and laid a tentative hand on my arm. "There's something I should tell you."

"Now?"

"I think...."

"Henry?" Elizabeth had one hand raised like a drowning woman, and a taut, wide-eyed look. "We could use another bottle of wine. And I think Alice is ready for more beer."

My father hesitated, his hand splayed on my wrist. "The thing is," he whispered, "I just wanted you to have fun."

"I am having fun. Can't you tell?"

"And, Henry...?" my mother called again. "You might see if there are any more peanuts."

With a pallid smile he turned and headed toward the kitchen as the bell rang again. I stepped forward, unsuspecting, and opened the door.

Mona wore black tights, a short red skirt and a bright yellow blouse that wasn't quite the same shade as her hair. The clothes seemed at war with one another, and together they bleached all the warmth from her skin, but there was something about her that seemed suddenly more real and solid than anything else in the room. All at once I realized how long it had been since I'd seen her last, and I had to fight the urge to grab hold of her and run. She held a bottle of wine unsuspecting in both hands like a sign of the festivities to come, but her smile was already fading before the expression on my face. "Hi."

"What are you doing here?"

"Cut it out," she said. "I'm not that late, am I?"

She stepped inside just as Henry came hurrying back with an open bottle of wine in one hand, a can of peanuts in the other, and a nest of fresh beer cans in the crook of his arm. He offered a warm and anxious smile. "You look great."

"Thanks," said Mona. "I thought maybe I had the wrong night."

"No. This is it," he said. "Come on in. Let me introduce you."

But as he ushered her ahead, I caught the tail of his jacket and drew him back. "Henry?"

"I ran into her the other day," he said in a rushed whisper. "I thought you'd invited her. You said you were going to."

"No, I didn't."

"Well, you should have!" he snapped, and hurried after her.

Mona stood for a moment in the door of the living room gazing down at the sofa, trying to figure out what Alice could be doing there and who she was with. I could see the exact moment when she figured it out.

She would have shoved past and headed straight for the door if Henry hadn't laid a firm and fatherly arm around her shoulders. "You know Betsy, of course. And you remember Alice...." He hesitated, glanced back helplessly.

"Raeburn," I said weakly. "With an R."

"This is Mona Brown."

"Pleased to meet you," said Alice.

Mona barely nodded.

"I'm thinking maybe you could use a drink," said Henry.

He poured her a large glass of wine and settled her on the end of the sofa beside me. She looked thinner than usual, and her hair, instead of fading with time, had grown more lurid. But even pale and pinched as it was, her face looked beautiful in a way I hadn't remembered. I tried to replace the jagged sense of regret that was opening in my chest with a sense of righteous anger. What were my parents thinking, that they should drag her into this little performance of theirs? But as she glanced over at me there was no hiding from the hurt in her eyes. "I didn't know you were coming," I whispered, but that didn't seem to help.

"Have I seen you at Mom's?" asked Alice.

"I've been there," Mona said.

"I thought so. I never forget a face. Are you a sort of friend of the family?"

Mona scowled and opened her mouth, but Henry leaned forward hurriedly. "Mona is a private detective."

"Really? Isn't that something. I didn't know they really existed. Are you investigating something now?"

"Not at the moment."

Elizabeth had settled back in her chair with a cool hospitable smile. She no longer looked stunned or uneasy, as if Mona's discomfort had somehow relieved her of her own. She said, "Finally. I'm glad you could make it. I'm Elizabeth Drew."

"I know," said Mona.

"Of course you do. Would you like some artichoke hearts?"

"No, thank you."

"I've been wanting to meet you for a while. Of course, you know so much about me, it must feel as if we've already met."

"Not really," said Mona.

"Well, good. I'd hate to think I was such an open book."

I was startled by the edge to her voice. She seemed to have drifted away from the one, big, happy family scenario, but it wasn't clear why. What was the point of the evening, if it wasn't to demonstrate our private little happy ending?

Maybe Mona was wondering the same thing because she was watching with something like caution as Elizabeth continued. "I was just saying to Henry that you must be very good at your job. To have found me, I mean."

"Thanks."

"I hope it wasn't too much trouble."

"Not too much, no." Mona had her grim, business face on. Her voice was low.

At the other end of the sofa Alice was starting to look perplexed. "I don't get it," she said. "You were looking for her?"

"She found me," said Elizabeth.

"You mean professionally? Someone hired you to find her?"

"That's right," said Mona.

"You mean like some kind of a process server?"

"No," I said. "It's nothing like that."

"Man," muttered Alice. "I had one of those on my ass once—you don't want to know what for. But he was like a blood hound. He was all over me. Every time I turned, there he was."

"It wasn't like that."

But she was shaking her head, growing outraged even at the memory of it. "What an asshole. I'd almost forgotten. He was always poking his nose into my business. I think he even went through my garbage." She peered at Mona with a new light in her eye. "Is that what you do?"

Mona sat there, stubborn and small, like a canary facing down an alley cat. "Something like that."

"It is not!" I snapped.

"Well," said Alice grimly. "You've got some nerve."

"Thank you."

"She finds people who are lost, " I said. "That's what she does. She helps people get their lives back. She brings people together who couldn't do it on their own."

But Alice wasn't listening. She turned to Elizabeth. "And she was after you? Honey, I don't envy you."

"It was a little surprising," said Elizabeth. "I was living in Chicago, and out of the blue, she found me."

Alice nodded sympathetically. "Hiding out?"

"I wasn't hiding. I was just living there. But she tracked me down, anyway."

"Just like that? Minding your own business? You must have been pissed."

Elizabeth smiled demurely. "I was definitely surprised."

"Surprised?" I said. "That's it? That's all you felt?"

"No, of course not," she said. "That's not all. But you've got to admit, it was unexpected."

Alice turned to Mona. "Why would you do that?"

"What do you mean, why?" I snapped. "Because she was trying to help. Why do you think? She doesn't just do it for fun."

"Yeah, but still...."

"Maybe we should go to the table," said Henry quickly. He'd been silent all this time, subsiding under the sharpening tone of the conversation, but now he roused himself with an anxious smile. "It must be just about time."

"Not yet, dear," my mother said coolly. "It's not quite ready."

Henry's glance was imploring. "I hope you're all hungry. Betsy's made Beef Wellington. She spent the whole afternoon on it. I'm sure we'll really enjoy it."

"I thought you didn't cook," I said.

"It's a special occasion. I thought I'd try something nice. To make up for all those awful casseroles."

"I liked those casseroles."

"Well, you'll love this," said Henry hurriedly.

But Alice was undeterred. "I just think it's weird, that's all. Butting into someone else's business like that."

"She doesn't butt in," I said. "She helps out. If someone's lost, she finds them."

Alice crooked her head at my mother. "She didn't say she was lost."

"No," agreed Elizabeth.

"Besides," said Alice. "Don't people have the right to get lost if they want?"

"Why?" I said. "Why should they? The inalienable right to just go away? Without a word? Without an explanation?"

"Hey," said Alice. "It's not against the law to want to start over. I knew a guy once. He was good looking. Made pretty good money. But he was all over me. All lovey-dovey, but real demanding? We were at a bar, in West Des Moines. Not a great place, but not bad. After a while I went to the ladies' room, and then I just walked out the door." She grinned. "I don't know when he figured out I was gone."

"Did he come looking for you?" asked Henry.

"I don't know. He sure as hell never found me." She laughed. "I don't know anybody who couldn't use a fresh start, every once in a while."

Nobody replied. My mother was gazing speculatively over at Mona. After a moment she said, "Sometimes I can't help thinking that I must have made it too easy for you."

"It wasn't that easy."

"But you have to admit, if I'd really wanted to hide I'd have gone further than Chicago."

"If you'd really wanted to hide?" I said. "What do you mean? Instead of just pretending? Tell me." I turned to Mona. "If someone really wants to hide, how do they do it? How is it different? Disappearing suddenly. Driving off. No phone calls. No letters."

"I phoned," said Elizabeth, frowning slightly.

Mona glanced at me, uncertain if I really wanted to know. But after a moment she said, "They change their names. They change their habits. If you want to disappear, it's not enough just to move. That's what's hard. People tend to slip back into the old routines."

"Is that how you found me?"

Mona seemed to measure my expression. "I don't really want to talk about it."

"Professional secrets?"

"Something like that."

"But I'm interested."

"Why?" I asked. "So you can do a better job next time?"

"I'm just curious."

"What does it matter?" said Henry hurriedly. "We're all just happy how things turned out."

"Of course," said Elizabeth. "Of course we are. But I'm just curious. If I were hiding? Could you still have found me?"

"It might have taken a little longer," Mona conceded. "If you didn't want to be found."

"Do most people?" she asked. "Want to be found, I mean. In your experience?"

"Sometimes. Sometimes it's like a test. They want to find out how far someone's willing to go for them. The harder they make it, the greater the proof."

"Betsy?" my father said. "We should probably see about dinner."

"Just a second, Henry. Please."

I glanced over. My father was smiling hopefully, but not with any assurance. Here he was. He had proved his love. He had tracked her down. But how could he be sure that it was really what she'd wanted?

And I thought of Mona's father, drifting from bar to bar, waiting for his daughter to find him, then later, drifting away altogether. Had he meant to get so far lost? Or had he wanted her to follow him even there? And I thought of Elizabeth simply driving away one day. Were they both just testing the limits of what it would take nearly to escape, or did they simply want to be gone?

"And if it isn't?" said Elizabeth. "If that's not what they want? Then, as Alice says, what business is it of yours?"

I turned angrily. "But you wanted to be found, didn't you?" Though at that moment I remembered what Mona had said, all those weeks ago. People don't hide, because they want to be found. And that was true. I knew it was true. I just stared with a clenched and sinking feeling, marveling that I could be caught again on my own barbed hopes. "I mean, you're glad, aren't you? That you were found? You're not sorry."

"Yes," said my mother. And then, as if realizing what she'd said. "Of course I'm glad."

"Then, what's the problem?"

"The important thing," said Henry soothingly, "is that we found you. Isn't that right? I mean, that's what's important. That you're back."

"Of course it is," she said. "Harry, there's no reason to get upset."

"I'm not upset."

"We don't need to talk about it any more. I didn't mean to upset anyone."

"Good," I said. "Fine."

"I think Alice could use another beer."

And sure enough there she was, picking through the empty cans for one she might have overlooked. Without a word I stood and headed toward the kitchen.

It was as I stepped in through the doorway that I noticed the thin silver haze hanging on the air by the ceiling and the wispy cloud spilling out from the lip of the oven. I stood there for a long moment with a hot grim ingot of satisfaction glowing in my chest, then I turned in the doorway. "Is it just me," I said, "or does anyone else smell smoke?"

"Damn it!" My mother leapt to her feet and rushed to the kitchen. The others followed in her wake, drawn like a crowd to the promise of bad news. She opened the oven, and the gentle wisps of cloud became a torrent. "God damn it!" She waved an oven mitt angrily at the smoke, and then reached in. The Beef Wellington had seen better days. Charred to the consistency of a moon rock, it sat at the center of an oval stain of burned fat, looking sad and disappointed in its sagging puff pastry.

"It'll be fine," said my father, all unflagging hope.

"For God's sake, Henry! It's burned to a crisp! Look at it!" She glared around, looking for someone whose fault this could be. And I thought of all the cookies she had burned, all the casseroles she'd overcooked and, in a world of fresh starts and new beginnings, I marveled at the power of the past to reach out and reclaim you when you least expect it.

34

The party broke up early.

In all my preparations I had never thought ahead to the end of the evening, though by the time it came, there weren't many options—a disastrous party had its own kind of awful momentum that carried the whole night along. Mona drove off without a word. My parents stood in the doorway, wrapped tightly in their own conversation. And when Alice climbed in behind the wheel of her car and started it up, there was nothing for me to do but climb in beside her. She drove us away with a kind of bleary expectancy, peering ahead through the windshield as the road materialized foot by foot in the glare of her headlights.

I'd been drinking diligently all evening long, but my mind remained dispiritingly clear. Houses slipped past in a kind of heightened focus, and I tried not to think of Mona. Or if I did, I tried to focus on her parting expression, the clenched jaw and narrowed eyes, and to see only the anger smoldering there and not the hurt. But other memories of her invested the darkness, shallow-breasted and pale as a ghost, and I carried them with me as we drove.

"That was some party," observed Alice.

"Yeah."

She shook her head, marveling. "Boy. That beef Wilmington."

"Wellington."

"What was that all about?"

"It's not supposed to look like that."

"And what about that Maura? What's her story? Talk about one pissed off chick."

"Yeah," I said. "She's funny that way."

The last time I'd driven home with Alice I'd been woozy from shock and loss of blood, and events had kept slipping out of my grasp. I wasn't bleeding now, but the night had that same shifting, uncertain quality. So much so that, when Alice parked in front of her apartment, the familiarity of it startled me the way a person who has dreamed of a landscape is startled to find it actually exists.

She turned in her seat. "You want to come in?"

Reluctantly I nodded. "I could maybe do that."

I was thinking of Mona's parting glance, fierce and angry. I had pretty much burned my bridges. And what was left? A night alone at the bar? The ache in my chest was nothing Alice could cure, but the thought of being alone seemed more than I could imagine. And so, without plans or desire I trudged along beside her up the walk to the shadowy doorway and watched as she wedged her hand into the tight pocket of her jeans and drew out a single key. She held it up as if we should both be equally surprised that it was there, then using both hands to guide it in, unlocked the door.

The house smelled surprisingly cozy, a mixture of baby powder and burned toast, and as Alice moved through the small living room turning on lights, we were gradually surrounded by a warm and unexpected encroachment of peach. The walls, the furniture, the lampshades, the curtains, everything was draped or molded or painted in various shades. There was nothing frilly or feminine about it. No ruffles or bows or little exuberances of fabric. Instead the warm walls and the low glow of the lamps gave the whole apartment the vaguely disturbing feel of surrounding flesh, as if we'd been swallowed by something with an improbably neat digestive tract.

Alice halted in the kitchen doorway, swaying gently. "What'll you have? I've got beer. I might have some wine somewhere." Then she added with a suddenly shy gruffness, "Unless, you know, you want to lie down."

And though I'd done nothing but drink all night, I said. "Maybe we should have another beer."

Alice hesitated. Then giving in to her own shifting balance, she leaned heavily against the door frame. "You're not a little tired?"

"I'm okay."

"I think maybe I'll lie down," she said. "If you don't mind."

She turned, and reluctantly I followed her down a narrow peach hallway. "You can get yourself a beer, if you want," she said.

"That's okay."

"You don't snore, do you?"

"I don't think so."

She nodded. "I'm a very light sleeper."

The bedroom was narrow and more pink than peach, as if we were working our way up the color spectrum. Alice sat heavily on the edge of the bed. She smiled and started to unbutton her shirt. I told myself, okay. This is okay. Though I wished my head wasn't quite so clear. "Maybe I will have that beer."

She looked up, startled. "Okay. They're out in the kitchen." She pointed a little vaguely down the hall.

"Do you want one?"

"No. I don't know. Sure. Why not?"

I found my way to the kitchen and drew two beers from the fridge. It was surprisingly well stocked with vegetables, cold cuts, food of all sorts. Somehow that made it even stranger, wandering in the house of someone who made lunches and dinners for herself; who, upon waking in the morning, would go about a normal day. It was odd to think this night was part of anyone's normal life, least of all my own.

When I got back to the bedroom Alice was naked beneath the covers. A single lamp glowed. Her clothes lay piled on a chair: jeans, flannel shirt, socks, and the limp drape of bra and underpants. I stood there, foolish and awkward, the two bottles turning clammy in my hands. "You could just put them on the table," she suggested.

"Okay."

Without the bottles there was nothing for me to do with my hands except undress. I draped my clothes on the chair over hers, and skinning off my shorts climbed hurriedly in beside her. The sheets were cold. The mattress had a soft and unfamiliar droop.

"This is cozy," she said.

"I'm afraid my hands are a little cold."

She smiled, and taking my excuse for an invitation she drew one cold hand under the covers to the warmth of her belly. "I'll heat them up." Her flesh, unconfined by flannel or denim, felt slack and smooth, and I could trace under my touch the cross-hatched line where the waistband dug in. "That's nice," she murmured. Her breath was warm and beerily humid. Her voice had the vague tone of someone floating between drunkenness and sleep, and for a moment I thought she might just drift off, but her hand, releasing mine, slipped purposefully down to where my poor, doleful flesh, caught up in the general air of troubled distraction, was showing distressingly few signs of life.

"Um. I guess I'm a little tired."

She smiled conspiratorially. "I know what you need."

"No, really. It's okay."

But she had already reared up and, dragging the covers down, huddled over me like some hardy pioneer woman breathing life into a dying campfire. I closed my eyes and tried to concentrate as her mouth, hot in the darkness, enveloped me in a moist and unemphatic grip. I tried to conjure up impure thoughts, I tried to will the troops into action, but all I felt was nerveless and distant. Alice worked diligently at first as I sank into a deepening pool of embarrassment and shame, but nothing happened, and after a while she slowed to a soft and ruminative stillness, as if she'd lost track of where she was going.

I reached down a tentative hand. "I'm sorry," I said awkwardly. "Maybe I could do something for you...."

But she said nothing. And as I lay there wordlessly in a bleak cloud of mortification and relief, Alice laid her cheek heavily against my thigh and fell asleep.

I eased out from under her head, tucking the covers in around her, and slipped out down the peach hallway, through the peach living room, and away. But once outside, beneath the shadowy trees, I realized I had no further plan. I didn't want to go home now, not to Henry and Elizabeth. I could go to the bar, but the idea seemed so bleak and dreary that I turned and started blindly up the street without any real confidence that it could take me anywhere I'd want to be.

The sounds of a drunken party floated on the breeze; someone was having fun at least. There were a few loud voices, and then nothing. I kept walking. After a moment I heard the low whine of a car engine, oddly comforting in the silence. Someone else wandering around the dark end of town. At least I wasn't alone. With a flash of headlights, the car turned the corner behind me and after a moment, as if making up its mind, drew closer. It moved slowly, creeping along behind me, just keeping pace. Out of the corner of my eye, I caught a glimpse of red, and I had the sudden, unreasoning conviction that Mona, who was after all a private detective, had managed to find me. Never mind that she had no earthly reason to want to try. I turned. But it was a Jeep, not a Mustang.

I should have run, but I was too tired, and the sight of Biff grinning coldly behind the wheel seemed less a threat than simply the next obvious step in an evening gone so far wrong. So, when he held up the heavy black revolver, not so much pointing it as simply showing it to me, as if it were something interesting I might enjoy, I walked over and climbed in beside him.

"Have you ever had one of those nights?" I asked.

"Feel like a little drive?"

"No."

But he just shrugged and put the car in gear. We didn't drive far. After a few minutes, turning a corner, he pulled off to the side of the road in front of a darkened house. He killed the engine and sat looking down at the pistol cradled in his lap. It glinted in the darkness. He had the weary expression of someone who thought he had already been through all this once. "Didn't I tell you not to bother Jean?"

"Would it do any good to say we didn't?"

"Tell me you haven't seen her lately."

"A couple of weeks ago. She came by. She wanted to tell us not to bother you."

Biff nodded, smiling thinly, as if the gun in his lap were saying something funny. "How'd she seem?"

"A little anxious."

"She didn't happen to mention my money?"

"She said you didn't have it."

"I know I don't have it. Why do you think I'm asking for?"

"She said she didn't have it either."

He considered that. "Did you believe her?"

"She's your girlfriend."

"Did she say where she put it?"

"No."

"And I'm supposed to believe you?"

I said nothing. Biff was peering down at the dark pistol glinting in his hands. "You married?"

"No."

"Got a girlfriend, though."

"Tell you the truth," I said, "I don't know what I've got."

"Do you love her?"

"I'm not even sure how to tell anymore."

He smiled grimly at that. "Does she make you mad?"

"Yeah."

"How mad?"

"Pretty mad."

"'Cause that's the test," he said. "You take it from me. It's the only way to know for sure. Everything else... it's bullshit. All that stuff about romance? All that candlelight and shit? That's nothing. You can do that with anyone. All that lovey-dovey stuff. But if she makes you mad, really mad. I mean if she just bugs the shit out of you. You know? And she takes your stuff, and hides it? I mean, if she really just gets under your skin. So you just want to slap her. Or you just want to get away as far as you can....” He shook his head.

“Yeah?”

“All of that, and you still can’t leave? I mean, you get in the car, and you start it up, and you drive, and you stop. You think you’re headed for Colorado and you end up at some bar down by the river ‘cause that’s as far as you could get? Well. The rest of it’s just fun and games. But when you can’t leave...? That’s when it’s serious.”

“Jean’ll be happy to hear that.”

Biff looked curious. “Your girlfriend’s name is Jean?”

“Mona.”

“Oh,” he said. “Yeah. But you can’t tell her, man. What do you think? She’ll just walk all over you.”

“She sort of does that anyway,” I said. “At least, she did.”

He nodded companionably. “They do bug the shit out of you sometimes.”

“I just don’t like being lied to,” I said. “That doesn’t seem like too much to ask, does it?”

“Oh, man. Lying… That’s what I’m saying. It’s all lies. I mean, she says what she has to, or what she thinks you want to hear, or maybe she even says what she’s really thinking. But you can never know for sure. She doesn’t even know, herself, what she means most of the time, and it’s a cinch you never will. So you can’t get hung up on that. It’s not about what she says. It’s how she feels. And how she makes you feel.”

I thought about that for a while. “Even if that all made any kind of sense, which it doesn’t, that’s still the problem,” I said. “How do you know how you feel?”

Biff frowned angrily, pointing the gun at me. “Don’t give me that shit. You know. Deep down inside you do. So don’t go telling me you don’t.”

"I don't."

"Then leave her," he said

"I did."

He shrugged. "Then there's your answer. What's the problem?"

"Who said I had a problem?" I said glumly.

Biff hefted the revolver. It looked heavy and thick-barreled in his hand. I stiffened. "You're not going to bother us anymore," he said.

"Is that a question?"

"No."

"No," I agreed.

"Put this over there." He waved the gun toward the glove compartment. I took it. It weighed even more than I expected. I put it away and closed the hatch. "You want a lift some-where?" said Biff.

"No. Thanks. I'll walk." I climbed out, and hesitated. "So, what about the money?"

"What about it?"

"What if she hasn't got it?"

"She's got it," he said. "No big deal. She'll tell me where it is. She wants to."

"You know, maybe if you just told her you loved her...."

"Man, did you tell your girlfriend you loved her?"

"Yeah."

"And how did that work out?"

I hesitated.

"Shut the door," he said.

I shut the door. The jeep roared away, spitting gravel all over my shoes.

35.

The Blue Diner was almost empty. There were a couple of college students studying at the tables along the side, and a janitor off the night shift at the hospital was working his way implacably through a plate of chicken-fried steak. The booth I chose had a constellation of toast crumbs and a few moist fragments of scrambled eggs lingering on the tabletop, and I had brushed the eggs together into a pile and was writing brief messages to myself in the toast crumbs when Rusty wandered over with a damp cloth and wiped the table clean.

I gazed up at her weakly. "How's your day been?"

"Just peachy. You want a menu?"

"I don't suppose you have any tuna casserole?"

"Sorry. The chef's opposed to seafood on principle. You want to try something in a pork chop?"

"Actually, I was hoping for something a little more comforting."

Rusty looked suddenly concerned. "You're not here to see Jane, are you?"

"What if I were?"

She shook her head gravely. "She says you've been kind of an asshole lately."

"Did she actually say asshole?"

"Yeah, she did."

"Did she look like she might be open to reconsider her position?"

"I wouldn't count on it." She drew out her pad and made a few marks. "How about stroganoff? It's served with noodles and a side salad or vegetable. That's pretty much as comforting as she comes."

The plate came piled with overcooked noodles drowned beneath a spill of beef and cream sauce. I considered it with mild alarm. "Do I look that hungry?"

"You look that sad," said Rusty. "You want cheese?"

"On stroganoff?"

"Some do."

"No, thanks."

She turned and wandered away, and I picked up my fork. The sauce had the rich, chalky flavor of too much sour cream, and it clung to the noodles with a viscous tenacity that could, I supposed, be considered comforting. The meat was as chewy as the noodles weren't, but I liked the fact that you didn't have to cut it, that all you had to do was eat, though after a while even that seemed too much effort.

When Rusty wandered back again she gazed down at the plate, still nearly full. "Anything you want me to pass on to the chef?"

"Do you think she'll ever forgive me?"

"I don't know. She's pretty mad."

"Have you seen her this mad before? What about with Carlisle? He was a jerk, right? He must have made her this mad."

But Rusty just shook her head.

I thought about Mona. I thought about how little we had in common. It was pretty much Henry. That was it. And Jean Tipton. What else had we ever done together? How had we spent our time? Spying on Jean, waiting for her life to go bad. That was it. And how could sitting in a dark car, waiting for someone else's troubles to catch up with them, be any sort of basis for love? We'd built our relationship on Jean's shaky hopes and Henry's love life. And now Jean was gone, and Henry was as far away as he could be.

"Are you busy?" I asked.

"I'm not going to cut your meat for you."

"Have you got your cards?"

She didn't actually look surprised, but she let her impassive gaze rest on me a moment longer than necessary. "I got a special rate for friends of the family."

"I don't suppose I qualify."

She disappeared into the kitchen and returned a moment later with the deck of Tarot cards wrapped in their red silk scarf. I pushed my plate aside and gave the table a quick wipe as Rusty unwrapped the deck and tied the scarf around her head. "So?"

"I want you to tell my fortune."

"I don't do fortunes."

"My future, then."

"It's not like that."

"What's it like, then?" I asked peevishly.

"You've seen it. It's not a set of directions."

"But that's just what I need. Where do I go for a set of directions?"

She frowned, her fingers hovering over the deck. "Okay. We'll try it, but don't blame me if it doesn't work." She sat up very straight and began shuffling the cards. "Do you have a specific question?"

"Just the whole thing. The future."

"It doesn't work like that. What part of your future? What's the focus of the reading?"

"Is it just my future? Can it be someone else's as well?"

"Only where it overlaps yours. But you need to narrow it down. Money, career, romance."

I hesitated. "Do people still call it romance?"

"Some do. More than most."

"What if you don't believe in romance any more?"

Rusty regarded me dourly for a moment. "Choose five. Don't look at them."

I closed my eyes and chose with great care.

"Keep them in order. Don't turn them."

"How do most people do this?"

"That's fine," she said.

She gathered the remaining cards and set them in a neat pile precisely at the corner of the table. Then she picked up the five I'd chosen. "Empty your mind of doubt and worry."

"Is there another option?"

"Just do your best."

She laid the cards face down in a row. "This is Affirmation. It's what's going to happen. This is Negation. What can prevent it. This is the Explanation. Why you're in this situation."

"But that's just it," I said. "What's the situation? That's what I need to know."

She ignored me completely and, laying down the last two cards, said, "This is the Solution. What you can do about it. This is the Determination. What will happen in the end."

"Just like that?"

"Depending on the steps you take."

"Which steps? That's what I need to--"

"Shush," said Rusty not unkindly. Then she reached out and turned the first card.

A skeleton swathed in a long black robe. He had a grim and lipless smile and carried a scythe arching over his shoulder, caught in mid-swing. I gazed down at it, and even though it was just a card, even though I knew this was all just a matter of chance, it took me a moment to be able to swallow. "That can't be good."

Even Rusty seemed a little shaken. "This is the Affirmation."

"So this is the best I can expect?"

"This is what's going to happen. Or might, if you don't change it."

"So, what are you saying? I'm going to die?"

"Not necessarily. It could mean a sudden change or an end to things as they are."

"That's all? Just a sudden change?"

"Maybe." She didn't sound all that convinced. "Or inevitability. Something that can't be avoided. A sudden change of plans, or a personal failure."

"Could you be a little less specific?"

"Or it could really mean death," she said.

"Mine?"

"Or someone close to you."

"You know, I don't really believe in this."

"It's too late for that now." She was reaching for the second card. "This is Negation."

"This is what can prevent it?"

"Maybe."

It was an old stone tower crumbling beneath a bleak sky, tipping at an anxious angle as if it couldn't stay upright much longer. "Oh," said Rusty.

I tried to smile. "We're not looking all that upbeat, are we?" She was frowning over the card. "This is a joke, isn't it?" I said. "You're doing this for Mona, to get back at me."

She shook her head. "Disruption. Adversity of some sort. An unforeseen ending."

"Is it all going to be downhill from here?"

"It could mean disgrace, or misery. Maybe a personal loss."

"What sort of loss?"

"It could be financial. Do you have any investments?"

"No."

"It could be personal. The break up of a marriage or a relationship."

"You know," I said slowly, "it would probably be okay if you just stopped right now."

But she was already reaching for the third card. "It can't go on like this. There's got to be some good news somewhere."

"So this looks pretty bad to you?"

"Not bad. I didn't mean bad. It's not a question of good or bad."

"Death and destruction? That doesn't sound bad to you?"

She turned the card over. The Devil. A smiling character in red tights and a cape, leaping across the card as if taunting me. "It's reversed," Rusty, said. "Upside down."

"Is that good or bad? I know. There's no such thing. But what if there were?"

"It's the card of blindness."

"I'm going to go blind?"

"It's the Explanation card. Why you're where you are. It's about blindness, jealousy, or an illness of some sort. Or an evil fate. Or wrong choices. Pettiness, weakness."

Blindness, pettiness, the break up of a relationship. It was as much about my past and present, as it was about my future. Maybe that was the secret of fortune telling: your life never really changed. Despite all your greatest hopes and fears, you remained what you were, and the only trick to telling the future was just to mark closely the confusion of the present.

Rusty was shaking her head, staring down at the cards. "You don't get a hand like this very often."

"I don't suppose I could have gotten somebody else's cards by mistake."

She didn't even bother to reply. "This is the Solution." She reached down and uncovered the image of a man hanging upside down from a rope around his ankle. He seemed remarkably calm about it all, considering. His face wore a look of bland patience. And then I noticed that the rope was looped up over a tree branch and down behind his back, where he appeared to be holding it in one tight fist.

"Is he doing that to himself?"

"It's the image of self-sacrifice. It brings a growth of wisdom or intuition. Giving something up for the sake of something better. But there's a need for caution as well. There's hidden danger."

"He's hanging upside down. How hidden is that?"

"That's not the danger. That's the self-sacrifice. The danger's somewhere else. There's strife, disillusionment. But something more. There are occult forces in operation around you, but the card suggests a growth of intuition. Or maybe latent psychic abilities."

I looked up bleakly. "I have psychic abilities?"

"But you don't know you have them."

"What makes you think I don't?" But Rusty wasn't smiling. I nodded down at the one remaining card. "So, what's that last one, then? Is that the answer to everything?"

She shook her head. "There is no answer. You didn't ask a question. But it's the Determination. What's likely to happen."

"I don't suppose we could just leave it where it is."

"Of course." And she moved with sudden eagerness to gather up the cards.

"Wait." Reluctantly, I reached out and flipped the card over. It showed an old man in a cloak holding a lamp up against the darkness, alone on an empty plain.

"Well," said Rusty after a moment. "That could be worse. It's the Hermit. Actually, considering everything else, it's a good card."

"How good?"

She straightened it nervously in its place. "It means self-examination, moderation, wisdom, silence. Prudence, withdrawal, solitude."

"So I'm going to learn wisdom through self-examination and moderation?"

"Maybe."

Hurriedly she gathered up the cards and slipped the scarf from her head as I gazed down at the blank table where they used to be. It was a parlor trick, I told myself. The last resort of wacky old women and wandering minds, and it didn't mean anything more than the fifteen minutes of lost time it took. It was no more an omen than the plate of congealed stroganoff, sitting cold and forgotten by the edge of the table. But there was something in my mind that couldn't shake it, and I wondered if the true meaning of that last card wasn't simply that I was going to be alone for the rest of my life.

"You know," said Rusty as she stood up and slipped the cards into the pocket of her apron. "It's probably not as bad as it seems."

"Really?"

She shrugged, then nodded at the plate of cold stroganoff. "You through with that?"

Outside I found the bright red Mustang, newly repaired and parked at the curb, but there was no sign of Mona. The door up to her apartment was closed and silent. I stood there for a moment, debating, then spotted the folded scrap of paper on her windshield. It had my name on it. She must have seen me in the diner. I pulled it out from under the wiper blade and opened it up. It was written in lipstick, two words alone in the middle of the page. One of them was 'you.' I turned and started walking. There were definitely occult powers at work. With the first stirrings of my latent psychic abilities I could tell without the slightest doubt that I had screwed up my life in a huge and irrevocable way.

At the corner of Washington, meditating on a red light, I saw something that momentarily raised my spirits. Another loser in love. Standing in the shadow of an alley a man was shouting at a parked taxi. I couldn't see clearly, but in the glare of the headlights I could make out the figure of a woman, hunched in the back seat, with her hands up as if protecting herself or just refusing to argue. Her window was open, and the taxi was just sitting there, waiting for them to finish.

I stood, watching with a quick rush of sympathy. Was love always this hard? It started out all comfort and excitement, and ended with what? A five-card spread of some glowering future or a simple and unoccult argument in an alley on a Saturday night. But maybe the problem lay in thinking of it as a comfort. Love was nothing as gentle as that. It was fiercer and more dangerous: affection with a razor's edge, all exhilaration and loss.

I couldn't hear what they were saying. The man's voice rebounded off the half-closed window, muffled and distorted in the darkness, and the woman's voice, if she was answering at all, was lost in the cab. She sat hunched and unmoving as the anger vibrated around her until, as if the time had run out, she leaned forward and signaled the driver. The cab started up.

It caught the man by surprise. He was drawn off balance, as if tied to the car by his fury, so that he stumbled into a jagged run. He was shouting now, not into the window but out into the night, waving his arms, shaking his fists, twisting in a pantomime of angry futility to deliver a swinging kick that fell far short of the taxi's bumper. It spun him around so he had to catch hold of a parking meter to keep his balance, and he stood there sagging as the anger ebbed out of him like stuffing from a doll. And only then did I recognize him.

By the time I'd crossed the street Henry was breathing like a man trapped in a bell jar. At first I thought he was drunk. The wine from dinner was sour on his breath. "Henry! What the hell?"

"Harry?" He looked up, startled. "Don't let her. You need to stop her. Wait." But when he turned again, stricken, the cab had already vanished.

"Are you all right? What is it? What's going on?"

"She's gone," he said. "She left." He was panting still, each thought vanishing in a wisp of breath, as if some part inside of him continued to rush around, using up oxygen faster than he could take it in.

"Henry! Calm down. Don't worry. It's okay."

But my father was shaking his head. He seemed to lose his balance again, and shifted his grip from the parking meter to the front of my jacket. "God damn her!" His first complete thought. Then, a look of surprise bloomed on his face. "Harry...?" And without another word he crumpled within the slow circle of my arms, sliding to the ground.

Like the pistol an hour before, he was heavier than I would have thought possible, as if the weight of his sadness lent itself to the otherwise modest bulk. I hoisted him up, staring around at the empty street. Where was everybody? How could it be so deserted on a Saturday night? I staggered into motion.

The hospital was five blocks away, and in the endless time

it took to get there, lungs bursting, heart pounding like a fist against a locked door, I didn't see a single, solitary soul. The whole town might have been empty. And all I could think of was that first card turned over back at the diner, and the grim fleshless smile leering up at me.

The emergency room seemed familiar, almost comforting. The ordinary carpet and the black and chrome chairs were unchanged, while at the front desk sat the same receptionist from all those weeks ago. I felt a kind of drifting lack of surprise. Each separate thing unfolded step by step. The orderlies, moving in a leisurely rush, lifted Henry onto a gurney and wheeled him out of sight, as a woman led me through a series of questions and typed my answers into her computer with a calm expression that I could read as compassion if I chose.

"I've got to see him."

"He's being taken care of."

"Is he going to be all right?"

"They're doing all they can."

When I was finally led back to a curtained alcove I found him, looking old and orphan-like in the childish drape of the hospital gown. His eyes were closed, his head propped against a pillow, with a respirator taped to his mouth and the sharp, reassuring beep of the monitor announcing, at hurried and irregular intervals, the thin reprieve of each heartbeat.

36

I stepped into the silence of the house and into the stale haze of burned meat still hanging on the air. On the counter the empty wine bottles were gathered like a crowd around the charred relic of the Beef Wellington, and the sink was piled with saucepans turning sour in the warmth. Whatever else my parents had done after the rest of us left, they hadn't bothered to clean up. I hesitated. "Anybody home?"

But of course, there wasn't.

All these years I'd been worried about the possibility of a stroke. I'd fretted about his blood pressure, about the bacon, the cheese, the coffee, the eggs, about the numbness in his arm and the hidden frangibility of all the tiniest blood vessels in the depths of his brain. But I should have known. I should have seen it. The problem was never his brain. It was always his heart that I should have worried about.

Is he going to be all right?

The doctor had been a narrow, gray man, curt and impatient, as if there were any number of other places he'd rather have been. He'd glanced up from Henry's chart with a frown. Was I aware my father's cholesterol was quite high, and there was a history of high blood pressure? Did he seem to be under any extra stress lately? Were there any problems at home? Yes, yes, yes. He looked grimly satisfied at the sense it all made. In some of these cases, he said, it was just a matter of time.

"But is he going to be all right?"

At this point they couldn't be sure. He was out of danger. But there might have been some collateral damage; portions of the brain might have been compromised, though they wouldn't know the extent until he regained consciousness. There was no need for me to stay. There was nothing I could do. I should just go home and rest.

Upstairs, the master bedroom was empty and forlorn, the bedspread as smooth and unmarked as a new snowfall. There was no sign of my mother. No toothbrush in the bathroom, no hairbrush on the bureau, no clothing. Not even a hint of perfume in the air. I stood there and wondered what to do. Sleep, the doctor had said, but the house was too silent for sleep. I gathered together Henry's toothbrush, toothpaste, his razor, his pillow, and, as an afterthought, the little Panasonic radio, gray and dirty, that he listened to when he was working out in the garden. I made a little pile on the bed to take to him tomorrow. I told myself he'd need them when he woke up. Then I stopped.

I sank down onto the bed, beside the silent phone. I dialed Directory Assistance. No, there was no listing for an Elizabeth Drew. Not in Chicago, not in Rogers Park, or Northbrook, Glencoe, Winnetka, Hyde Park. I worked my way north and south through the suburbs, but there was nothing. It wasn't that uncommon a name. There should have been at least one, even if it wasn't the right one, but the absence was like a proof of impossibility. She had vanished completely. I got up and searched the closet, the bedside tables, every bureau drawer, looking for a scrap of paper, a matchbook, a business card, a little torn sheet with her familiar fine and tangled handwriting, anything that would tell me where she lived. But there was nothing. It might all have been a mirage—her return, even her existence—except that I found, in the back of Henry's closet, a box of photographs.

I had thought they were gone. I'd thought they had long ago been fed to the fire. When Henry took them from the parlor I had said we should just burn them, and he had reluctantly agreed. But in the end I suppose it was more than he could do. There weren't that many; I guess we weren't a particularly photographic family. Maybe we thought we didn't need them to remember. Maybe there just hadn't been a chance. But here they were, like a thin reminder of forgotten times: everybody looking so young and optimistic, everybody smiling for the camera.

I could picture him now, all these years, alone in his bedroom, leafing through the photos, preserving them. Henry, his young wife, his infant son—all the irredeemable years preserved in changeless, smiling faces. While in real life, the actual wife and the actual son, in their own respective ways, had wanted to do nothing but forget. He must have thought he was the only one holding us all together, despite our best efforts, despite the past and the present, binding us by some tenuous web of affection and will until he could finally get her back. And for what?

Oh, Henry. Poor Henry. What had he thought? That it would be enough if he changed? If he made a new man of himself? The two Bailey boys, getting back on the horse again. I thought of all the courage it must have taken to reach back for a life that had left you behind. I thought of what he must have felt when, after all his efforts to re-make himself, after his brand new leaf had been turned over and he had coaxed her back, she had told him that she just couldn't stick it. Sure, he had managed to change. But then, he hadn't been the problem to begin with. It was Henry she had telephoned. It was Henry she'd been dancing with, laughing with. And if it was Henry who drew her back, then, as clear as the silence of the house at this moment, it couldn't have been Henry who had first driven her away.

What else could I believe?

Clearly, she had waited until the time was right, until I should have been long gone, until she had every right to think she'd be able to return without having to face an evening like tonight. Without having to share her husband with a son who clearly had no clue what was going on. Who kept trying to entice her with meals she had grown tired of years ago. Who kept trying to bind her with guilt and anger, as if that could possibly have done anything but drive her away.

I'd never heard the house so quiet. The silence crowded into the room, muffling the air. It was speaking to me. It was reminding me of all that Henry wasn't saying. All the noise he wasn't making. The house was more about Henry's absence than it had ever been about my presence. Henry's absence, and now Elizabeth's. She hadn't spent more than four weeks here in the last six years, but even in that desperately short time she'd intruded back into this life more thoroughly than I ever had.

I felt myself disappearing. How could this have happened? How could I have been living all these years and have left myself behind? I felt how lightly I'd been skating over the surface of my own life, as if I'd had no place in it. As if this were some young stranger in the photographs, smiling so determinedly.

It was four in the morning when I left the house. I walked because I was in no hurry, and because I was too tired to do anything else. The diner was as dark as all the other storefronts on the street, but the red Mustang looked shiny and scornful under the streetlights. I climbed the stairs slowly, resting at the second floor landing before continuing to the top. I knocked.

She came slowly to the door, not as if she'd been asleep, but as if she knew who was knocking and had to decide whether to answer. She was wearing a gray sweatshirt over black sweatpants with the uneven hem of an undershirt hanging out like a little ruffle. She looked at me. "You've got to be kidding."

"I need to see you."

"It's fucking four o'clock in the morning."

"Please."

"What if I don't want to see you? What if it's not such a good time? What if I've got a fucking man in my bedroom?"

"Do you? Is Carlisle here?"

"Fuck you."

"I need to come in."

"Can you think of a single goddam reason why you should?" But after a moment longer she stepped back, letting the door swing open. "You look like shit," she said.

In the light of the living room she was taut and pale, except for her left eyebrow, which puffed out, pink and infected, around the shaft of a tiny silver barbell. "You pierced your eyebrow."

"Pretty great, isn't it?" she said sourly.

"Henry's in the hospital. I just took him there. The emergency room. I think they remembered me. It was just like old times."

"What do you mean? What is it? What happened?"

"A heart attack. I don't know how bad. He was standing on the street yelling at my mother."

"He was yelling?"

"Screaming."

"Henry?"

"He just collapsed. She's left again."

"Oh, no."

"She was driving off in a cab. There's nothing at the house. No sign of her. No toothbrush."

"Poor Henry," she murmured.

"I need to find her. I need her address. Her phone number. I need to get in touch with her. I don't even know where she is now." I thought how strange it was to be saying this as if it were something new, as if it hadn't been the rule of my life for so many years.

"Close the door," said Mona. "I've got it in my files."

"It's late," I said, as if it had only just occurred to me. "I am so tired."

Mona glanced coldly up. She seemed on the verge of saying something, but in the end just turned to the file cabinet and opened a drawer. "Have you got a piece of paper?"

"What? No."

Irritably she reached into her desk and took out a yellow legal pad. She threw it to me. I caught it clumsily, pages ruffling and folding under my fingers. "The number's 518--."

"Wait. I don't have a pen."

"Jesus Christ." She snatched a pen from the desk top. I thought she was going to throw it for a moment, but she just held it out.

"Thanks."

"518-361-5286. The address is 1417 Western Avenue in Evanston." She closed the file and threw it onto the desk. "Now get the hell out of here."

I held the pad awkwardly, looking down at the numbers. They hung there in the middle of the page as if referring to nothing at all. "Were you asleep?"

"No."

I touched my eyebrow where hers was so angry and swollen. "Did you do that yourself?"

"You got a problem with it?"

I shook my head. "I didn't know you were going to be there tonight. Honest."

"Henry invited me."

"I know. He didn't tell me. I didn't..." I shrugged. "It wasn't about you."

"Well, doesn't that make me feel better," she said. "And what was with that lumberjack?"

"I don't know. I just thought she was someone my mother would hate."

"You're supposed to stop doing that after high school," said Mona.

"I know."

"Did you sleep with her?"

"No. Not quite."

"Swell."

I felt the last of my energy draining away. "I've got to sit down."

I sank onto the arm of the sofa and slumped there, not so much sitting as failing to fall completely. I felt like a hollow vase, fragile and tippy. Beside me I noticed another figure, slumped in the same posture at the other end of the sofa. Paddington the Bear looking fresh and cheerful, even after all that had happened. "I like your friend."

"Shut up," said Mona. "You can sit, but it doesn't mean I have to talk to you."

"What's he doing here?"

"Jean left him behind. I'm babysitting."

And I thought back to that night when she had stormed out, empty handed in every sense, even this one. "He looks right at home." I reached over and lifted him onto my lap. It felt instantly comforting. "I can see how you'd get attached to these things." I leaned back wearily.

"Don't get too comfortable."

"I can't believe she's gone again."

"I thought you said you wanted her to leave."

"I did, didn't I?"

After a moment she gave me an irritable shove, and I shifted over. She sat down. "Is Henry going to be okay?"

"They don't know. He had a heart attack. Did I say that already?"

"He'll be okay."

But I just shook my head. "This is my fault."

"No, it's not. It's not anybody's fault."

"You don't believe that."

Mona sighed. "You should get some sleep."

"How can I sleep?" But I could feel my eyelids drifting down in spite of everything. "I don't want to go home. Not tonight."

"He's going to be all right."

"Please?"

Mona glared at me. "Just like that?"

"No," I said. "That's not what I meant."

"You got your address. Now get the hell out."

"Yeah." I nodded. But the prospect of climbing up off the sofa seemed far beyond my powers. I wondered how I'd ever managed it before. It was so soft. I could feel myself sinking….

"Hey! Wake up."

"I'm awake."

Mona glared at me, then she stood up. She brought a blanket from the bedroom closet and a fitted sheet, bright with a green and orange jungle print. "Get up," she snapped. She shook the sheet out over the cushions of the sofa, folding it like a tortilla, and laid the blanket over it. "You can use one of the cushions for a pillow."

"Thanks."

"He's going to be fine," she said brusquely.

I shook my head. "He loves her more than anything in the world, and I just drove her away. I don't think he's going to be fine."

"Go to sleep."

She turned off the light. The glow from the bedroom spilled in through the open door. She started to close it.

"Wait!" My chest was suddenly tight as a fist. "Would you leave it open?"

She frowned.

"I just need the light."

I waited for her sarcastic reply, but she said nothing. She crossed to the desk and turned on the lamp there. It lit up the piles of papers and the telephone and the photograph of Young Jane in a little tented glow. "Go to sleep," she said again.

I didn't even hear the door close.

But later something woke me, some dream. I started up with a sensation of falling, and jerked awake with a grip on the covers like a drowning man. I tried to remember where I was, but the room kept shifting. I saw the lamp, the desk, and I was straining at my memory to force it into this new shape as the door opened. Mona, her hair a shock of pale feathers, stood in a t-shirt, squinting against the light from the desk. "You okay?"

I looked up, aware of the bear still clutched fiercely in my arms. "Did I make a noise?"

"I thought you were dying in here."

"I didn't know where I was."

She sighed. "You're okay."

"I don't know," I said. "I don't think that's true."

She hesitated, then gave a jerk of her head. "Move over."

I dropped Paddington onto the floor and squeezed back against the cushions. The sofa wasn't all that wide. I held up the sheet, and Mona climbed in, backing into a snug, curving fit against me. I reached an arm around her. She was solid and warm. Her hair tickled my nose.

"I am so sorry," I whispered.

Her sigh was a faint, despairing breath against the bright sheets.

"Jane?" I pleaded. "Don't be mad at me. I've fucked up so many things. Please tell me I haven't fucked this up, too."

"Shut up," she said and slowly, reluctantly, laid a hand over mine. "Now go to sleep."

37

I woke to the warm and solid puzzle of Mona lying in the curve of my arm. A long way off the phone was ringing, but it stopped before I was fully awake, so I opened my eyes to the troubled awareness of silence and the vague premonition of something gone wrong. Henry? But there was no way the hospital could have known to reach me here; I hadn't told them where I'd be. And I realized, even in this, I was letting him down.

Mona shifted under my arm. "Did you answer that?" she murmured.

"No." On her eyebrow the angry pinch of flesh, skewered on the tiny barbell, was flecked at either end with a crust of blood. It looked ugly and painful and permanent, and that, too, was my fault. "Go back to sleep," I said.

"What time is it?"

"Twelve-thirty."

"Midnight?"

"No." The windows were bright with day. I wasn't sure when city employees had to be at work, but Alice must have long since risen from a groggy sleep to look, puzzled and half-remembering, at the empty bed beside her. I wondered what she made of it. Already it seemed distant and unreal.

"I had a terrible dream," Mona whispered.

"I know. I'm so sorry."

She reached up and touched her eyebrow with a tentative finger. "Do you hate it?"

"No."

"It'll be a little ring, eventually."

"It'll be nice."

She prodded the swollen flesh, and winced.

"Stop that."

"What? You think you're the only one who gets to hurt me?"

"That's right," I said. "Only me."

She let her hand come to rest on my arm just above the old wound, and I could feel her fingers pressing it lightly, testing it, tracing the thin angry scar bending across my wrist. "Does this hurt?"

"No."

"Too bad." But still her touch was light, as if the former pain was still part of whatever meaning it held. She gave a little shove. "Move. I've got to get going."

"You want some breakfast?"

"No."

"Coffee?"

She shrugged.

"You should put some disinfectant on that," I said.

"Just the coffee, thanks." She stood up. The t-shirt, wrinkled from the night, didn't quite cover the glint of festive green panties. She must have worn them last night to the dinner party. A long, long time ago. Now they looked too bright for the morning. "I'm going to take a bath," she said, and trudged blearily to the bedroom door, then paused. "That's not an invitation."

When she was gone I eased my feet to the floor, feeling stiff and rumpled from sleep, as if I were nothing more than my clothes. I walked over to the desk and dialed the hospital. It took them a while to locate the doctor in charge, time enough to imagine all sorts of disasters.

"He's stable," the doctor said. "He's sleeping."

"Has he woken up?"

"Not yet."

"You mean he's in a coma?"

"No. It's not a coma."

"But he's asleep."

"It's a good sign," the man said patiently.

I hung up. From the bathroom came the sound of running

water. Mona had left the door ajar, but I didn't know what that meant. What was the difference between a door left open a crack and one just incompletely closed? In the kitchen I made my way through the clutter of dirty dishes and brewed the coffee, but the only milk in the fridge had gone bad, so I poured it black and added sugar. I knocked on the bathroom door. "Coffee's ready."

"So, now you're afraid to come in?" she said peevishly.

I opened the door. The t-shirt and panties lay on the floor like bright scraps of shed skin. Beneath the water her breasts rose delicately. She wore her glasses. They were already misting up at the edges, but she gazed through them with an angry, challenging look, daring me to say anything at all.

"There's no milk."

"You can be such an asshole, you know?"

I nodded. "Your mother told me. I used to think it was a family trait, but now I realize it's something all my own." I set the mug down on the chair beside her. "I called the hospital. Henry's asleep."

"Is he going to be all right?"

"They don't know. They said it's a good sign, but what else are they going to say? I should probably call Elizabeth." I hesitated. "I don't suppose you know why she left? Did she tell you?"

"No."

"When your father left, how did your mother take it?"

Mona frowned impatiently. "There's not a lot of choice. There's only one way to take it."

"And you? What did you think?"

She hesitated. "It isn't your fault," she said finally. "You don't want to think like that."

"I don't know. Last night. I was an asshole. You said so yourself."

"That wasn't enough to drive her away."

"But what if it was? What if I've always been an asshole, and just didn't know it?"

"You're not," she said. "Not always. You can be really nice sometimes. When you don't mean to be."

The telephone rang. "I gave them this number," I said, and reluctantly stood up, but there seemed no rush to answer it. I no longer had any faith in good news, and bad news always arrived too soon, no matter what you did.

It was a man's voice, nobody I'd heard before. And the moment he spoke I felt the sudden conviction that the worst had happened and they'd found some stranger to give me the news. Some administrator who specialized in breaking it carefully. He said, "Mona Brown?"

"It's okay. This is his son. You can tell me."

"I need to speak to Mona Brown."

I was gripping the phone hard. "She's just going to tell me anyway! Why don't you just save yourself the goddam effort and tell me what's going on!"

"Is she there?" the man said patiently.

I carried the phone in and handed it to her. She held it to her ear, angling it up to keep it out of the water. "Mona Brown," she said. "Yes. That's right. Oh." Her shoulders sagged. The phone dipped, almost into the bath. "Shit," she whispered. And there was a long silence. "Okay." She turned off the phone and peered up at me, her face stunned and pale.

"Oh, God," I whispered. "I knew it. Everything's not okay, is it?"

Jean Tipton's street looked unremarkable in the afternoon light, and even the police cars in front of the blue Swiss chalet seemed almost ordinary, their flashing lights lost in the broad, bright sunshine. Inside, the house was a wreck. The living room had been ripped apart, the furniture upended, cushions scattered. Fistfuls of white stuffing bulged from the seams and lay on the carpet like stubborn clumps of snow, refusing to melt. The kitchen, in contrast, was tidy and neat. The only disarray was the plate of cheese and crackers, untouched on the table, and the shattered remains of two wine glasses on the floor beside a glaze of pink zinfandel and a darker, fist-sized smear, more crimson than pink. There was no chalk outline. Maybe they didn't do that except in the movies. Or maybe they'd already tidied it away with everything else, to make room for all the policemen.

There was no reason for us to be there, nothing more we could do. We had already talked to police and explained why Mona's business card should be in the possession of the deceased. We had given our statements. But we didn't want to leave until the paramedics had lifted the stretcher carefully through the doorway and down over the front step, then wheeled it the rest of the way to the darkened ambulance. It was the only vehicle whose flashers weren't on. There was no need for them, and no need for hurry. Lying on the stretcher Jean Tipton looked sad and bereft, lonely as a child without her stuffed bear.

38

Despite our best judgment we cling to the notion that love is the opposite of disaster. That it might yet be our guard against all that is random and at risk. In spite of everything it remains our last, hopeful refuge from the pangs of loneliness and fate. But if love is our protection, our best defense, if love is where we go to hide from the disappointments of life, then where do we go to hide from love?

That evening I sat on the sofa in Mona's living room, listening to the radio playing love songs from the seventies and eighties. A hit list of romance and misery from longer ago than I could remember. Outside, the evening was drifting into darkness, but the desk lamp threw a little campfire of light across the carpet at my feet. Beside me Mona held Paddington on her lap. The bear sat slouched and stunned like the lone survivor of some terrible accident.

"There was nothing you could do," I said.

But Mona just shook her head. "She came to me. I could have protected her."

"She didn't want to be protected."

"Then I could have done something."

"You did all you could."

"Really?" she said.

"Yes."

She breathed a low, despairing sigh. "Tell me again."

"You can't save someone who doesn't want to be saved."

"But that's no answer. That's as bad as anything."

I laid my arm gently across her shoulders, and her voice died away. She leaned into me, and we sat huddled together, the three of us. Mona, Paddington, and me. Our own little bleak and fragile family. "You told her to leave. You told her to walk away. You told her to go to the police," I said. "She should have."

"But why didn't she? Why does love always have to be such a tragedy?"

I felt the words like a sudden congestion of the heart. I said, "Does it? Always?"

"Tell me any good it's ever done. Tell me who's happier because of it."

I wondered if I were happier now. I wondered if I would even know. It's not so much that you become happier with love. Sometimes it's just that, without it, you would be so much emptier than you could possibly imagine. I thought about what Biff had said, that in the end all that love means is not being able to leave. Could that possibly be true? Nothing about romance, nothing about happiness? "No one ever said it's supposed to make things easy," I said.

"But then what's the point? Everything is hard enough already. Do me a favor," Mona added softly. She was resting her chin on the bear's slouching head, peering glumly down at his little skewed legs. "Whatever else you do, don't ever tell me you love me again."

I held her without a word.

There was a knock on the door, muffled and tentative in the dim light. I glanced over. "Are you expecting anyone?"

She shook her head. I levered myself up off the sofa and trudged to the door. After all that had happened, a knock on the door seemed perfectly ordinary and safe. Bad news would only come by phone. So I opened it, and there was Biff, just like that.

He looked thinner, more ragged than I remembered. His face was still clenched like a fist, but his eyes were red and pouchy, and he looked like someone who'd only just realized he would never sleep again.

"The police are looking for you," I said.

He didn't seem to hear. "There was nothing I could do." He said it in a whisper dry as sand. "I called the ambulance."

"We saw it."

"Is she all right?"

"No."

His breath was like the last thin puff of air from an empty chest. He stared at me desperately, as if he'd come all this way just to tell me this one thing. "She slipped," he said. "I swear. I didn't touch her. She just slipped, and hit her head on the counter."

"Just like that?"

"I got angry, I broke the glasses. The wine spilled. She slipped in that. I swear to God. It wasn't anything I meant." He gazed bleakly over at me. "I loved her. You know I loved her. I didn't want to. I tried to leave."

"You should have," said Mona harshly. "You should have left her alone."

But he just shook his head as if that was the problem, as if that was exactly what made it so terrible and strange. He took a step toward the sofa and stood unsteadily above her. "It was an awful noise," he said softly. "Just once, sudden. Loud. Like a piece of clay hitting the floor. Jesus Christ, I never want to hear that sound again." But he looked as if he were hearing it now. I stepped closer, edging between him and Mona. He said, "There wasn't much blood."

"We saw."

"I should have left." He said it as if returning to the words against his will. "I told her that. I should have just gone away. Just left her alone. We'd have been fine then."

"She loved you," said Mona.

"And what kind of an answer is that?" He sounded wounded and furious. "You think that's some kind of help? You think that's some kind of explanation?" And he reached into his pocket and jerked out a knife, flicking it open with his thumb. The blade was maybe four inches long, the color of well-used pewter.

I threw up my hands. "Wait!"

"Don't!" he said, holding up his fist with the blade growing out if it. "Don't be stupid." Then he turned back to Mona, glaring down at her now as if she held all the sadness in the world on her lap. "Give it to me."

She stared up uncomprehendingly.

"Give it!" And then reaching down he snatched the teddy bear out of her hands. He wrapped his arm around it, hugging it to his chest, and just for a moment he looked like an orphan, fierce and homeless. He looked as if he were about to cry. "This stupid bear," he muttered. "She loved this bear." And he jabbed the blade up to the knuckles in the bear's furry stomach.

"Jesus!"

But Biff paid no attention. He was sawing upwards, opening a jagged slit in the bear with a muffled ripping sound. Ragged strands of fur and stuffing leaked out, but Paddington remained unmoved, as if this, too, were simply part of it all.

Biff pulled out the knife and folded the blade away. Then he reached inside the gaping wound and drew out a bulky plastic bag that had been taking up most of the space in the bear's overstuffed body. He pulled it free and held it dangling. The clear plastic sagged under the weight of the bills. Twenties, fifties, some hundreds, all mixed together, dense and compacted. He dropped the bear onto the floor, where it lay, silent and surprised, coming undone.

Then he moved to the door. But even as he stepped through he turned. "This isn't the way I wanted it," he said. "It isn't what I meant to happen." He was staring fiercely at Mona, then back at me, as if daring us to forgive him.

39

You tell yourself things will look better in the morning. Lying awake in the middle of the night you swear if you can just get to daylight then all your worst fears will retreat back into your dreams. But I woke the next day with a bleak and haunted feeling that no rising of daylight could dispel, and as I opened my eyes to the unremarkable order of Mona's living room, everything seemed to resist recognition, as if after all that had happened even the most familiar things were changed forever. I eased off the sofa and walked silently to the bedroom door. She lay curled under the covers, solid and reassuring in the early light, and I had to fight the urge to crawl in beside her. Quietly I dressed, pulling on my clothes, limp with two days of wear, and slipped out the door. I bought coffee downstairs and carried it straight to the hardware store, opening more or less on time. I felt tight-skinned and exhausted, hollowed out by circumstance, but none of the customers seemed to notice. Maybe they had their own worries, or maybe they just didn't have mine.

A little before noon Mona stalked in looking bright and angry as a coral snake in a red checked shirt and yellow pants, but her voice softened when she saw how awful I looked. "Jesus," she said. "What time did you get up?"

"About six."

"I didn't know you were leaving. Just tell me next time, all right? Before you go?"

"I didn't want to wake you."

"I woke up. I didn't know where you'd gone." She glanced down at my clothes. "I guess you didn't go home?"

I shook my head wearily. "Some guy came in this morning; he bought two of every size screw we had. Then he came back three hours later and returned half of them. One of each. Said he'd over-estimated. Another guy bought twelve thousand feet of clothes line. All we had. He cleaned us out. And a lawn chair. Asked us if we sold any helium weather balloons. He said it was for an experiment."

"I called the hospital," Mona said.

I nodded. "Me, too. He's still asleep."

"He must be resting comfortably."

"I'm not sure that's what it means."

"Did you call Chicago?"

"First thing. About seven. All I got was voice mail, but I told her what happened."

"Don't worry," said Mona gently. "I'm sure she'll come as soon as she can."

But all I could do was shake my head. "It's strange that I could ever have thought that might solve anything."

"I'm going to Motor Vehicles in Des Moines this afternoon. I'll be back late." She hesitated. Then, reaching into her pocket she held out a key, pinched between fingertips. "In case you need it." She was scowling as if she'd been caught doing something stupid again.

But sometimes, I thought, all we had was our mistakes, and the courage to make them over and over. I took the key without a word. She gave a little shrug and turned toward the door. I wanted to stop her. I wanted to wrap my arms around her and bury my face in that wild yellow hair, but I felt so tired and undone I could barely speak. "Jane?" I whispered. "I'll make it up to you somehow. All of this. I promise." But in that moment I sounded so much like my father I almost wept. And I wondered if we were destined, we Bailey men, to a lifetime of apology and expiation, as if sadness itself were simply part of my patrimony.

"Just tell me next time, when you leave. Okay? I hate that."

"I will. Drive carefully," I said.

"Yeah. Whatever."

At six I turned off the lights and closed the shop, aware of

every step as if I'd never done it before. I felt the utter black-
ness as I closed the door, the aisles and shelves subsiding in that
last wedge of light, and I had the image of it all—the chia pets
and screw drivers and plastic tubing and coffee makers—just
sitting there in a kind of suspended animation, like one of those
old science fiction stories where space travelers slept through
hundreds of years to reach some distant star, and the most dangerous part was that something might malfunction and there
would be nothing to wake them up. I walked out of the building
clutching Mona's key.

At the curb in front of the house I parked with the flashers
going and hurried inside. I found the little pile of things for Henry still on the bed and stuffed them into a plastic grocery bag.
Then I added a pair of pajamas, my father's slippers and the
magic burgundy dinner jacket, just for luck. I went to my own
room and into a second bag I stuffed a clean shirt, underwear,
socks, a clean pair of jeans, working as quickly as I could. The
silence of the house felt like a maze I'd wandered into by accident, and I had to concentrate on every step if I wanted to get
out again.

I hurried through the clutter of the living room, through the
kitchen with the sinkful of dishes and the soggy, sour smell,
pausing only to check the silent answering machine. The wine
glasses stood tinged with the dried remnants of what might
have been blood. It looked like the scene of a crime, and I left it
all just as it was.

At the hospital Henry was asleep. The monitor beeped steadily. They had taken him off the ventilator, but he still wore an
oxygen tube over his upper lip. He lay with his mouth ajar as
if surprised by sleep in the middle of a low moan. His face was
ashen. He didn't move. He didn't even twitch in his sleep.

I sat by the bedside watching the slow rise and fall of his chest,
listening to the metronomic beep of the monitor. After almost an
hour his eyes fluttered open. He peered up into the room with
blank uncertainty, like a trout peering up through the surface of

a stream.

"Hi, there," I said.

He blinked and turned his head, moving against a great weight. His lips were dry. They fluttered for a moment before any sound came out. "Where am I?"

"You're in the hospital. You had a heart attack. You're going to be fine."

His face sagged into creases it had never had before. He swallowed. "Do I know you?"

"Dad?" I leaned forward, laying an urgent hand on my father's dry wrist. "Dad, it's me."

But Henry closed his eyes. "Just kidding," he whispered.

I left after an hour-and-a-half and parked the truck in front of the diner in an all night spot. I trudged up the stairs. I couldn't have imagined being so tired, but despite the stunned fatigue everything was impossibly clear: the banister scuffed and worn as an old dance-floor, the blank bulbs in the ceiling looking startled and bare. I unlocked the door and let myself in, then walked around turning on every lamp in the place.

Mona's kitchen, too, was a mess, but this one I could deal with. I filled the sink with water and, since I couldn't find any dish soap, added a scoop of laundry detergent from the broom closet. I had to scrub at the dried food. I found a box of steel wool and a stiff brush that might have been used on the floor, though not recently. I washed the dishes, dried them, put them away as best I could. Then I scrubbed the counters, mopped the floor, and filling a saucepan with soapy water, washed the refrigerator inside and out. The effort seemed to stretch me like taffy. When I finished I left the apartment and drove to the Eagle Market where I bought eggs, milk, butter, bread, a head of lettuce, spaghetti, hamburger, marinara sauce. I was standing at the stove stirring when I heard the front door open.

"What have you been doing?" Mona stood on her tiptoes in the kitchen doorway as if afraid of the clean floor.

"How was Des Moines?"

"Awful. Five hours at the DMV, and nothing." She stepped in cautiously, glancing around at the empty sink, the clean counters. "What's that?"

"Spaghetti. Maybe you've heard of it."

"You didn't need to."

"You didn't eat already, did you?"

She hesitated. "I stopped at a McDonald's on the way home. I didn't know you'd be cooking."

"Oh." I was so tired the disappointment felt sharp as despair. I frowned down at the sauce.

"It smells good," she said hurriedly.

"It's just canned sauce."

"I might have a little."

"You don't have to."

"Just a little."

I put a small portion on a plate for Mona, and a larger one for myself. She had no dining table so we sat at her desk, my knees bumping against the steel front. I had to lean forward over the edge to eat, but with the first bite I realized I was too tired anyway. I tore off tiny fragments of bread and drank the wine in silence.

When it was time for bed we stood awkwardly in the middle of the bedroom. "Do you want a bath or anything?" Mona asked. "A shower?"

"I think I'd better. If you want to use the bathroom first."

"Okay. Yeah."

We moved awkwardly around each other, as if the room were suddenly much smaller and we had to squeeze past.

"There's toothpaste."

"I've got some." I hesitated. "Don't worry. I'm not staying long. I just couldn't bear to go home. Not just yet. That's all."

"So, why don't you go stay with--?"

"Please don't say Alice. Please? I said I was sorry."

"Okay," she said gruffly. "So, go take a bath why don't you."

Mona had a collection of bubble bath canisters on a shelf behind the sink. I poured in a scoop of Lavender Mist. It said *Revitalization* on the label in bright letters. That sounded right to me; that sounded like what I needed. I climbed in, stepping high over the rim. The hot water drew the ache from my muscles, but it left nothing behind. I lay there drifting to the sound of pipes creaking and the scuff of movement as Mona prowled around the apartment. Every time the footsteps paused I waited for a knock on the door, but it never came. I could have called out, invited her in, but I didn't have the courage.

Later, when I stepped out, the bedroom was dark, with only a faint glow spilling in from the front room. Mona was already in bed, curled like a question mark under the covers.

"Good night," I whispered, but she didn't reply.

I crept past, into the living room. The sofa was innocent of covers. The blanket and sheet from the night before were nowhere to be found. Hesitantly I turned and again approached the bed. She was lying off-center, leaving a space that, while sufficient, didn't seem deliberate. My heart was thumping. "Mona?"

"You can sleep," she growled. "But don't try anything."

I slipped beneath the covers like a swimmer into cold water. She didn't stir. We lay without touching. No longer a question mark, but a pair of parentheses. I fell asleep without a word.

In the morning I woke to feel Mona's foot pressed, warm and furry, against my own. She shifted and turned, squinting over at me, her hair bent and metallic in the gray light. "Jesus. I'm still wearing my socks."

"I've got to go open the store."

"What time is it?"

"Six-thirty."

"Want me to make you some coffee?"

"That's okay. I'll pick some up."

She buried her face in the pillow again. "Good answer."

I drank my coffee standing at the cash register, poring over the lists of the monthly inventory. On my lunch hour I drove to the hospital.

Henry was sitting up with a tray on his lap. The unused oxygen tube lay draped over the corner of the bed like a long strand of Lucite macaroni. Lunch was mostly liquids: tomato soup, Jello, applesauce. He gripped the spoon, but seemed too tired to lift it from his lap. As I walked in he glanced up and offered a weak smile that seemed to die away at the left edge of his mouth. He looked like a man who'd had an afternoon of dental work and was waiting for the Novocaine to wear off.

"Hi. How are you feeling?"

"M'fine," he murmured shapelessly.

"You scared the shit out of me."

"M' too. Sorry."

"The doctor said it's just temporary, the…" I gestured vaguely at my own cheek, unable to say the work paralysis for fear it might be true. "….the numbness. He said your hand was tingling?"

Henry nodded and flexed his left hand. "Feels like's gone t' sleep."

"The doctor says it'll come back. It's just about blood flow or something. He says you're going to be fine."

Henry was gazing down at his hand, opening and closing, as if he were trying to catch something out of the air but couldn't move nearly fast enough.

"Dad?"

"I'm really sorr' about all this."

"Cut it out," I said. "You don't have anything to be sorry for."

But he just shook his head. "What a mess."

"It's not. Everything's going to be fine. The store's great. Mona sends her love."

Henry glanced up and mustered that smile again. His silence itself was a question.

"I called her," I said. "She wasn't in. I left a message."

"She sai' she was goin' t' be busy. She ha' a lot of work pilin' up, spendin' all this time here."

"I'm sure she'll come as soon as she can."

Henry leaned back against the pillow. "You think I'd learn. You think I'd smarten up…all this time. But, maybe you jus' never do. Maybe tha's the joke. You jus' make the same mistakes over an' over. You get smar' enough to know wha' to do, but no' enough to do it." He smiled sadly. "I tol' her I didn't wan' her t'go. Tha's all. You can't go, I said. How dare you?" He shook his head, marveling. "I said that. How dare you. All this time, and tha's all I came up with. Isn't tha' what I sai' las' time? D'you remember?"

"No. Sorry."

He shrugged. "You think I could've come up with somethi' better."

I leaned closer. I took his hand, the one that was still tingling, the one that felt asleep. "Henry? Could you maybe just learn not to love her? You know, just practice a little bit more each day?"

But my father just closed his eyes wearily. "S' funny, tha' someone can be the bes' and the wors' thing that ever happened? There should be a riddle or a joke or somethin' tha' goes like tha'."

I swallowed hard. "You're going to be great. You're going to be up and around. Better than ever."

"Yeah," he said. "Tha's right. Tha's the spirit."

After work I drove home, down the alley this time, and pulled into the driveway. She was sitting in the last of the evening light at the red patio table, beneath the pergola. She'd plugged in the string of lights, and they were sparkling like so many electric bees above her head, their brightness throwing the sky into darker relief.

She watched as I came slowly down the path. "I don't have a key," she said.

"How long have you been waiting?"

"A few hours."

"You could have come to the hospital."

"I was afraid to. How is he?"

"He's fine. Or at least, he's better. His arm. His cheek." I shrugged. "They say it's probably just temporary."

"But he's all right?"

"I'm not sure what that means anymore."

I stepped past her and unlocked the door. "The place is a mess. But you know that."

The ruined meat and vegetables had been sitting out in the heat for days, and the house held the stench, still and stagnant. Elizabeth wrinkled her nose. "Phew."

"I was saving it for you."

She looked at me for a moment. Then she lifted the apron off the top of the fire extinguisher, and slipped it on. "Why don't you open some windows," she said as she rolled up the sleeves of her blouse.

I moved through the downstairs, turning on lights, opening every window wide. The faint pressure of the evening air curled in, hesitating at the rank stillness inside. I heard the sound of running water, the chunky splash of dishes being done. I swept up the peanut crumbs and carried the beer cans out to the garbage. By the time I'd finished, Elizabeth had the plates stacked in the drying rack and was working at the wine stains on the glasses. She concentrated on each one, squeezing the sponge down into the narrow dimple at the bottom, rinsing them delicately under the faucet. It reminded me of pictures I'd seen of Greenpeace workers after an oil spill trying to clean the feathers of a wild gull, and I marveled that she would bother. Only later did it occur to him that the wine glasses, like the champagne flutes, had been wedding presents all those years before, and there was no telling what she was thinking as she sponged them clean.

"Are you hungry?"

She smiled grimly. "Even after this."

From the freezer I took a pack of chicken breasts, and thawed them under the faucet. Then I poured a cup of rice into the bottom of the casserole, laid the chicken on top, and opened a can of mushroom soup.

"You're kidding," she said.

"This is what we're having."

I opened the last bottle of wine from the party and filled a couple of the newly clean glasses, and we waited out on the patio while the chicken cooked. Elizabeth sat upright, legs tightly crossed. I listened to the sounds of the cicadas and the distant creak and thump of trains hooking and unhooking in the switching yard.

"You know," I said, "you're killing him."

She managed a crooked smile. "Haven't you heard? Nobody dies of a broken heart." But she didn't look as if she believed it. "How about you?" she asked. "Am I killing you as well?"

"Why did you have to leave in the first place? And if you had to leave, why did you have to come back? And if you had to come back, why did you have to leave again?"

She smiled bleakly. "I didn't want to hurt him. I didn't want to hurt either of you." And she stared down into her wine glass. "You know what these are from?"

"Yes."

"I loved them. They were like the promise of something. I thought if we drank our wine every night from these, like a couple of magic goblets, it would transform our lives. I was what, twenty-one? What did I know? We didn't drink much wine. We barely used the glasses." She glanced over at me. "You think that's trivial, don't you?"

"I've been drinking wine out of jelly glasses with little pictures of Fred Flintstone." But I thought of the new glasses Mona had bought.

My mother shook her head sadly. "Do you remember what it was like? All the arguments? The fights?"

"Everybody fights."

"We were so wrong for each other."

"I don't believe that."

"Oh, sweetie." She reached out.

I sat stiffly under her hand, but I'd spent so long waiting for exactly that touch, I couldn't pull away. Her face was drawn tight. "I had to leave. You've got to believe that. This was my life. This was all I was going to have. I couldn't let it all slip past in a blur of arguments and frustration."

"Just like that?"

She gazed up at me. "No. Of course not. Not just like that. But is it so awful to want a fresh start? Is that so terrible?"

"But what about us?" I said. "You got a fresh start. What did we get?"

"I am so sorry. I am. What is there I can say? That I'm not a good mother? I'm sorry, but I'm not. I'm not a good wife. I'm not a good mother. Is that what you want me to tell you? I wanted to be. I tried. But I'm just not."

"You seem to have come to grips with it pretty easily."

"Do you really think hating myself would have made you feel better?"

"I don't know. It might have been worth a shot."

She shook her head grimly. "It wouldn't have made any difference. It was too late from the very beginning. From the first moment I left. If I were a better person. I don't know. If I were more selfless. But even then, what? More arguments? More fights? What would you have done, if you were in my place? Do you think you'd have stayed?"

I remembered all the college pamphlets spread out on my desk like wings just waiting to fly. My throat felt tight. "But what about me?"

"Oh, sweetie."

"I need to know. It's not a big deal, but I just need to ask. Was it me? Is that why you left? Because of me?"

She looked startled and impulsively she reached out again. "How could you think that? No. Of course not."

"It's okay," I said. "You can tell me."

She smiled again sadly. "I loved you. You were my little boy.

"But you stayed away."

"I called," she said. "Henry sent me pictures."

"That's not enough."

"No," she agreed. "It's not. But that's all I could do. I couldn't come back. And would it have been any better to keep getting your hopes up again and again?"

"Maybe," I said.

"No. And what about my hopes?"

Something in her sadness was like a spark on tinder. I felt myself scowling furiously. "So, why the hell did you come back? You had your happy life. What could be more fulfilling than commercial real estate in Evanston, Illinois? Why the hell didn't you just stay there and leave us alone?"

And she was gazing at me marveling, as if she couldn't imagine how anyone could be so blind. "Because," she said, "I'm crazy about your father. I'm absolutely, crazy in love with him."

"Oh, stop it! You don't even know what that means."

"It means we're stuck," she said. "That's what it means. It means there's a tiny little spot where my heart should be that's empty when I'm not with him. And sometimes I think if we just try it again, if we do it a little differently." She gave a thin, tragic little laugh.

"What the hell are you laughing for? This is my life you're screwing with."

"That's right. That's exactly right," she said. "And mine. And his. Don't you think I know that? Don't you think I'd like to forget that every once in a while?" She took a deep, tired breath. "I know what you think. You think happiness is there if you can just figure it out, if you can just make it that far. But it's not like that. It's a few years, a few weeks, a few days at a time. It's a balancing act between what makes you so miserable you curl up inside and what you absolutely-can't-help-yourself, got-to-have."

She set the wine glass down on the patio table painted red for remembrance, beneath the arbor and the scattering of lights. "I'd make you happy if I could," she said. "Henry, too. If it were just up to me."

"It is up to you."

"No. Not any more." She gave a weary sigh. "God knows I messed up. I did an awful job. I hurt you, I know. And I couldn't be more sorry. But you're a big boy now, Harry. You're all grown up, and you're on your own now, sweetie. Just like the rest of us. It can't be all my fault anymore."

I peered up at her for a long moment. On a little puff of breeze I caught her perfume like a distant cry. "You really love him?"

"I do," she said. "Sometimes I wish I didn't."

"Do you love me?"

"Yes."

"Do you sometimes wish you didn't?"

She shook her head. "No."

"That's not much," I said, "if it's supposed to make up for all these years. For just walking away."

She smiled sadly. "What would make up for it?"

"Nothing. Not a goddam thing."

"I know."

I was scowling again helplessly. "You think this is enough? What am I supposed to do with all this now?"

"I don't know. I'm sorry. I can't help you there. I wish I could." And after a moment longer, "Is he very mad?"

"You know Henry. How can you tell? I would be."

"You are."

"That's right."

"Do you think you'll ever forgive me?"

"Does it matter?"

"Of course it matters."

But I knew in some fundamental way it didn't. Not really. Forgiveness was somehow beside the point, and that, in itself, was a kind of relief. It didn't all rest on my shoulders anymore— neither the fault nor the expiation. Love was more complex than I'd imagined, more intricate than the mixture of affection and comfort I had envisioned up until now. But it bound us together, forgiveness or not, with a lifetime of all we had thought or done or meant to do for each other.

"I guess," I said, "you'll just have to wait and see."

She nodded. After a moment she stood up. "Can I take the truck? I got a cab from the airport."

"What about dinner?"

"I'll pick up something at the hospital."

I reached into my pocket and held out the keys. "Say hello to Henry for me."

She reached out hesitantly again, and smoothed the shirt over my shoulder. "You look nice. Did I tell you that? I meant to. You turned out really well."

"No thanks to you."

"Well," she said. "Maybe a little thanks to me."

She picked up her purse and strode down the path, out of the canopy of lights and into the darkness.

I sat there in the silence. Even the trains had settled down for the night. In the kitchen the timer went off with a thin, persistent ding, and when I stepped inside, the aroma of Persian Army Chicken was warm on the sour air. I lifted the casserole and set it on the stove. It hissed and bubbled. I stood there alone in the empty house until it was cold as a stone.

40

I climbed the stairs to the apartment and rang the bell. I held the casserole in the crook of my arm the way men in old daguerreotypes held their hats. Mona opened the door and glanced without a word at the suitcase in my other hand.

"You told me to tell you when I left," I said. "I came to say goodbye. Can I come in? Just for a minute? I promise I won't stay."

She stepped back. I carried the suitcase in and sank down onto the sofa, cradling the casserole on my lap. I felt like some strange sort of immigrant, just arrived at Ellis Island with the last unsavory remnant of my former life grown cold in my hands.

Mona wore an expression of bleak uncertainty, like someone with a list of questions she doesn't really want answered. "How's Henry?"

"He's okay. A lot better, actually. My mother's with him now."

"She's back?"

"She says she loves him. That's why she keeps breaking his heart. I said, if she really loved him, maybe she should just stay away."

"What did she say?"

In the corner of the sofa Paddington the Bear sat slouched, thin and peaked, with a yellow scarf tied like a tourniquet around his middle. I picked him up, and immediately the extent of the damage became more apparent. He felt limp and hollow. If you held him delicately he retained most of his usual shape, but at the slightest pressure he collapsed. "She said she loved him too much to stay away. I think they're going to kill each other."

"You don't really think that."

"They should just give it up. Call it quits and cut their losses."

"They're in love," said Mona. And after a moment's hesitation, "Don't you think that's worth the effort?"

"I don't know. Where's it going to lead?" I looked up pleadingly. "How is it going to end?"

"The way everything ends," said Mona angrily. "In a hundred years we'll all be dea. So? Is that what you're going to worry about?"

I gazed at her helplessly. "You and me...?" I began, and then just faded off.

"Is that a question?"

"What are we supposed to do?"

She gazed forlornly down at my suitcase, as if the answer were already right in front of us, and she was just too tired to argue. After a moment she said, "When was the last time you were happy?"

I shook my head. I wanted to say I wasn't even sure I'd recognize it anymore, but I was already thinking of the night of our stakeout, the darkness and the cozy proximity prickling with expectation. And the night after. And the night after that. "I don't remember."

"You are such a liar."

"All right. I do. So?"

"So, you tell me," she said.

All these years I'd spent so much of my energy waiting. For my mother to get back, for my father to get going, for my life to start. All that time thinking it was my parents who were lost, one to distance and one to heartbreak. And never realizing I was the one who so desperately needed to be found. How much time would it have saved, if I'd just come to Mona and said, I think I'm missing. Can you find me? But now it was too late.

"I'm leaving town," I said.

"Is that right?"

"I decided I need my own life. It's a little late, I know. But I think it's time."

She stood gazing stiffly down without expression, and it occurred to me this was the first time I'd seen her without even a glint of anger. All feeling withdrawn, the moment itself receding. "Just like that?" she said.

I looked up at her. I was thinking about what Elizabeth had said. That love didn't promise happiness. The only thing it promised was love. You loved someone because you had to, because you didn't have a choice, because it was all you could do. I thought about what Biff had said in the car, about the only true measure of love. It could be nothing less than desperate.

"Don't you see?" I whispered. "How it's going to end? Two people. They make each other mad. They make each other crazy. They break each other's hearts. It's terrible. Or worse."

"It doesn't have to be."

"Look at Jean. Look at my parents. Look at me. Jesus Christ, Jane! What chance have we got?"

"You aren't your parents. What do you think? You're trapped in their life?"

"Yes! Look what I've done so far. What kind of a mess is this? What kind of a life? What if it's genetic? What if I don't do any better than they have?"

"Stop it!" she said. "Just stop!" Her voice sounded tight in her throat. "Right now, right at this moment, do you think your parents are unhappy?"

"At this very moment?" I glanced at my watch. It was ten-thirty. I had stopped at the hospital on my way over and poked my head into my father's room. He'd been sitting up, propped against the pillows. He'd raised a hand in greeting. Beside him curled on top of the covers lay Elizabeth. She looked rumpled and exhausted in her skirt and blouse, and even fast asleep she clutched the sleeve of Henry's pajamas as if she'd never let go.

"No," I said. "At this moment they're probably as happy as they can be."

"Then what are you afraid of?"

I felt the heavy beat of my heart. I thought about that last taro reading and my final card. The Hermit, and all of his solitude, wisdom, prudence, caution. And then what? No mention of happiness. No mention of love. I said, "What if I'm just not good at this? What's going to happen then?"

Mona didn't reply. I sat there, the wounded bear in one arm, the cold casserole in the other. There was a strange pressure in my chest, hollow and bursting at the same time. I said, "Do you love me?"

"You don't deserve to know."

"What does that mean?"

"It means that life is hard," she said. "And you deserve what you settle for."

I sat there. I'd been a coward for so long, hiding behind Henry's fears and my own. But in the end what breaks your heart might be the same thing that keeps it alive. There's no safety without danger. No protection that doesn't inflict its own cost. You need to risk something for love: it's the impurity that gives the stone its color.

After a moment Mona sank down beside me. She reached over and lifted the lid from the casserole. It was cold as the earth. The chicken lay naked beneath a crinkled drapery of pale, congealed soup. "That looks disgusting."

"This was my favorite meal for the last six years."

Mona said not a word.

"I missed you," I whispered. "I missed you a lot."

She reached out a tentative hand, and smoothed the t-shirt over my ribs. "Are you going to make me sorry?"

"No," I said. "No. I hope not."

She leaned against my shoulder. I felt her hair soft as feathers on my cheek. Her voice was low and rough, velvet rubbed against the nap. "This doesn't mean I'm not still mad at you."

"I know," I said. My voice was a whisper. "I'm a little scared."

"Okay, then," she said. After a moment she tucked her hand under my arm. "Okay."

About the author

D. K. Smith is a graduate of Yale and the Iowa Writers' Workshop. He is the author of two additional novels: *Nothing Disappears,* and *Bunny, a romance.* He teaches Medieval and Renaissance literature at Kansas State University.

Lightning Source UK Ltd.
Milton Keynes UK
UKOW04n0437261017
311650UK00001B/2/P